DOMINIC

a slater brothers novel

NEW YORK TIMES & USA TODAY BESTSELLING AUTHOR

L. A. CASEY

DOMINIC
a slater brothers novel
Copyright © 2014, 2016 by L.A. Casey
Published by L.A. Casey
www.lacaseyauthor.com

Cover Design by Mayhem Cover Creations | Editing by JaVa Editing
Formatting by JT Formatting

This book is licensed for your personal enjoyment only.
This book may not be re-sold or given away to other people. If you would like to
share this book with another person, please purchase an additional copy for each
recipient. If you're reading this book and did not purchase it, or it wasn't purchased
for your use only, then please return to your favorite book retailer and purchase your
own copy. Thank you for respecting the hard work of this author.
All rights reserved.
Except as permitted under S.I. No. 337/2011 – European Communities (Electronic
Communications Networks and Services) (Universal Service and Users' Rights)
Regulations 2011, no part of this publication may be reproduced, distributed, or
transmitted in any form or by any means, or stored in a database or retrieval system,
without prior written permission of the author. The scanning, uploading, and
distribution of this book via the Internet or via other means without the permission of
the publisher is illegal and punishable by law. Please purchase only authorized
electronic editions and do not participate in or encourage electronic piracy of
copyrighted materials. This is a work of fiction. Names, characters, places, brands,
media, and incidents are either the product of the author's imagination or are used
fictitiously. The author acknowledges the trademarked status and trademark owners
of various products referenced in this work of fiction, which have been used without
permission. The publication/use of these trademarks is not authorized, associated
with, or sponsored by the trademark owners.

DOMINIC / L.A. Casey – 2nd ed.
ISBN-13: 978-1496174093 | ISBN-10: 1496174097

DEDICATION

To my little sister,
I wouldn't have been able to write *DOMINIC* and plot the rest of the
books in the *Slater Brothers* series without our midnight
brainstorming sessions. I love you!

TABLE OF CONTENTS

Reader's Note

DOMINIC is set in Ireland; most of the characters are Irish, and the Irish have a dialect that is completely different from any other dialect in the world. We tend to break words down when speaking and jumble them up; we're weird like that.

I want to make it clear that when you see an Irish (South Dublin) character in *DOMINIC* and the rest of the Slater Brothers series know that they are based on my accent and how I speak, when the say the word 'me' where 'my' should be, it is **supposed** to be written that way. Of course, not *everyone* in Ireland says 'me', this is again just based on my own accent and how I speak. I replace 'my' with 'me' nearly 100% of the time.

Here in South Dublin, where the book is set, it is also more common for *most* people (**not everyone!**) to leave out the letter G on *most* words when we speak, again, this is just another part of our dialect.

This note in here for readers who aren't familiar with Irish dialect, so you don't read a sentence and think, "What the fuck?"

CHAPTER ONE

I was late for school today, but it wasn't my fault; it was Branna's fault.

Branna was my older sister and became my legal guardian nine years ago when our parents died in a car accident. She was twenty-eight years old while I was pushing eighteen. She might be my guardian, but the girl was a total sibling when it came to pissing me off. She hogged the bathroom for twenty-five minutes this morning.

Twenty-five bloody minutes!

She was the sole reason I was fifteen minutes late for school and why I looked like shite. I was currently entering the school when the urge to 'fix' myself got the better of me. I paused mid-stride and then turned in the direction of the girl's bathroom. I wasn't one for constantly thinking about my appearance but I *did* want to be as put together as I could before I went to class.

When I got to the girl's bathroom, I did my business in the toilet and then went to the sink to wash my hands. When I was finished I looked up at the small mirror over the sink and frowned at my appearance. My bright green eyes looked tired, the bags under them proved me correct. I was a bit of a mess today. I didn't have time to do much more than French plait my waist length, chocolate brown hair to keep it under control, then put a few strokes of mascara on

1

each set of long lashes and brush my damn teeth. My chubby cheeks were red from windburn, and my usually pale pink lips were a little chapped and puffy. I was pretty sure that if death were a person, then that person would resemble me.

I stood up straight and moved to the full-length mirror in the bathroom to stare at myself. I sighed; I was so white I could give Casper a run for his money. Being Irish, my skin repelled any sort of tanning. *Natural* tanning anyway. I was probably the only girl in school who didn't put on fake tan and wore makeup that actually matched my skin tone instead of trying to make myself appear darker than I was. Why try to be something I wasn't? I had porcelain white skin with a splash of light freckles across my upper nose and under my eyes. Branna said they made me look adorable and that I should embrace it; so embracing my whiteness and freckles was what I was doing.

I fixed my school skirt, pulled up my stockings, and adjusted my school jumper. I ran my hand over my uniform to smooth it out. I tilted my head to the left as I studied myself. I liked how I looked. I had big hips and a small waist; I didn't have a big bust, but I had something else that was huge. I turned to the side and rolled my eyes; if I could change one thing about my body it would be my arse. It was big, and more than a few times I have gotten crude comments about it. It made me mad because it messed with my need to be ignored.

I liked being practically invisible.

I grunted as I left the bathroom and proceeded down the corridor to registration class. It was a stupid class we had every morning; our tutor—the person we went to if we got in trouble or needed the bathroom pass—took attendance and then let us do whatever we wanted for forty minutes until the class was over.

Usually everyone chatted about random stuff, but I didn't have any friends so I just kept to myself. That sounded pathetic, but I really didn't have any friends. It wasn't for lack of trying on my classmates' part; it was all down to me really. Ever since my parents died,

I had been closed off and guarded. I didn't like the idea of getting attached to someone new knowing that they could be taken away from me. That's why I chose not to make friends with anyone in school, or anyone at all, it was just too risky. Branna said it was stupid and that I couldn't be closed off from people forever because it wasn't healthy. I got that it was weird—I *was* weird—for just wanting to be on my own all the time, but I was content this way so I didn't let her words get to me.

When I reached my classroom, I opened the door and looked directly at my tutor. "Sorry that I'm late, miss," I said, hoping that I looked like I cared about my tardiness.

My tutor nodded her head at me like I knew she would. I was never late for class, and if I did make it a habit, I doubted she would give me late stamps in my school journal because she liked me. I was her quietest student and never gave her any trouble.

I moved across the room and, as usual, none of my classmates bothered with me but for some reason today everyone was very talkative and giddy. It was when I walked towards my desk that I realised why.

I looked to the lads that were seated at my desk; they were identical twins, that much was obvious. One had hair as white as snow while the other had a colour much like my own, dark chocolate brown. I didn't linger on looking at them, because they seemed to be enjoying the suggestive stares of my fellow female classmates, so I kept my eyes downcast as I neared them.

"That's me desk," I said when I reached them, my tone flat.

The twin with white hair made a move to get up but his dark-haired brother, the one who was in my seat, placed a hand on his shoulder and halted his movements.

"*Your* desk?" he asked with an eyebrow raised. "Does it have your name on it or something?"

His accent made him stick out like a sore thumb. It wasn't Irish. My guess was American, but I didn't ask. I looked down at him and glared. He had grey eyes that looked slightly silver when the light hit

3

them. I inwardly kicked myself for even noticing that about him and refocused. I leaned over the table and pointed to the corner of the desk.

"Yeah, it does," I replied as I pointed my name out on the desk.

I had carved it on the desk in first year when I was bored.

"Bro-what?" Dark-haired twin read aloud in a confused tone that made me roll my eyes.

"*Bronagh*," I said clearly.

I disliked when foreign people pronounced my name, they completely butchered it and could never say it the way one was supposed to.

"Bro-nah?" Dark-haired twin correctly sounded it out, then muttered about the stupidity of the G being silent.

I cocked an eyebrow. "Yeah, that's how you say me name and it is on *my* desk as you can clearly see."

The white-haired twin snorted. "She has you by the balls on that, bro. Let's just move out of this *lovely* woman's way and sit down in the back row next to the pretty ladies."

The fact that the girls in my class giggled, and the twins grinned over this, made my stomach lurch in disgust. I didn't like pretty boys who were full of themselves; we already had one lad like that in this school, and he was an absolute dickhead. We didn't need another one, let alone *two* more.

The white-haired twin winked at me when he stood up, but I didn't smile back at him. The dark-haired twin slowly stood up from my seat. He didn't smile at me, he grinned. My hardened stare only caused his grin to curl up into a devilish smirk.

"I warmed it up for you," he teased.

"Be sure to thank your arse for me." I said as I moved past him and sat down in my seat, and pulled it into my desk. I put my bag onto the chair next to me and tugged it close. It was obvious I was stating that no one was to sit next to me.

I heard the dark-haired twin chuckle as he moved to the back of the class.

"What's her problem?" he asked, aloud.

"Who? Bronagh? Nothin'," Alannah Ryan replied. "She just doesn't like attention, or people that much. She prefers to be by herself."

Alannah was a nice girl; she always smiled at me when she passed me by and unlike every other student in our year, she left me alone. She seemed to understand that I was just content with being on my own, and I really liked that about her. I thought she was pretty cool because of that.

"She doesn't like people?" Dark-haired twin grunted as he asked, "Is there something wrong with her?"

I might be a quiet person who liked to be ignored but I wasn't a pushover; if someone pissed me off, you could bet your arse I would speak my mind to them. My mind didn't have a filter either. I tended to say what I was thinking *without* thinking.

"I'm sure there are many things wrong with me accordin' to you, but I assure you pretty boy," I said aloud without turning around. "Me hearin' is perfectly fine."

I heard some chuckles then and when I glanced up, I caught Miss McKesson grinning down into her book.

"Inside voice, bro," white-haired twin's voice snickered.

"*Pretty boy?*" dark-haired twin growled then muttered to whom I assumed was either himself or his brother. "Who does that bitch think she is talking to?"

He thought I was a bitch? My mind snickered. *Like I gave a shit.*

"Okay, less of that," Miss McKesson said, standing up once she heard the word bitch. "Bronagh, these lads are our new students, all the way from the United States of America."

When I realised my classmates were looking at me for some sort of reaction, I twirled my finger around in the air trying to be enthusiastic even though I couldn't care less.

"Go US of A."

Miss McKesson bit down on her bottom lip and shook her head.

"The Slater boys are twins, obviously. It's easy to tell them apart with them havin' different hair colour. Nico has brown hair and Damien has blond hair, well, more white than blond."

Nico was *its* name?

"I'll be sure to remember that miss, thank you," I sarcastically said with a beaming smile.

A few snorts later Miss McKesson introduced me. "And this lovely lady, lads, is Bronagh Murphy."

"It's a *pleasure*, Miss. Murphy," Nico purred.

I shook my head. "I seriously doubt that, Mr. Slater," I replied, making the class laugh.

I didn't care that they were probably laughing at me because it was obviously *not* a pleasure to meet me, but whatever, I didn't care.

"Okay, back to whatever it was that you were all doin' before Bronagh came to class," Miss McKesson said with a wave of her hand.

Not a second later, the questions fired left, right, and centre from the girls to the twins, and it made me sigh. I hoped it wasn't going to be like this every day, because that shite would get old and annoy me pretty quickly.

"Miss?" I muttered to my tutor.

When Miss McKesson looked up, I shook my iTouch at her, and she nodded, giving me silent permission to listen to it.

"Shit, you're allowed to listen to iPods here?" I heard Nico ask.

"Huh? Oh no, just Bronagh. She gets her work done every day, so she is allowed to listen to it as long as the volume is low," Alannah's voice replied to Nico.

I knew that made me out to be a geek, but I kind of was, not in the I-was-seriously-smart kind of way but just in the I-got-my-work-done-on-time kind of way. I didn't really have much else to do in school other than work, so having it done on time was never a problem.

I didn't hear Nico's response to Alannah because I turned my music on. I welcomed it the pulsing beats and enjoyed the fact that the beautiful sound drowned everyone else out.

I took out my English copybook and read over the essay I wrote last night for class later today. I corrected any mistakes I spotted, and then re-read it again. When I was satisfied with it, I put it back in my bag and zipped it closed. I checked the time and saw that there was less than two minutes left in class. I sat up straight and took out my earphones then switched off my iTouch and pocketed it.

I stood up at the same time the bell rang. I pushed my chair under my desk, walked out of the room, and headed towards the woodwork room. I *loved* this class; I really enjoyed making new things for projects. I always made jewellery boxes, makeup holders for Branna or cool shelves and bookcases. I got more creative with each one I made, and Branna loved them, so it made me happy.

When I got to class, I waved to Mr. Kelly. He was the woodwork teacher, and he was nice. He always left me alone and only came over to me when I needed help. He was cool like that; he seemed to know how I worked, and I liked that about him.

"Mornin', Bronagh," the sir beamed.

"Mornin', sir, can I listen to me iTouch? I'm just sandin' down all the pieces I cut up on Friday then I'm puttin' them together. I won't be near any dangerous machines that music would distract me from. Promise."

The sir bobbed his head up and down. "No problem, kid. If you need to cut or saw somethin' just make sure you take the earphones out, okay?" I saluted him which made him chuckle as he waved me on.

I put my bag under my woodwork desktop and moved down to the walk-in storage press at the back of the room; I grabbed an apron and put it on then put my earphones back in my ears and switched on my music. I moved back out into the classroom and noticed out of the corner of my eye that the rest of my classmates were coming in. I was the only girl in the class; all the other girls chose metalwork over woodwork, which was fine by me. I didn't have to listen to them chitchat about who was going out with who when I didn't have my earphones in.

While the lads put their stuff under their desks, I moved to the right of the room and went into the supply room that was connected to the woodwork room. I got some new sandpaper, and then headed back into the classroom to get a handheld sander from the holder on the wall. I was minding my own business when I headed back to my desk, only to come to a halt.

"Get *out* of me seat," I snarled as I all but ripped my earphones out of my ears.

Nico looked up at me and grinned as he sarcastically asked, "Is your name on this desk as well?"

He obviously thought he was funny, but he wasn't. I didn't find him amusing in the slightest, I found him extremely annoying. Our first interaction wasn't the best, but I now knew that he was purposely trying to make me mad, and I instantly didn't like him because of it.

"Move," I replied, ignoring his question.

He shook his head, so I gripped my sander like a bat and moved towards him only to be blocked by the sir's body.

"Bronagh, put the sander down," Mr. Kelly said calmly with his hands raised in an I-am-unarmed-don't-hurt-me motion.

I blinked, dumbly.

"I wasn't goin' to hit 'em with it," I lied.

I *was* going to hit him with it. Probably not that hard, but I was still going to hit him with it nonetheless.

"Why are you holdin' it like a weapon then?" the sir asked me with a raised eyebrow.

I grunted, "He is in me seat! Tell 'em to move."

The sir sighed and turned around. "That's Bronagh's worktop—wait, are you new here, son?"

"Son?" I spluttered. "Don't call 'em that, he is a gobshite—"

"Bronagh!" the sir cut me off in a low warning tone.

Some of the lads in the class cracked up at what I said while I fumed in silence.

"Yes, sir, I'm new." Nico replied. "I just started today."

The sir looked around to me with raised eyebrows. "You were goin' to attack a *new* student?" he questioned.

Would I be in less trouble if I attacked an old one? I thought. "I don't like 'em," I quipped, making the sir sigh and shake his head while pinching the bridge of his nose.

"That doesn't mean you can attack 'em, Bronagh."

I glowered over that fact. "I know, the school rules are stupid."

The sir looked like he was fighting off a smile before he turned and put his back to me again.

"What's your name, son?" he asked the *new* student.

I huffed.

"Nico," Fuckface replied.

I inwardly smiled; I liked calling him Fuckface instead of Nico.

"What's that short for?" the sir asked, curiously.

"Dominic, but everyone just calls me Nico. I prefer it that way," *Dominic* replied.

Everyone might call him Nico, and he might prefer it that way, but I wasn't everyone so if I ever had to address him, it would be as Dominic or Fuckface. Most likely the latter.

"Well, it's very nice to meet you Nico but this here is usually just Bronagh's worktop. But you can have the other end of the table since she has this one to herself."

"No!" I shouted at the same time Dominic said, "Thanks, sir."

This could *not* be happening!

"Sir, that's not fair," I protested. "I've *never* had to share me worktop with anyone. I like havin' it to meself, you *know* that."

The sir sighed when he turned to face me. "I know, kid, but all the other worktops are filled since I'm repairin' the two near the doorway."

"This is fuckin' bullshit," I muttered.

The sir grinned—he was great like that, he never cared about students cursing—and patted me on the back. "Put your earphones in and you will be grand, Bronagh."

I huffed when the sir moved away.

"Are you finished with your little temper tantrum, sweetie?" Fuckface asked me, batting his long eyelashes.

I glared at him as I placed my sander on my worktop then pressed my hands down next to it and leaned forward. "Listen to me, you annoyin' little prick. I don't like you and want you to stay the hell away from me, otherwise I'll imbed this sander into your stupid lookin' skull. Are we clear on that, *Dominic*?" I snarled, my voice ice-cold.

Dominic's lip twitched. He looked me up and down like he was assessing me. "Crystal clear, sweetheart," he replied when his grey eyes landed on mine.

"Good," I hissed. "Now bloody *move*."

I was a little shocked that I was so angry; the only other person who could get to me so easily without actually doing much was Jason Bane. He was the main pretty boy in this school and had always been a dick to me. He was currently on holiday somewhere in Australia and had been for the entire summer. He wouldn't get back until late September, the end of this month. It had been the best summer and start of the school year without him around to bully me. He was an evil, good-looking bastard, and the fact that this Dominic prick might be an American version of Jason scared the hell out of me.

I thought this over while I waited for Dominic to move to the other end of the worktop we now shared. I put my earphones in and turned my music back on when he was away from me. I could feel his eyes on me, probably to try and annoy me but little did he know that I was *very* good at ignoring people.

After the first five minutes of not getting a response from me, he got bored, I knew this because he got up and went over to the sir. I looked up as the sir was pointing out some different wood materials to Dominic, and I knew he was about to get started on his first project. This pleased me; hopefully he would keep busy and stay away from me.

It was the end of second period when I finished sanding down all of the pieces for Branna's new makeup box. It was going to be big with lots of spacious compartments. My sister had a lot of makeup so she would be delighted with it.

I took my base pieces and moved over to the glue gun station. I picked up a glue gun, grabbed a new glue stick, fitted it into the back of the gun then switched it on. I waited two minutes for the gun to heat up and melt the glue stick. I aligned my pieces how I wanted them to be, then generously applied glue to the wood, carefully placing the pieces together.

I put the glue gun down and stepped back, looking over my piece. I bent forward and pressed down hard on the wood, forcing any air bubbles out from between the wood's open spaces and used my free hand to get a piece of card to swipe the now lukewarm excess glue away. I did this for about twenty seconds, and then got some used sandpaper from my worktop to go over some of the areas that I had missed. While doing this I felt like I was being watched so when I glanced over my shoulder, I was startled when I found that some of the lads in the class were looking at me. Some looked amused while others were grinning at Dominic, who was grinning at me.

"What's so funny?" I asked when I took out my earphones.

"Nothin'," the lads who were looking at me said in unison, and then turned back to their work.

That obviously meant something, so I looked at Dominic.

"What did you do, Fuckface?"

Dominic dropped his jaw a little at my insult before composing himself. "Fuckface? That's sort of mean, *Bronagh*."

I narrowed my eyes. "What did you do, *Dominic*?" I repeated through gritted teeth.

Dominic smirked and said, "I just took a picture."

I mentally counted to ten.

"A picture of *what*?" I eventually asked.

"I'm not saying. I'll be a real *ass* if I do," Dominic replied, snickering.

I balled my hands into fists and contemplated hitting him, but I instead put my earphones back in and ignored him. I knew he took a picture of my arse; it was obvious with what he said and the way the lads were chuckling and grinning at him. I forced myself not to care though.

Fuck him and fuck this school day. It was turning out to be a bitch of one!

CHAPTER TWO

"**W**hat the hell has been up your arse all week, Bronagh?" Branna's voice shouted at the same time my covers were violently torn from my body.

I jolted awake and groaned out in tiredness and annoyance. I just wanted to be left alone in peace so I could sleep.

"Branna, feck off, I'm sleepin' here!" I snapped into my pillow, keeping my eyes tightly closed.

I felt a whack on my arse, which made me yelp, and caused me to jump upright to my feet so that I was standing on my bed. "That's child abuse!" I shouted to Branna, who stood at the end of my bed with her arms folded and her eyes narrowed at me.

She didn't look amused in the slightest.

I did something wrong, my mind whispered.

"What did I do?" I asked. "Why are you in here wakin' me up and hittin' me? I'm your little sister you shouldn't—"

"Save it, I heard you this mornin' turnin' off your alarm and go-in' back to bed." She frowned. "You ditched school today and that is *not* cool. You have been a walkin' hormone since you came home from school on Monday. What on Earth is goin' on with you?"

I groaned, not wanting to explain why I've been off all week.

"Nothin'," I mumbled. "I just don't feel good today."

I really didn't feel very good, but the entire truth was that I didn't want to go to school today because I didn't want to deal with another day of Dominic Slater while I felt ill.

If Branna knew that he was bullying me, she would call the school and demand a meeting, which would embarrass me. Or she would find out where Dominic lived and murder him. And that would leave me homeless since she technically owned our house and paid for everything. Plus, killing Dominic would land her arse in Mountjoy Prison and I would be left all on my own.

I could *never* let that happen. I could never be on my own.

"I'll let it slide this once because you're always in school but in the future, tell me if you're sick, okay?" My sister said. "I'll make a doctor's appointment for you."

I shook my head. "I'm due me monthly, I think that's what has me sore and cranky."

I *was* due my period but what had me all wound up was an American dickhead named Dominic. After that first meeting at school Monday morning, he made it his personal mission to get as close to me as he could throughout the school week, because he knew how much I hated it. I restored to slapping him across the face on Wednesday when he grabbed my arse. He said there was a spider on it, and he was just wiping it off for me.

It was utter bullshit and he knew it. He fucking squeezed my arse cheek to the point of pain, and that's why he had a grin on his face while pretending to be a do-gooder. I was *really* grateful, so grateful that I left a pretty decent handprint on his cheek that was visible for the rest of the day, which had him grumbling and his brother grinning.

Speaking of his brother, it turned out that Damien Slater was the polar opposite of Dominic; he was nice and didn't piss me off. I got paired with him for a science experiment and during that class he apologised for Dominic's behaviour and kindly asked me not to fol-low-through on any plans I might have formed to murder him, be-cause he preferred him alive and breathing, but only a little.

He was *extremely* flirtatious, but I paid him no mind and just focused on the project we had together. He seemed to get that I wasn't interested in flirting or talking with him at all. He didn't even try after the first few minutes of getting no response from me, which I silently celebrated over. Now, if only his brother gave up as easily, then I would be on cloud nine.

Branna's loud snort pulled me from my thoughts and caused me to look at her.

"What?" I asked.

"Nothin'," she chuckled. "Just thinkin' of you bein' in labour with a baby. You wouldn't be able to handle any aspect of childbirth if you can't even handle period pains."

I rolled my eyes. "Oh, and you are such an expert on childbirth?"

Stupid question, my mind taunted.

"No, but compared to you on the subject I *am* an expert. I'm a medical student studyin' to be a midwife, after all. I'm in my fourth year, which means I get to be present in the delivery room now while women give birth so I can get a proper understandin' of what I'm goin' to be doin' when I graduate at the end of the year."

I shivered in disgust. "You're so nasty, you actually want to *look* at a ten pound ham comin' out of a vagina."

Branna burst out laughing. "Don't call a baby a ham, you bitch!"

I cringed before I scrubbed my face a few times with my hands. "Now I'm picturin' someone givin' birth. Damn it, Branna!"

My sister shook her head at me, then moved to my window and opened my curtains, making me hiss at the sunlight that streamed into my room.

"Get up and get dressed, vampire." She chirped. "Since you aren't in school you can do the shoppin' while I'm at the hospital workin'."

That was fair.

I scratched my neck. "Are you at the hospital all day?"

When Branna wasn't in college doing a million assignments,

writing essay papers, or studying for crazy hard tests, she was at the maternity hospital volunteering. All medical students in her chosen field had to volunteer so many hours of their time to get some live experience of childbirth.

It's not required that she get paid, because she has to volunteer for experience, but her hospital did pay her. It wasn't much but it was enough for us to live on. We didn't really need Branna's wages to get by. We still had lots of money left to us by our parents, which would get us by until Branna became a midwife and had a steady income. Once I finished my final year in school and graduated, I'd get a summer job that would hopefully roll into a permanent job by the time I started college so that I didn't have to leech off Branna for everything.

"Yeah, I get to see babies come into the world today, isn't that brilliant?" Branna beamed and clapped her hands together, getting my attention again.

I gave her a disgusted look, making her snort. "Well, okay, I know you don't like it because you flip out at stuff like what I do but just think, one day *you* will be givin' birth, and *I* could be helpin' you deliver!"

Branna sounded way too excited about that thought.

"I will *never* have children," I declared. "Why have kids only to worry about their health and safety for the rest of me life? That's *way* too much stress for me to deal with, thank you very much."

Branna waddled her index finger at me. "Someone is goin' to change your way of thinkin' one day, little sister. I won't be the only person you love and care for. Someone will claw their way into that boxed off heart of yours and set up camp for the long haul, and there won't be a thing you can do about it."

"Don't threaten me!" I snapped.

Branna gleefully laughed and asked, "Wishin' you find love is a threat?"

I nodded. "Yes."

My sister shook her head. "Bronagh, you *really* need to get out more."

I rolled my eyes but decided to humour her. "Okay, sis, I'll make a start on findin' love by goin' to the supermarket and doin' the shoppin'. You never know, I might find him in the poultry aisle."

"Wow, great start," she said sarcastically before giving me a wink and leaving my room to get ready for her shift at work.

I rolled my eyes heavenward and fell backwards onto my bed. Groaning, I closed my eyes. I stayed that way for so long that I eventually dozed back off, and when I awoke it wasn't so bright out anymore. I checked the clock in my room and saw it read 4:32 p.m.

I yawned and got up from my bed and stretched; I held my belly when light cramp pains attacked. I went into the bathroom and groaned. Sure enough, my period had arrived as predicted. I got cleaned up, washed, and dressed before heading downstairs to take some painkillers.

Branna had already left for work hours ago and had left the shopping list I needed on the counter along with cash to pay for the items. I tucked the list and money into my jeans, and then plaited my hair back out of my face.

I didn't bother with putting makeup on because I felt like shite and would be going to bed when I got home anyway, so I left the house barefaced. I put my earphones in my ears as I walked down the street and hit shuffle on my iTouch.

I passed two people on the pathway, but if I passed more I didn't notice because I was too busy taking in the stunning view I had on my left. I sighed a little; living on the bottom side of the Dublin Mountains really did have its perks. I would never tire of the view it offered; the mountain cliffs, the trails, the multiple shades of green, the huge trees, and of course, a few sheep off in the distance. Content and happy, I looked away from my left and glanced to my right, which only deepened my feeling of happiness. To my left I had a mountain view and to my right, a town view.

My housing estate was higher up than the rest of the estates in my area because we were right on the mountainside. That meant I overlooked the entire town, which was brilliant. I never usually thought where I lived was beautiful, but it was, once you looked hard enough.

My walk to Citywest Shopping Centre was a quick one and before I knew it, I was in Dunnes Stores, walking around pushing a trolley. I took out the list Branna made and began picking up the items she wrote down. I added some cookies and other treats into the trolley, because it was that time of the month, and I needed them.

I bent down to get the triple chocolate cookies—the best cookies ever—on the bottom shelf. I had to go down on my knees because there were only two packets left, and they were at the very back. I got them though, and when I stood up and turned to toss them in my trolley I froze mid-step.

"What the heck are *you* doin' here?" I asked, blinking rapidly as if I were seeing things.

Dominic Slater's face morphed into a teasing one. "What do you think I'm doing in a grocery store? Taking a shower?"

I pulled a face at him. "It's called a *supermarket*, you bloody ee-jit," I said coolly before moving towards my trolley.

Dominic stepped in front of me, blocking my way.

I blew out a big breath. "Move. Now."

"Why weren't you in school today?" he asked, ignoring my demand.

He noticed I wasn't in class today? I thought. *Probably because he had no one else to bully since I wasn't there.*

"I'm sick," I said and tried to get around him once more.

He blocked my way again by stepping to the same side as me at the same time.

"You don't look sick," he commented, his eyes scanning my face.

I glared at him.

"Shows how much you know, doesn't it?" I growled.

I hunched forward a little when pressure erupted across my lower abdomen and caused me immense pain.

"Dominic, move out of me way!" I pleaded.

"Are you going to puke?" he asked, *still* blocking my way.

"Yeah, I'm goin' to puke, and I'm aimin' for you, so move!" I warned.

He chuckled. "Nah, you don't look like you'll be sick. You're obviously having stomach pain though."

Don't attack him, my mind whispered. *He isn't worth it.*

"Thank you for that observation doctor Fuckface, now move!" I spat.

Dominic merrily laughed at me then glanced to my hands. "I'll happily move... when you give me those cookies."

I cuddled the cookies to my chest as I would with a newly born infant.

"No way," I growled. "I got them first!"

Dominic rolled his grey eyes. "They are most likely the *last* triple chocolate cookies in the entire store since you had to get them from the very back of the shelf. This is the first time in weeks I have a break in my training routine, and I'm craving cookies. If you want me to move, then you will give them to me."

Training routine? My mind whispered. *What bloody training routine?*

I desperately wanted to ask the question on my mind, but the pain in my stomach demanded otherwise.

"They *were* the last two packets in the shop, but I'm not givin' you either of them, and if you don't move I'll scream!" I warned.

He tipped his head back and laughed, so I took the opportunity and manoeuvred around him. I used one hand to hold the cookies to my chest and the other to grab my trolley.

"Oh no you don't!" He grumbled.

When I felt hands come around my stomach from behind, I almost died. He was touching me! Dominic Slater had his large hands on my stomach and had his hard body pressed into my back.

Did this motherfucker have a death wish? I angrily thought.

"I'll give you three seconds to get your hands and body away from me," I threatened, "otherwise I *will* knock you out!"

Dominic's soft chuckle in my ear made my body tense up even more than it already was. The hairs on the back on my neck rose, and shivers ran up and down my spine at the close contact.

"You think you can take me, pretty girl?" he asked as his hot breath spread out over my neck.

I resisted the urge to roll my eyes back as my skin tingled with delighted. I quickly refocused my attention to what he said, and I stiffened.

Pretty girl? I thought. *Was he trying to be funny or something?*

"I do!" I barked then said, "Don't call me that again!"

"I can call you what I like and say what I like to you," he quipped. "Freedom of speech and all that."

I struggled against his hold.

"Get off me!" I snapped then gasped when one of his arms came up and made a blatant grab for my cookies.

No. Fecking. Way!

I lifted my leg and kicked back against Dominic's shin; he hissed as he jumped back away from me. I whirled around and glared at him while he shook out his leg, probably trying to shake the pain away.

"You bitch!" he bit out. "You kicked me!"

I evilly smiled at him. "That will be your balls if you ever touch me again. Have you not learned your lesson? Touchin' me results in me hittin' you."

Dominic rubbed his cheek as if still feeling the pain of the slap I delivered to him on Wednesday for touching my arse. He dropped his hand and grinned at me.

"You have a phat ass," he shrugged. "I couldn't help myself from having a feel."

He just called me fat. He *actually* just called me fat.

I didn't care if I looked the size of a whale; you just didn't call a girl fat, *especially* to her damn face.

The insult hurt me and I hated that. I detested that I let Dominic get to me enough to make me feel something other than annoyance. I needed to toughen up around him otherwise he could ruin all the years I've spent building up my protective wall.

"*You* are fat!" I immaturely retorted, then turned and grabbed my trolley with one hand to push it away.

Fuckface stopped me though.

He wedged himself between my trolley and my body. I didn't like it how my body betrayed me and got all tingly and hyper sensitive whenever he got close to me.

"I didn't call you fat." Dominic said, looking down at me.

The dirty liar!

I growled at him. "You did too, you lyin' sack of shite!"

"I said you have a phat ass, there's a difference," he stated.

What? My mind bellowed.

"No there isn't," I argued. "You said me arse is fat—"

"Phat as in sexy," he purred.

I stared at him, suppressing the urge to beat him to death with my cookies.

"Fat is *not* sexy," I specified.

"When you have a phat ass it is," Dominic countered, still standing in front of me. "You have a big butt, and that *is* sexy."

Why were we having this conversation about my fat but not fat arse? I wondered.

"I don't give a shite." I stated. "Me and me fat arse want to move on with our trolley so get outta the way."

Dominic smirked and held out his hand and said, "Cookies first."

I gripped the cookies tighter. "You will have to pry them from me cold, dead fingers, you lanky bastard."

He took a threatening step towards me; I panicked and swung my arm catching him across the face with the cookie packet. He stumbled to the side and out of my way as he gripped his face. I shot forward, grabbed my trolley, and all but sprinted up the aisle.

"Bronagh!" he roared.

I turned and headed straight for a checkout till, more than ready to pay for the items and get home. People obviously heard Dominic shouting and were looking down the aisle where I just shot out from. I pretended to be confused as well; I didn't want anyone thinking I was the Bronagh that Dominic was shouting after.

I jumped into a queue and began to unload my trolley items onto the conveyor belt while mentally shouting at the woman in front of me to hurry up and pack her things.

"I could have you arrested for assault, you know that right?" His voice all but snarled. "That's *twice* you hit me back there."

I sighed, wishing he would just go away.

"It was self-defence, *you* put your hands on *me* first without permission," I stated as I nudged my trolley forward without looking around at him.

"That's bullshit," Dominic spat.

I swallowed; trying not to falter even though it was obvious he was pissed at me.

"Get over it." I mumbled.

I surged forward when the lady in front of me was finished and, thankfully, the woman serving me had my stuff scanned and helped me bag them in record time.

"Those cookies are the nicest ones in the entire shop, they are always sold out." The woman commented when she tucked them into a bag.

I looked up at Dominic who was glaring at me. It made me smile before I looked at the woman.

"I agree," I beamed. "They *are* delicious."

"Evil bitch," Dominic muttered, making the woman snap her head to him, which caused me to grin a little.

I paid the woman, grabbed the three carrier bags, and heaved them down. They were heavy and I hated that Branna wasn't here with her car to help me bring them home.

I sucked in a large breath and headed for the exit of the shop on-ly to pause at the doors, almost whimpering right there and then. It was absolutely lashing rain outside. I didn't know why I was so surprised, it always happened. It could be mild and cool here in Dublin one minute then belting rain the next.

I sighed and looked up at the sky after a full minute of just staring out at the rain. "You just can't cut me a break, can you, Jesus?"

"I don't think he replies to people who assault innocents."

I jumped at his voice, which he laughed at.

I shook my head without looking at Dominic when he came to stand next to me. "How the hell did you pack your things and pay for them so quickly?" I questioned.

"Magic," he replied.

I grunted. "Well, use some magic and disappear from me presence."

Dominic snorted. "You would love that, wouldn't you?"

I looked at him, and narrowed my eyes. "I would love nothin' more than for you to disappear from the face of the earth, Fuckface."

His lip quirked as he said, "No wonder you bought tampons, it must be that time of the month."

He saw my tampons? My mind screamed.

I felt heat spread out over my cheeks. "Shut up."

There was a gleam of wickedness in his eyes as he said, "You're seriously mean on your period."

Oh, my God!

"This was horrible," I stated. "I hope we don't run into each other here—or anywhere—ever again. Bad day to you, sir." I bowed my head and stepped out into the rain.

I felt a chill run up my spine, so I straightened myself up, ignored the pain of the plastic bags digging into my fingers, and pushed on walking.

"Do you want a ride?" I heard Dominic's voice shout from my far left.

I gasped and spun in his direction, noticing that he was moving towards a large black Jeep.

"You dirty bastard!" I snapped. "How *dare* you ask me that!"

Dominic paused his stride and looked at me with his eyebrows raised before he burst into laughter.

"I meant a lift as in a *lift home in my car*. I didn't mean a ride as in the meaning of what a ride is over here... I'm not asking you to ride *me*, Bronagh."

I was mortified.

"Whatever, I don't need a *lift!*" I turned and continue brisk walking out of the car park and onto the pathway.

The rain was coming down so hard that it was dribbling down into my eyes making it hard to see. I rubbed my eyes against my shoulder and pressed on.

I never cared about the rain—I was used to it and actually liked walking in it when it rained hard. But not when I was carrying heavy things. I glared at Dominic's Jeep when it passed me by then screamed when he came close to the path and splashed dirty water all over me.

"You arsehole!" I screamed as loud as I could.

I had dropped my shopping bags during the soaking, so I quickly bent down to pick them up. Dominic was lucky everything I bought was in sealed packaging and wouldn't be destroyed by the water.

"I know you won't believe me but I was actually pulling up beside you to offer you a ride again. I really didn't mean to get you all wet," Dominic's voice shouted out from his car—the passenger side window was rolled down—then followed with a laugh.

He was actually laughing at me!

I growled as I looked to my right and glared at him. I used my shoulder to get the water out of my eyes again before spitting some out of my mouth.

"Piss off," I bellowed. "Just leave me the hell alone!"

His eyebrows jumped a little at my shouting, but I didn't care. Screw him. I turned and pretty much jogged away and the rest of the way home. I didn't stop moving until I was safely inside my house. I sank down to my arse with the hall door pressed to my back.

"Bronagh? Is that you? I got off early and tried ringin' you to see if you needed—" Branna's voice was cut off mid-sentence before a muffled laugh quickly filled up the silence. "You look like a soaked rat!"

I growled and leaned my head back against the door and closed my eyes. I winced a little when my stomach began to cramp up, adding further horribleness to my already shitty day.

"I didn't think it was rainin' *that* hard. You're seriously soaked, Bee. What happened?"

I grunted as I continued to sit on the floor with my shopping bags gathered around me. I could easily tell her that an American boy soaked me with his car after harassing me inside the supermarket but I honestly didn't want to talk about Dominic or even think about the arsehole.

"I don't want to talk about it." I grumbled.

I was fuming that I was soaked to the bone and annoyed that I had a female reproductive system, I leaned my head back against the door and closed my eyes again before exhaling loudly.

I *hated* Dominic Slater.

CHAPTER THREE

66 I don't want to go class, I still feel like shite. Please, Branna, don't make me go. If you love me at all, you *won't* make me do this," I complained and flung my limbs around like it was nobody's business.

Branna grunted as she continued to pull at my waist, trying to get me to release the handle of the passenger door of her car.

"I'm goin' to be late for class and so are you, so let go and get goin'!"

I gripped the handle of the car tighter. "Never!"

Branna sighed loudly. "I didn't want to have to do this but you leave me no choice."

I furrowed my eyebrows together and wondered what was she talking about—"Ahh!" I screamed, cutting my thoughts off. "No, Branna, don't tickle me! Mercy, *mercy*!"

She showed *no* mercy, she tickled under my armpits and down my ribs until I was a convulsing mess and jumped away from the car and her. She quickly locked up the car by pressing a button on her keys as soon as I was a metre or two away.

I was straightening my clothes out and shivering a little in my tickle aftermath while Branna folded her arms across her chest and cocked her eyebrow at me, daring me to come at her and the car again.

I groaned. "You're the worst sister ever, I'm *dyin'* here!"

Branna rolled her eyes. "You took your painkillers and ate some food, you can't miss class just to stay in bed and do nothin' so get!"

I narrowed my eyes at her. "When the day comes that you're in labour with a child I'm goin' to laugh at you and remind you of this day!" With that said, I turned and stomped across the car park towards my school's entrance.

"Have a nice day, you big baby!" Branna shouted after me, laughing.

Bitch!

I entered school just as the class bell rang, so I picked up my pace to a little jog. I didn't want to get a late stamp and be told off by teachers because that would just make me feel even worse. I got to registration class roughly three minutes after class started so when I entered the room, everyone was already seated and looked at the door when it opened. I didn't look at anyone, only my tutor who smiled at me when I walked in.

She looked a little *too* happy to see me.

"Welcome back, Bronagh, we missed you on Friday."

Sure.

"Uh, sorry I'm late, I overslept," I muttered.

The miss waved me off. "Not a bother, you're actually the girl I need to do a job for me since you're already on your feet."

Oh bollocks, I thought.

"Uh, okay," I said, and scratched my neck awkwardly.

She turned to the rest of the class. "I need another female volunteer for this *special* job."

Not one single girl raised her hand and I didn't blame them, doing 'jobs' for teachers was always shite.

The miss sighed. "Okay, I'll just pick someone then... Destiny."

Destiny groaned out loud making everyone except me chuckle.

"Fine, what's the job?" she asked in defeat.

"Well, as you all know, it's our annual Raise To Praise event day today, and this year the second year classes and tutors are in charge of decoratin' the hall and organisin' the games. But as usual, there is only one job that two senior girls must do, no younger girls can do it. I've been asked to choose two lovely girls from my tutor class for the job."

A smile lit up on Destiny's face while a look of sheer horror overtook mine. I forgot all about the Raise To Praise event today; I would have locked myself in my bedroom if I had remembered it!

"The kissin' booth!" Destiny and I said in unison, only my tone was that of disgust while Destiny's tone was one of excitement.

"That's the one," the miss beamed.

Some of the boys in class whooped making Destiny playfully laugh.

I moved towards the miss. "Miss, pick someone else, please. This day is to *raise* money for the sports team; you will *lose* money if I help out at the kissin' booth. I guarantee you that."

Some people laughed, but I didn't care; they and I both knew it was true. I didn't look like Destiny at all; she was slim with curvy hips, big boobs, flaming red hair, and a beautiful face that was hardly ever in need of makeup. She was naturally stunning while I... wasn't.

I knew I wasn't fat, but I wasn't slim like Destiny either. Like I mentioned before, I had a pear shape frame, which meant I was all small boobs and waist with a big arse and thighs that made me look huge unless I wore the right clothing.

"Oh, nonsense, don't even go there. You and Destiny are both pretty as can be so *no* backin' out," the miss stated, pulling me from my thoughts and making me sigh.

"Whatever," I mumbled and dragged my feet as I walked over to my desk, not looking down at the back row.

Down in the back was where *it* sat.

Unfortunately, first period was over like the snap of my fingers, and it made me inwardly groan and wish the class went on for longer.

"Everyone can head to the main hall now; have fun, and don't do anythin' that will wind up in me givin' out detention. Understood?"

Everyone mumbled a yeah to the miss, which made her happy, as we all headed out of class and towards the main hall. I felt a firm tap on my shoulder when I got inside and it made me jump a little.

"Sorry," Destiny's voice chuckled as she rounded on me. "Didn't mean to scare you."

Yeah, like I believed that.

"You didn't," I lied.

Destiny smirked a little before fully smiling. "Let's go to the kissin' booth and get workin'."

She turned and pranced off towards the back of the hall where the kissing booth was always set up. I reluctantly followed her with my head down and my shoulders slumped.

When I got to the booth, Destiny was already settled into hers. So I slid into mine, put my bag on the floor next to me, closed my eyes, and proceeded to wish I were dead.

"Two Euro per kiss, ladies. Get the money first."

I opened my eyes and nodded to the male teacher who was talking to Destiny and me.

"The kissin' booth is open, everyone," the sir then shouted.

I groaned, and then dropped my head to my hands; this was *so* bloody embarrassing. About two minutes passed until a group of first year lads got the courage to inch their way towards the booth.

"We have money," one of the lads said.

I couldn't help but recoil a little; these lads were all only thirteen or so, and it was possible that Destiny or I was about to be their first kiss. That thought didn't sit well with me.

"Okay, lads. No blondes this year so those who prefer redheads line up in front of me and those who prefer brunettes line up in front of Bronagh," Destiny said taking charge with the line that the girls working the booth each year had to use.

It was a quick way to get the lines formed in front of the girls doing the kissing and made things less awkward in case the lad didn't know whom to choose.

There were eight lads and five of them lined up in front of me, which shocked the hell out of me. I figured they would pick Destiny even if they preferred brunettes because she was so much better looking than me, even on a bad day.

I blinked when the first lad stepped towards me, held out his two Euro coin, and dropped it in my collection basket.

"I'm Toby." He smiled and revealed the cutest gap between his front teeth.

"Hi Toby, I'm Bronagh." I smiled and forced myself not to puke.

This kid was so cute and I felt like I was about to violate him.

He shifted his stance and just looked at me like he was waiting for the green light to kiss me so I blew out a breath, puckered my lips, and leaned towards him. He jumped a little, smiled, then mimicked my actions and met my lips, pressing his against mine.

It was the type of kiss that was five seconds long and tight-lipped. The kind you would give someone as a quick peck on the cheek, but instead it was on my lips and Toby seemed to be thrilled with that.

"Thanks," he breathed.

When I pulled back from him, he just stood staring at me with a bright smile and wide eyes.

"Toby, it's *my* turn to kiss 'er now," a lad from behind Toby hollered.

Toby frowned but quickly smiled at me again before moving off. The four lads that followed Toby all got the same five-second long, closed-mouthed kiss, and afterwards they acted like I had flashed them my boobs with the way they gazed at me.

"This is fun," Destiny chirped from my left.

I looked at her, my face scrunched up in horror. "They were practically babies!"

She rolled her eyes. "Puh-lease, we're only like four to five years older than them. Besides, it was only for two seconds."

Five seconds.

I shook my head. "I still didn't think it was fun."

"You will when the older lads pile in and come over." Destiny beamed.

I snorted and said, "I will happily leave you to deal with them since you seem to enjoy this."

"Really?" she said excitedly. "Deadly, thanks!"

You're more than welcome, I thought.

I turned my head and looked around the hall at the rest of the set-ups to earn money. There were games, baked goods for sale, dancing, and other stuff that I couldn't see from where I was sitting.

"You know that Jason is back from his holiday early, right? And that he prefers brunettes over redheads?"

Why did she keep talking to me? My mind grumbled. *Wait. Did she say Jason was back from his holiday... early?*

I groaned aloud. "That news just made me die inside."

Destiny giggled so I looked at her and said, "He will choose you over me. He knows I don't like him."

That was an understatement; Jason knew I hated him.

Jason was the captain of the football team and had been a pain in my arse since second class in primary school when he decided to bully me for his personal amusement.

The captain of each sports team always had to hit up the kissing booth and bring their players along. For some reason other boys in the school did the same shite they did, and the teachers knew that, so they made a deal with the teams to promote the kissing booth so they could earn more money for their uniforms and stuff.

I mean, the money we all raised went directly to their teams, so they got pretty hands—and lips—on about it each year and made sure the kissing booth made the most money. Because, according to them, it was the most fun during the whole event.

Destiny's laughter got my attention. "Exactly, which is why he will choose you because it will make you mad, and he lives for that."

"He doesn't like me either," I argued. "Why would he want to kiss me just to piss me off?"

"I don't know," Destiny grinned. "But you can ask him 'cause here he and the football team comes now."

"Ladies." Jason's obnoxious voice rang in my ear as I turned my gaze to his. He looked the same as the last time I saw him, just tanner. He grinned and rubbed his hands together when he came to a stop in front of the booths. "Well, lady and Bronagh."

I glared at him then at the team and took charge instead of Destiny.

"You know the drill," I announced. "If you like redheads line up in front of Destiny and if you want a dig in the face, line up in front of me 'cause I'm your girl."

I hated that an even amount of the team separated into lines. A good few chose me, and it made me blink.

"Did you not hear me sayin' I'll dig you in the face?" I questioned them.

I got back grins, smirks, and even a bold 'I'll risk it'.

"I have a cold sore," I blurted out, hoping they would run away in terror.

They didn't, they only laughed.

"We're payin' costumers, you have to kiss us. It's in the rules." Gavin Collins grinned when he shoved his way to the front of the line.

I was in a lot of Gavin's classes, and he seemed like a really nice lad. He was really cute as well, so when my face turned red it wasn't because I was angry with him. He was one of those lads that was seriously good looking, tall and lean but still remained nice and not arrogant. Which made him many girls' perfect dream man.

"Whatever," I muttered, trying to downplay my blush.

Gavin stepped forward, dropped four Euros into my basket, and smirked at my raised eyebrows. "I want an *extra* long kiss."

I felt horrified and flattered at the same time.

"What?" I whispered. "*Why?*"

Gavin gave me a 'duh' look but I didn't understand what I was supposed to get so I just stared back at him until he laughed and leaned the whole one hundred percent of the way into me, put his hand on the back of my neck, and pulled my head to his.

Then he kissed me and because I was so shocked, I opened my mouth, which he filled with his hot tongue. I couldn't pull away and the way his hand cupped my face, I could do nothing but mimic his actions and kiss him back.

This was my first *real* kiss.

That's all I could think of during the kiss; it didn't leave a lot of time to actually enjoy it. I blinked my eyes open when Gavin pulled away from me grinning.

"That was more than four Euros worth so here is another two." He chuckled and flipped another two Euro into my basket.

I just blinked at him before clearing my throat. "Uh, thanks?"

Gavin laughed then winked as he moved aside in the line. The next couple of lads kissed me exactly like Gavin did, and it made me feel weird. These lads never paid attention to me at all during our time in school, not that I paid them any either, and yet they kissed me like I was their one and only. I kissed them back just like they kissed me but there was no intensity behind my kisses. I was merely just moving my mouth and tongue.

My lips were starting to hurt and felt a little puffy, so by the time the last lad from the team in line stepped up to me, I was happy it was nearly over. I wasn't happy when I saw who the lad was though.

"No way," I hissed, "go to Destiny!"

Jason smirked at me and said, "I'm a brunette man, Bronagh, can't bend the rules."

I hissed at him. "That's bullshit, you hate me, and I hate you. This is *not* happenin'!"

He stepped towards me and I growled.

"Problem with kissin' me, Bronagh?" Jason asked, snickering.

"I have a list a fuckin' mile long!" I snapped.

I hated him so much, probably even more than I hated Dominic.

I groaned then; Jason was back in school, and Dominic was here as well now. They both made my life hell and would totally be to blame if I ever killed myself.

Jason stepped towards me again so I swung at him with my right fist making him laugh and jump back. I heard a deep chuckle from behind Jason—a chuckle that made me want to shrivel up and die.

"I'm feeling a little jealous here, Bronagh, I thought *I* was the only guy that you physically assaulted around here."

I growled when Dominic stepped out from behind Jason and grinned down at me. The lanky bastard!

"You must be Nico?" Jason said getting Dominic's attention.

Dominic looked to him and nodded, which made Jason smile as he said, "Some of the lads told me you filled in on tormentin' Bronagh while I was away. It's much appreciated, man. I didn't want her to get too bored while I was away."

What a dickhead!

"When you're both done blowin' each other, you can kindly piss off," I bit out making them both turn to me and grin.

I glared at them both.

"Rules say you *have* to kiss anyone from the ages of thirteen and eighteen if they are payin'," Jason smirked at me.

I wanted to kick him in the face.

"I know the poxy rules but why me? Why not Destiny? You both hate me, and I hate you!"

They both smiled, and I snarled.

I flicked my eyes behind the lads' forms and spotted a girl that for once made me happy at the sight of her.

"Micah," I shouted, "your boyfriend is tryin' to buy a kiss!"

Jason's face turned red when he looked over his shoulder and spotted Micah Daley, his equally evil girlfriend, storming towards us.

"You fuckin' bitch!" Jason hissed to me.

He turned to face Micah and held his hands up by his face. "I'm team captain; I *have* to kiss one of them, and I had to pick a brunette because they are my preference, but I was only goin' to plant one on her cheek. I swear."

Micah glared at him.

"Like I'd kiss any girl when I have you, babe." Jason continued. "Especially *Bronagh*. Micah, she is disgustin'."

Thanks for the vote of confidence, prick, my mind growled.

"Give me the money," Micah snapped and held out her hand.

Jason gave her his money then turned his body to look at her when she moved by him and headed towards me. Fuck!

"I wasn't goin' to let him kiss me cheek, I swear," I blurted out and resisted throwing my arms in front of my face.

You see, Micah was a kickboxer and could probably kill me with one punch or kick, and I really didn't want to die like that.

Micah rolled her eyes. "It's mandatory for the sports teams to help out at the kissin' booth since it makes the most money but Jason won't be kissin' you or Destiny. *I* will fill in for him."

I flicked my eyes to Jason and noticed his mouth dropped open; his friends and Dominic looked just as shocked as him. I looked back at Micah and shrugged, I preferred her kissing my cheek over Jason any day. I was game.

"Okay."

Micah rolled her eyes at my stiffness and leaned forward towards me. I turned my head to let her kiss my cheek but she caught my chin with her hand and forced me to look at her. She did something then that made the lads almost collapse and me almost have a heart attack.

She kissed me. On the lips. In front of everyone—and she stuck her tongue inside my mouth.

I guessed the rumours about her swinging both ways were true after all. I had the same problem with gay people, bi people, straight people, and pretty much any people in general who touched me. I didn't like being touched, talked to, or noticed in any way. Micah was fucking that up big time, because she was really going to town on kissing me and drawing *lots* of attention because of it.

I had my eyes wide open and my mouth agape when she pulled back from me. She laughed at my facial expression before turning and strutting off like she was on some sort of catwalk.

"I'm so happy that was you and not me; she all but wore the face off you," Destiny cackled.

"Piss off, Destiny!" I spat before wiping my mouth with the back of my hand.

"That was—"

"So fuckin'—"

"Sexy."

My eyes landed on Dominic when his voice said the word sexy; he was staring at me and licking his lips. I looked at the other males close by and noticed they were doing the same thing. It set off alarm bells in my head.

"One kiss per... *person*!" I stated out loud which made some of the lads mutter curses before moving away.

I couldn't exactly say one kiss per lad since Micah had just kissed me in front of everyone. That would make me sexist and homophobic.

Dominic stepped directly in front of me, but I ignored him while I continued to wipe at my mouth.

"I take it you didn't like a girl kissing you?" he asked.

I felt my eye twitch. "No, I'm straight and feel a little traumatised over what just happened, but I'll call Micah back for round two if it will get you to fuck off or step into Destiny's line instead."

Dominic laughed. "As erotic as you and Micah kissing was, I think I want a turn at your lips."

I blushed, I actually fucking blushed!

"You have to be jokin' me, right?"

He shook his head.

"But... but... you hate me!" I spluttered.

Dominic smirked. "Be that as it may, I'm a brunette man."

"You told me you were a redhead man this week, Dominic." Destiny's voice said from my left. "You said next week is blonde week and this week was redhead week, remember you said that?"

I gave Dominic a disgusted look, the prick actually sorted out which girls he would shag by hair colour and separated them into weeks. The bloody slut—wait, if he said he was a redhead man this week that meant I was off the hook for a kiss since I was a brunette. I swear I saw fireworks light up around me because of that.

"Oh, *really*? You can't break the rules Dominic. They are there for a reason, so go over to Destiny, redhead of the week, for your kiss, please."

He growled at my happiness and quickly leaned into me with his lips puckered. I, however, turned my head so fast that his lips pressed against my cheek.

"Ha!" I laughed and snatched his two Euros from his hand. "*That* was your one kiss from me, bitch!"

He looked so mad when he pulled back from me and then even angrier when I did a little victory dance whilst sitting down on my stool.

He dug out another two Euros from his pocket, and spat some curses and insults at me. He stepped over to Destiny, tossed the money into her basket, and then grabbed her face and crashed his mouth down on hers.

I felt so uncomfortable; they were seriously necking on and were just short of pulling each other's clothes off ten seconds into the kissing. I couldn't do anything other than remain next to them. So while they kissed, I made a huge show of looking at the posters around the hall. A couple of minutes passed and some third years came to the kissing booths. Even the ones who wanted to kiss Destiny had to kiss me because Dominic and she were *still* necking on.

By the time they stopped kissing, I had aged twenty years.

"Wow," Destiny's voice whispered in awe.

I couldn't help but snort as I applied some lip balm to my sore lips.

Dominic's gaze cut to me. "Jealous, phat ass?" he asked me with a growl.

I bristled a little at the insult before evilly chuckling. "Jealous? Of kissin' *you*? Not a chance in hell, Fuckface." I flicked my gaze to Destiny then and said, "He owes you at least a tenner for that kiss. Two Euros won't cut it."

She snorted then looked back at Dominic who rolled his eyes. He dug out a note from his pocket and put it in her basket.

"T'was a pleasure, my lady." Dominic bowed making Destiny giggle.

I gave him the finger before he turned and trotted off to some of the game stands.

"Holy shite, he kissed the fuck outta me. Me lips are *actually* kiss swollen!" Destiny squealed while touching her red and puffy lips.

I could relate since my lips felt so swollen you would have thought someone punched me.

I snickered at how stupid Destiny was over *that* specimen and said, "I personally think he is a dickhead and don't want to say anythin' nice about 'em but he is *so* into you, you should get stuck into 'em. No lad would kiss a girl like that if he didn't like her."

"You're right, you're *so* right!" Destiny beamed, then took out her phone and began tapping on the screen.

I inwardly smiled.

I had a feeling Dominic kissed Destiny the way he did just to make me uncomfortable because I was sitting next to her and had made a fool out of him by tricking him into kissing only my cheek. Destiny pursuing him might annoy him though, and I was all for annoying him.

You could actually say that after Dominic called me fat arse in front of Destiny, annoying him was what I now lived for.

CHAPTER FOUR

"**M**otherfucker!"

I bit down hard on my lip so I didn't laugh. If I laughed it would make me his number one target. So I did what everyone else in the class did when Dominic shrieked and cursed like a girl. I jumped with fright and swung my head around to see what was wrong with him.

"What? What is it?" Miss McKesson shouted.

Dominic was on his feet, his hands on his arse cheeks with his forehead pressed against the wall at the back of the class. Everyone watched him as he removed his hands from his arse with a hard tug that caused him to hiss in pain. When he turned and dropped thumb tacks on his desk, we all winced.

I winced for show, but what I really wanted to do was cackle like an evil witch. You see, I was no good at getting revenge on someone because I usually just had to deal with Jason and all he did was annoy me with words. But Dominic, he got in my personal space and really tried to get under my skin. His fat arse comment in front of Destiny last week during the Raise To Praise event really annoyed me; I decided to get him back by putting thumb tacks on his chair so when he sat down the needle-like pins stuck into his arse and obviously hurt like hell.

Let *his* arse hurt over calling *my* arse fat!

Ha, ha, fucking, ha!

The fact that today was my eighteenth birthday made it all the merrier. I didn't care if that made me a sadist; this was the best birthday present ever!

"*Who* put them there?" Dominic growled as his eyes flickered around the room.

I, like everyone else, shrugged my shoulders.

"I'm sure they were left there by accident—"

"There are ten pins; this is *no* accident," Dominic cut the miss off with a growl.

Damien leaned back in his chair and looked at his brother's arse. "I think you're bleeding a little, bro."

"Fuck," Dominic grunted and put his hands on his arse again.

When he removed them, there was indeed blood on his hands. Not loads, but more than pin pricks should have caused.

I guessed they pricked the prick pretty good, my mind jabbed.

I hated that I snorted at my thoughts because it got everyone's attention, and I mean *everyone*.

"You!" Dominic growled in my direction.

I raised my eyebrows in shock and raised my hands up. "Me? I didn't do anythin'. I was about to sneeze, that's all."

Dominic glared at me. "I don't believe you. You're the first person in here every day. You had the perfect opportunity to put them on my seat."

I blinked, dumbly. "I don't appreciate these false accusations, Mr. Slater."

When the students chuckled, Dominic's face reddened with anger.

"I *know* you did this." He snarled.

I shook my head. "Well, you're wrong."

"Open your bag," he snapped.

I felt my stomach lurch.

"What? Why?" I asked, trying not to sound panicked even though I could actually feel myself starting to break out in a sweat.

He was *so* not looking inside my bag.

"Why are you so nervous, slut?" Dominic questioned.

Slut? I was the most frigid person in this entire school, including the juniors! I was definitely *not* a fucking slut.

I glared at him. "'Cause you're blamin' me on somethin' I didn't do, faggot!"

Collective gasps sounded around the room at our nasty name-calling.

"That's it, the pair of you get your bags and get out into the hall. Now!" Miss McKesson snapped.

I dropped my jaw. "But miss, *he* is the one—"

"You *both* used foul, disgustin' language and disrupted my class, get out into the hall and stay there until class is over, and I am ready to speak to you both!"

I was shocked.

Miss McKesson had never raised her voice to me or kicked me out of class; I've never been kicked out of any class.

Ever.

"Okay," I mumbled as I stood up, grabbed my bag, and did the walk of shame out of the classroom along with Dominic.

He tried to walk out first, but I shouldered him into a desk making some students laugh and him growl. When we got outside and the door to the classroom was closed he instantly backed me up against the wall, placed his hands on either side of my head and leaned towards me. There were literally only a few inches of space between his face and mine.

"I *know* you did it," he growled as he leaned his head down to me, closing the gap between us even further.

I hated that he intimidated me. He was almost a good foot taller than me, broader than me, and had muscle on him. I weighed one fifty something and stood at five foot three. I couldn't exactly scare him off with my body, but I probably could with my snarky replies and attitude, so I focused and looked directly into his grey eyes.

"No," I spat. "You want me to have done it so you can bully me some more!"

He narrowed his eyes to slits and growled, "I don't bully you."

I scoffed. "Yeah, you do and you know it. You're pathetic, pickin' on a girl because it gives you kicks. You're a sad, sad *little* lad."

Dominic's eye twitched. "There is nothin' little about me, sweetheart."

He clearly wasn't talking about his height.

"I'm sure two inches is nothin' to brag about, *sweetheart*." I grinned.

Obviously I had no idea the size of his penis but saying anything less than five inches had to be a hit to the ego since I read in a magazine that five inches was the average penis size for men.

"Two?" Dominic asked, his voice high like he couldn't breathe right. "Try adding six more onto that baby, and you'll get the size of my cock."

He actually measured his penis? I thought. *That would mean he was eight inches long? Yeah, right.*

"Don't all lads say somethin' like that to make themselves look good?" I teased.

Dominic was getting red in the face again so when he pressed his body against mine, I was convinced he was going to smother me. I was shocked, however, when he tried to grab my hand and place it down *there* on his body.

"Feel for yourself." He challenged.

"Get off me you pervert," I gasped and pulled my hand from his. "I'm not touchin' you... down *there* or anywhere else!"

"Afraid you might like it?" Dominic sneered.

I scoffed. "I'd rather get off with Jason Bane than touch you, Fuckface."

I was shocked that I actually meant what I said, which clearly meant that I hated Dominic more than I did Jason.

I never thought that would happen!

Dominic clearly didn't like what I had said because he growled down at me like a dog... a murderous looking dog.

"You'd be lucky to touch me, bitch." He bit out. "You're lucky I'm this close to you right now!"

Who the fuck did he think he was? I angrily thought.

"Yeah," I argued. "'Cause I feel very lucky right now, *little* dick!"

I felt pressure on my head before I realised what was happening. Dominic fisted my hair in his hand and pressed even closer to me causing my mouth to go dry. I tried to focus on his hold on me instead of his head being bent, and his forehead touching mine. I closed my eyes as I inhaled his scent and let it wrap around me like a warm blanket. He smelled *so* good.

Bronagh, my mind growled. *Focus.*

I blinked my eyes open and stared into his grey eyes, noticing they lit up like fire. I could feel his grip on my hair tighten as my breathing turned rapid, but it didn't hurt.

Dominic tried to stick to glowering at me, but he slipped a couple of times and licked his lips when he flicked his eyes down to mine. He felt my breath on his face as I panted with fear, and he *liked* it. I saw his eyes flutter closed, and felt his lower half slightly grind into me.

"Dominic," I breathed.

He snapped out of whatever had hold of him, and locked his narrowed eyes back on mine.

"Keep running that smart mouth of yours and I'll bend you over, smack that phat ass and fuck you until you scream."

Holy shite.

My legs began to tremble. "What... you... how *dare* you say somethin' like that to me! Get away from me before I scream!"

Dominic only glared at me then looked down to my chest and stared. It was hot today, and we were allowed take off our uniform jumpers to cool down. I had my school shirt on underneath so when I looked down to see what Dominic was looking at, I gasped.

My nipples were beaded and visible, but I couldn't allow Dominic to know that it was his doing that made them hard.

"It's the material on me bra," I stated, angrily.

His grin told me he didn't believe me.

I growled. "I'm serious, it's just the material. Like I would ever be turned on by the likes of you. You aren't me type."

Dominic pulled back a little and drew his eyebrows together. "I'm *everyone's* type."

I raised an eyebrow. "Not mine, now back the fuck away."

He did, but with a grin on his face. It was only then that I realised he had my school bag in his hand; I blinked.

How the hell did he take the straps off my shoulder without me noticing? I felt my eye twitch when I realised what he did. He got close to me to distract me so he could get my bag.

"Give it back!" I snarled.

His eyes narrowed. "I will… *after* I look through it."

Before I could move forward and grab the bag or even warn him not to look into it, he stuck his hand inside the bag, rooted around, then pulled out a small box of thumbtacks. A box of thirty thumbtacks that were missing ten tacks, if he'd have taken the time to count them.

"I knew it," he hissed, glaring at the tacks then at me.

I nervously swallowed. "That proves nothin', lots of people have thumbtacks in their school bags."

"You're seriously trying to convince me you aren't to blame when I have the evidence in my hand?" he questioned.

I grunted; he had me on that.

"Fine," I grumbled. "Whatever, it was me."

He stepped towards me and I instinctively threw my hands up in front of me and pressed back against the wall. "It was payback for sayin' me arse is fat."

He just looked at me like I was ten kinds of stupid.

"Your ass *is* phat." He stated.

He just didn't get it.

"Whether it's fat or not, you don't *say* it to me." I stressed. "It's a horrible thing to say to a person!"

Dominic rubbed his temples, like our arguing was giving him a bad headache. "I told you two weeks ago in the grocery store that when I say you have a phat ass, I mean it in the best fucking way possible."

I groaned, not understanding his logic. "This here is Ireland, buddy, fat *just* means fat here!"

He shook his head and glanced at my bag before tossing it back to me, I caught it then closed it up.

"Can I have me thumbtacks back?" I asked.

Dominic pocketed the box. "Nope."

I glared at the thieving bastard.

"Fine," I huffed. "Keep them. I didn't want them anyway."

He leaned back against the wall across from me but winced when his arse rested against the wall. I tried to muffle a laugh but failed miserably.

"You know I'm going to get you back for this, right?" he warned and it shut up my snickering

I widened my eyes, which made his lip quirk.

"Seriously?" I frowned. "But I'm not good at pranks, it took me a whole week to think of puttin' tacks on your chair!"

"I'm not good at pranks either, but that's not how I'll be getting you back." He said, his lip quirked.

I cowered away from him. "Are you goin' to hurt me or somethin'?"

Dominic scanned his eyes over me. "No, I won't hurt you. I might just up my ante in bugging you since it clearly gets to you."

That was worse!

"I'll stab you in the eye with a pen if you annoy me more than you already do!" I warned him.

He wasn't fazed. "I'm not worried, pretty girl, I think I can hold my own against you."

Shite, he was right. He was bigger than me and clearly stronger. I didn't stand much of a chance against him if I was to try and hurt him and we both knew it.

45

"I'll tell on you." I threatened.

He full on laughed then. "I like you, pretty girl."

He liked that he made me miserable. He was all about it.

I shook my head." *Stop* callin' me that!"

"Why?" he quizzed.

I folded my arms across my chest. "Because I don't like it."

He winked. "Which is exactly why I call you that. Plus it suits you."

I hated that I felt heat stain my cheeks.

"Shut up, Dominic."

I turned away from him while he chuckled. "Come on, you have to know that you're pretty."

The eejit was teasing me now.

"Drop it," I growled, my back still to him.

My breath left my body when he put his arms around my waist and stroked my sides with his thumbs. I felt his breath on my ear, and the sensation I felt caused my eyes to drift closed. I really wanted to shove him away from me, but I just couldn't move. I felt like I was stuck.

"I don't think you know just how pretty you are, Bronagh," Dominic purred in my ear. "You're different from every other girl in this school. You aren't in the same league as them. You're in one of your own."

I snapped my eyes open.

This school had a lot of gorgeous girls and for him to say that I couldn't even compete in the same league with them hurt, and I didn't know why, but it did. I moved away from him as the bell rang out, and the classroom door opened.

Our classmates piled out of the room, nearly all of them greeting Dominic or slapping their hand against his as they passed him by. Damien stopped by his brother and said something, making him laugh, before moving on.

I kept my eyes glued on the floor during all of this, and I kept them aimed downwards when Miss McKesson stepped out into the hallway and stood in front of us.

"I never want a repeat of what happened in my class earlier on, do you both understand me? *Never*! The things that came out of your mouths were disgustin', and if you ever react like that to one another or anybody again I will suspend you. Do you both understand me?"

"Yes, miss," Dominic and I replied in unison.

"I'm not goin' to ask what riled you both up so much because it's over now and I hope you have both learned your lesson not to treat each other so badly or call each other such mean names. Do I need to give you both detention to drive me point home?" Miss McKesson threatened.

"No, miss," we again replied in unison.

"Good," she quipped. "Now get to class."

I moved away while the miss stopped Dominic and quietly asked, "Do you need to see the school nurse for your behind to have your wounds treated?"

Wounds?

They were tiny pinpricks for goodness sake, it's not like he just got back from war and was riddled with bullets! I didn't say anything though; I instead tilted my head down and quickly moved away before I snickered a little at my thoughts.

"No, I'm fine," Dominic replied to the miss then walked in the same direction as me.

"You'll be sorry for this Bronagh, *very* sorry," his voice growled from behind me.

I sighed because I knew that he would follow through with his threat and make me sorry.

Very sorry.

47

CHAPTER FIVE

"**S**orry, I wasn't watchin' where I was goin'," I gasped when I literally walked into somebody and knocked him or her over as I exited the school gates.

I was in a world of my own, replaying what Dominic had said to me this morning in my head. I felt sick over it all day, but felt even worse when I spotted whom I knocked over. It was Jason.

Bollocks, my mind screamed.

I reached down to help Jason to his feet. I might not like him, but I wasn't above helping someone when I was in the wrong. He didn't want my help though, and slapped my hand away. I jumped back a little and snatched my hand away, cradling it with my other hand. His slap hurt my hand; it was stinging. But I jumped back more so in shock that he actually hit me rather than the pain I felt.

"You stupid fuckin' bitch, *look* what you did to me new runners! They're all scratched up!" Jason bellowed as he got to his feet; he started forward and grabbed hold of my arm making me tense up.

He pulled me forward making me stumble into his chest. "You're payin' for these, you ugly, fat cunt!" he growled.

I nodded frantically, feeling tears well up in my eyes. He had never been physical with me before; I was used to the name-calling, but him actually hurting me upset me a lot.

"I will, I'm so sorry," I blurted out.

48

I was terrified and also was genuinely shocked. I couldn't believe he was manhandling me, especially in front of passing students.

Jason glared at me for a moment, his eyes scanning my face and landing on my mouth before grunting and shoving me away from him, which made me fly backwards. I tensed up when I lost my footing; I prepared for my arse hitting the ground, but arms caught me instead.

I breathed in relief but then gasped when the person who caught me straightened me upright and rounded on me. I didn't even try to hide my surprise and widened my eyes to the point that they stung me.

"*Dominic?*" I said, staring at his grey eyes, which were narrowed and slightly twitched.

He looked furious.

"Are you okay?" he asked me looking at my cheeks.

It was only then that I felt the fat tears from before stream down my cheeks. I quickly wiped them away and nodded. The hiccup and fresh batch of tears that followed proved me a liar though.

Dominic set his jaw as he looked at my face. "Step back and then *don't* move a muscle," he said to me; his voice sounded deeper than usual, and it freaked me out a little.

I did as he asked without question, for once, then I watched in confusion as he handed me his school bag from off his back and turned his back to me. When he started towards Jason, my stomach flip-flopped.

He wasn't going to do what I thought he was, my mind screamed, *was he?*

"Can you believe that tramp, man?" Jason asked Dominic, chuckling.

Dominic didn't say a word as he swung his fist, connecting with Jason's jaw. Jason's face snapped to the side; he was still for a moment before he realised what was happening and then suddenly speared Dominic to the ground. I heard myself scream when I heard the thud of his back hitting the ground.

I even tried to move towards the lads to stop the fight, but an arm around my waist held me in place.

"Don't interfere, it will only make him angrier because he told you not to move."

I twisted my head around and saw Dominic's face, only with white hair framing it.

Damien.

"Damien," I whimpered. "Stop them!"

Damien smiled at me, and I was a little surprised that I noticed how different his smile was from Dominic's. He had the same dimples, and exact mouth shape, but his lips were slightly rosier, and I hated myself for noticing that.

I turned my gazed from Damien, and focused on his brother.

"Stop!" I pleaded when Dominic's fist cracked into Jason's jaw causing some girls who were observing the fight scream and gasp.

I winced along with some others when we heard a really high-pitched scream.

"Stop." The voice screamed. "Oh, my God, *stop!*"

I looked and saw Jason's girlfriend, Micah, run from the school gates towards us at high speed.

This was going to be so bad. Once she found out that I was the reason the lads were fighting, she was going to kill me. She hated me as it was, thanks to Jason's attempt to kiss me last week at the kissing booth.

When Dominic landed another hit on Jason's face, some of Jason's friends who were standing back and letting them go at it because it was a fair fight, suddenly stepped in to break it up. Jason got a decent punch on Dominic's jaw first though, and it made me wince.

When Jason's friends pulled them apart, I twisted out of Damien's hold and started forward.

"Dominic, stop!" I said when I noticed him trying to go for Jason again.

I put my body in front of him and placed a hand on his chest.

He was looking over my head with his eyes narrowed. When I touched him he looked down at me and his face changed; it softened. I frowned when I spotted the cut on his eyebrow. It was starting to swell and blood was surrounding it.

"Please," I whispered and pressed on his chest in a last ditched effort to get him to back away from Jason.

I couldn't believe he fought Jason and, to make matters worse, it was because of me.

"Come on, bro, you beat his ass." Damien said as he landed a firm hand on Dominic's shoulder. "Nothing left to prove."

Dominic was trembling with rage.

"He put his hand on what's mine, don't fucking tell me I don't have something to prove."

His, my mind gasped. *What did that mean?*

"Nico!" Jason's voice shouted from behind me. "What the fuck is your problem, man?"

Dominic turned my body and carefully pushed me behind him.

"*My* problem?" He bellowed. "What the fuck is *yours*?"

"Mine?" Jason hissed. "What the hell do you mean?"

"You fucking touched her!" Dominic roared, making me jump with fright.

"Who?" Jason asked then laughed when I poked my head out from behind Dominic only to quickly retreat back behind him. "Bronagh? You jumped on me because of *that* fat bitch?"

I dropped his bag and gripped onto Dominic's waist when he tried to dart forward. "Stop!" I screamed. "Please!"

Dominic tried to shake me off him but, in doing so, his elbow hit off my cheekbone, making me hiss. Dominic didn't notice that he hit me, but his brother did.

"Dominic!" Damien roared.

Dominic snapped his head in his direction.

Damien held his brother's gaze. "You're scaring her, bro."

Dominic tensed as he turned and looked back to Jason and snarled. "Put a finger on her again and I'll kill you. Call her names again and I'll kill you. If you so much as *look* at her again I'll fucking kill you. Do you understand, *man*?"

Jason shook his head at Dominic. "What fuckin' ever, man," he said then turned to Micah, who was fussing over his face and kissing him, which Jason's friends found amusing.

Dominic turned and bent down to pick up his bag, he threw it to Damien then looked to me. "Turn around and walk," he said, his voice gruff.

I turned and began to walk through the crowd of students that had formed to watch the fight. I carefully made my way through until I was walking down the path on my own. I lifted my hand to my right cheekbone and held it there because it was throbbing pretty badly. My eye was hurting as well and I resisted the urge to cry again because if I started, I probably wouldn't stop.

"Bronagh!" I heard Dominic's voice call from behind me.

I couldn't face him, not after what he had done and what he said, I still couldn't believe he said I was his. I broke out into a run when he called me and winced every time my feet pounded against the ground because the pounding of my body made my trembling face hurt even more.

"Bronagh, for fuck's sake," he bellowed. "Don't run from me!"

I ran faster; I cut through some gardens until I was in a housing estate lower down the mountainside and yet I still kept running. It was my top speed, but it still wasn't good enough. His arms enclosed around me, and he actually lifted me up into the air to stop me running completely.

"Oh my God!" I squeaked out, not liking the sensation of being held up off the ground.

"Will you *stop* running from me?" Dominic panted into my hair.

I didn't know whether he meant every time I saw him or just now.

"No!" I snapped, not liking him telling me what to do.

I felt the vibrations of his growl against the back of my head as he adjusted his hold on me. I was acutely aware of his arms wrapped around me, his body pressed against mine.

I felt *everything*.

"Put me down, Dominic!" I grunted, trying to sound really mad rather than breathless.

"No," he replied, calmly.

I squealed in frustration.

"What do you mean, no?" I snarled. "Put me down, you big bastard!"

I heard a chuckle escape from Dominic, and it made me see red.

"I swear to God, I'm goin' to pummel you for doin' this to me!" I promised.

In one swift motion, I was placed on the ground and turned to face him. It made me gasp, because I wasn't expecting him to do that.

"Doing what to you?" Dominic asked, his eyes narrowed. "*Defending* you?"

Great, now he was mad at me.

"Eh, yeah!" I breathed. "Ever since I met you—which unbelievably has only been a few weeks—you have been nothin' but a pain in me arse. You tease me, make fun of me, and today you made me feel like absolute crap, so excuse the fuck out of me for bein' pissed at your mood swings. You go from bullyin' me to defendin' me all in the space of a few hours. Who does that?"

Dominic looked at my eyes before zoning his gaze on my right cheek.

"Did he fucking hit you in the face?" he asked, his voice venomous.

I rolled my eyes at the subject change.

"No," I quipped. "*You* did that!"

Dominic looked like I slapped him across the face.

"Me?" he whispered. "I didn't—"

"Yeah, you did." I cut him off. "When I tried to stop you from goin' for Jason the second time, your elbow hit me in the face."

His face visibly paled.

"Bronagh, I'm… I'm so sorry. I would *never* hit a girl; I swear I didn't mean it," he insisted as he lifted his hands and ran his fingertips over my cheekbone, making me wince because it was really tender.

He looked distraught by this and pulled me towards him. "Come with me, please?" he pleaded.

I pulled out of his hold.

"No, I have to go home and get ice—"

"I'll ice it for you." He offered. "Please, pretty girl, it would make me feel better if you let me take care of you."

I stared at him; I still couldn't believe he gave me *that* nickname.

I continued to stare at him and wondered what the hell was happening. I was so confused that it actually made my head hurt.

"Are you Damien?" I asked curiously, my left eyebrow quirked.

"Are you serious?" Dominic blinked. "Can you not tell the differences between us?"

"Sure I can," I said. "Your hair colour is different, and you have paler lips than he does. He is right-handed, and you are left. He's nice and you aren't. That's exactly why I'm askin' if you're him because you've been awfully nice to me these last twenty minutes, gettin' your face smashed in and all."

Dominic sort of smiled for a moment before he glared at me. "I handed that prick's ass to him, not the other way around, babe."

"Babe?" I spluttered. "You're sayin' I'm yours and callin' me babe now? I think Jason hit you too hard on the head there, *buddy*."

He rolled his eyes and muttered, "Shut up."

I sighed, closed my eyes and rubbed my temples. Dominic stepped towards me again; I could *feel* how close he was to me.

"Come back to my house with me so I can help you." He hesitated for a moment then said, "Damien will be there in case you're afraid. He took my car home for me when I came after you."

I opened my eyes and studied his face; his eyebrow was cut and some blood surrounded it, his jaw was swollen, and his chin looked like it was bruising also.

"I think you need the help more than I do." I commented. "Your face is pretty messed up."

Dominic smiled, and it messed with my already confused mind. I sighed then, shocked that I was actually agreeing to this.

"Okay," I said and waved my hand. "Lead the way."

Dominic's lip twitched and gestured for me to walk back the way I just ran from. I did so and he fell in step with me. We didn't speak, but it wasn't awkward or anything. We walked until we headed past our school, and I whistled when we entered Upton.

"You live in Upton?" I muttered. "You must have a shitload of money,"

"And why is that?" Dominic asked, amused.

I shrugged as we walked through the very clean housing estate. "Because it's not a council estate. You own the houses and nobody rents them out because they are too nice *not* to live in."

Dominic played with his hands as we walked like he was nervous, which caught my attention, but I didn't say anything about it.

"Where do you live?" he asked me after a moment.

"About a ten minute walk from here," I said. "Down on Old Isle Green. It's practically a dump compared to this estate."

"Does that matter to you?" he asked.

I shook my head, kind of shocked that I was having a legit conversation with him. While that was mildly shocking, the extreme shock factor was that I was actually *enjoying* it.

"No," I answered honestly. "I like where I live. I like me house and me road. I'm sort of intimidated by bein' here for some reason, and I don't know why. Wait, I do, it's probably because it's perfect and me bein' here messes that up."

I stopped walked when Dominic was suddenly in front of me; his head lowered to mine.

"Don't do that!" he growled at me.

I swallowed as I looked up at him and asked, "Do what?"

"Put yourself down the way you just did," he frowned.

I furrowed my eyebrows. "So *I* can't put meself down but *you* can? You said the same thing today to me. You said that I didn't fit in with the girls in our school when it came to looks. You said I was in a different league than them all!"

Dominic sighed. "I didn't mean it like that."

I shook my head. "Don't lie, it may hurt me feelin's like it did today when you said it, but don't lie just to make me feel better. If you think I'm ugly then that's fine—"

Dominic moved his head down and pressed his forehead against mine, and it made me hold my breath which cut me off.

"I didn't mean it like *that*," he said clearly. "I don't think you're ugly. When I said you were in a different league than any girl here, I meant you're more beautiful than them. You're the best-looking girl I've ever seen, period. I call you pretty girl for a reason other than to piss you off, Bronagh."

I felt my legs shake and my next breath escape in a big puff making Dominic grin because he felt it on his face. I felt like I was going to do something seriously stupid like *kiss him* so I stepped back a little and looked down. My insides were swimming because while I still strongly didn't like him, I felt a little flushed now just looking at him.

"Are we near your house yet?" I asked.

"Yeah, it's just up here," he replied in a tone that made me think he was smiling.

I didn't look up at him though; I just gestured for him to walk, which he did, so I followed him. When he entered the garden of a big four-story house, I stood at the gate and openly gaped at it.

"Fuck me sideways." I whistled.

"Is that an invitation?" I heard Dominic ask.

I snapped my head to him.

"*What*?" I almost shouted.

He pointed to my foot; I looked down and saw a flyer under my foot. I picked it up and read it; it was an invite to a four-year-old's birthday party this weekend.

"Um, yeah, it is," I muttered and let the wind take the piece of paper away.

I felt my cheeks heat up as Dominic looked at me, grinning.

"What did you think I meant?" he asked.

I didn't dare look at him.

"Nothin'," I replied and followed him into his garden.

We paused outside the door while Dominic fished out his keys from his pocket. When he got them out and opened the door he shouted, "I'm home."

I heard a chorus of rude greetings, and it made me freeze.

"That's *not* just Damien in there," I muttered.

Dominic looked down at me. "Correct, our three older brothers are in there, too."

My jaw dropped.

"I'm goin' home," I stated and turned.

I barely made it halfway out of the garden before I was lifted up from behind again.

"Oh my God," I screamed. "What the hell is your deal with pickin' me up? Put me down or I'll kick the shite outta you!"

I heard some snorts that weren't from Dominic and it made me freeze.

"I hate you," I whispered to Dominic.

He grunted.

"I know," he replied as he put me down on the ground but didn't let me go.

He turned me to face him. "I have to ice that pretty face of yours, remember?"

I hated that I turned red again, and I hated Dominic even more for smiling at me because of it. When he turned us both to face his house, I stared wide-eyed. The two men that stood leaning against the door frame were seriously sexy.

"Wow," I whispered.

Dominic snapped his head at me and glared.

"Who's the little beauty, bro?" the lad on the left asked.

Little beauty? Me?

Oh.

My.

God.

The man had dark hair like Dominic but it was long, it almost reached his shoulders. He had the same dimples when he grinned, his arms were huge with muscle and he had multiple tattoos. I could see this because he was shirtless. One tattoo was really colourful and wrapped around his arm and slithered up to his shoulder and neck.

The other lad was bare-chested as well; he had some tattoos and was muscular also. His hair was tightly cut to his head and he had a lot of scars on his torso and face that I could see from a good distance away, but he was still strikingly hot.

I found it very hard not to look at the V lines they were both sporting, but I managed it, and I think I deserved a medal for it.

"Don't even think about it Alec, she's *mine*," Dominic snarled making both the men grin.

Again with that? I thought. *Seriously?*

"Ahh," the brother with the longer hair grinned. "You must be Bronagh then?"

"How do you know me name?" I asked, confused.

Both the men grinned when Dominic snarled at them.

"Don't mind them. The asshole talking to you is Alec, the prick on the right is Kane, and my other brother Ryder is in the house with Damien."

Dominic, Damien, Alec, Kane and Ryder.

Oh, my God. Their names were just as sexy as they were.

"It's a pleasure." Kane said to me after a moment.

He looked like he was glaring at me, but when Alec murmured something to him; he smiled and scanned his eyes over my body openly.

I melted; he had such a stunning smile, which caused me to smile back at him. I didn't even pay attention to the scar curved around his mouth because his smile was simply breath taking.

"The pleasure is all *mine*, Mr. Slater." I purred.

Dominic's hand suddenly grabbed hold of mine. "All right, that's enough of *that*," he said tugging me into him.

I felt my face and neck flush as I tried to push away from him. "What the hell, Dominic?" I snapped. "The past few weeks you annoy me from a distance but within the last half hour you won't stop touchin' me. What the hell, man?"

"Man," Alec and Kane mimicked my accent in unison making each other chuckle.

I flicked my eyes towards them; I had them narrowed but when Kane laughed at my trying to get away from Dominic, I couldn't keep it up for long.

"How old are you both?" I asked, smiling.

"Twenty-five," Alec replied.

Kane cocked his brow. "I'm twenty-three, how old are you?"

"I'm eighteen today." I replied.

"Happy birthday," Alec and Kane said in unison making my insides flutter with delight.

"What?" Dominic asked, gaining my attention. "*Today* is your birthday?"

I looked at him and nodded.

He frowned. "Now I feel even worse for hitting you."

"What?" Alec and Kane roared.

I jumped while Dominic flung his hands up in front of him in an 'I surrender' motion.

"It was an accident," he stated. "Some prick hit her in school so I kicked his ass, but when she tried to pull me back, my elbow hit her face. I brought her here to ice it."

Alec waved us forward. "Yeah, Dame told us about the fight but left *her* out of it."

I was obviously *her*.

Dominic tugged me forward then, so I followed him back up the steps to his house. I had to turn so I could get by Alec's shirtless, muscular body.

"I li-like your tattoos," I stuttered.

And your mouth-watering face and body, I thought.

"Bronagh!" Dominic scowled at me when we got inside the beautiful house. "Stop it."

I pulled my hand from his.

"What? I just said I liked his tattoos." I frowned then pointed my finger dangerously at him. "I don't know where you're gettin' off thinkin' you can tell me what to do, Dominic, because you can't, so stop it before I break a bone."

He smirked at me. "You want to get physical with me, darling?"

"What?" I spluttered before licking my suddenly dry lips. "I think we need to go to the hospital with you, you're sayin' weird things and just actin' out of character since that fight. I *really* think Jason hit you too hard on the head."

Dominic's brothers chuckled as they moved around us. I watched as they went into what I would have guessed to be a sitting room but turned out to be a home gym. That explained why they were shirtless and so buff; they were working out and clearly did it often.

"Are you going to stare at my brothers all day or are you going to come with me?" Dominic asked in an impatient tone.

I bit down on my lower lip. "If that is a legit question, I vote to stay here and stare at your brothers all day."

He grabbed my hand and roughly pulled me down the hall and away from the view of Alec and Kane.

"It was *really* nice to meet you both," I shouted to them.

"You too," they both shouted back in unison.

I grunted when Dominic and I entered what was obviously the kitchen. He was tugging me along behind him but when he stopped I collided with his back. I didn't even try to pull my hand from his, because he had a good grip on me.

"'Bout time you showed up. Why are you getting into fights at school Dominic? We don't need attention drawn to us, you fucking *know* this!" a deep voice bellowed.

I froze and decided to stay behind Dominic. That was obviously his eldest brother, Ryder, shouting and I didn't want to be a target of his anger so I stayed put. Also, I wanted to see if he would elaborate on what he just said.

I mean, *why* didn't they need attention drawn to them?

"I'm aware of that, and I'm sure Dame already told you why I got into a fight," Dominic replied calmly regaining my attention.

"He did," the deep voice said. "I just want to hear it from you.".

"He put his hands on her, even if he didn't hurt her I still would have beaten the shit out of him for the names he called her," Dominic said casually.

My stomach was flip-flopping left, right and centre.

What the hell was going on?

"Bronagh?" deep voice inquired.

I stepped out from behind Dominic and waved a little. "Heya."

"I'm Ryder, Dominic and Damien's oldest brother."

Holy shite.

He looked like Matt Bomber, only hotter because he was buff and covered in tattoos!

"Nice to meet you," I murmured and just flat-out stared at him.

Dominic shook his head at my reaction to his brother, but I didn't care. This family had beautiful genes, like I wasn't going to ogle them.

"How is your face?" Ryder asked me.

I thought about what he asked then touched my face and hissed. "It's sore."

Dominic moved across the room, opened what looked like a freezer and pulled out an ice pack, then grabbed a small hand towel on his way back over to me.

I frowned at him. "You are the one with the cut eyebrow and busted up face. You need the ice more than I do, princess."

Dominic's brothers snickered.

"I like her," Ryder mused.

"I like her more and more each time she insults him," Damien teased.

"Fuck you both," Dominic grinned as he continued to move towards me.

He turned me around and applied pressure to my back, making me walk forward.

"This is startin' to piss me off, Dominic." I grunted. "Stop pushin' me around. Stop touchin' me altogether!"

"That's the appeal then?" Ryder said softly then murmured. "He wants what he can't have."

"That, her accent, and I'm sure the fact that she's smoking hot has something to do with it as well," Damien's voice chimed in.

Dominic grunted as he directed me upstairs. We walked all the way to the fourth floor, which I wasn't happy about.

"Why are we comin' up here?" I asked, huffing and puffing.

Dominic laughed from behind me. "Do you do any cardio? You sound like you're going to collapse."

I snarled as I entered the room he directed me into. "No, I don't do cardio; there is a reason I look the way I do, and it's not because I enjoy doin' cardio in me spare time."

"I wasn't saying you need cardio, you look damn fine from where I'm standing—"

"Oh, my God." I suddenly shouted. "Stop. Just *stop!*"

Dominic closed the door behind us and just stared at me for a moment.

"Stop what?" he asked.

I gaped at him. "Are you serious? Stop being overly nice to me, stop commentin' on me looks and body, and for the love of God stop pushin' me around!"

Dominic pointed behind me. "Okay, I will do all that if you sit on my bed so I can ice your face."

I widened my eyes and looked behind me to the king-size bed; it was bloody huge.

I hesitated. "Uh…"

I heard Dominic chuckle. "I'm not just trying to get you into my bed; not for the reasons you're probably thinking anyway."

I flushed.

"I wasn't thinkin' anythin'," I lied.

"Go sit down then," he challenged.

I did, and I was stiff as a board while I did it.

"Okay, I'm sittin' on your bed." I announced. "Can I have the ice pack now?"

Dominic nodded, wrapped the towel around the ice pack and carefully placed it on my cheekbone.

I instantly sighed. "That feels good."

"I'm glad," Dominic said as he sat down next to me.

I looked at him and frowned. "Do you have a first aid kit?" I asked.

He raised his uncut eyebrow and nodded before he got up and went to his bathroom. He had one connected to his room!

He came back out with a small first aid kit, sat back beside me and handed me the kit. I put my ice pack down and stood up; I opened the kit, took out a cleaning gauze and a small bottle of purified water. I soaked the gauze then leaned towards Dominic.

"Stay still," I murmured before I began wiping around his cut eyebrow.

He hissed a little, and it made me smile.

"I'm nearly done, princess."

Dominic growled and hissed at the same time. He remained still while I wiped away all the dry blood from his face. The cut on his eyebrow was only a little deep and was already clotted, so I just put a clear plaster over it. Then I picked up my ice pack and placed it on his face. I tried not to fumble with what I was doing, but it was difficult. Dominic was silent as he studied me and allowed me to clean him up.

"Thank you," he murmured.

I nodded. "You're welcome."

Those words were the first nice things we had ever said to one another without being sarcastic.

Dominic lifted his hand and placed it on top of mine on his ice pack. I froze and looked into his eyes, wondering what he was doing. I started to sweat when his other hand touched my back and pulled me close to him. My heart rate picked up and began to pound into my ribs.

"Dominic," I whispered, my voice trembling. "What are you doin'?"

"Why do you call me Dominic?" he asked me, ignoring my question and my trembling.

My mind was getting all mushy, and my stomach was fluttering with butterflies.

"Because it's your name."

His lip twitched. "Everyone calls me Nico though, only my brothers call me Dominic."

I shrugged. "I'm not like everyone else."

He pulled me closer to him then.

"You torment me," he whispered to me.

His scent filled my nose making me feel a little lightheaded.

"You started it," I said through my slight swaying.

He grinned at me and said, "I don't mean it like that; I mean you do torment me on a daily basis, but you torment me constantly, day *and* night."

I just looked at him in confusion, which made him laugh.

"Bronagh, you get under my skin, you make me crazy," he clarified.

What? I thought. *How is that possible?*

I ignored him as much as I could at school and when he got too close to me, I physically and verbally assaulted him. I'm not saying I was proud of it... but I also wasn't saying I wouldn't do it again.

I narrowed my eyes at him. "Did you bring me up here just to tell me how much I annoy you? Because if you did, you could have done it back at school and saved me walkin' all the way up here—"

He cut me off with a soul-crushing kiss.

I opened my mouth to protest but instead of words leaving my mouth. I moaned when a warm, wet tongue entered. I dropped my hand away from the ice pack and Dominic caught it and grabbed my other hand and pulled me onto him. I felt his hands go under my school skirt and land on the back of my bare thighs before he hoisted me up onto his body.

I gasped and then groaned when he nibbled on my bottom lip. He positioned me so I was straddling him. His left arm was tightly wrapped around my waist while his right arm was lower, and I found out why it was lower down when his hand slid around my right arse cheek.

"Dominic!"

I was shocked in myself at how that came out; it was meant to be sobering, but it sounded more like a soft moan.

Dominic growled into my mouth then he captured it with another kiss. My hands found their way to his hair and when I twisted my fingers around his dark locks he stood up with me still wrapped around him. He turned us and lay me down on the bed with his body hovering over me.

This may not have been my first kiss, but it *felt* like it was because all I could do was feel and I felt *so* good with Dominic kissing me.

He stopped kissing me long enough to sit up and pull his t-shirt from his body. I blew out a breath when I caught sight of his toned and tanned chest followed by his visible abs and very visible V line.

He must work out, too!

My eyes flicked to his right side and I groaned; he had a tribal tattoo curling from his ribs around to his back and up onto his shoulder. It looked like it wasn't finished though and that it was going to be a tribal tattoo sleeve down the entire length of his right arm.

Jesus, help me.

"Sit up," Dominic ordered, his voice husky.

I did and when he lifted my school jumper from my body and starting unbuttoning my shirt I didn't stop him. My mind was literally screaming that this wasn't right, and I wasn't the type of girl to do this stuff with someone I didn't really know. My body replied with a simple 'fuck you' and won the battle.

"So fucking hot," Dominic growled when he pulled my shirt away from me.

I couldn't believe I was letting this happen. I was aware of what was going to happen if I let this continue on, but I chose to let it. It might be wrong but at this moment and time, it didn't feel wrong.

Dominic reached around to unhook my bra straps at the exact same time his bedroom door opened.

"Dominic, are you coming for a run with—oh shit, sorry."

I shrieked and covered myself up even though Dominic's body was hiding me from view.

"Alec, bro," Dominic bellowed, looking over his shoulder. "Get the fuck out!"

"Leaving," Alec said, as the door clicked shut.

I closed my eyes and could only imagine what Alec thought. From his view, he would have seen Dominic's bare back with my bare legs wrapped around the back of his because my skirt was rising up.

"Oh, my God," I whispered.

"I'm sorry about that, babe." Dominic murmured in a seductive tone. "Now where were we?"

Was he serious?

"I was about to get dressed and go home," I answered and pushed him back away from me.

I was red faced as I scrambled around picking up my school shirt and jumper. I quickly got my shirt back on and buttoned and fixed it into my skirt, then pulled my jumper over my head. I picked up my school bag and put the straps over my shoulders.

I moved towards the door without speaking to Dominic, and this made him mad.

"You're just going to leave," he snapped. "Just like that?"

I turned and didn't look at his face, just at his still bare torso. "This is wrong, we don't even like each other so we shouldn't be kissin' or doin' anythin' other than ignorin' each other. I appreciate what you did for me today; I *really* do but that won't fix anythin', I still don't like you."

Dominic frowned. "I get that but I thought that we could hash it out—"

"By havin' sex?" I gasped.

"Uh, that's a good a way as any but-"

"You arsehole! You thought by seducin' me it would make me magically *not* hate you?" I asked then widened my eyes. "Is *that* what you meant this mornin' when you said you would get me back without physically hurtin' me? You wanted to take me virginity when you knew I would regret that, and it would hurt me emotionally? Is *that* what is happenin' here?"

Dominic shook his head. "No, I'm saying this all wrong, babe."

"*Don't* call me that." I bellowed. "Get the hell out of me way, now!"

He didn't move, his own eyes narrowed now. "Stop being such a crazy bitch for a second and just *listen* to me—"

"Oh, that's a great way to get a girl to listen, call her names," I spat sarcastically as I stormed out of his room and down the stairs.

When I got to the bottom of the stairs, Dominic suddenly jumped around me. The sight of his bareback and his tattoo before he turned around tormented me. It was rippled with muscle and for some reason I wanted to bite him.

"Will you just *stop*," he pleaded. "You're overreacting right now."

"Bro," a voice whispered from my right. "You don't *ever* say that to an angry woman. Especially not an angry *Irish* woman."

"Fuck off, Alec," Dominic snapped without looking away from me.

"Why wouldn't I overreact?" I quipped. "You have been a bloody dick to me ever since I met you, and now, all of a sudden, you want to hash things out between us by havin' sex? You're a class A fuckin' arsehole!"

I angrily shoved at his chest.

"You know what?" he laughed. "I thought you would be somewhat nice to me for doing you a favour by defending you today, but I guess you really are an ice-cold bitch. No wonder nobody at school wants to be your friend. Get the fuck out, no pussy is worth this bullshit."

Pussy? That's all I was?

He really was only trying to get laid and he hoped to hurt me in the process. I hated that my eyes welled up, but I hated even more that Dominic noticed it and shook his head at me.

"If you want to do me a favour then stay the fuck away from me," I said in a cold tone before turning and walking away.

I paused at the door when I opened it. It was raining out, but that wasn't why I stopped. I looked over my shoulder and evilly smiled at Dominic, ignoring the fact that all his brothers were watching and listening from out of the sitting/gym room doorway.

Dominic hurt me with his words, worse than when he elbowed me in the face, and I wanted to hurt him back.

"And don't get big headed thinkin' I wanted to sleep with you, because I pretended you were Damien the *whole* time up there," I said sweetly then walked out the door and slammed it behind me.

"You fucking slut!" I heard Dominic's voice roar.

I heard his brothers shout at each other to grab him. The noise of their shouting stopped when I got a good bit away from their house.

I was so mad at myself; I should have known better than to go to his house. He was just another typical slimy lad who thought about nothing but having sex and he thought that defending me would get him into my knickers. The fucking sad fact was that if Alec hadn't walked into the bedroom, he *would* have succeeded.

Apparently I *was* that easy!

I was fuming mad all the way home from Dominic's house and when I finally did get inside my house, I was completely soaked and freezing.

"I'm home," I called out as I closed the front door behind me.

"I'm in the kitchen," Branna shouted. "Happy birthday, baby."

Shite, I cringed. *I forgot it was my birthday.*

I groaned when I walked into the kitchen of my house.

"Thanks, Bran," I said to my sister.

"We're going to the cinema to see Magic Mike for your birthday tonight, Aideen is meetin' us there with her friend Keela!" Branna announced with a bright smile on her face only for it to drop and her eyes to widen.

"What the hell happened to you, Bronagh?" she shouted when her eyes zeroed in on my face. She pushed away from the kitchen table and ran towards me. I sighed and stood still as she examined my battered flesh.

"Put the kettle on," I grumbled. "It's a long story."

CHAPTER SIX

I was the first person in class the next morning, which was the usual. The classroom door was unlocked, so I walked in and sat in my usual seat at my usual desk. I took out my iTouch, put my earphones in my ears, took out a notepad from my bag and started doodling out some pumpkins, ghosts, and other random scary things. Halloween was only two weeks away. I didn't like the holiday at all, but I was bored and just felt like drawing them.

I yawned after a moment; I was up for ages last night telling Branna about the Dominic and what my life had been like since he started at school before we went out for my birthday to cinema with her friends. I didn't know why, but I left Damien out of the briefing completely, and I referred to Dominic as Nico. I felt like since he told me that only his brothers called him Dominic, it was something special for me and only me, which was so pathetic.

Branna found some of my interactions with Dominic amusing, but she didn't like what he did yesterday. Trying to get sex out of me in order to hurt me for hurting him with thumbtacks. She also didn't like what Jason did to me; I had to talk her out of going to his house and beating him with a hammer.

I assured her Dominic's beating was punishment enough. It took her a while, and even though she wanted to hurt him, she accepted it and put the hammer back in her toolbox.

After my yawn, I rubbed my eyes only to hiss in pain. Thanks to Dominic's elbow in the face yesterday my cheekbone and eye were bruised; I actually had a black eye. I didn't know how it was black and blue since he hit me in the cheek but whatever, it was bruised and there wasn't a thing I could do to hide it. Not even makeup could be applied because it was too painful to touch, so I would be baring all to see.

I didn't even bother to try and hide it by framing my face with my hair because it would still be visible, so I bit another bullet and French plaited my hair back, keeping my hair tight to my head and completely out of my face.

I heard the class bell ring at the same time some students walked into the classroom. As usual, I didn't look up or acknowledge anyone. I continued to scribble on my copybook but when a shadow fell over my desk, I glanced up.

It was only Alannah passing my table by, but when I looked to the left it was at the exact moment Dominic stepped into the classroom with his arm around Destiny's shoulder.

Seriously? My mind hissed. *He was going to parade around with another girl not even twenty hours after he almost successfully seduced me?*

And that fucker had the nerve to call *me* a slut.

I couldn't help the snort that erupted out of me. Dominic looked at me the same time I snorted and it gave me a perfect look at his face. His chin was bruised and so was a little of his cheek. Above his eyebrow was cut and bruised also. He looked practically perfect for someone who was in a fight while I got hit once and had the mother of all black eyes.

Fucking typical.

Dominic's eyes were directly on my black eye while he stared at me. Destiny got his attention though when she tickled his belly.

I turned my attention back to my copybook and continued scribbling away. I only looked up when I heard Miss McKesson's voice over my music, so I took out my earphones.

71

She was calling out names while ticking them off on the attendance sheet.

"Bronagh Murphy," she called out.

"Here," I replied.

She looked up, smiled at me then gasped and actually dropped her pen to the floor.

"What happened to you?" she asked as she moved over to me.

Even though I had a black eye, nobody but Dominic noticed it since I had only looked at him. My other classmates didn't pay attention to me because that was the norm; I didn't bother with them, and they didn't bother with me. Thanks to Miss McKesson though, everyone was looking at me now.

"Holy shite, Bronagh, that's some shiner," Alannah's voice said from my left.

I nodded, because she was right.

I looked at Miss McKesson and smiled. "I'm fine, it's nothin'."

"It's not nothin', you have a black eye for goodness sake," she breathed.

I smiled again; her concern was nice.

"I'm honestly fine; it was just a misunderstandin', the other person is dead now."

That lightened up the tension because everyone, including Miss McKesson, chuckled. The tension came right back when she looked around the room and gasped as she looked to the back.

"Nico, what happened to you… *this* time?" she gasped, again.

I wanted to laugh at the 'this time' part of her question. She knew he was a troublemaker considering the amount of times he rolled into school with bruises and whatnot on his face over the last five, almost six, weeks. His fight with Jason was the only one I had heard of him being in since he and his brother started here so where he got all the bruises from was beyond me.

"Nothing, just shitty decision making on my part. Chose to defend someone who wasn't worth it, it was my mistake."

I gritted my teeth and muttered, "You *are* a mistake."

I didn't mean for this to be audible but it was and my classmates actually *oh'd*. I meant that Dominic was my mistake and that kissing him was a mistake, but the class probably thought I meant his existence was a mistake, which right now, honestly wasn't that far off the bat with the way I was feeling.

Miss McKesson looked between Dominic and myself for a few moments. "The two of you stay after class."

Again? I thought.

I wanted to protest, but her tone was a serious one, so I just sighed and put my earphones back in. Class flew by; I noticed Damien entering class about thirty minutes late with another girl from class, Lexi Mars. I was instantly disgusted by the state of her hair and clothes and the shit-eating grin Damien was sporting.

That girl and Damien—because I heard from passing conversations that he had shagged multiple girls since moving here—were the definition of a slut, not me.

When class ended, I didn't move from my seat. I waited for everyone to leave before I took out my earphones.

"As much as the students of this school think us teachers are stupid, we aren't. We heard about the altercation between you and Jason after school yesterday, Nico. Care to explain what that was over?"

"It was over Bronagh," Dominic answered seconds later.

I humourlessly laughed. "No, he stuck his nose in other people's business then blamed it on me because he didn't get what he wanted out of the situation."

"And what did he want out of the situation?" Miss McKesson asked.

I looked at her with raised eyebrows. Did she really expect me to have a heart to heart with her?

"A lovin' hug," I replied sarcastically.

She looked at Dominic then flicked her eyes between us. "I don't know what is goin' on between you both but sort it out between yourselves and don't bring any more violence into it. No more fightin', leave each other alone if you can't get along, understand?"

I saluted her, which made her roll her eyes.

"Go on," she sighed. "The pair of you, get to class."

I stood up and pushed my chair into my desk then quickly left the classroom. The hallways were already emptying because second period had already started, so I quickened my pace until an arm gripped onto mine, bringing me to a halt.

"What's the rush, pretty girl?" his voice sneered.

I jerked my arm free from Dominic's hold and started walking to class again.

"Don't fuckin' touch me, you dick," I snapped.

Dominic snickered and caught up with me. "You wanted my dick buried in you to the hilt yesterday, didn't you?"

"Damien's, not yours," I corrected trying not to blush with embarrassment of what was the truth. I did want him yesterday.

What I just said about Damien was an honest to God lie, but Dominic didn't need to know that. I wasn't attracted to Damien at all, even though he was Dominic's clone.

Dominic laughed, clearly amused. "No, you wanted *my* cock. I could smell how wet you were for me—"

I whirled around and jumped for him, intending to break something on his body, but he caught me mid-air, turned us both, and pressed me against the wall in the corridor. My tiptoes were touching the ground, but not fully because Dominic's body was pressed between my legs, literally pinning me against the wall.

"I like this side of you," Dominic grinned as he brought his bruised face to mine. "Makes me want to fuck you even more knowing you'll fight for dominance."

"Get off me, now!" I snapped. "Miss McKesson said you have to stay away from me!"

Dominic smirked and looked down to where his body was pressed against mine. "I'm thinking you're enjoying this, babe."

I narrowed my eyes. "I'm not your babe, your possession, or your aggressive bitch. I'm nothin' to you, now let me go!"

Dominic seemed unaffected as he said, "Don't think too highly of yourself, *babe*. I wanted to get laid by the ice-cold bitch that roams these school's hallways. I wanted to see if the only bit of heat in you was located deep, deep in your pussy—"

"You're horrible! I hate you, get off me!" I hissed and tried to slap him, but he grabbed my hands with his.

He rotated his pelvis into me, still grinning. "Give it a minute, I'll get you good and wet enough so I can smell—"

"Shut the fuck up!" I growled. "That was a mistake, you said so yourself, so just forget it. Let go of me and stay the fuck away from me."

Dominic laughed as he let me drop and watched me stumble a little. He stepped backwards and gestured me towards class with his hands. "I like messing around with you too much to stay away from you, darling." He winked.

"You're a vile, disgustin' creature," I snarled to him as I turned and stormed down the corridor, ignoring some lingering students who got an eyeful and earful of that 'conversation'.

"A vile, disgusting creature that you near enough fucked yester-day!" Dominic called out after me just as I opened the woodwork room door.

Everyone heard him, even Mr. Kelly.

I slammed the door shut behind me. "Move him to a different worktop, sir. I swear to God, I'll stab him if you don't!" I stated to Mr. Kelly, who was just looking at me with wide eyes.

When the door opened to the woodwork room and Dominic strolled in, he headed for my desk, but Mr. Kelly quickly got up to intercept him.

"Actually, Nico, switch seats with Gavin for today." He quickly ordered. "Bronagh seems to be very cross with you, son."

Under-fucking-statement!

"Sure thing, sir," Dominic replied happily.

I was fuming while I shoved my bag under my desk and stormed to the back room to get an apron. When I came back out, the lads in the room, including Dominic and the sir, were looking at me.

"What?" I angrily snapped.

"Nothin'," they all replied in unison and busied themselves with whatever was in front of them.

I glared at them all before moving to the supply room and re-trieving the timber that I hid so Dominic wouldn't use it on me. He didn't mess with any of my projects, but I wasn't taking any risks, so I hid my stuff just in case.

When I re-entered the room, nobody paid me any attention, which was good so I went to my worktop and pencilled out a design on the wood, marking where I would have to saw and sand.

Gavin took his time moving over to my desk.

"Hey, Bronagh." He smiled.

I returned his smile, because it seemed genuine.

"Hey, Gav," I replied, shocking myself that I used the nickname I've heard the other lads in class call him.

I was allowed to call him that, though, since he was technically my first proper kiss ever.

"Are you okay?" he asked. "You seem pretty heated."

I sighed. "I'm fine, just that American prick annoyin' me."

Gavin snorted at me, which made me grin; it was nice that someone else agreed Dominic was a prick.

"You do know what he is sayin' to the lads back there, don't you?" Gavin murmured.

I looked to the back of the room and noticed some of the lads were gathered around Dominic, grinning and knuckle touching him.

"What's he sayin'?" I asked.

"That he was very close to findin' heat in you. He called you an ice-cold bitch. Pretty obvious he was sayin' he almost fucked you."

I gaped at Gavin's bluntness then quickly composed myself. "He is lyin'. We kissed, but it was a horrible mistake. He is just blowin' it out of proportion!"

Gavin looked at me for a moment then nodded. "I believe you, he is probably just sore that he didn't get to go all the way with you.

His ego is clearly takin' it bad; that's why he is bein' a prick."

I groaned.

"He is *naturally* a prick," I said making Gavin laugh which got the prick's attention.

I looked at Dominic and noticed him glaring at Gavin's back before switching his gaze on me, winking at me and blowing me a kiss.

"Fuck you," I snarled in his direction.

"Now or later?" he replied.

The lads in the class laughed, and laughed hard. I couldn't help it when my eyes filled with tears, so I looked down and quickly grabbed my bag while they fell down my cheeks.

"Bronagh," Gavin sighed when he heard me sniffle. "Don't cry, babe."

I didn't look to him or anyone else as I practically ran out of class. I didn't even ask the sir for permission, I just left.

"Nice goin', man." Gavin's voice hissed. "Does makin' girls cry get you hard or somethin'?"

"Fuck you, asshole." Dominic shot back. "Don't be inserting yourself into my business, and while you're at it, don't look or even talk to Bronagh again, I'll kick your ass otherwise."

I didn't hear what Gavin said in response to Dominic. I only heard Mr. Kelly's voice roaring for them to stop whatever it was they were currently doing and to get away from each other.

I was walking briskly down the hallway when I heard a loud bang sound from behind me.

"Bronagh!"

I jumped as I looked over my shoulder; Dominic was jogging towards me. I screamed; I didn't know why but I did, and I did it loudly. Another bang sounded and this time Gavin and Mr. Kelly as well as my other classmates poured from the woodwork room.

I stopped screaming when Dominic pressed himself to me and put his arms around me.

"I'm sorry, okay?" he breathed. "I'm *so* sorry, I'm a fucking dick. I won't be horrible anymore, I swear. I didn't mean to make you cry, forgive me."

I shook my head.

"No, I know you aren't sorry," I sniffled. "Leave. Me. Alone."

He was about to say something else but was suddenly pulled away from me, which caused me to stumble backwards and fall to the ground on my arse.

It hurt like hell, and I knew that there was going to be a fresh bruise on my arse because of the pain. I looked up as Dominic looked down at me; his face turned red as I hissed in pain. He turned and speared the person who pulled him off me and caused me to fall. That person turned out to be Gavin.

"Stop!" I screamed and scrambled to my feet.

I felt the blood drain from my face as Dominic dished out blow after blow to Gavin. It wasn't one-sided though; Gavin was just as good, and even head butted Dominic at one point. But no matter what he did, Dominic was better.

It was like the hits he received didn't even hurt him. He was like a bull on a rampage, and it terrified the crap out of me.

"Stop!" I screamed again and tried to pull Dominic off him, but Conner, a boy in our woodwork class, lifted me back.

"You will only get hurt," he told me when I struggled against him.

I pushed away from him and sprinted towards the metalwork room while Mr. Kelly tried to stop the fight to no avail.

"Damien!" I screamed when I flung the door open.

Damien sat at the back of the class, surrounded by girls, but when he heard me he was on his feet and moved towards me like the speed of light.

"Dominic is goin' to kill Gavin, make 'em stop!" I bawled.

Damien ran out of the room ahead of me and followed the shouts. Everyone else in the class, the teacher included, followed to see what was happening while I lingered in the class on my own.

I was afraid to go back out there. I had to stay away from Dominic because he was dangerous, and I didn't do dangerous.

CHAPTER SEVEN

"I thought I said *no* more fightin' with Nico, Bronagh?" Miss McKesson said to me at the end of school my first day back from suspension.

After Damien stopped the fight two weeks ago, both Dominic and Gavin were suspended because their fight was on school grounds while I was suspended for leaving class without permission and apparently inciting a fight between the lads. I was suspended for two weeks and was told not to come back to school until after Halloween. I wasn't sure how long the lads would be suspended for but I heard they were lucky to each receive just a suspension because their fight was so violent, the school principal wanted to call the Guards but somehow Mr. Kelly talked him out of it, which was really good for the lads.

"Bronagh, are you even listenin' to me?" Miss McKesson's voice snapped making me jump and look to her.

I nodded. "I am, miss."

"Then answer me question," she challenged.

I sighed. "I wasn't involved in any of the fightin', miss. Dominic was the one who chased me and grabbed me after I left class; Gavin was tryin' to defend me, and he got smashed up for it."

Miss McKesson rubbed her temples. "Which one of those lads is your boyfriend?"

I widened my eyes in utter shock.

"Neither of them. I hate Dominic and I hardly know Gavin."

Miss McKesson shook her head. "Are you sure you aren't goin' out with one of them, Nico perhaps?"

I gaped at her. "Miss, Dominic is *not* me boyfriend!"

She cocked an eyebrow. "Does he know that? Because he really did a number on Gavin for touchin' you."

I gasped, again. "Gavin didn't *touch* me, he tried to shove Dominic off me and it knocked me to the ground."

"The fact that you got knocked to the ground enraged Nico, he said so himself durin' the meetin' held between me, him, his brother, Gavin, his dad, and the principal."

There was a meeting over what happened?

I groaned and scrubbed my face. "He had no right to get enraged over me fallin', it wouldn't have happened if he hadn't grabbed me in the first place!"

Miss McKesson chewed on her lip. "I think he feels very protective of you."

I rolled my eyes. "He is a dick who gets a hard on from makin' me miserable, don't confuse him 'fightin' to defend me' as anythin' other that a nasty pit bull protectin' its favourite chew toy."

Miss McKesson looked at me with her eyes wide for a few moments before she frowned at me. "Does Nico do things that you don't approve of, Bronagh?"

I furrowed my eyebrows at her. "He just annoys me miss, he takes joy in pissin' me off."

"I understand that, but look at this from *my* point of view; it looks to me like you're a couple and Nico is the protective teenage boyfriend... or possibly the abusive teenage boyfriend. He comes into school more days than I can count with new bruises and lately, so have you."

"I can't comment on why he's busted up all the time because I don't know anythin' about why he comes into school like that, but you couldn't be more wrong about thinkin' he is me fella, miss," I stated.

She blew out a breath in relief. "So he hasn't done anythin' to you that you might be afraid to tell someone?"

Where was she going with this? I wondered.

"Like what?" I asked, curiously.

She lowered her voice. "He hasn't touched you sexually without your permission or anything of that nature, has he?"

I flushed red; she was asking if Dominic had raped me? Holy shite, how the hell did Dominic fightin' with Jason and then Gavin over me come to this type of questioning?

"No, miss, he hasn't done anythin' like that at all," I stated, clearly.

I might despise the lad, but I wasn't about to say he raped me when he hadn't.

Miss McKesson visibly relaxed. "Good, that is very good. I'm sorry if I have upset you by askin' these questions, I just needed to make sure that you're okay and that the arguments and fights involvin' Nico aren't anythin' beyond your control."

I didn't think I could ever handle, or control, Dominic or any situation we were in.

"Don't be worryin', I've got everythin' under control, Miss," I lied, smiling.

She nodded to me. "Good woman yourself, go on and get goin' before it gets dark out."

I nodded. "See you Monday, miss."

She gave me a wave as I left her classroom and walked down the now empty school hallways. School ended twenty minutes ago and even though it was only 4:20 p.m. the sun had already set and the skies were growing darker by the minute, which wasn't surprising since it was already November.

I shook my head a little; I couldn't believe it was only November, but it felt like a lifetime since Dominic came into my life and turned it upside down instead of only ten weeks.

It was crazy to think about.

The first thing that hit me as I exited the school and began my walk home was the cold, the second thing was a fist when someone stepped out from behind a pillar that led into a housing estate I had to pass by to get home.

I screeched as I fell back to the ground and then whimpered as the items in my bag dug into my back when it made contact with the ground. I felt pain in my face then; my right cheek had just fully healed up from when Dominic hit me in the face a couple of weeks ago, and I could already tell a new bruise would form and cover the old one up.

"Did you really think I wouldn't do somethin' to you after all the trouble you have caused between Nico and Jason over the last few weeks, bitch?"

I winced as I pushed myself up to my feet and looked towards Micah, behind her stood two of her friends watching us with amusement.

"That wasn't me fa-fault Micah, I don't know why Dominic did what he did, I swear," I said to her as I held my now throbbing cheek.

Micah rolled her eyes. "Because he is your fella and since I can't hit him for hurtin' *my* fella, I'm hurtin' *you* instead."

"Dominic isn't me fella, Micah, I swear—" she cut me off by jumping at me, knocking me back to the ground.

I could do little more than cover my face with my arms while she pulled at my hair and punched at any visible bit of skin she could make contact with. I screamed when she stood up off me and kicked me directly in the stomach; it made me dry heave with the force of it.

"Don't look at Jason or even in his direction again because if you do, and it pisses off Nico and results in Jason gettin' hurt again, I'll kill you. Understand, fatso?" she asked and kicked me again.

"Yeah," I rasped.

"Good." She spat on me then turned and walked off with her friends.

I lay on the ground for a few moments until the cold got to me and forced me to move. I hissed and winced as I got to my feet, it was darker out now, and there wasn't a soul out on the street, which wasn't surprising.

I coughed and the action caused my stomach to erupt in pain, I felt like crying but didn't in case Micah was somewhere near and could see or hear me. She beat me up with ease, but I wouldn't give her the satisfaction of seeing or hearing me cry.

I didn't know what hurt more, my stomach, my face, or my head. I settled on my nose hurting the most when a trickle of blood seeped from my nostril, slid down over my lips and chin where it dripped down onto my school uniform jumper. I didn't even bother to wipe it away because I was sure it would stop eventually. I slowly made my way home and as soon as I got inside, I headed to the bathroom, drew a bath, stripped down and sunk into it.

I didn't cry until a minute and a half into my bath, and I didn't stop until I got out. I dried myself then and carefully used a dry wash cloth to pat my face dry, my nose was now blood free and just red and a little swollen, my right cheek was a bit swollen, and so was my jaw. I could already see the bruise that was beginning to form around my jaw, but none around my eye, which gave me hope that it wouldn't bruise again.

After I left the bathroom, I went into my room and changed into some pyjama trousers, a tank top, and a blue hoodie that used to be owned by my father. I carefully brushed out my hair because it was tender as hell from Micah pulling on it. When I was done, I did a very loose plait in my hair and flung it over my shoulders then headed downstairs for some food.

Lots of food.

I heard the hall door open as I poured some custard and whipped cream over my giant bowl of ice-cream. I heard the door close, keys being put on the key hook on the hall wall then footsteps into the kitchen.

"Hey, honey, how was your first day back—omigod!"

I winced when I turned; Branna's screams could be pretty loud.

"I'm goin' to find out where he lives and fuckin' kill him!" my sister vowed then turned and stormed out of the kitchen.

Him?

"Branna, a girl did this, not a lad," I shouted after her.

Her steps paused then pattered back into the kitchen.

"That Nico kid didn't do that or cause it?" she asked, boring her eyes into mine to see if I was lying.

She thought Dominic did this to me or was the cause of it? Not surprising since the only times I ever had bruises or got into trouble he was usually involved.

"No, I haven't seen or spoken to him since I was suspended two weeks ago," I assured her.

She eyed me for a moment. "Who did this then? Give me names and I'll fix it."

I blinked with surprise. She was acting like a hit man... or woman.

"I don't know who she was but I think she thought I was someone else. She called me Sarah and told me to stay away from her fella," I lied and felt horrible about it.

I couldn't tell her it was Micah because Branna would find her and do damage to Micah's face like she did to mine, and I couldn't let that happen. She was a medical student studying to be a midwife and I doubted she would be hired anywhere if she had a rap sheet for assaulting a minor since Micah was only seventeen.

Branna frowned at me but continued to stare at me for signs of lies. I was usually a terrible liar, but the fact that I had to lie to keep her from potentially destroying her career made me hold a steady face.

"Oh sweetheart, that is horrible luck." She frowned. "It's the last thing you need after that stupid suspension and especially after the black eye you got off that Nico kid."

I wanted to fall to the floor in relief but I didn't, I forced myself to snort. "Tell me about it."

I starting chuckling but winced over my side and gripped it.

"Show me," Branna ordered.

I lifted my hoodie and tank top upwards.

"Your stomach is black and blue!"

I looked down and groaned. Branna was right; my left side was bruised from my lower ribs to my hipbone. It looked like Micah's kickboxing classes paid off because she did substantial damage to me in only a matter of seconds.

"I took a bath, it helped with the pain but to make me feel even better I'm eatin' this," I said and gestured to my large serving of ice-cream, custard, and whipped cream.

Branna chuckled and shook her head. "Thank God you pick out the low fat on everything we buy. You'd be as big a house if you keep up this comfort eatin' thing you've got goin'."

I rolled my eyes. "I haven't even gained weight so clearly me comfort eatin' isn't bad."

Branna huffed. "Give it a while, your jeans will suddenly feel a bit too tight and then, after that, all hell breaks loose."

I shook my head and lifted up my bowl. "If you need me, I'll be eatin' me feelin's in me room while watchin' *Dear John*."

"Baby," Branna frowned and lightly chuckled.

She felt sorry for me and watched me exit the kitchen.

I headed up to my room, settled into my bed, turned on my television, and dug into my food. I snorted at Branna's logic; there wasn't anything wrong with comfort eating, so what if I gained some weight? Honestly, who gave a shite?

Not me. I'd rather deal with my worries by comfort eating and have some extra pounds than sit around afraid that Micah might beat me up again or what would happen when I saw Dominic again.

I groaned at the thought of him and all the trouble he had caused me in the short time I've known him. I shook my head; one bowl of ice-cream was nowhere near enough to deal with this bullshit.

CHAPTER EIGHT

"I can't believe we're this high up the mountains," I growled to Branna and quickly glanced around my surroundings.

I was mad that she brought me up here but when I caught sight of the view overlooking Dublin at night I was shocked I hadn't come up here before just to look at it. All the lights and patches of darkness from the fields were just stunning.

My sister rolled her eyes when I looked back at her. "We're ten minutes from the house. We live on the bottom of the mountain so what's the big deal about bein' higher up on it?" she asked.

I shrugged. "You said we were goin' clubbin' so I figured we would go to Temple Bar, Sin nightclub in town, or even The Playhouse down the Tallaght Bypass but not up the fuckin' mountains!" I snapped lowly and rubbed my bare arms to generate some heat.

My sister rolled her eyes at me again. "This place is exclusive; it's based up here because a lot of people with money come here who don't want to venture near town or anywhere like that."

I shook my head at her.

"You know, Branna, a *normal* older sister would take their little sister out for dinner or order takeaway or even go to the cinema when tryin' to make her feel better about gettin' jumped on. They don't bring said little sister to an underground night club," I hissed as we stood in a queue waiting to be assessed by the bouncers of

Darkness, an underground nightclub that was apparently *very* exclusive after seeing the amount of people that had been turned away since Branna and I got into the queue.

Branna shushed me as she kept looking ahead.

"I don't have any form of identification yet though." I whispered in her ear as we moved forward in the queue. "I just turned eighteen, Branna, they won't let me in."

I was starting to sweat; I didn't want to be embarrassed by being turned down entry into the club. Branna brought me here to get me out of the funk I was in since Micah attacked me a week ago but embarrassing me wasn't going to help me in anyway.

"Close your mouth before I put me fist in it!" Branna warned in a very low tone that honestly scared the crap out of me.

"Okay," I murmured and looked down.

I felt like my parents were chastising me. I mentally snorted at that, and then gasped when Branna's hand pressed against the small of my back and urged me forward. I looked at my sister then looked forward; we were next, and the bouncers were waiting for us to approach.

"Branna, sweetheart," beamed a tall bouncer with zero hair and a large black spiral tattoo circling his right cheek and down his neck, disappearing under his shirt.

I was horrified. Branna had been here before; I knew that because she told me when I asked about how she knew about the club that I'd never heard of, but what's worse was that this obvious criminal knew her by the excited way he addressed her.

"He looks like a serial killer, I'm fuckin' out!" I hissed to Branna and was about to move out of line only for her to hold me in place by moving her hand from my back to my hip, keeping me next to her. I winced a little because her hand was directly on my bruise, but I stayed put despite the pain.

"Hey Skull, this is me little sister. Her eighteenth was a few weeks ago. I thought I'd bring her to watch the fight and get her first alcoholic drink as an adult," Branna chirped making Skull chuckle.

"She knows the rules of the club?" he questioned.

Branna nodded her head. "Yep, I gave her a rundown of them twice and made her leave her phone at home so no videos or pictures can be taken of any fight inside the club."

Skull nodded his head at Branna then flickered his eyes back in my direction. I wondered if he would still ask me for I.D. then I wondered what 'fight' Branna was talking about and why phones were banned. Skull gave me a once-over and grinned at me getting my full attention before nodding Branna and myself past the red rope and into the club.

"Tell John to stamp the both of you for free drinks," Skull called after us.

Branna looked over her shoulder. "Thanks, babe." She grinned to Skull.

Skull.

My God, his name was *actually* Skull.

My sweating over my nerves of being rejected passed and instead fear pricked at me as Branna held my hand and led me down four flights of stairs. This was literally an underground nightclub; we were deep into the mountain. To be honest, that freaked me out more than a little.

"They must be horrible to walk up when you're drunk," I voiced my thought aloud when I looked down to the steps.

"They are," Branna answered with a cackle.

When we reached the bottom of the stairs, there were two huge black doors. They were closed and in front of them stood two huge bouncers.

"H-Hi." I smiled when they looked at my sister then to me.

"Skull said for you to stamp us, John," Branna beamed.

The man on my right chuckled, so I guessed him to be John.

"You have Skull in ribbons when you show off those pretty legs of yours, Branna." He teased. "The poor lad can't think straight."

Branna chuckled. "Whatever, he just likes me 'cause I'm mates with his misses."

John chortled and said, "Yeah, *right*."

They nodded to us then, and I noticed Branna holding her right arm out so I did the same with mine. The bouncers then took out a stamp from their pockets and turned our hands around and pressed the stamp on the inside of our wrists.

Free was stamped across my wrist in thick black ink. The bouncer who stamped me picked up my other wrist and stamped it with a different stamp. When I glanced at my left wrist, *Darkness* was stamped on my skin in the same thick black ink.

I held my hands out for a few seconds not wanting to smudge the ink, but I found it had practically dried straight away so I didn't have to worry.

"Have fun in the Darkness ladies," John said with a grin and pushed on the side of the double doors.

I jumped when pounding music filled my ears. It frightened me; the stairway and door area was deathly quiet until the doors opened up into the club. They were seriously soundproof, because when they were closed you honestly couldn't hear a thing outside.

Branna led me into the club. The name Darkness suited it because the entryway was virtually black until flashing strobe lights attacked my eyes.

I ducked my head and huddled closely to Branna.

"This place is an epileptic's worst nightmare," I shouted to her.

I felt the vibrations of her body indicating she was laughing, but I couldn't hear her because of the music that was currently blaring into my eardrums. I once again huddled close to Branna when the view of a huge crowd of people swaying their bodies got my attention.

The strobe lights made everything look crazy. It was like I was daydreaming and everything was happening in slow motion. Branna's hands encased mine as she led me to the left of the dance floor, and that's when I spotted a massive bar that stretched around the entire room only stopping a few feet away from a darkened area of the club.

I leaned into Branna, putting my mouth by her ear. "What's that area for?" I asked, pointing to the darkened section.

Branna looked to the area then back to me and grinned.

"That, me darlin' baby sister, is where girls soak their knickers at the mere sight of big, bad, scary men."

I felt the blood drain from my face.

"Is this a *sex club*?" I shouted, horrified.

Branna laughed at my facial expression and shook her head. "No, it's not a *sex club*." She cackled and leaned into my ear and said, "It's actually an underground fightin' club."

I leaned back and stared at Branna. "An underground fightin' club?" I repeated and she nodded.

"A real fight club? Like in the film *Fight Club*?" I questioned, my eyebrows raised.

Branna made me watch those films. She was really into the whole underground fighting thing, and I liked watching the films, but being here in an actual underground fighting club was actually a little scary.

"Bronagh, how many times do I have to tell you? You *don't* talk about fight club," my sister smirked.

I playfully rolled my eyes. "I don't know if I'm comfortable with this."

Branna sighed. "It will be fine; you can hang back here and watch the fight. You don't have to be circle side. Okay?"

I nodded. "Okay."

She smiled. "I'm serious, though, about what I said before. You don't talk about this fight club; this place is well-known but only to certain people. It is illegal after all."

I gaped at Branna. "I thought you were just referencin' the film!"

She laughed. "I was because I've *always* wanted to say that but it actually applies here. Don't talk about this fightin' club, ever. That was what Skull was talkin' about outside; this place is very exclusive so don't speak of it. Not to anyone, okay?"

I didn't talk to anybody so I wouldn't have anyone to tell even if I wanted to, but I still nodded firmly. I couldn't believe my big sister brought me to a nightclub that condoned illegal acts. It was freaky, scary, and sort of exciting at the same time.

"So what do we do here?" I shouted.

Branna laughed as she turned, shouted some orders to a man behind the bar and then turned back to me.

"We drink, dance, watch hot lads fight, and have a hell of a good fuckin' time," she cheered.

I burst out laughing; thank God she remained my sister once she became my guardian. It would have been horrible if she completely fell into the role of being my mam and dad. I would literally have no one to introduce me to anything wild, and I would certainly have no one to do stupid stuff with me.

"I've never drank before so what will I order—"

"I ordered you a glass of blue WKD already, it's just an alco-pop. Don't want you legless leavin' here with me." Branna said.

I shrugged; I trusted her so blue WKD it was.

"Okay."

When the bartender came back with a glass full of bright blue liquid and what looked like a glass of Coke I licked my lips. Branna showed him her right wrist that had *Free* stamped written across it. The bartender nodded and then looked at me, so I showed him my stamp, and he nodded again before walking off to take more orders.

"How come we got the *Free* stamp?" I leaned in and asked Branna.

She smiled. "I used to have a thing with Skull, but that was forever ago. Now he goes out with Aideen."

I nodded. Aideen Collins was Branna's friend since they were in primary school; she was also Gavin Collins' big sister.

"Yeah, so we're all pretty good friends. It pays to have friends like her, literally," Branna said and gestured to our drinks, which made me chuckle.

She handed me my large glass of blue liquid and watched me

take a sip. She laughed when I widened my eyes and suddenly downed a huge gulp.

"This tastes like a cool pop. We used to eat them when we were younger, remember?" I gushed.

Branna chuckled and nodded. "I do remember but take it easy; there is alcohol in it even though it may not taste like it."

I nodded my head and settled on taking small mouthfuls of the drink instead of gulps. After thirty minutes I was on my third large glass of WKD, and Branna was on her third vodka and Coke. She had told me what she was drinking when I asked.

"I have to wee," I said just as Branna jumped up to dance along to *Scream* by Usher.

"Do you want me to come with you?" Branna shouted.

I looked over my shoulder; near the darkened area was a neon sign for the ladies' toilets. I turned and shook my head. "Nope, it's just over there. I'll be back in a second."

Branna looked at me for a moment then nodded. "Don't go off with anyone and don't accept drinks or anythin' else if someone offers it, understood?"

I nodded firmly. "Yeah, I understand."

I turned then and walked around some people and across a bit more of a clearer area to head into the ladies' bathroom. I did my business, washed my hands, and then exited the bathroom.

Literally two steps outside of the bathroom a girl tripped and stumbled forward. I knew she was going to go face-first onto the ground if I didn't grab her, so that's what I did even though it killed my bruised side.

"Omigod!" the girl screamed then laughed once I steadied her.

"Are you okay?" I asked her, letting go of her arm and placing my hand across my stomach.

She nodded and looked up to me; the strobe lights were back on, so it made getting a good look of her face hard.

"Thanks babe, that was seriously close. You saved me," she beamed then turned around. "She saved me," she shouted to no one and everyone.

I laughed a little, more out of awkwardness than amusement and bowed my head, ready to move away from her. That was until a body suddenly stepped in front of me from my left from out of the darkened area of the club.

"What the hell are *you* doing here?"

I instantly knew the voice, because I loathed that fucking voice. So when I tilted my head back and met the bright grey eyes of Dominic Slater, I growled.

"None of your fuckin' business, now move!" I snapped, trying to sound mad and not turned on, which was what I was whenever I was around him lately. My entire body became hypersensitive when he was near.

He grinned and stepped an inch towards me. An inch was the only free space there was between us, so Dominic was now pressed fully against me.

I hated that my control slipped whenever this fucker was around; anyone on the planet could annoy the hell out of me and I would keep my cool and ignore him or he with the exception of Dominic. I didn't know what it was about him, but he got to me way too easily and he knew it. Even though he intimidated me I was ready to argue and kiss him at the same time. It was very frustrating and confusing.

I raised my hands with the intent to push shove him away, but he caught my hand, twirled me around, and encased his arms around me from behind, pinning my back to his chest.

How did he do that? My mind screeched.

I knew I was a shite fighter, but what he just did was too fast. My movement was too fast for me as well, because I hurt my side more than anything, and it made me hiss.

"Let go!" I shouted.

The girl whom I saved from face planting on the ground was gone when I looked to her for help, so I cursed her. That's the thanks I got for preserving her pretty face? The bitch!

"Seriously, babe, what are you doing here?" Dominic asked into my hair close to my ear so I could hear him over the music.

I cringed because his breath on my ear tickled me. It caused me to shiver and my eyes to drift closed for a few moments. I took in a deep breath and his scent filled me and made me a little woozy, but I remembered whom I was swooning over and shook my head clear.

"I came here with me sister," I replied. "Now let me go."

He let me go so I jumped away from him. I whirled around, and gave him the finger, which made him laugh. I walked around him and headed back to Branna. When I got to the place I left Branna at she wasn't there and I instantly began panicking.

"Hey, lifesaver, your sister asked me to come get you. She's sitting with us."

I turned around and recognised the girl I saved from falling and raised an eyebrow but I followed her. When we walked towards the darkened area and turned off to the right, I noticed seated booths. They were large and cool looking. The seats were black and the table was silver looking marble with a glow ball thing in the middle; it looked awesome.

I searched the strange faces until my eyes landed on someone I knew.

Alec Slater?

I continued to look to the right and saw Kane and Damien. I nearly fell over when I spotted Dominic smirking at me. I glared at him before continuing to look to the right, and when I spotted my sister, sitting on Ryder's lap, I gasped.

This could not be happening!

"No! No fuckin' way," I bellowed. "Get up, now!"

Branna gaped at me; Ryder looked ill when he saw me while the rest of the table either snorted or looked at me like I was mental.

"Bronagh, don't be so rude. This is Ryder, I was goin' to introduce—"

"Fuck that, you are literally sitting with the enemy. That is Nico! The lad who you are all but dry humpin' up is his *brother*!" I growled and pointed to the smug-looking American bastard.

Branna widened her eyes. "Dominic is *Nico*? That Nico kid that tried to—"

"Yeah!" I snapped, cutting Branna off.

My sister was like Muhammad Ali when she reached out and punched Dominic; it was so fast, none of us had time to react. Dominic's head snapped to the side, but he turned his head back just as fast to glare at Branna. Ryder jumped up, and all but pushed her off him like she was dirt, and that enraged me.

"Don't you *dare* push me sister, you big bastard!" I snapped and tried to get revenge by hitting Ryder, but he ducked out of my reach.

"Fuck off Branna, we're done," he then hissed to at my sister, clearly mad that she hit his little brother.

Branna humourlessly laughed as she grabbed my hand. "Believe me, sweetie, I'm goin'." She growled. "I'd *kill* your pervy little brother for doin' what he did to me little sister otherwise!"

I didn't get a chance to give Dominic the finger again or even rattle off an insult in farewell because Branna pulled me away with her.

I hugged her when we were back at the dance floor. "Holy shite, Bran, you were amazin'. You punched Dominic in the face; I'm so jealous!" I gushed in awe and delight.

Branna smiled and hugged me tightly. "Nobody messes with *my* sister, especially not a pretty little batty boy."

She was brilliant, she seriously was!

I was about to ask her how she knew Ryder, but she cut me off by shouting, "Now, let's dance!"

I didn't need to be told twice; I let Branna lead me into the crowd of swaying bodies. I was a little nervous at first, but I literally just let go along with Branna, shoved my hands in the air, and got lost in the music. It was so much fun, possibly the most fun I had ever had.

I knew I needed to get out more, but this, being here right now, was a huge step from hiding behind my Kindle at home or behind my iTouch at school. It was progress, and I was happy about it.

After five songs and some serious carefree dancing, Branna and I were parched. She ordered me a small vodka and Coke because I didn't feel any drunken effects from the three glasses of WKD that I had already drunk. She was pretty buzzed by the time she finished her fifth glass of vodka and Coke. I was still on my first one because it tasted strong; I was sipping it every few minutes instead of gulping it down like I did with the WKD.

Branna and I were laughing at a joke she told when lights from our right suddenly lit up the darkened side of the club, earning loud cheers and screams. The majority of the dance floor and bar area emptied as everyone ran towards the lights. I focused my eyes and noticed there was a round platform a few feet up in the air in the centre of the now lit up area. A single black line went around the edges of the circled platform that looked important, so I asked Branna what it was.

"It's just showin' the no cross point of the circle. If a fighter gets knocked out of it, it's an automatic knockout. It's a pretty big circle, so no strong fighter ever falls off; it's usually the weak fighters who get beat up so bad they unknowingly move backwards, makin' it easier for them to be knocked off," Branna explained.

I widened my eyes and pointed. "What about the people standin' around the platform?" I questioned.

"They usually move back quick enough to avoid a body landin' on top of them."

I gasped. "That's horrible!"

"That's the sport." Branna shrugged. "It's a mixture of different things, the main things being hot, sexy, sweaty, dangerous, fierce men—"

"Oh, shut up," I muttered, making Branna chuckle.

"Ladies and gents, welcome to Darkness!" A deep voice suddenly blared through the speakers around the club where music was playing just seconds ago.

The voice caused loud cheers to erupt around the club.

"It's Friday night here at Darkness and you all know what that means…"

"Fight Night!" the crowd that surrounded the platform screamed out in answer, making the deep voice chuckle through the speakers.

"That's right, it's Fight Night, but tonight is a little different. Instead of our usual three fights, tonight we have four."

More cheers.

"The first two lads up are still newcomers so go easy on them, because they sure as hell won't go easy on each other. They have both fought a few of times over the past few weeks so you may recognise them."

Cheers and screams came from next to me, causing me to roll my eyes; Branna was so into this.

"Make way for our new boys, you all get to choose their fight names durin' the fight tonight so for now, welcome Nico and Drake!"

I widened my eyes.

No fucking way!

"Bronagh, it's Nico, *your* Nico!" Branna gasped.

My Nico?

"He isn't mine!" I bit out. "And please, call him Dominic, I distaste his stupid nickname."

Branna waved me off because she was watching the show so I turned to look as well and watched as Dominic pulled himself up onto the platform and sort of bounced on his feet while he shook his limbs out. He was shirtless, and even though I hated him with a passion, my mind automatically flashed back to when that shirtless body was pressed against mine, making me shudder before shaking my head and the thoughts away.

I studied the rest of Dominic; he had on black shorts that ended a little above the knee and wore padded fingerless gloves. His hair was pushed back out of his face; I guessed there was some gel in it now because it stayed the way it was pushed back, making it look messy.

I widened my eyes as I got sight of his right arm and back when he bounced around. I had seen his back in his room when I was running away from him, and it was only partial curled at the shoulder with a tribal tattoo. Now, though, there was more detail on his shoulder and his sleeve was complete.

"Nice tat," Branna mused.

I growled, "We don't like him, remember?"

She shrugged. "Yeah but that doesn't mean we can't say he has a nice tattoo, because he does."

I huffed. "It's new, the sleeve wasn't complete a few weeks ago."

My sister side looked at me. "Yeah, you got a *good* look at his body back then, didn't you?"

I growled at her, making her laugh as she reached for her vodka and Coke. I reached for my own and gulped it down. I welcomed the burning in my throat and chest since it took my mind off Dominic. Well, until I looked back up at him that is.

I blew out a breath when another lad the same height and build climbed up on the platform. He was wearing the same thing as Dominic except his shorts and gloves were a dark blue.

"That Drake kid is hot," Branna gushed.

I looked him over and agreed with her; he was hot. He had a sexy lean body, blond hair, and I could only guess that he had pretty blue eyes to match.

"Here we go," Branna beamed as she pulled me from my seat and towards the crowd.

I went with her without protest and laughed when she screamed, "Kill him, Drake!"

Drake heard this and grinned around his mouth guard, while Dominic quickly glanced down. And out of everyone, he made eye contact with me and glared like he thought I had said that to Drake.

Whatever, I was thinking it.

Dominic returned his focus to Drake and attacked him when a loud beep sounded. I gasped when Dominic landed a solid punch to

Drake's face; it reminded me of when he beat up Jason and Gavin. How he fought then should have given me some indication that he did this a lot, and the fact that he rolled into school some days with bruises on his face and swollen bits of flesh everywhere. But it didn't, which was why I was still surprised to be watching him in action now.

"Come on, Drake!" I cheered, making Branna whoop and some people around us chuckle.

There was a low chant of Drake that somehow turned into The Destroyer, and that got the announcer's attention.

"Seems as though Drake has got his fightin' nickname, he is *The Destroyer*," the voice boomed getting loud screams in return.

We started to chant 'The Destroyer'.

Drake seemed to get a boost of confidence from our chanting because he speared Dominic to the ground and began pounding on him.

"Woohoo!" I cheered and clapped my hands together.

Every punch Drake landed on Dominic, in my mind, was payback for all the bullshit he had put me through since he first started school with his brother.

My smile was wiped from my face when Dominic got his leg up under Drake and kicked his body off him. Dominic jumped to his feet and kicked Drake to the floor when he tried to stand back up. Dominic pounced on him then and unleashed a series of bullet fast punches to Drake's guarded head and unguarded chest and stomach. I had seen him like this before when he fought with Gavin in school, it was like he lost it completely and went crazy with punches and other hits.

"Whoa! Nico is goin' on a bit of a rampage here, this might be over quick folks!" the voice stated.

The chant 'Rampage' was heard then, and I instantly knew that was going to be Dominic's fight nickname. It made me scowl, because it was a good nickname that suited him.

I glared hard at Dominic's back that was now covered in a layer of sweat. One punch later, and the same beep that started the fight ended it.

Dominic got off Drake and turned his body in my direction; his eyes found me, and he glared hard at me while smirking at my shocked expression. I couldn't believe he just destroyed The Destroyer!

"Rampage wins; The Destroyer cannot continue. Give it up for, *RAMPAGE!*"

I scoffed while everyone around me went crazy; Dominic lifted his arms above his head in victory as he continued to smirk down at me.

I gave him the finger and mouthed, "Fuck you!"

He winked at me so I shook my head then turned to Branna, who was looking between Dominic and myself with wide eyes.

"What?" I asked her.

"He purposely looked at you after he kicked the shite outta that lad." She blinked. "I think he has a *thing* for you."

I rolled my eyes. "He just wanted to make sure I saw him win. He is a cocky bastard like that," I assured her to which she shrugged in response.

When Dominic and a battered Drake got down from the platform, the voice announced two more fighters that looked older than Dominic and Drake. It continued like this for two more fights until all the fights were over. I was shocked that I was cheering and screaming when whomever I was rooting for won or lost. It was exciting in a twisted sort of way; I mean I was getting enjoyment out of lads kicking the shite out of each other but so was everyone else here. I wasn't alone; they were all just as sick and twisted as me.

When the fights were over it was past two in the morning because aside from Dominic's fight, there were no knockouts until twenty minutes or more into each fight. Yeah, that's right, these things actually went on that long.

My vision was making me see double and my head was dizzy so I got a glass of water from the bartender before Branna and I started to leave. I came to the conclusion that I was drunk when I fell walking up the stairs of Darkness and then burst out laughing. Branna was drunk as well, but she seemed to be walking fine and only laughing a little when I did or said something stupid.

"Come on, let's get home," Branna announced when we got outside.

I waved to Skull, who didn't look so much like a serial killer to me anymore with his smiling, happy face. "That was deadly!" I shouted to him.

He laughed and waved. "Get home safe, ladies."

"We will." Branna waved back to him.

Branna had her arm around me as we walked down the path with people in front and behind us. I shook my head, trying to fight off the light-headedness that was wrapping around me.

"Hey babe," a voice said from my left.

I looked to the voice and instantly beamed.

"Drake!" I shouted. "You're The Destroyer! I saw you fi-fight tonight! You were deadly!"

His face was pretty busted up but he was still smiling, which meant he couldn't be hurting that badly.

"I got me arse handed to me but thanks," he chuckled. "I'll get better once I get a decent practice routine."

I nodded my head, suddenly feeling on cloud nine. "I bet you wi-will."

He grinned at me and glanced to Branna. "Do you and your friend wanna come to a party?"

Branna perked up.

"A party?" she asked, making Drake grin. "Where?"

"In Upton," she replied. "Nico is havin' a party to celebrate his win tonight."

I instantly scowled. "We can't go."

Drake frowned. "Why?" he asked.

"Because Dominic and I hate each other, plus me sister here punched him in the face earlier tonight so we won't be invited," I snorted then cracked up when Branna cackled after she remembered what she did.

"I'm sure Nico won't mind you comin'," Drake continued as his eyes flicked over my shoulder.

I was chuckling now.

"No, seriously," I stressed. "He would mind."

"I wouldn't mind at all, pretty girl."

I froze.

Why did he appear at the most unnecessary times? My mind sneered. *He was like fucking herpes.*

I tensed. "Go fuck yourself, Dominic."

Drake raised his eyebrows as he looked over my shoulder and asked, "She your misses, man?"

I erupted into laughter like what he said was the funniest thing ever.

"His misses?" I said with distaste. "In his fu-fuckin' dreams—"

"Yeah," Dominic cut me off. "She's mine."

Drake nodded his head, though he didn't look happy anymore. "I'll catch you around then, babe. See you back at yours, man."

"Yeah bro, later."

I spun around, taking Branna with me, to face Dominic... and all his brothers. My mind choose that moment to start spinning

I glared at all of them, except Damien, and then lifted my free hand that wasn't wrapped around Branna and pointed it into Dominic's red and slightly swollen face. He folded his arms across his chest and looked at me with a raised eyebrow and smirk playing on his swollen lips.

"Yo-you little cock sucker, I am not yours." I snarled I am no-not anythin' to you and if you so much as hint th-that I am again, I'll—"

I cut myself off when I heard Branna heave and felt her body droop, which caused me great pain since I had to use my strength to hold her up.

"No Branna, don't do this." I pleaded. "Don't you pu-puke on me or die, I can't carry you home; I'm we-weak as shite!"

When I heard the lads laugh, I looked up and growled.

"Fuck all of you... except you Damien, you're ni-nice," I said, making Damien laugh and Dominic growl.

"Give me her, I'll carry her back to the house."

I looked up at Ryder when he spoke. "Eh, no, she thinks you're a pr-prick—as do I—and will punch you if she realises you're wi-with her."

Ryder smirked and looked down to Branna as he said, "I'll take my chances."

I rolled my eyes shut and swayed a little because the movement made me feel dizzy again.

"I got you."

I felt the weight of Branna's body leave my arms, and I forced my eyes open and glared at the grey ones staring down at me. "Let. Me. Go," I growled.

"Okay," Dominic chirped and let me go, only to grab me again when my knees buckled from under me.

His chuckle was low and rumbling as he lifted me up and held me against his hard body. "It looks like you *need* me, pretty girl."

I hated that I was starting to love when he called me that.

"I don't even look pr-pretty," I replied, groggily overlooking the comment about me needing him, there was no way in hell I would admit to that. Ever.

Dominic's reply was a snicker as he hoisted me into his arms and carried me off somewhere. My last coherent thought before everything went black was that Dominic Slater was going to cut me, and my sister, up into hundreds of little pieces and his brothers would part take in the evil scheme.

Except Damien, my mine reasoned. *He wouldn't help them because he was nice.*

CHAPTER NINE

Pain.

That was all I could feel in my head and body as I blinked my eyes open only to squeeze them shut seconds later. It wasn't bright; my room was actually dark indicating the curtains were pulled, so that wasn't what hurt my head. My own doing caused the awful pounding in my head, and recoil of my stomach. If I didn't remember drinking myself silly then the nasty taste in my mouth pretty much confirmed I did this to myself.

Alcohol, I thought, and almost wished bad things upon Branna for taking me out last night.

I relaxed into my bed, stirring a little before slowly sitting up.

"Branna?" I called, hoping she would reply so I could ask her for some water.

The last thing I remembered from last night was Ryder Slater offering to help me with her. I remembered Dominic talking to me but then things went black.

"Lie back down, I wasn't done cuddling that body of yours yet," a husky male voice said, making me scream at the top of my lungs.

I scrambled off my bed only to fall and land arse first on the floor. I cried out in pain but quickly got to my feet with my arms raised ready to fight off my attacker.

"Are you actually planning to fight me with your eyes closed?"

the voice asked, sounding amused now.

I forced my eyes to fully open, and when they landed on the owner of the voice, I gasped and then screamed again.

"What… what am I… what am I—"

"You're currently stuttering which is making it hard to understand you. Your accent is thick as it is, add stuttering to the loop, and you're practically speaking Chinese."

My accent was *that* hard to understand.

"Fuck you," I barked. "What am I doin' here? In your house, in your room, in your fuckin' *bed*?"

Dominic grinned at me, and my stomach lurched at the sight.

"Please," I whispered. "Don't tell me we… we… did… *it*."

"It?" Dominic repeated as he raised both his hands behind his head and grinned at me. "What would *it* be, pretty girl?".

I hated that my eyes flicked down to his chest; I could see his arm muscles flex as they were raised behind his head and also the tattoo that curled from around his back onto the side of his waist, up to his shoulder and down his right arm.

"Enjoying the view?"

I snapped my eyes up to Dominic's and glared.

"Did we have sex?" I growled.

He shook his head. "No, we didn't. If we did, you would remember it because you would have been fully sober during it."

I let out a huge breath of relief.

I didn't have sex with him, I thought. *Thank God.*

"Thank you, Jesus," I said to the heavens then looked back down and snarled at Dominic, who was sizing me up with his eyes.

"How dare you put me in your bed when I wasn't in me right mind? How fuckin' dare you—"

"How dare *I*?" Dominic suddenly snapped and jumped from the bed to his feet and stalked towards me.

I was pissed at him, but I noticed he was in just his boxers and that he had a couple of bruises on his chest, shoulders, and his face. They were all obviously from the fight last night.

"You were the one who was so drunk she couldn't stand. You were trying to help your sister when you could barely stand yourself. And just so you know, you wanted in my bed instead of partying downstairs with everyone else. You told me you wanted me to sleep with you and hold you. *You* asked for that, *not* fucking me."

I was wide-eyed by the time he finished speaking; my throat felt a little dry as I swallowed.

"I don't believe you-"

"Well, you better start because it's true!" he growled as he got in my space and lowered his head to mine, scaring the crap out of me.

"I was drunk, so that's why I said whatever I did last night. I can't remember it so it didn't happen—"

"It happened, and you liked it. You fucking purred when I cuddled you."

I purred?

What the fuck did he think I was, a cat? I thought.

"Humans don't purr-"

"Baby, you made a rumbling purr sound because you were so relaxed and content in my arms. Whether you like it or not, you enjoyed sleeping with me!"

I narrowed my eyes to slits. "I was drunk."

"That's your excuse? You acted like you did because you were drunk?"

Eh, yes!

"Obviously." I quipped. "Dominic, I can't stand you so I would have to be drunk out of me mind to willingly crawl into your bed and want you to touch me!"

His silver eyes flared.

"You know what, Bronagh?" He glared. "You can go and fuck *yourself*, and you can take the stick out of your phat ass while you're at it."

I slapped him across the face.

I didn't even care if he hit me back, it wouldn't be about a male hitting a female because at this stage I put my hands on him more than any person should to another person, but he asked for it.

I turned to storm out of Dominic's room, but a hand gripped my hair and an arm came around my waist, halting my movements.

"Let me go!" I shouted, my hands flying to grab the hand on my hair.

"No," he growled in my ear, "because you hit me *again*."

"You cursed at me, so I don't give a damn!" I screamed.

His teeth, yes, his teeth, latched onto my neck and bit down. I knew it wouldn't have been hard enough to break the skin, but it hurt; it hurt a fucking lot.

I screamed again and swung my hands back, punching at any piece of him I could hit.

"I'll kill you!" I swore.

He suddenly released me with his mouth and hands, so I swirled around and literally jumped on him with my hands swinging.

We collided and fell back onto his bed; I was on top for about three seconds before Dominic rolled us over and pinned me under him. I was acutely aware that I was in just my dress from last night, and it had risen up to the very top of my thighs showing off my underwear and bare thighs.

"Blue lacy? I would have pegged you for the granny type of panties—"

"Get off!" I demanded and tried to kick him since he had my arms pinned down, but he pressed himself between my legs to stop me from hurting him that way.

"Calm down, you aren't doing any good acting like a psychopathic!"

"Oh, my God, do you know *anythin'* about women or people in general? Don't insult someone when tryin' to calm them down because it has the opposite effect you fuckin' eejit!"

I ignored the fact that I should take my own advice because Dominic was just as mad as me right now and calling him names wouldn't make him any happier.

He shook his head, hissing at me. "I could honestly throttle you right now, you're un-fucking-real!'"

"If it wasn't illegal, I'd murder you!" I snarled back.

Dominic's lip curled then before he shook his head. "Right back at ya, pretty girl."

I growled, and he glared back at me.

He lowered his head down to mine, and I held my breath when the tip of his nose rubbed against mine, making my heart pound into my chest.

"I hate you!" I forced out.

Dominic's left eye twitched. "I hate you, too."

He then slammed his mouth down on mine and kissed me with a hunger and intensity that surprised me.

I fluttered my eyes closed and tried to squeeze my legs together because the shivers I was currently experiencing were shooting straight down to one location. The fact that Dominic was between my legs only made my legs squeeze his hips making him growl down at me.

My hips bucked forward into his.

I despised him so much for making my body react this way to him. I loathed him even more when I opened my mouth to him and kissed him back, hard!

"You drive me fucking crazy," he growled into my mouth.

Back at you, mate! My mind quipped.

He released my pinned hands and put his weight on his elbows as he leaned over me. I should have used my hands to push him off me or to claw at his face or something along those lines, but I didn't. I did a stupid thing and put my arms around his neck and pulled his head as close to mine as I could.

We kissed each other, and it was an exact replay of the scene from the last time in his bedroom. He had me on my back, on his bed, ready to give him something that wasn't his to take.

"Bronagh?" I heard Branna's voice shout loudly, and then she started banging on Dominic's door.

Dominic groaned into my mouth, and then growled when I pulled away from him.

"We're busy!" he shouted to my sister.

Whoever was outside with Branna laughed then yelped.

"Get away from me sister you pervy little fucker or I'll end you!" she bellowed.

I pushed at Dominic. "Get off me," I breathed.

He did so I quickly stood up and fixed my dress. I grabbed my bag that was on the floor and looked around for my shoes, but I couldn't find them, so I just rushed over to Dominic's door and opened it.

"I can't remember anythin' or how I got up here, but I didn't do anythin' with him. I swear!" I gushed to Branna who looked as bad as I felt.

She looked me over, and her eyes landed on my neck and her face turned red.

"You better not have touched her without permission—"

"I didn't!" Dominic bellowed. "I'm not a fucking rapist!"

Branna growled. "You better not be because I'll fuckin' rape *you* if you harmed her in any way!"

Dominic's smirk was enough to put me back in a bad mood with him. "You can rape me anytime you want, gorgeous."

I gasped.

"You're a prick!" I snapped.

He flicked his eyes to me and rolled them while sighing. "I'm kidding, don't be mad at me for that. Even though your sister *is* smoking hot, you're hotter."

Was that meant to be a compliment or something?

"Piss off, Dominic."

I turned to Branna and grabbed her hand. "We're leavin'!"

She nodded then looked back to the figure behind her. "Move!" she snapped to him.

"I'm not letting you leave until you hear me out!" Ryder said in a firm voice.

I scoffed. "You can't keep her here, arsehole."

He flicked his eyes to me and narrowed them. I sort of moved behind Branna because it was only then that I realised how much bigger he was than me; he was even bigger than Dominic.

"Don't look at me sister like that, do you hear me? You're scarin' her!" Branna shouted.

Ryder scrubbed his face with his hands. "Bran, baby, I didn't know Bronagh was your sister. You called her Bee when you talked about her. If I had known who she was I would have told you so you didn't look at me like you did last night."

I widened my eyes.

They knew each other?

"Hold up, rewind and freeze. Branna... are you seein' him?" I asked, blatant shock laced in my tone.

She looked to me and frowned. "I wasn't keepin' it from you, sweetie. I met him at Darkness a few weeks ago when I was there with Aideen. We hit it off and went on some dates since then; I wasn't goin' to tell you about him until I was sure about him. I know how you feel about people, and I didn't want to bring him around unless I was sure he was goin' to stick around." She cut her eyes to Ryder then, and he was looking at her with such intensity that *I* gasped.

"What is your deal with people, Bronagh?" Dominic's voice asked from behind me, making me tense up.

Branna felt my hand grip hers so she looked at Dominic. "It's *none* of your business," she snapped then looked back to Ryder. "I'm not doin' this to her. She doesn't like you, and that means it won't work between us."

Ryder looked beyond mad as he reached for her and pulled her away from me so they could talk in private, but it was pointless because I could still hear everything that was said.

"You can't just dump me because you sister doesn't like getting close to people, Branna. I really like you and I care about you a *lot*. I know you feel the same way about me. I don't want to end this; I want you to be my girl. We can take things slow; I won't press Bronagh out of her comfort zone but please don't give up on me, on us."

My heart broke for him; I didn't know he and Branna had a thing. I thought he just pulled her last night when I found her sitting on his lap at the table, but I guess they were sort of a couple, and that's why they were sitting the way they were. It made sense when I thought about how Branna said she wanted to introduce me to Ryder before I cut her off in the club last night. Things had clearly escalated since then because they weren't smiling and acting all loved up with each other anymore like they were before all hell broke loose last night. They had obviously fought over Dominic, and me, and that made me feel like crap. They shouldn't not be together because of us or, more importantly, because of me.

"Branna," I mumbled.

She looked at me, tears in her eyes. She clearly felt the same way about Ryder; she didn't want to break up with him, and I didn't want her to.

"Don't break up with him." I said, lowering my head. "I'll... I'll try harder for you; I promise."

Branna cried then and said, "Baby, you don't have to try for me. Try for yourself, this outlook you have isn't healthy. I want you to let other people in; you can't only have me in your life. If anythin' ever happened to me, you would be all alone, and that terrifies me Bee, more than anythin'."

I nodded my head; I knew it was weird to only limit myself to one person in my life but I was afraid to allow anyone else to become a part of my life simply because I knew they could leave as quick as they entered, and I hated the worry that came with that.

"Okay, I'll try harder. I promise." I nodded my head.

She kissed my cheek and hugged me tight. When we pulled apart, I looked at Ryder and awkwardly met his gaze.

"Sorry for causin' trouble for you, Ryder."

He smiled at me. "I think you just saved me a lot of trouble,

Bronagh."

I smiled a little at him then, because when he looked at Branna, he looked really happy.

I couldn't believe I didn't know about him.

"I can't believe you didn't tell me about him. You usually can't keep shite to yourself, so how you didn't let on about him is beyond me."

Branna laughed, sniffled, and then rubbed under her nose. "It was horrible. I wanted to tell you so many times but had to bite my lip or talk about somethin' random."

I chuckled. "So, you're both like a real couple? Boyfriend and girlfriend?"

They looked at each other, smiled, and nodded.

I grumbled. "This should be interestin'."

Ryder looked to me. "Why is that?"

"Because she is a freak, and you will soon learn things about her that will have you runnin' for the hills. For example, she is an OCD cleaner and has multiple personalities. I'm not even jokin', she could be me sister one minute then me ma and da the next."

Branna slapped my arm while Ryder laughed.

"Why would she be your mom or dad?" Dominic asked from behind me.

I instantly looked down; I had forgotten he was there. He just overheard all of that conversation.

Oh, my God.

"Our parents both died nine years ago, Dominic, I've been her guardian since I turned nineteen. I took over raisin' her when our parents passed away, so she considers me her sister, her ma, and da all wrapped into one. Her memories with them are limited, because she was so young when they passed. She doesn't talk about them at all."

I squeezed my eyes shut when the image of my mother's beautiful face framed with her dark chocolate-coloured hair flying in the wind as she ran while my tall father chased her around our back garden filled my mind. Branna looked like our mother with her heart shaped face and blue eyes while I looked like my dad with his white complexion and bright green eyes. That much about them I could remember without seeing their pictures.

I didn't know why but I couldn't remember anything but that single memory of my parents messing around in our back garden. I refused to see a therapist when I was younger but one made an educated guess to Branna that the impact and trauma of losing them made my mind completely block them out.

I loved my parents and my chest hurt when I thought about them, which was why I didn't do it often. I thought it was good that I could barely remember them. It made losing them sort of bearable even after all these years. Some people liked talking about their lost loved ones and decorating their house with their pictures, but not me and Branna. We acknowledged certain things like their birthdays, their wedding anniversary, and their death anniversary but other than that, we didn't have reminders of them, because it was just easier that way. It hurt less.

I blinked my eyes open when the memory went away and found things were quiet for a moment until Dominic spoke again. "Is *that* why you have people issues, you won't get close to anyone in school, or people in general, because you're afraid you could lose them like you did your parents?"

I widened my eyes; he had hit the nail directly on the head.

"Dominic," Ryder snapped. "Show some compassion!"

"I was just asking a question." He defended. "When our parents were killed you took over the mother and father role like Branna did, but I didn't push everyone away from me because I was afraid they might die. That's a pretty shitty way to live."

Those words hurt me hard because they were completely true.

"I want to go home," I said as tears filled my eyes.

"Bronagh," Branna whispered and quickly followed me as I pushed past Ryder and ran for the stairs. I heard Ryder shouting. Then I heard roars from Dominic for me to wait and that he was sorry.

I ignored everyone and everything and ran down the stairs at full speed. It amazed me how I didn't trip and fall to my death because a couple of times I missed my footing and stumbled a little. I eventually had to slow down, though, because some random people were sort of lying on the stairs on the bottom floor, which reminded me of the reason I was here.

The party.

I felt Branna's hand come into mine as she caught up with me and manoeuvred around the sleeping, drunken bodies that littered the bottom floor of the house. I heard a giggle and kissing noises so I turned and watched Damien walk a girl out of the kitchen and towards the hallway to the front door.

"Bronagh!" the girl gasped when her eyes landed on me.

It was Destiny.

Oh, Jesus!

I flicked my eyes between her and Damien; she was shocked while he was grinning at me.

"Babe, just hear me out before you leave—"

"Dominic, leave her alone!"

I blinked when Ryder and Dominic were suddenly in front of me. This caused Destiny's eyes to practically pop out of her head.

"*You* and Nico?" she gasped, looking at him in his boxers.

I frantically shook my head. She had such a big mouth and would have a rumour spread around school by the end of first period on Monday if I let her think what she was thinking.

"No, no. I'm here with me sister and her boyfriend, Ryder. He is Dominic and Damien's big brother. That's all."

Destiny blew out a breath and looked like she believed me until Dominic got in my face.

"So what was upstairs then? You didn't sleep with your sister last night Bronagh; it was my bed you slept in and I was the person you slept with!"

"Oh, my God! You *slept* together?" Destiny squeaked as her

face twisted in rage. "*Seriously?*"

Her version of slept was clearly not what mine was.

Damien all but carried her down the hallway and out of the house once Branna lunged for Dominic and Ryder had to restrain her.

"That girl thinks Bronagh slept with you!" she shouted.

Dominic glared at Branna. "She *did* sleep with me!"

Branna snapped her head to me, so I held up my hands. "He means slept as in the literal term. We literally did *just* sleep next to each other."

Branna threw her hands up in the air and pointed at Dominic. "I see why she can't stand you. You're a word twistin' little fuck!"

Dominic actually smirked, and it made Branna angrier than she already was. I pushed Dominic in the sitting/gym room that was littered with drinks and rubbish. I slammed the double doors behind us and swirled around to face him.

"You know Destiny will tell everyone what she saw and heard. Everyone will think we had sex and that I'm with you or somethin'!"

Dominic shrugged. "So?"

I gaped at him. "So it's a lie, none of that is true!"

He stepped towards me. "The being together part could be true."

I laughed. "You're havin' me on!"

He glared at me. "You know I'm not. I do hate you Bronagh, and I can't stand you at times. But I'm also attracted to you more than I have ever been to a girl in my life. I want you."

I just looked at him. "So you want us to be together because you fancy me even though you hate me?"

Dominic shrugged. "If fancy means having a crush then yes. I have a crush on you and once we work through our feelings, I bet we will like each other just fine—"

"There is somethin' wrong with you, you have a fucked up way of thinkin'!"

He smiled. "Trust me, I know."

I sighed. "Dominic, just leave me alone. Please?"

I locked eyes with him, and he stared at me hard before blowing out a big breath.

"Fine, if you want to go and not give us a shot then go. Leave."

The relief I felt come off my shoulders was as immense as the horrible pain that suddenly filled my chest. I didn't know why it hurt when I should have felt nothing but relief. I forced myself not to think about it.

"Okay." I nodded then turned and walked back out into the hall where Ryder was waking people up and pretty much kicking them out of the house.

"Are we good to go?" Branna asked.

The gym door slammed shut behind me and music suddenly blared making Ryder sigh.

"He is *pissed*," he murmured while looking at the door, then looked at me. "What did you say to him?"

I shrugged. "He wanted us to be together, for me to be his girl-friend, but I told him no, because it wouldn't work between us."

Ryder stared at me for a moment before he smiled and said, "I think you're the only girl he has ever asked to be his girl, and you rejected him. That might knock him back a bit and make him realise he's not God."

Branna snorted. "I doubt that, your brother has too big of an ego not to bounce back from this."

I was fed up with all things related to this conversation.

"Can we just go home now?" I asked Branna.

She nodded. "Yeah, I need food and sleep."

"Yeah, we didn't get much of *that* last night." Ryder grinned down at her.

I felt sick.

"Look, Ryder," I began. "I'm tryin' to be understandin' about your sudden entrance into my life with you bein' me sister's new boyfriend, I really am, but never and I mean never, talk about sex with her around me. I will puke on you otherwise. Got that, *bro*?"

Branna face-palmed herself while Ryder bit down on his lip and cleared his throat. "Understood, Bronagh."

"Great."

Ryder drove us home and thankfully the car ride was silent. I didn't know what to say or talk about with him, so I just remained quiet.

When we got to our house, Branna leaned over and pecked Ryder's lips with hers, then reached for my hand. "Call you later."

He nodded and watched her walk away as we walked up our garden to the porch of our house; she waved while I unlocked the door. When we were inside I just stood still and looked around.

"Nothin' has changed in here and yet everythin' feels so different," I murmured.

Branna's arms came around me from behind. "It's a new chapter for us. Somethin' new is happenin', and it will take some gettin' used to for both of us."

I nodded because she was right; I just hoped I did get used to Ryder being around because if I didn't, it would break Branna's heart.

CHAPTER TEN

"I think your arse is gettin' bigger by the day, Bronagh." Jason's voice hollered.

I closed my eyes and sighed as I stepped into P.E. class in the main hall of my school. All four of the senior classes merged together for P.E., because our classes aren't very big and we need the numbers to play football or other games after we finish running and other horrible exercises.

After Jason's dig about the size of my bum, I wanted nothing more than to go back to the girls' changing rooms, get my school tracksuit jumper, and tie it around my hips. But I didn't, I just shrugged instead.

"I don't see how anythin' to do with me arse is any concern of yours," I replied as I walked over to the line-up section of the huge hall where we would be running laps.

"I beg to differ, you see, it's *very* distractin'," Jason continued, grinning as his friends made some crude remarks about what use my arse could be to them.

"Don't look at it then," I growled.

"I think the point Jason is making, Bronagh, is that your ass is hard to miss because of its size, therefore, it *is* distracting."

Oh God, apart I could somewhat deal with them, but together? I might just crumble and die!

"The two of you run ahead of me then, and it won't be a fuckin' distraction!" I snapped.

Dominic and Jason laughed along with Jason's friends.

I shook my head. "You two are serious dicks. I bet you would make each other's perfect bum boy."

I regretted the words as soon as they were out of my mouth, because the grin that took over Jason's face told me he was about to say something that would probably make me want to kill him or go home and cry.

"I don't think that would work out too well seein' as Nico's dick has been up your arse, mine wouldn't hold much appeal to him after that."

Oh.

My.

God.

"That's a fuckin' lie!" I bellowed.

Jason and his friends laughed and flicked their eyes to Dominic, who was only watching me with a sly grin on his face. I stepped forward to him and shoved his shoulder; he didn't even stumble.

"Tell them it's a lie!" I ordered.

It was Monday today, the party after Darkness was on Friday and upon arriving at school this morning it became clear that Destiny and her mouth had been very busy over the weekend because everyone knew that Dominic and I slept together. Only thing was they thought we had sex, and we didn't!

"That what is a lie?" Dominic asked innocently.

I felt my left eye twitch. "Tell them we didn't sleep together!"

He raised an eyebrow. "But we *did* sleep together."

Jason and his friends laughed, hooted, and cheered while I felt my entire body flush with anger.

"We didn't have sex though!" I growled.

Dominic was about to open his mouth when Jason suddenly moved and appeared at my side.

"When is it my turn to test ride that arse and pussy of yours seein' as you aren't a little virgin Mary anymore?"

Dominic raised his eyebrows and cut his eyes to Jason and gave him a look, which made Jason pipe down, but only a little.

I wanted to cry. All this honestly wasn't fair; I really was a virgin, and I didn't have sex with Dominic, but everyone else thought I did so suddenly I had morphed into the school slut.

I swallowed the bile that was rising in my throat, and I growled at Jason. "I'll tell Micah what you said if you don't get away from me."

Jason sighed, shook his head, and moved back next to Dominic.

"Fuckin' bitch," Jason spat at me, making his buddies laugh.

I rolled my eyes. "*You* are a bitch, you little prick!"

That set them all off laughing so without a word, I turned and stormed away. I stopped next to the water cooler so I could get a drink, but I froze when arms came around my waist and a chest moulded into my back. It made me tense up and melt at the same time, because he made me feel safe and guarded.

"Go away, Dominic."

He chuckled as he lowered his mouth to my ear. "How did you know it was me?"

I set my jaw. "Because you're the only person who ever touches me or gets in me personal space, *that's* how I know."

"Hmmm, you didn't seem to mind those times we were kissing." He said and he nuzzled my ear. "You seemed to enjoy that *a lot*, pretty girl."

I growled and turned to face him; the dickhead didn't step back, so I did.

"Those two moments were me havin' a brain fart."

Dominic chuckled and shook his head. "Whatever you say, pretty girl."

"I really hate you," I spat.

He smiled, his dimples waving at me. "I really hate you too, sweetheart. Catch you later."

Why was he acting like I didn't reject him on Saturday morning, and why the hell did he move back over to Jason and his gang? I shook my head. They fought a few weeks ago, literally kicked and punched the hell out of each other, and now they were buddies? Dominic literally warned Jason off me and now they are hanging out in school?

I will *never* understand men!

"You okay, Bronagh?"

I jumped and whirled around, my hand flying to my chest.

"You scared me," I breathed.

Gavin smiled at me, the bruise on his jawline almost faded but still slightly visible.

"Sorry."

I shook my head. "Don't be, I was in a world of my own. Today is your first day back from suspension, right? How are you?"

He smiled again; he had such a cute smile. "Yeah, it is, and I'm good, thanks."

I frowned, suddenly feeling horrible and guilty. "Gavin, I've never thanked you for helpin' me with Dominic. I really appreciate you standin' up for me, and you tryin' to get him away from me a few of weeks ago."

Gavin waved his hand and gestured to his still healing face. "I don't think I helped much at all."

I shook my head. "No, you did. He didn't like hearin' someone else call him out on what he has been doin' to me. He's being a possessive fucker lately, whether it's bullyin' me or tryin' it on with me."

Gavin frowned. "Are you *with* him?"

I shook my head. "He asked me to be his girlfriend but I said no. I don't know why he keeps at me so much. I think he really just enjoys pissin' me off."

Gavin snorted. "He clearly wants you, and even though you rejected him, he still wants to be close to you. Bullyin' seems to be his only ticket to get to you. He might enjoy rufflin' your feathers a little as well though."

More than a little.

I grimaced. "Tell me about it."

He smiled. "I kind of owe him in a way though, we all do. You aren't just a shadow around school anymore; you're just like the rest of us since he started here."

I smiled a little and joked, "Who knew it would take a stuck-up American to drag me from my comfort zone?"

"Not me, that's for damn sure," Gavin chuckled.

I smiled at him, shocked at how easy it was to talk to him.

"Lookin' forward to ten wonderful laps of this fine hall?" he then asked sarcastically while gesturing to our surroundings.

I snorted. "Oh yeah, cannot wait to feel like my legs are about to fall off. I've been dyin' for it all weekend."

Gavin chuckled at me then gestured for me to stand next to him. "You can catch me if I fall," he teased.

I laughed, loudly. "Can you imagine if you did fall and I tried to catch you? We would both hit the ground in a matter of seconds."

Gavin laughed when he thought about it. He snorted mid-laugh, and it made me laugh louder, which Gavin found extra amusing. When we started our laps, I jogged side by side around the hall with Gavin laughing at me when I tried to talk through my breathlessness.

As per usual, I got to the fourth lap and had to stop because I honestly felt like I was about to die. I was *always* the first person to stop jogging, all the other girls and lads were fitter than me. I never usually cared because no one ever said anything, not even Jason, but this time Fuckface opened his mouth when he neared me on his jog.

"Don't stop, keep going Bronagh."

I gave him the finger over my head and rasped out, "Fuck off!"

He laughed and slapped my arse hard as he passed me by.

"You bastard!" I snapped.

I wasn't even about to try and chase after him for two reasons: reason one was that I was dying, and reason two was that I knew I wouldn't catch him even if I tried.

I angrily walked over to the mats and began stretching after passing our P.E. teacher. Our P.E. teacher was Mr. Rivers. He never bothered with the girls very much. If we stopped running or didn't do our stretches, he just didn't care. His only concern was the boys in the class because the majority of them played for his football team and they had to be match fit to be considered for the team. Even though their training days were after school, he used P.E. to make them sweat also.

It was a pretty good thing us girls—me—had going because when we got tired, we could bow out and not be shouted at like the boys would be. I did attempt to run as long as I could, but I was just not fit so I didn't last very long. I did, however, stretch very well.

I was bent forward, my legs shoulder width apart and my palms pressed to the ground in front of me when I heard commotion behind me.

"Slater, you may not be on the team lad but that doesn't mean you can just stop runnin' and cause me players to crash into you and fall!" Mr. Rivers yelled.

"I'm sorry but, Jesus Christ, how do you expect me to run when I have a view like *that* mere feet away?"

What in God's name was that lad yapping on about now? Why couldn't he just run without causing people problems?

He was like a damn virus!

"Stop lookin' at her!" Mr. Rivers bellowed. "I won't have you oglin' female students and distractin' the lads, so either get back to runnin' or go stretch-"

"I vote on stretching," Dominic cut the sir off, getting some chuckles.

"Leave her alone."

I knew it was Gavin's voice, and I was instantly scared because the last time Gavin interfered with something to do with Dominic, he ended up in a fight with him.

I carefully stood upright, shook my legs out then turned to see what the big deal was about when I suddenly shot forward. Dominic was squaring up to Gavin, and everyone else had backed away from them as if they weren't going to attempt to stop a fight if it happened.

"Stop!" I snapped to both of them and pushed my body between their bodies.

My arse and back were pressed against Gavin's front while my front was pressed against Dominic's. I tilted my head back and looked up at him.

"Just give it a rest, will you?" I pleaded. "Stop causin' trouble. I'm fed up with you doin' this!"

Dominic narrowed his eyes when he looked down at me, then he started breathing a little heavy when Gavin took a step back and took me with him, his arm securely around my waist keeping me tight against him.

"Get. Your. Hand. Off. Her," Dominic snarled in a low, dangerous warning tone.

I wanted to scream and cry at the same time.

Where did he get off telling people what do to with me? I rejected him yet he still had the nerve to try and control who could and couldn't touch me?

"She doesn't want you, just accept that already and back fuckin' off. It's gettin' pathetic at this stage, man!" Gavin said to Dominic while taking another step back bringing me with him.

Dominic looked ready to blow a fuse when Damien suddenly appeared next to him. "Leave it, bro."

"I want to hear her say it," Dominic growled.

Hear me say what?

Damien sighed then looked to me. "Bee, you want to be with Gavin, right?"

What did he mean by *that*?

"Huh?" I murmured, confused.

Damien smiled a little and was about to say something when Gavin spoke. "She's goin' on a date with me tonight so I guess that's a yeah to your question, Damien."

That was news to me.

Dominic's left eye twitched and his face slightly reddened. "You don't want to date me, but you will go on a date with that sorry excuse for a—"

"Hey! That's enough!" I suddenly snapped, not liking Dominic trying to put Gavin down.

I realised then what Gavin was doing; he was obviously handing me a ticket to get off Dominic's radar by saying we were going on a date.

"Fuck you, Bronagh, and fuck you, prick," Dominic growled to Gavin.

Gavin tensed around me. "Look man, you win some, you lose some. She's mine so just stay the fuck away from her, understand?"

Holy hell, Gavin had this down. He sounded so serious and actually came off like a protective boyfriend.

Dominic laughed and so did Jason, which made his friends laugh.

"What are you gonna do if I don't, bitch? I know you can't fight worth a shit. What exactly are you gonna do to me if I *don't* leave her alone?" Dominic grinned evilly.

He might be grinning, but I could tell that he was still fuming mad. He looked downright evil right now and I really didn't like it.

"He won't do anythin' but I'm sure Ryder will. You know your big brother who just happens to be *my* big sister's *boyfriend*," I cut in, smiling sweetly.

Damien grinned. "Little Bee can hold her own, I'm proud."

I looked to him and smiled a genuine smile; he was lovely, so different from his crazy-arse brother.

"Shut up, you," I said, playfully making Damien snort.

"Not that this episode of Irish/American Teenage Drama isn't interestin', but can you all get a move on?" Mr. Rivers suddenly shouted.

All the guys on the team launched straight back into their laps, and the girls moved to the mats where gossip was clearly flying back and forth. Gavin kept his arm around me, and his body pressed to mine while Dominic glowered at us.

He looked me directly in the eye. "Fuck you, Bronagh."

I felt like he was stating a fact like he was done with me and I was horrified because it actually hurt.

I cleared my throat and forced myself to say, "Not in this lifetime or the next, Fuckface."

If looks could kill, I would have been dead and buried with the look Dominic shot me. His entire body tensed, his hands were clenched together, and veins were popping out everywhere.

"Walk away," Damien murmured to Dominic.

Dominic bore his eyes into mine, and I found I couldn't look back into his so I lowered my head and completely avoided his gaze. I watched his feet as he turned and jogged off, joining the rest of the lads who were being shouted at by Mr. Rivers.

"Sorry about him bro, he has a bit of a temper," Damien said.

I looked up and snorted while Gavin chuckled behind me.

A bit of a temper?

That was an understatement if I've ever heard one.

Damien winked at me. "Catch you later, Bee."

I smiled at him, liking the fact that he called me Bee like Branna did.

"Later."

When Damien jogged off, I turned to Gavin, who smiled down at me.

"I'm really expectin' a date from you, it's the least you can do since Dominic might just murder me soon."

I playfully rolled my eyes. "I feel weird though; I've never been on a date."

Gavin raised his eyebrows. *"Never?"*

He seemed very shocked.

I shook my head. "No, I've never been asked out by anyone. I mean, lads aren't into me. Sure you were me first kiss."

"What?" Gavin asked and dropped his jaw.

"Why are you actin' so surprised?" I quizzed.

He stared at me blankly, blinking.

"Gavin?" I prompted him.

"Collins!" Mr. Rivers screamed making me jump with fright.

"Sir?" Gavin asked after a moment of doing nothin' but staring at me.

"Leave the female alone and get your head and legs back into your laps!"

I rolled my eyes at Mr. Rivers and looked back at Gavin, who was looking at me again.

"You're startin' to freak me out by just starin' at me, Gav," I teased.

Gavin blinked. "Sorry, but you have no idea how happy you just made me."

"How?" I asked.

He shook his head. "Never mind Bee. I've to run, literally, but give me your number? I'm cashin' in on that date I made up for Dominic's benefit."

I punched his shoulder, making him laugh.

I tired to downplay the blush that was creeping up my neck. He just called me Bee; I guess that was my official nickname. Between Branna always calling me it and Damien now calling me it, it was obvious it was sticking. Even Gavin using it was sort of making me want to giggle. I was also trying to will away the sweat that started to fill my palms.

"Gavin, a lot of new things are happenin' to me lately. I was invisible for a long time and now all of a sudden I'm not and crazy shite—"

"It's a date Bronagh, not a weddin'. Chill," Gavin chuckled.

I chuckled a little along with him. I knew a date wasn't anything to be freaking out over, but a date for me *was* something to freak out over because I honestly had *no* clue about anything like that. I mean, I didn't even know how to accept the invite correctly.

"You're right," I breathed. "I mean, it's just for fun, right?"

Gavin nodded. "Yeah, we can go see a film. I might even let

you pick." He winked.

Was he flirting with me?

I wasn't sure but blushed either way in case he was.

"Okay."

"Yeah?" Gavin smiled.

He had such a pretty smile.

"Yeah," I smiled back at him.

He took his phone from his shorts and handed it to me; I quickly typed in my number and handed it back to him.

"I'm gonna annoy the shite outta you with texts," he grinned devilishly.

Surprisingly, the thought of that didn't bother me in the slightest.

"Oh God, did I just give a potential stalker my number?" I teasingly gasped.

Gavin pulled a face and playfully shoved me making me laugh.

"Collins! Girlfriend time is for home time, you're on my time now so move!"

"Girlfriend?" a voice called out from my left. "That was quick work, pretty girl."

I forced myself not to turn around and correct Dominic, because for some reason I *wanted* him to think I was Gavin's girlfriend in hopes that it would hurt him like he has hurt me.

"Don't let him get to you," Gavin murmured as he leaned down and put his arms around me.

I jumped a little before giving him a quick squeeze like I've seen girls do with lads.

"Text you later, okay?" he smiled then turned and jogged away.

Obviously his question was rhetorical since he didn't stick around for an answer. It was a good thing that he moved away because I was a few seconds away from collapsing into a melted puddle over the smile he shot me over his shoulder.

How had I not perved on him since first year started?

I've noticed his looks a little since we did go to school together, but holy hell, I've never really looked at him. He was fucking stunning, and his smile was a serious contender against Dominic's, even though he didn't have dimples. I paused mid thought and grunted. How did that fucker work his way into my Gavin filled thoughts? He just couldn't leave me alone, even inside my damn head!

I shook my head, turned, and walked over to the area of the hall where the skipping ropes were. I never participated in any of the sports that involved me being part of a team, so this was like my own little area. However, the girls came over and crowded me today, which made me feel really uncomfortable.

"What's the story, Bronagh?" Micah asked me.

I was instantly afraid as I cleared my throat.

"Nothin'," I murmured. "What're you up to?"

She shrugged. "Bored of this class, figured we'd chill here for a bit. That cool with you?"

No.

I nodded. "Sure."

"Cool," she replied.

I was tense as fuck as she moved beside me and gripped a skipping rope. I had no idea why, but I was expecting her to lash out and hit me with it and I wanted to be ready to take the blow so it would hurt less. I licked my dry lips and looked to my right, willing Mr. Rivers to call the girls away for something, but my eyes caught Dominic's eyes instead, because he was already staring at me.

I froze then quickly looked away and back towards Micah, who glanced Dominic's way and nodded her head a little when he nodded for her to move away from me. I heard he had a 'talk' with her after rumours spread that Micah attacked me after school almost two weeks ago. It was obviously true because Micah looked terrified of him and hadn't so much as looked at me since the night she attacked me.

"I'm actually gonna do some more runnin'. Later, Bronagh." Micah smiled.

"Bye, Micah," I breathed.

Micah and her two friends, whose names I never bothered to learn, moved off and left Destiny, Lexi, and three other girls playing around with the ropes near me. Alannah was across the hall sitting on a bench reading on her Kindle like she always did after she had finished running and stretching. I felt eyes on me and it made me self-conscious and not want to jump rope. I made a move to put my rope back but Destiny was suddenly in front of me.

"I shagged Nico last night," she said as casually as saying hello.

Why the hell did that feel like being kicked in the stomach?

"Congratulations," I said, forcing my tone to come off as flat and bored.

Destiny cocked an eyebrow. "You aren't bothered that I shagged your fella?"

"He is not me fella and regardless of what you saw on Saturday and what Dominic is sayin', I didn't have sex with him." I was going to move around her when I paused and glared at her. "And it's dis- gustin' that you thought he was me boyfriend and yet you're actin' so proud that you shagged him. Honestly, why would you brag about being a slut and home wrecker?" I questioned.

I wished I had kept my mouth shut because I knew she was go- ing to shout at me before she even opened her mouth.

"I am not a slut, you're just jealous of me!" she screamed.

The whole hall went quiet. I felt my hand twitch and my blood boil. How fucking dare she scream in my face and say I was jealous of her?!

"Are you jokin'? You bragged only last week that you rode five lads in one week. If that isn't a slut, then I don't know what is! And why in God's name would I be jealous of you? You just openly told me you shagged Dominic last night even though you thought I was his girlfriend. You're a pathetic, STD riddin' little knacker and if you don't get out of me face, I'm goin' to—"

I didn't get to finish my sentence because with a roar she came at me. But, unlike last time when I was attacked, I wasn't unsuspect- ing and afraid, I was ready and mad. I lifted my arms and shoved

Destiny back away from me and leaned my head to the left, avoiding the hand that reached out to grab me. She landed back on her arse with a thud.

"Cat fight!" one of the lads shouted.

"Stop!" Mr. Rivers yelled.

"First and *last* warnin', stay the fuck away from me, Destiny," I snarled and she whimpered on the ground and cowered back like I was about to jump on her.

I wasn't going to hit her but whoever lifted me away from where I stood wasn't taking any chances.

"You're a magnet for trouble, Bee."

I began laughing. "All this shite only started happenin' when you and your evil twin rolled into town!"

Damien snorted into my ear then murmured, "Fights, mad girls, sex, parties… all that crap happens in every town we go to."

Did that mean they moved around a lot?

"Well, I don't want any part of it yet somehow I got dragged into it!" I snapped.

"Because Dominic wants you." Damien sighed.

I growled. "He can't have me!"

"And *that* is one of the reasons why he won't leave you alone."

I groaned. "I hate men."

Damien laughed then moved on when Gavin appeared in front of me.

"You okay? Do you need anythin'?" he asked me, a frown on his face.

"Straight to the principal's office Bronagh and Destiny, now!"

I cringed at Mr. Rivers' roar.

I groaned and said to Gavin, "Yeah, I need an ambulance because when me sister hears about this she is gonna kill me."

CHAPTER ELEVEN

"Y ou're so lucky you weren't suspended again!"

I kept my head down as I got into the back of Ryder's Jeep; it was like the Slater family car since all the lads drove it at one time or another.

"Dame, sit in the middle," my sister ordered. "I'm not listenin' to those two tear at each other's throats."

I completely and totally ignored Branna. She was making me take a ride home from Ryder knowing Dominic was going to be in the car, and I was mad at her for it. I was also mad that she was mad at me over what went down with Destiny.

I mean, I explained *exactly* what happened, and she was still pissed at me. I buckled my seatbelt, hugged my school bag to my chest and looked out of the car window.

"What were you thinkin', Bronagh?" she shouted.

I clenched my school bag and ignored her again.

Branna twisted around in her seat and looked at me, her eyes narrowed. "Answer me!"

I swallowed, looked at her calmly said, "I was thinkin' that I'm sick and tired of people walkin' all over me like I'm a doormat just because I'm quiet; I was stickin' up for meself!"

Branna shook her head. "By fuckin' *fightin'*?"

I lost it.

"I didn't fight her!" I snapped. "She got in me face and tried to humiliate me by braggin' that she shagged that prick over there and then she said I was jealous of her! Plus, she was the one who came at me; I pushed her away from me in an attempt to defend meself, unless you wanted me to let her beat me up like Micah did?"

Her eyes flashed; she only recently learned that Micah was the one who beat me up a couple of weeks ago, and that I had lied when I said I didn't know who hurt me. She understood my reasons, but she was still upset about that.

"You know I never want that to happen to you again, your fuckin' stomach is still only healin' from what that Micah girl done to you!"

I felt his eyes on me.

"What did she do to your stomach?" he asked me.

I ignored him.

I wasn't talking to him, because once again what happened was because of him; Destiny tried to rub having sex with him in my face.

"It was black and blue from that girl kickin' her when she was on the ground. The bruises are nearly faded but it's takin' a long time for them to heal."

I growled at Branna. "It's none of his business because *that* was his fault, *this* is his fault, *everything* is his fault."

I couldn't believe my voice cracked at the end of my sentence. I was going to cry; I knew it and so did everyone else. I looked out the window as Ryder began to pull out of the space he had parked in the school car park. I bit down on my lip and prayed that my tears would dry up but they didn't.

When I blinked, they fell onto my cheeks and then a little sniffle came from my nose.

Damien sighed next to me and put his arm around my shoulder. He didn't say a word or pull me into a side hug, he just left his arm around me for comfort. I usually didn't like anything like this. I could tell he didn't either but I was glad of it because it made me feel a little bit better.

The car journey wasn't long so I wiped my face as discreetly as I could when Ryder pulled up to mine and Branna's house.

"Later, Bee," Damien said.

I glanced at him and gave him a little smile then flicked my surely red and puffy eyes to Dominic and narrowed them. "I hate you," I said before turning and getting out of the car, closing the door and stalking up the garden.

"Bye, sweetie," I heard Branna say, and it made me scoff.

Ryder was bigger than both Branna and me put together. There was no way in hell a man his size should be called sweetie, it was just wrong. I thought this over while I rooted through my bag for my keys. When I found them I unlocked the door and headed straight for my room. I heard Branna follow me and it caused me to inwardly groan. I needed to lie down and just be on my own for a while, but apparently she wasn't going to let that happen.

When I got into my room, I kicked off my shoes and began to take off my uniform. I pulled on some pyjama trousers under my school skirt then took off the shirt once the trousers were up. I settled on my bed once I had a tank top on and gestured for Branna—who was leaning against my door—to come into the room.

"Please, continue to belittle and shout at me, I didn't get enough of that at school or in the car."

Branna's eyes narrowed as she walked into my room and sat down on my bed. "I'm not belittlin' you. Shoutin' at you was just from the shock at being called from class to come to your school because you were in a fight!"

I groaned. "It wasn't a fight, I don't know how many times I have to say that for you to believe me!"

"You shoved Destiny to the ground. That has means for a fight, Bronagh."

I grunted. "She deserved it. She got in my face and tried to upset me by throwin' her shaggin' Dominic in me face, the slut!"

Branna sighed and muttered, "That lad does nothin' but 'cause trouble."

"I know! I've been sayin' that for *weeks*!" I exclaimed.

Branna settled me with a wave of her hand. "I understand how much he gets to you and the trouble he is causin' you. Ryder is talkin' to him about it tonight. It won't magically fix things, but if you both can at least say hello to one another, and be around each other without war eruptin', myself, and everyone else, will be forever grateful."

I grumbled, "I can't stand him though, he thinks he is God's gift or somethin'. I mean, he practically begged me to get with him, and when I say no, he goes and shags Destiny not a day later then tries to act like nothin' happened. Who does that?"

Branna shrugged her shoulders. "His ego took a hit at your rejection. Did you talk to him about it?"

I shook my head.

"Then how do you know if it's true?" she questioned.

I shrugged because I didn't have an answer.

"Let's say he did sleep with her," Branna suggested. "You both aren't in a relationship because you turned him down so he can be with anyone and that's okay because you aren't his girl."

I glowered. "I know that. It still doesn't make *me* feel better if he slept with her whether we're together or not. He shouldn't be with anyone if he is trying to court me—"

I cut myself off once I realised what I was rambling on about.

"Wait," Branna gasped. "Are you upset that Nico might have had sex in general? Not just because it might have been with Destiny?"

No.

Heavens no.

Heavens *and* Hell no!

"You are!" Branna gasped again. "You *like* him!"

"I do not, I hate him," I countered. "I can't stand the sight of him—"

"Give it up Bee, you're gettin' defensive and that's a dead giveaway."

I growled at Branna. "Thinkin' someone, even an evil bastard, is attractive does not mean you like them."

I couldn't believe that I admitted out loud, or at all, that I found Dominic attractive!

Branna nodded. "You're right, it doesn't. But if said attractive bastard had sex with another girl, and it upsets you then yeah, it does mean you like him."

I swallowed the retort that was climbing up my throat and settled on giving Branna a dirty look, which made her laugh.

"Oh God, you hate that you like him, don't you?" she cackled.

I grunted and kicked at her, which she laughed even harder over. I gave up on trying to shut her up and angrily folded my arms across my chest until she stopped—which wasn't for a solid two minutes.

"When the hell did all *this* start to happen?" Branna asked me as she wiped her eyes.

I groaned and covered my face with my hands. "I have no idea… I honestly think it was when he first kissed me in his room after he defended me from Jason. I liked how he acted then; he wasn't mean or anythin', and he seemed nice, we had an actual conversation. I guess it just went from there." I frowned. "Don't get me wrong though, I do hate him for the times—which is pretty much all the time—he is an arsehole, but I always find myself looking out for him, or just plain lookin' at him. I hate that Destiny might have been with him or that he could be with other girls or that he wants to be with them. I never really thought about it, but it makes me so mad and my chest hurts. It's horrible Branna, how do I make it stop?"

Branna started laughing again. "Bee, you can't just turn off your feelin's. If you like Nico then you will continue to like him until you get over him or until you start to like someone else who takes up all your attention from Nico."

I perked up at that. "There is another lad that I think I could like, his name is Gavin Collins—"

"Aideen's little brother?" Branna questioned with a raised brow. "The kid who fought Dominic and got you suspended?"

That didn't put Gavin in the best light.

I winced. "Yeah, but he is the *complete* opposite of Dominic so you would like him. I swear."

Branna grinned at me. "I can't believe this is finally happenin'."

I frowned. "You can't believe *what* is finally happenin'?"

"You're startin' to let people in," she gushed. "You're *actually* havin' boy problems and not only with one lad but two of them! I thought this day would never come, I'm so bloody happy!"

I was a little freaked because what she was saying was true, but what freaked me out the most was that Branna actually started to cry. I was instantly crawling to her side and wrapping my arms around her, hugging her tight.

"Why are you cryin'?" I asked her, panicked.

She shrugged. "I'm just happy."

I pulled back and glared at her. "You're happy that I'm havin' boy problems?"

"Yes!" she squealed and burst into tears again.

Oh Christ.

"I need you to woman up, stop cryin', and help me figure all this out. I am in unknown territory here, what the hell do I do?"

Branna sat back and wiped her face but was still sniffling a little. I couldn't believe she cried because I was having boy troubles; there was something very weird and just plain wrong with that.

"Datin' Nico is out, right?" Branna asked me.

Was that a serious question?

"Eh, yeah! I barely like him Branna. Honestly, the qualities I like are things he's showed like twice. The rest of the time he is a thorn in me side and I can't get rid of him."

Branna nodded her head in understanding. "Okay, Nico and you datin' is out, what about you and Gavin?"

I chewed on my lip. "He asked me out on a date today. At first it was just a front he put on to make Dominic take a step back from me, to make him think we're together or somethin', but because Dominic seemed to get mad over it, he wanted a real date just in case he dies by Dominic's hand… or foot."

Branna laughed. "That explains why Nico is more pissed than usual, it's because you rejected him on Saturday mornin' and today, only two days later, you're apparently in a relationship with another lad. The very lad that fought him a few weeks ago tryin' to defend you… that has got to be a major shot to the ego for him."

I groaned and rubbed my face with my hands. "I don't know how all this has happened, Branna. It's like the more I try to push Dominic away, the more he forces himself in. Why won't he take no for an answer and just leave me alone? I mean he may want to kiss me, but he doesn't like me for me, he actually hates me."

Branna sighed. "Maybe he just isn't used to hearin' a girl tell him no. Maybe he feels you're a challenge, and we all know he loves a challenge."

I grunted. "He knows I'm not playin' hard to get, I told him I just wasn't interested in him."

"Was that before or after the two times you made out with him?" she asked in an American accent.

I growled at my sister making her smile with glee.

I eventually shrugged, not being able to remember and said, "Me body and me mind seem to run on two different circuit boards where Dominic is involved, much to my displeasure."

"That much is obvious." Branna mused.

I grunted.

My sister pressed on. "It's an odd situation, but there *does* seem to be a solution to it."

I perked up. "Really? What is it? What is the solution?"

"Gavin Collins." Branna grinned devilishly.

Uh, oh.

"Gavin?" I repeated.

Branna nodded. "You said yourself that you could like him and the best way to get over a lad is to get under another," she paused when I snorted. "I don't mean it like *that*, you don't have to get under Gavin—"

"I get the metaphor Bran, I'm just teasin'."

She rolled her eyes. "Okay, good. Anyway, as I was sayin', if you get with Gavin it will help you move on, and it might just hit home with Nico that you really don't want him and that he should just move on too. Understand?"

I shook my head. "Do you mean really date Gavin or just pretend date him, because I don't think I can do either, I hardly know him."

Branna rolled her eyes. "You said you like him, the like starts the gettin' to know him, Bee. Besides, that's what dates are for, you to get to know one another. You have already secured one date so we can just see how it goes; you never know, you might just find yourself happy with Gavin."

I rolled my eyes. "I don't think anyone can know whether they would be happy with someone after one date."

Branna smiled. "I knew after my first date with Ryder."

I raised my brows. "Really?"

She nodded. "It was a gut feelin' that I knew I could really like him and that we could be good together. It might be different for everyone else, but I just knew."

I whistled then gaped at her. "You don't mean you know he is the one, do you?"

Branna just beamed, and I groaned.

Ryder was her one.

"Why did *your* one have to be closely related to *my* nemesis?"

She snorted. "Maybe God is findin' your and Nico's situation amusin'. I am for the most part."

I rolled my eyes skyward and spoke to my ceiling. "Can you cut me a break, Jesus? This bullshit isn't funny anymore—"

I yelped as Branna dove on me and knocked me back onto my bed.

"She didn't mean that, she takes it back," Branna shouted.

I laughed at her, which made her elbow me. "Don't curse when you're talkin' to Jesus. That is like askin' to be struck down."

I grunted. "Havin' Dominic in me life is punishment enough, trust me."

Branna rolled off me onto her back and lay beside me. I heard my phone vibrate on my locker; I grabbed it and saw I had a text from an unknown number.

I opened the text and felt myself blush.

I said to Dominic today that I was taking you out tonight; I'm keeping good on my word. Is eight okay? ;)

He sent me a wink face.

What did that mean?

"Gavin wants to take me out tonight at eight," I murmured.

Branna clapped her hands together. "Perfect, we can start operation get over Nico by gettin' under Gavin."

I looked at Branna and shook my head. "There is somethin' seriously wrong with you. I'm your little sister!"

Branna rolled her eyes. "You're eighteen Bee, you aren't a baby anymore."

I grunted. "I understand that."

She smiled at me. "Where is he takin' you?"

I shrugged. "He mentioned the cinema in school."

Branna nodded. "Text him back that eight is great and then get up and get your arse into the shower."

I nodded, texted Gavin back, then looked at Branna while she muttered curse words as she looked through my wardrobe. I walked into the bathroom when Branna turned and headed into her room.

"What are you doin'?" I shouted.

She grunted. "Your black jeans are good, but you have zero decent tops. I'm pickin' out one of mine."

When she bounced back into my room with a red top that was low cut and made of lace, I stared at her with my jaw hangin' open.

She expected me to wear that piece of cloth?

"I can't wear that, it's practically non-existent!" I argued.

Branna snorted. "Puh-lease, it's only a little low-cut and will look amazing under a cardigan. You need to work your best assets when goin' on a date. Your jeans will hug your arse and showcase your hips; this top will show off the fact that you actually do possess a pair of breasts even if they are small. You will be showin' off hardly any skin and yet your body will be on show, it's perfect."

I continued to stare at Branna like she had grown an extra ear on her head.

She shook her head at me. "I'm goin' to have me work cut out for me, go on and get your shower. I'll iron your clothes and then get my makeup and hair products for when you're done. I'll make you look even more gorgeous than you already are. Gavin won't know what hit him."

I opened my mouth to speak then closed it again before mutely walking into the bathroom and stripping down for my shower. I was nervous; I was nervous about what Branna was going to do to me, nervous about what Gavin would think once he saw me, and nervous in general for our date.

I honestly felt like puking.

Is this how girls felt before every date they had with a boy or did it get worse on the actual date?

I hope not because spitting chunks on Gavin's shoes would seriously mess with operation get over Dominic by—not literally—getting under Gavin.

This operation *needed* to be a success.

CHAPTER TWELVE

"Gavin is here Bronagh, and he looks hot!" My sister gushed. "No lad notices you for years and now all of a sudden you have two hotties chasin' after you. This is so excitin'!"

Exciting?

More like bloody nerve wrecking.

I remained hidden inside the bathroom while Branna lightly knocked on the door. "Yay, lucky me," I murmured to her as I stared at myself in the full-length mirror on the bathroom wall.

I looked like me but at the same time I didn't. It was still my face, just with some extra makeup on it. My hair was big and curly. Honestly, it was huge. My body looked the same only more outlined; skinnies always hugged a person's lower half but combined with a fitted shirt up top, it made me feel naked.

"I can't wear this Bran, you can see all my—barely there—cleavage," I groaned when I opened the door to the bathroom and let Branna come inside.

She rolled her eyes at me. "Stop bein' so dramatic, you can only see a little of your cleavage which is normal in that top. You have jeans on, and the cardigan covers up your arms. Some cleavage, a little bit of your neck and face is the only skin on show."

I grunted. "Everythin' is so fittin' and tight it feels like a second skin. I might as well be naked!"

Branna pinched the bridge of her nose and shook her head. "This is the wrong way around. You should be wantin' to dress like this and I should be opposed because I'm older and your guardian."

I snorted. "You're just excited because I'm like a doll you can play dress up with now and talk lads."

My sister clapped her hands excitedly. "Isn't it great?"

No.

"The greatest," I deadpanned.

Branna playfully swatted me. "Whatever, I'll be excited for you."

I sighed; I was excited but I was way too nervous about this date with Gavin. I mean, what the hell do I do?

"Stop thinkin' and come on, he is waitin'."

Before I could stall for a few more minutes, Branna took my arm and pulled me from the bathroom and down the stairs. I pulled my arm free from Branna's hold, and was about to tell her off when I caught sight of Gavin and had to stop myself from gasping.

He had on grey jeans, a black tee, and a black coat. His hair was gelled upwards; I liked it because you could completely see his face with that style. I realised I was staring when Branna elbowed me in the side.

"Say somethin'," she grumbled.

I quickly cleared my throat. "Hey, Gav."

He flicked his eyes up from my chest and gave me a dazzling smile. "Hey, you look gorgeous."

I flushed.

"Awe," Branna cooed. "I told her the same thing, but she doesn't believe me."

What the hell did she just say? My mind growled. *Was she trying to embarrass me?*

"I'll just have to remind her often tonight then just how gorgeous she is," Gavin smiled and winked, making me stare at him in a trance.

Seriously, how did I not notice him growing up?

I heard the hall door open and close and alarm shot through me. Who the hell was that and how did the person get in so easily? I had no idea why, but when I glanced over my shoulder and saw the body of a man, I shrieked and jumped in Gavin's direction. His arms went around my waist, and my head went to his throat.

"It's just Ryder!" Branna shouted over my screaming.

I pulled my head from Gavin's neck and looked at the man again. Sure enough Ryder stood in the hallway with his eyebrows raised, pizza boxes in his hands and a key in his mouth.

"Really? You find me so ugly that you scream and run for cover?" he mumbled around the key.

Branna snorted at him, and even Gavin chuckled.

I composed myself before glaring at Ryder. "I didn't know it was you, did I? Since when do you have a key to me house?"

I knew I was supposed to be nice to him, but having him around was taking some getting used to. No man that Branna was ever seeing was in the house when I was at home. I didn't think she actually ever brought one home, so it was weird that Ryder was coming and going like he owned the place the past few days.

"Since this mornin' when I gave him one," Branna said to me, slightly glaring.

I glared right back at her. "Well, you should have let me know. I live here too, you know?"

Her shoulders slumped a little, and her glare vanished. "Right, I'm sorry. I guess I forgot."

I nodded to her then looked to Ryder, who was looking at Gavin.

"This is Gavin—"

"We've met." Ryder cut me off, still staring at Gavin.

They met?

"When did you meet?" I asked.

"The meeting a few weeks ago when he and Dominic got into it in school," Ryder cut me off again and continued to look at Gavin.

I widened my eyes a little; I had forgotten all about that meeting.

Crap.

This was turning out to be very awkward, and we hadn't even left the house yet.

"So… you two, huh?" Ryder asked Gavin.

I felt Gavin shrug. "We're goin' on a date so yeah, I guess so."

Ryder flicked his eyes to me but didn't say anything.

"I'm going to dish up the pizza, babe," he said to Branna, then looked back to Gavin and me. "Have a great time."

"Thanks," Gavin and I said in unison.

Silence fell then, and luckily Gavin cleared his throat breaking it.

"We better go, the film starts at half eight."

I nodded my head and said bye to Ryder—who headed into the kitchen—and Branna—who was bouncing on her toes—as I left the house with Gavin.

"I'm… I'm so sorry about… whatever the hell that was back there," I said when Gavin and I neared his car.

At least I thought it was his car.

"Don't even worry about it. I remember you said in school that Nico's older brother was your sister's boyfriend. I was mentally prepared to see him." Gavin snorted.

I snickered a little too and smiled when he opened the car door for me like a gentleman. I slid inside, buckled my seatbelt, and folded my hands across my lap.

"Me da let me use this car since I don't have one yet. Passed me full drivin' test last week, so he is being very trustin' of me tonight," Gavin said when he got into his side of the car.

I looked at Gavin, my face expressionless. "Please tell me you passed everythin' on your drivin' test with flyin' colours."

He looked me dead in the eye, the corner of his lip curling upwards. "I passed me test with flyin' colours."

I yelped. "I'm goin' to die!"

Gavin cracked up laughing. "I'm a good driver, Bee, no worries.

You're safe with me, promise."

I glanced at him from the corner of my eye and smiled a little.

Okay, once we got past the awkwardness in the house, this was a good start to my first date. I was feeling excited now and not nervous at all.

As we drove to the cinema, Gavin and I talked about his football team at school and how hard Mr. Rivers makes the team's training sessions. I honestly couldn't give a hoot about football, but Gavin clearly adored the sport and loved playing it, so I was all ears while he talked. I asked relevant questions here and there making myself appear interested.

It didn't take long to get to the cinema. After getting out of the car and walking inside, Gavin took my hand and smiled down at me. "What do you want to eat? My treat."

I was blushing over him holding my hand, but snorted at his wording. "That rhymed," I mused.

Gavin grinned. "I am poet, and I know it."

I chuckled then and continued to smile as we walked hand in hand up to an open till. I wanted popcorn, M&M's, and a Coke. Gavin wanted the same, so he got us a couple's combo with extra M&M's. My face was burning, a couple's meal. Couple!

I was giddy and sort of sick with excitement the more I thought about what it meant.

Were we a couple or was that just the smart thing to buy for two people?

I had no idea!

After paying for our tickets—Gavin refused my money—and our food, Gavin held the drinks and M&M's while I held the big tub of popcorn. We headed down to the screen that the film we were seeing was at and settled into our seats in the middle row.

Everything was going great until I spotted Kane, Dominic and Damien's older brother, near the back row seated between two blondes. He locked eyes with me, flicked his eyes in Gavin's direction then back to mine, and sort of glared at me. I had no idea why he was glaring, but when I noticed the light on his face and the device in his hand I groaned, then slumped down into my seat.

"What's wrong?" Gavin asked as he settled in next to me and handed me my drink and M&M's.

I looked at him and smiled. "Nothin'."

He gave me a knowing look, and I found myself sighing before leaning into him a little. "The lad in the back row between the two blondes is Dominic and Damien's older brother. He looked at you, and me, and then glared. He took out his phone and began textin' on it. It could be nothin', but I'd bet money that he is tellin' Dominic that I'm here with you."

Gavin's eyes narrowed a little. "What the hell is that lad's problem? Is he obsessed with you or somethin'?"

I blushed. "No, I just think he thinks I'm playin' a hard to get game with him."

Gavin raised an eyebrow. "And are you playin' hard to get?"

I gaped at him. "No! Of course not."

Gavin nodded. "Good, I don't wanna play a game that I've no chance of winnin'."

I frowned at him and was about to say something when the room went dark and the screen lit up before us. The film was called *The Mortal Instruments: The City of Bones*. It was a good film, but I couldn't really concentrate for some reason so by the time it was over, I was a little relieved.

Gavin and I were the first to leave the cinema house, which I was grateful for because I didn't really want to have to say hello to Kane. I thought Gavin was going to bring me home but when he suggested going for some McDonald's, I agreed because I felt like we needed to talk about anything in order to stop the growing awkwardness after that conversation in the cinema.

After we got our food and sat down, we dug in and began talking about random stuff and laughing at silly things. I felt happy and relaxed and from the look of things, so did Gavin. That was until Kane strolled in with the two girls and Dominic in tow.

I felt my heart pump and my palms get sticky with sweat.

"No fuckin' way," I groaned and ducked my head a little.

Gavin frowned at me, then looked over his shoulder. His entire body went rigid and when he looked back at me, I swallowed nervously. He looked pissed.

"He is here because we're here, right?"

We both knew it was true, so I nodded my head.

Gavin sighed, and before he spoke I felt tears sting my eyes. I knew he was about to cut our date short and not ask me out for another one.

"Bronagh, I like you, I really do. You're gorgeous, down to earth, and an all-around great girl, but this thing with Nico is too much for me. If this thing between us went somewhere and we got together, I'd have to be on my guard around him and worry about what he would try and do to lure you away from me. He has it bad for you, and he obviously doesn't care about steppin' on me to get to you."

I bit the insides of my cheeks because this hurt, and I had no idea why.

"We can be friends; I wasn't jokin' when I said you're a great girl, you really are." Gavin continued.

Oh God, I was about to cry, and I didn't want to.

"I'm goin' to go to the bathroom for a minute, be right back." I whispered.

I jumped up and moved towards the toilet.

"Bronagh, wait-"

Gavin's voice cut off when I closed the bathroom door. I instantly fanned my hands at my eyes and tilted my head backwards, blinking rapidly to make the tears go away. I grabbed some tissue and dabbed around my eyes and took a few deep breaths. I felt sad but also really angry. I knew Gavin had a point; Dominic would always be meddling in our relationship if we formed one, so it's not really a surprise that Gavin didn't want anything more than a friendship. It was better that he let me down now instead of after more dates when I grew to care for him instead of just liking him.

It still hurt though.

This was the first time something like this had happened to me and on my first date nonetheless! I composed myself, fixed my hair in the mirror, and then headed back outside. Gavin was where I had left him, but Dominic now occupied my seat.

I stormed over to his side, gripped on his shoulder, and pulled. "Get up and leave us alone!"

He looked to his shoulder then looked up at me and glared. I moved my hand away from him but kept my glare in place.

"Dominic, leave." I repeated.

He smiled at me, but it didn't reach his eyes. "I'm only talking to your boyfriend—"

"Gavin isn't me boyfriend and won't ever be thanks to you, so just fuck off and leave us the hell alone. You have ruined me first date as it is so just go away!"

I hated that my voice cracked a little; everyone who was in the restaurant heard it when I shouted, and my embarrassment only upset me further.

I gave up on Dominic and looked to Gavin. "Can you take me home, please?"

He looked both pissed off and saddened as he nodded to me and stood up from his seat. He reached for my hand, but I found myself moved aside as Gavin's hand was pushed away from me.

I gaped when I got my footing and stared at Dominic. He actually moved himself in front of me, pushed Gavin's hand away from me, and got in his face.

"What the fuck are you doin'? You stupid yank-"

Dominic's fist flew into Gavin's jaw cutting his words off. I yelped when Gavin flew backwards onto the ground. I then screamed when Dominic tried to move after him raising his fist again. I flew into a rage and jumped on Dominic's back.

I wrapped my left arm around his neck, my legs around his hips, and thumped Dominic's head. Each blow was hurting my hand, but I

149

didn't care. I wanted to make him hurt because his stupid self had made me hurt tonight when Gavin broke off our date because of him.

"Damn it, Bronagh," Dominic snapped. "Get off me!"

"No!" I shouted and continued to smack at his head, shoulders, and back.

I was then pulled off Dominic and held off the ground like a rag doll.

"Calm down, hell cat," a voice chuckled into my ear.

I struggled against the hold on me. "Let me go, Kane. I'm goin' to kill that bastard!"

"That bastard is my little brother so I can't allow that," he said, lowly.

I struggled again but stopped when Gavin got to his feet and rubbed his red and slightly swollen jaw. He glared at Dominic then cut his eyes to me.

"I'm out of here, Bronagh," he announced. "I'm sorry, but this is too much to deal with."

With that said, he turned and stormed away.

I was wide-eyed and stared after him. "Gavin, wait, please-"

"Don't!" Dominic growled. "Don't call after him. He isn't man enough if he doesn't want to fight for you."

Fight for me?

"He doesn't have to fight for me!" I stated. "I was his if he wanted me, but he doesn't, and it's all because of you! Why can't you just leave me alone and stop interferin' in me life?"

Dominic held my gaze and said, "Because I want you."

I knew he wanted to have sex with me, he had told me that enough times before but for some reason I felt like he wasn't just saying he wanted that this time. It felt like he was saying he wanted all of me. Too fucking bad, he couldn't have me. He was dangerous; he made that clear each time I encountered him, and I just couldn't have him in my life like that.

He could break me.

"Dominic, I can't," I whispered. "You're too different from

me—"

"I'm calling bullshit on that. You were just on my back, pounding your fist onto my head in a blind rage. You're more like me than you think."

I glared at him. "Havin' a bad temper doesn't mean I'm like you. You fight for fun like a sick twisted fuck. I hit you to defend," I paused for a moment before clearing my throat, "to defend Gavin, not because I enjoyed it."

"I don't fight for fun, trust me on that," Dominic muttered catching my attention.

That confused me so I asked, "Why do you fight then if not for fun?"

He looked me in the eye. "I fight for my family, for my broth-"

"Dominic." Kane cut him off in a low warning tone.

I raised my eyebrows and wanted to thump Kane for cutting Dominic off. I couldn't ask him what he meant because all of a sudden throbbing spread throughout my hand, I let out a strangled cry and instantly cradled it.

"Oh shite, I think I broke me hand!"

Kane put me down—yeah, he held me up during that entire conversation which had to have killed his back under my weight— and came around to examine it with Dominic.

"Let me see," Dominic said softly.

I shook my head like a little kid and snapped, "No, it hurts! Go away!"

He smiled a little. "Come on, I'll take you to the hospital."

The hospital? Where they stick needles in people and cut them open?

I felt myself go pale, and before I knew it, I was swaying and then was encased in Dominic's arms.

"I've got you," he murmured into my ear.

That wasn't comforting!

He kept an arm around my waist as we walked out of the restaurant. We bumped into security guards who were piling in, and Dominic sighed and looked at them. "I know, I know. I'm never to enter the premises again."

I frowned as we left while he smiled down at me. "Not my first time being kicked out of a place for fighting."

"Shockin'," I grunted, which made him laugh.

Kane ventured off with his lady friends after Dominic assured him that I would be fine with him; I seriously doubted that because he was the reason my hand was killing me!

"I'm goin' to punch your brother in the face the next time I see him, I know he texted you where I was."

Dominic snorted as he buckled his seatbelt. "He actually texted me and asked me if I wanted to hit up McDonald's after his date with those girls. I had nothin' else to do so I said sure. I was just as surprised to see you and Gavin when I walked in as you were to see me."

Kane had a date with *two* girls?

I shook my head. "Your brother knew somethin' would come of it, the sadistic bastard."

Dominic laughed out right then, and I hated that I wanted to smile. My hand was now throbbing badly though, so instead I whimpered a little.

"Are you okay?" Dominic asked.

I snapped my head to him and glared. "Does it look like I'm okay?"

Dominic didn't reply, so I glared at him harder. "Answer me!"

He chewed on his lip. "No, because you're just going to yell at me no matter what I say, so I'm keeping my mouth shut."

I grunted. "That'd be a fuckin' first!"

Dominic didn't reply with a snotty retort, and it was sort of weird.

I looked at him, and he laughed and glanced to me. "I'm not going to argue with you babe so stop trying to bait me."

I growled. "I'm *not* your babe."

"I forgot," he smiled. "Sorry."

He wasn't sorry, the bastard.

I shook my head and groaned and held my hand to my chest. "God, this hurts so bad."

I felt tears stinging my eyes and I willed them away.

"Bronagh, please don't cry," Dominic pleaded.

I sniffled. "I can't help it, it really hurts."

"I know, but we're nearly at the hospital." He assured me. "I'll make them fix it, okay?"

I nodded my head still sniffling as I fished out my phone. I rang Branna before the pain got so bad that I couldn't talk.

"How is the date goin'?" Branna squealed when she answered.

I whimpered.

"Bronagh? Baby? What is it? What's wrong? Did Gavin hurt you? I'll fuckin' kill him—"

"Branna, shut up." I cut her off with a cry. "Gavin didn't hurt me, but I am hurt and I'm on my way to the hospital."

"The hospital?" she shrieked. "Why? What happened? Are you okay?"

I snorted through my pain. "Dominic happened."

Dominic sighed from next to me, and it made me grin a little even though I was hurting.

"Dominic?" she snapped then growled, "I'm goin' to kill your little brother."

"Not if I kill him first," I heard Ryder bellow.

Dominic heard it as well because he groaned out loud and it made my grin widen.

"We're on our way. I'll be there as soon as I can, Bee, okay?"

I nodded and sniffled. "'Kay."

I hung up just as Dominic pulled into the hospital, we found parking near A&E and got out so we could head inside. I felt Dominic at my back when I was giving my information to the woman behind the counter and it was distracting me. When I was checked in, we headed inside the waiting area that was absolutely packed with people.

I glared at Dominic. "I hate you."

He nodded his head. "I hate me, too. We're gonna be here all fucking night."

I growled, "Leave then, no one is askin' you to stay."

He gave me a look. "If you think I'm leaving you here, then you don't know me very well."

"I don't know you at all," I fired back.

He rolled his eyes and tugged on my good hand leading me towards the only spare seat in the room, which made me kick his shin and earned me a snort from a couple of people in the waiting area.

"Trouble in paradise?" a man asked Dominic, grinning.

Dominic snorted. "Nah bro, this is foreplay for us."

I gasped and Dominic instantly ducked away from me which the man and some others found funny. I was mortified; I could feel my face and neck burn.

"I'm sorry, I was only playing," Dominic murmured to me when he saw how red my face was.

I only glared at him, then widened my eyes when he sat down on the only seat available. What a dickhead! I was the one who was hurt; I should be sitting down not him. I was about to tell him that when he reached forward, placed his hands on my hips, turned me around and then pulled me down onto his lap.

I felt even more mortified than I already was when some people glanced at where I was sitting on Dominic. My arse was directly on his groin, my thighs were lined on top of his, my back was against his chest and the back of my head was on his shoulder.

It was a very intimate position, and it both thrilled and infuriated me.

"You can hit me later. Just relax now and let me hold you until you get seen by the doctor," Dominic said in my ear then kissed my cheek three times.

It was a surprisingly sweet gesture that did indeed shut me up. I felt my heart begin to pound as butterflies erupted across my stomach. He could make me so livid with one action then completely happy with another. I didn't know how to separate my feelings when it came to him.

I relaxed after a few moments and began looking around the hospital waiting room. There were four girls sitting across from us that were at least two years younger than us, smiling at Dominic and shooting him appreciative glances. One girl looked at my thighs and chewed on her lip before randomly looking away. I looked down and swallowed, my thighs tripled in size because I was sitting on Dominic and it made me uncomfortable. I remained seated on him, but I sat up and took off my cardigan and draped it over my legs, covering them.

"Are you warm?" Dominic asked when I settled back against him.

I shook my head and held my bad hand to my chest.

"Then why did you—"

"I was coverin' me legs," I mumbled.

Dominic was quiet for a moment. "I'm probably going to regret asking this, but why did you cover your legs?"

I blushed and whispered, "'Cause they triple in size when I sit down."

Silence.

I was about to speak when Dominic mumbled, "God save me from girls and their stupid way of thinking."

I gasped making him snort as he nuzzled his nose on my neck. "I happen to think you look fucking gorgeous tonight. I've never seen you wear clothes that actually *fit* you before. I must say, Bronagh, I like it *a lot*."

The tips of my ears felt on fire as I ducked my head, making him laugh.

"Bronagh Murphy?" called out a female voice.

I stood up and held onto my cardigan and moved towards the nurse who called my name. I felt Dominic follow me, but I didn't say anything. I knew I would need someone in there with me or I would probably pass out.

"Bronagh?" The nurse questioned when I stopped in front of her.

I nodded then chewed on my lip when she looked over my shoulder. "Family or partners only—"

"I'm her boyfriend," Dominic cut the woman off.

I felt myself blush while the nurse smiled, nodded and gestured us into the triage room. I moved inside and sat on the examination table. The nurse looked at the hand I was cradling and made a face.

"That looks painful." She winced.

"It is," I assured her.

"How did this happen?" she asked.

Dominic lowered his head behind her while I shrugged and said, "I punched a lad who told me I was fat and said I needed to go on a diet."

Dominic snapped his head up and stared at me from behind the nurse; I kept a straight face and looked at the nurse. "I don't usually act that way but the lad *really* hurt me feelin's."

I directed the last part of my sentence at Dominic making him frown.

The nurse shook her head. "I hope you hit the little shite hard enough to bruise. That is a disgustin' thing to say to a person!"

Go nurse!

I nodded my head to her. "I think I hurt him."

"You did," Dominic mouthed to me and rubbed the back of his head and winced, making me bite my lip so I wouldn't smile.

The nurse went about examining my hand, apologising every time I winced, groaned, and just plain screeched.

"I'll book you in for an X-Ray before you can see a doctor. You can tell from the waitin' room that we're pretty busy tonight. Our waitin' time right now is seven hours; it will be another two or three hours after you get seen before you can go home, okay?"

Guess I wouldn't be going to school tomorrow.

"That's fine, thank you. Me sister is on her way so she will stay with me—"

"*I'm* staying with you; Branna can argue with me all she wants, but I'm not going anywhere," Dominic cut me off.

I raised my eyebrows at him while the nurse beamed in his direction.

"That's very sweet of you to stay with your girlfriend." She said.

I was about to say Dominic wasn't my boyfriend but he smiled back at the nurse, and I forgot about what I was thinking. His dimples were standing at attention, and I couldn't *not* look at them.

I came to grips at that moment that his dimples were a huge weakness of mine, which was crazy because craters in someone's face shouldn't be so bloody attractive! I continued to look at Dominic while the nurse put my hand and arm in a sling and tied it off around my neck. He was watching what her hands were doing to me for a moment before he looked up at my face and found me looking at him.

I knew I was here because he had ruined my date with Gavin and any chance of a relationship with him and I was mad about that, but as much as I said I hated him, I couldn't force the feeling when it didn't exist. It existed at some stage, but not anymore.

Sure, he pissed me off something fierce, but I didn't hate him. We didn't see eye to eye on pretty much everything, but his persistence in wanting me was slowly but surely making me overlook the fact that we were probably the worst match. And having him in my life goes against everything I've ever built up about keeping people out. He was a risk and instead of shutting the idea down again, I was actually contemplating on whether to *take* the risk.

Holy shite.

"What are you thinking about?" Dominic asked me while the nurse was out getting me some painkillers and a slip for me to hold for my X-Ray when my name was called later.

"I'm thinkin' that you're dangerous, and that havin' you in me life would be doin' what Branna always wanted me to do, open up to someone. You're a risk that I'm thinkin' of takin'."

Dominic stared at me for a moment before he stepped forward and moved himself between my legs. "You want me?" he whispered.

I swallowed my pride. "You have to work on not makin' me so mad but yeah, I want you."

He cupped my cheeks with his hands and strummed his thumbs up and down.

"I'm not sayin' I'll be your girlfriend right away," I added. "I'm sayin' that I'm open to the idea."

He raised an eyebrow. "So I'm on a trial basis with you?"

I nodded. "Exactly, I just want to feel out how this could work with us before I put a title on us, is that okay with you?"

"Can I kiss you whenever I want?" he asked.

I rolled my eyes at him. "No kissin' in school because I'm not ready to deal with any of that drama, especially after what happened with Destiny, which, by the way I *never* want to talk about. We weren't anything over the weekend so anything that happened or didn't happen is none of me business. Apart from that though, yeah, you can kiss me whenever you want to."

"I'm fine with it then." Dominic breathed.

With that said, he crushed his mouth to mine and forced his tongue into my mouth, making me gasp and grip his arm with my good hand.

I barely had a chance to kiss him back because suddenly his body and mouth weren't pressed against mine anymore. I opened my eyes and found he was across the room with a female on top of him, swinging her fists down on him.

The female was my sister.

And she was beating the shite out of him.

Fuck!

CHAPTER THIRTEEN

"Are you sure you don't want to press charges, sweetie?"

I shook my head and scrubbed my face with my good hand while the female Garda asked Dominic the same question for the fifth time. She was young, twenty-five at the most, and was smiling and nodding her head at him every time he spoke, then cooing over him like the new nurse was when he winced over the needle digging into him while she stitched the cut under his eye that Branna's ring caused when she socked him.

"He already told you he doesn't want to press charges against me sister, *why* are you being so repetitive?" I asked the Garda, the snarl in my voice not going amiss.

The Garda snapped her gaze to me and glared. "It is me job to ask the victim of attacks these types of questions more than once to make sure they are solid on their decision."

Yeah, *sure* it was.

I asked, "Is it also your job to flirt with said victim while his *girlfriend* is sitting right next to him?"

The Garda had the decency to flush while the nurse stitching up Dominic's under eye went deathly quiet and stopped her cooing over him when he made noises of pain.

"Listen here, I wasn't flirtin'-"

"Yeah, you were, but you might as well give it up; he isn't interested in you. Right?" When I looked to Dominic, I found him already watching me, which made my insides jump a little because his gaze was dark, and it was entirely focused on me.

"Right." He grinned just as the nurse finished up his stitches and moved away from him but only by a couple of inches.

I nodded to him then looked back to the Garda. "See?"

The Garda was about to go off on me, but she stopped and gawked as Dominic cleared his throat then stretched his arms over his head, which caused his biceps, triceps, and all his other 'ceps to flex and contract. He was bare chested because Branna ripped his top when she 'attacked' him, and he had to throw it in the bin. This didn't bother me because he had such a sexy torso and I enjoyed getting the chance to admire it with my eyes.

Only my eyes weren't the sole pair doing the admiring and for the first time ever, I felt extremely jealous and extremely possessive of him. That's why I was pissy with the Garda and nurse; they openly raked their eyes over his body and shamelessly flirted with him while I sitting right next to him. They mistakenly took me for his sister at one stage, which was fucked up. Dominic was smoking hot but he wasn't a damn God, I wasn't unworthy of possibly being his girlfriend no matter what anyone thought.

He had flaws that his looks didn't cover, and I had been the one turning him down for the past few weeks, so clearly it's not as far-fetched of an idea as these women thought it was.

"Your tattoo is gorgeous," the nurse's voice said breaking me from my thoughts.

The Garda nodded her head in agreement.

I had a feeling I was about to be arrested for slapping both of these fools upside the head if they didn't quit while they were ahead.

"Thanks ladies, my *girlfriend* agrees with you both." Dominic smiled and put his left arm around my waist.

Both the women openly frowned at his gesture, and it made me roll my eyes. They looked like they were given a puppy only for it to be taken away again.

"Is he finished here?" I asked the Garda and the nurse.

They both nodded even though I could tell they didn't want to.

"So can we leave then?" I asked, my tone completely snotty.

The Garda cut her eyes to me. "Do you have a problem—"

"Yeah, she does," Dominic cut the Garda off and smiled to her. "She sprained her hand a few hours ago and hasn't had any painkillers yet. We're collecting them from the twenty-four hour pharmacy on our way home as soon as I'm done here."

The Garda smiled to Dominic again and I inwardly cursed her. She was clearly crap at her job if it all it took was a good-looking lad to distract her.

"I'll discharge you now," the nurse beamed to Dominic.

I rolled my eyes wishing the nurse who wrapped up my hand earlier were here instead. She was cool and not perverted like this young nurse.

"I'm done here, too, unless you do want to press charges. We can take this down to the station if you do."

I fucking bet she would just love to take him somewhere she had easy access to handcuffs!

"No thank you," Dominic smiled again. "I'm set on my decision."

The Garda nodded, said goodbye, and then left the room. I fumed quietly for a few moments until I felt his eyes staring at me.

"What?" I mumbled without looking at him.

"You're so fucking sexy," he growled and leaned into me, latching his lips onto my neck and sucking.

My body jerked as I jumped up away from him.

"Stop that, anyone could walk in here!" I scowled.

He only grinned at me. "Like I care, you being jealous and possessive of me has me hard as diamond. I fucking *love* this side of you."

Hard as diamond?

Oh, God!

"Dominic," I gasped as I felt the blood rush up my neck to my

161

cheeks.

He laughed at me. "You're going from sexy as fuck to adorable as hell. You're killing me here!"

I glared at him. "I'm about to kill you if you don't cut this out, I don't like it."

"Why are you crossing your legs then?" he asked me, grinning.

I looked down at myself and inwardly scowled. I was crossing my legs, and it was only then that I noticed the aching pain *between* my legs. I absentmindedly closed my legs to try and ease the ache, and Dominic noticed.

"Shut up." I whispered.

He licked his lips. "If you come over to me, I'll take that ache away and turn it into immense pleasure."

I felt my core throb; the ache was hurting me so bad like it needed to be rubbed away. I squeezed my thighs tighter together, and it made Dominic groan.

"I bet you're wet for me; I can practically feel how hot you are for me from all the way over here," he purred.

I closed my eyes and tried to ignore him and the throbbing.

"Come over to me, baby," he purred again.

I could feel my legs move before my brain registered anything; I opened my eyes when my knees knocked against Dominic's. He was grinning at me as he leaned his head down and brushed his nose against mine.

"What are you feeling right now?" he murmured. "*Tell me*, pretty girl."

My breathing got a little heavier as I opened my mouth and said, "I feel hot… and achy."

Dominic nodded like he understood exactly how I was feeling.

"Is it a teasing ache?" he whispered, brushing his lips over mine.

I nodded. "Uh huh."

Dominic sucked my bottom lip into his mouth for a moment, then released it. "Your body knows what it wants and the more you hold back, the more that pretty little clit of yours pulses away as it demands my attention. It wants just *my* attention, right?"

I felt my knees buckle a little, so I used my good hand to latch onto Dominic's bare shoulder. I squeezed it when his hands came around my waist then drifted south and gripped my behind.

"Why are you doin' this to me? I'll kill you for this when I'm thinkin' clearly," I groaned and kissed him when he squeezed my behind.

He kissed me hard and deep as he slid his right hand around to the front of my jeans and flicked his fingers over the front, unbuttoning and unzipping them within seconds.

"Dominic, please," I breathed against his mouth.

I wasn't sure if I was asking him *not* to touch me or begging him *to* touch, my mind was beyond dazed right now.

"Just relax baby and let me take care of you," he whispered as he dipped his hand down into the front of my knickers.

I gasped when his finger slid between my smooth, wet folds followed by his thumb as it brushed over the tiny bundle of nerves that was causing me such aching pains.

"Bronagh, baby, you're fucking *soaked*," Dominic growled as he caught my mouth in a kiss.

I couldn't kiss him back properly at all because when his thumb began a lazy pace of rotation around my swollen clit it caused me to go cross-eyed.

"Oh, God," I breathed against his mouth.

He watched my face like what I was feeling was somehow projected onto my facial expressions.

"Eyes on me," he ordered.

The throbbing intensified with his demands, and the need to have him touch me all over was becoming unbearable.

"Yes, yes! Don't stop," I pleaded and forced my eyes to stay on his.

"Not a fucking chance. Does that feel good, pretty girl?" he whispered, rotating his thumb faster.

My hips bucked, and he smiled. "I'll take that as a yes, open your legs a little wider for me."

I shamelessly did as he asked and moaned a little out louder when he slid his finger down my folds and carefully dipped inside of me.

"That's a tight fit for just one finger babe, I can't wait to feel you wrapped around my cock." He hissed. "You're going to be the undoing of me, pretty girl, I know it."

After a few pumps of his fingers in and out of me, he moved back to my clit and rotated with a faster pace than before, and it had me making noises I didn't know I could make.

"Oh God," I gasped when I felt like my body was about to light on fire. "Okay, you can stop no-now Dominic it's gettin' too much. I ca-can't—"

"You're about to come baby, that's all that is. Let me make you come, pretty girl," Dominic spoke over me and took my mouth in his when I began to moan out loud.

He held his free hand tightly around me and when I tried to pull away from him, he gripped me even harder.

It was too much, I couldn't take the sensation Dominic was causing, and I was about to scream for him to stop when dots suddenly spotted my vision and my body went limp as a hot tingling sensation attacked my body in waves, making me jerk and buck in his arms.

After a minute or two sound and sight returned to me and I blinked my eyes open. I was met with Dominic's face that was sporting a shit-eating grin.

"You look so fucking hot when you come, pretty girl," he said as he slowly removed his hand from my underwear and lifted it to his mouth where he licked and sucked his fingers clean. "Hmm, you taste even better."

That was the moment that I chose to feel mortified. He... he just tasted me on his fingers, the fingers that were inside me.

Oh my God, what did I just do?

"Oh, Jesus," I breathed and looked down making Dominic lightly chuckle.

"Don't do it, Bronagh." He warned. "Don't be embarrassed about what just happened. It was fucking beautiful, and I won't let you play it off as anything but, do you understand me?"

I couldn't speak to him. I couldn't even look at him so he lifted my head by my chin until my gaze found his.

"Understand me?" he repeated.

I groaned. "How can I not be embarrassed? You... you just did that to me and then you... you—"

"Licked your come off my fingers?" he questioned. "Yeah, I did, so what? It tasted great, and I'm already looking forward to seconds."

Oh, my fucking God!

"Dominic!" I breathed. "Don't say stuff like that to me, I've never done anythin' like this before, ever. Well, except for the times we almost had sex in your bedroom but still, this is *huge* for me, and I don't know how to process what I'm feelin'—"

"Baby, you need to take a breath and calm the fuck down. This is natural, you had an orgasm, an orgasm that I made you have. Big fucking deal, it made you feel incredible, so why should you be embarrassed about that? I'm your boyfriend, this is what I'm good for. It's pretty much all I'm good for."

I heard what he said, and I forced my mind to be as relaxed as my body was. Dominic was right—I'll never admit it though—this wasn't a big deal. If anything, it was an amazing thing because it clearly showed I had trust in him. I've never let any lad touch me like that before. He was the first, so yeah, this was a big step, a *good* step.

"Besides," he murmured. "I'm so fucking happy no one else has done that to you before. And I'm *panting* to be the first to have sex with you. I literally dream about it, pretty girl."

I felt my cheeks stain with heat.

"You do?" I murmured.

"Every night," he responded. "Ever since you told me you were

165

a virgin that day in my house after I fought Jason, I can't get it out of my head."

I swallowed. "Is it hard to believe?"

"Only because you're so beautiful, I'm just surprised no one else has gotten here before me." He grinned at me then. "I'm glad, though, because your virginity is *mine*."

I felt my lip quirk. "It's yours, huh?"

"I'm the boyfriend so yep," he winked, "all mine."

"I thought I said you're on a trial basis with me before I put a title on us?" I said and lazily smiled, which Dominic laughed at.

He kindly overlooked the fact that I titled myself as his girlfriend when the Garda was questioning him and that was good because so did I.

"Yeah, well, I'm promoting myself to boyfriend because I made you feel drunk on an orgasm. You're welcome by the way." He smirked.

I rolled my eyes. "I don't know why I bothered even saying you're on a trial basis with me. As soon as I said I'd take a risk with you, you pretty much took up root that you were me fella, right?"

Dominic shrugged. "Pretty much. I was going to let you think the ball was in your court and that you had all the power but as you already found out, I've all the power in the world right here in my fingertips." He grinned and wiggled his fingers at me making me flush.

"You're a dick," I giggled. "Stop embarrassin' me!"

He chuckled. "I'm sorry."

I pinched his arm with my good hand. "No, you aren't, you bastard!"

Dominic laughed and put his arms around me, hugging me to him. "You've made me happy, you know that, right?"

I smiled as my stomach fluttered.

I put my arm around him. "Yeah? Well, I'm happy too as long as you don't do somethin' to make me want to kill you."

He snorted and kissed the crown of my head. "Yeah, let's see how long that will last, shall we?"

I rolled my eyes and looked at his sore eye and frowned before murmuring, "For once I'd like to see your face *without* bruises or a cut."

Dominic smiled. "Sorry babe, cuts and bruises are part of a package deal you get once you start dating me."

I frowned. "Do you *have* to fight at Darkness? I mean, why can't you take up a hobby that won't possibly cause brain damage or other major bodily harm?"

Dominic looked at me with a raised eyebrow. "We're officially dating two minutes and already you're nagging me about fighting, really?"

I pulled back away from him a little. "I'm *not* naggin' you, I'm just askin' you questions. Sorry if I want to see you unharmed for a change."

He sighed and looked down at me. "Don't get pissy with me. I don't want to have our first official fight as a couple in a hospital examination room."

I raised my eyebrow. "Where would you like to have it then if not here?"

"In my bedroom where you can scream, shout, and throw things at me while I duck and try to avoid being hit by said objects. Then when you're least expecting it I can come at you, get you on my bed, and fuck you into submission or until you forget what I did to make you mad at me. It's easier to have makeup sex where we're comfortable."

Was he serious?

I gaped at him. "You're un-fuckin'-believable!"

He smiled. "I know, right?"

I didn't mean that as a compliment, and he knew it!

I shook my head at him. "Can we leave? I just want to go home. I've seen enough of this hospital to last me a lifetime."

The only good thing that came out of Branna bursting into the triage nurse's examination room and attacking Dominic like a wild animal was that I got bumped up to first on the list to see a doctor right along with Dominic. He needed stitches after Branna was peeled off him, but it cut our waiting time down by ninety percent, which I was happy about.

After being bumped to the top of the list, I got my X-Ray and found out that my hand wasn't broken after all. It was only sprained, which I was also happy about because I didn't have to wear a cast for six weeks, instead just a tight bandage wrap until my muscles healed.

I checked my watch and groaned. "It's half twelve, I'm usually in bed two hours by now!"

Dominic chuckled which made me frown.

"What?" I asked him.

"You go to sleep at ten thirty?" he asked, amused.

I huffed. "I can't help it, either I go to bed at that time, or I fall asleep where ever I am. I get up early so shut up."

He only smiled at me and pulled me in for another hug. I pulled back from him when I heard someone clear their throat.

"You're discharged Mr. Slater, you're free to go."

I looked round to the nurse who looked sad that Dominic was leaving and rolled my eyes.

"Let's get goin' before she changes her mind and locks you in the supply room," I grunted to Dominic and pulled him from the examination bed by the hand and produced a fake smile as we passed the nurse.

Dominic thanked her to which she giggled at.

"Are you seriously jealous right now?" he asked, putting his arm around me from behind as we walked, which probably made us look funny with our height being so different.

"Jealous of her and everybody else in here eye fuckin' you?" I sarcastically asked. "Nope, not jealous at all."

Dominic kissed my cheek. "Eye fucking? That's funny, I like that."

I scoffed. "Of course you would."

He chuckled as we entered the lobby of the A&E and spotted my sister and Ryder, which made him unwrap his arms from around me and move to my side.

"Is it broken?" Branna asked me as she jumped up from her seat and shot forward to me.

She was made to leave by the hospital security when she attacked Dominic; one male Garda questioned her while the female bitch questioned/flirted with Dominic.

"No, just sprained it. I've to rest it for a couple of weeks. If the muscles don't strengthen in two weeks, then I've to come back but until then, I'm grand," I explained.

Ryder looked at Dominic after I spoke, shook his head at his bare chest and then focused on his eye. "How many stitches?" he asked.

"Eight," Dominic replied and cut his eyes to Branna.

She held up her hands. "I'm not apologisin' to you; me sister was hurt because of you tonight in more ways than one!"

I flushed. "Branna, it's over and done with so just forget it."

She looked like she wanted to argue but just nodded once at me.

"Come on, I'm bringin' you home in my car. Ryder is going with Dominic in theirs."

Dominic's hand went to my back, and I knew he wanted to bring me home instead, but I wasn't up for another argument so I glanced at him. "Talk to you tomorrow, okay?" I murmured.

He set his jaw but nodded.

I didn't kiss him because Branna and Ryder were right there, and they didn't know we were together now. I wanted to wait a while before we told anyone.

I went home with Branna and thanked her when she got me an ice pack and a towel to rest my hand on while I lay in bed. I told her everything that happened with Gavin and Dominic before we went to the hospital but obviously left out the intimate stuff between Dominic and myself.

"Damn it, that kid just won't quit." Branna grunted.

I nodded. "He is persistent, I'll give him that."

"Just forget about him and get some sleep, you've had a hell of a night."

Branna kissed my head goodnight and left my room; I fell asleep almost straight away only to wake up what felt like minutes later to a throbbing pain in my hand. I moved it in my sleep and it hurt so I got up and went downstairs and took some of the painkillers Branna collected for me from the night chemist in the hospital before we came home.

It wasn't dark outside; it was sort of bright, so I checked the time and saw it was a quarter to eight. I knew I didn't have to go to school, but I decided just to go anyway. It beat lying around the house all day doing nothin'.

I got dressed and carefully avoided my hand. I left my hair down in a wavy mess because I couldn't tie it up or plait it and left my face bare because I wasn't bothered enough to put any makeup on.

I got my bag and popped my head into Branna's room only to find she was already gone.

She must have had an early shift at the hospital, I thought as I left my house and began the walk to school.

When I got there, it was business as usual. I was a ghost and took comfort in the peace and quiet of being ignored, until I stepped into my registration class and froze at what I saw.

"You have got to be fuckin' jokin' me!" I spat out loud.

Dominic snapped his head in my direction, away from her gaze to mine. He leisurely stood up, took a step around Destiny and slow-ly moved towards me with his hands in the air in an 'I surrender' motion. I took a step back and shook my head at him.

"Don't! Don't even fuckin' bother tryin' to talk your way out of it!" I snarled before I turned and stormed down the hallway towards the entrance of the school.

"Bronagh! It wasn't what it looked like, I swear it!" he shouted as he ran after me.

I laughed.

Yeah, fucking right.

He was about to kiss her, and we both fucking knew it.

I was so damn mad, the prick bent over backwards in destroying my life to get me to go out with him, and when I did, he attempted to cheat on me with his ex—or current for all I knew—fuck buddy not ten hours after we got together?

I stormed through the crowds of students and ignored Dominic's snarl for people to move out of his way. I flat-out ran when I got out of the school, I ran until I was in the middle of a quiet estate, and I was sure that Dominic wasn't following me.

It was only then that I noticed my hand was throbbing in pain, my chest was hurting, and tears were streaming down my cheeks.

I wasn't sure which pain I was crying over though; both were pretty bad.

CHAPTER FOURTEEN

Where are you? I got a text from Ryder, and Dominic said you ran out of school. Are you okay?

I sighed as I read my sister's text and hit reply.

I'm nearly at the house now; I just went on a long walk for most of the day. Talk to you in a few minutes, put the kettle on.

I pocketed my phone with a grunt; texting with my bad hand was harder than I thought it would be. I tugged my bag high up onto my shoulder and gazed around my road as I made the familiar trip down the path towards the gates of my garden.

I spotted Ryder's family Jeep in my garden and I groaned. Great, just what I needed, having the brother of that arsehole in my presence.

"I'm home," I shouted when I entered my house and closed the door behind me. "I'm goin' to bed though—"

"Come into the kitchen first, baby," Branna's voice shouted over me.

I sighed, rubbed the bridge of my nose and walked into the kitchen.

"I know you want an explanation, but I can't deal with talkin' right now, I just want to—" I stopped talking and pretty much stopped breathing when I looked to the kitchen table and found Dominic sitting at it with a cup of tea in his hands.

Was this son. Of. A. Bitch. Fucking with me?

I took in a really long, deep inhale before I exhaled and locked eyes with the ultimate prick. "You best be gettin' the hell out of me house before I lose it."

"Bronagh!" Branna gasped in outrage at the same time Dominic grinned and said, "Or what, pretty girl?"

No one had time to move because I turned, grabbed a cup that was on the counter, turned back and hurled it full-force at Dominic. It clocked him right on the head and he let out a very masculine roar for an eighteen-year-old as he jumped up and grabbed his forehead with his hand. The poor cup was in pieces on the floor, but I didn't care. I totally succeeded at having fabulous aim with my weaker arm.

I wasn't finished though. I turned, picked up a plate—it had biscuits on it—that was also on the counter and hurled it at him. He, however, used his arm this time to block the blow. It still had to hurt though because the plate smashed into pieces when it made contact.

"Let me go!"

It was Branna screaming at Ryder who had his arms clamped around her waist, keeping her from charging at me. That fucking traitor, how *dare* she try and come at me when she invited the enemy into my inner sanctum after what he did to me!

I turned to find more dishes to lob at Dominic, but there weren't any left. I was about to move towards the knives when a body smashed into my back and an arm clamped around me, pinning my arms to my sides.

I knew it was him.

"Get off me!" I bellowed. "I'm havin' you arrested for this. I'm sick and fuckin' tired of you touchin' and manhandlin' me, you big bastard!"

"Bronagh Jane Murphy!" Branna yelled.

I let my jaw drop and turned my head to the left. She just snapped my full name at me.

She. Was. Pissed!

"Your initials are BJ?" Dominic snorted in my ear making me scowl.

I ignored him and focused on Branna. "I don't care, Branna. He shouldn't be here, and I'm mad as hell that you've put Ryder and him before me, you cow!"

I was sort of grateful when Ryder held tightly onto Branna this time, because when she tried to charge me, her eyes were murderous, and I knew without a doubt that if she got a hold of me, she would kick seven shades of shite out of me.

"You disrespectful little bitch!" She snapped. "How dare you talk to me like that. I'm your sister! I'm goin' to deck you when I get me hands on you!"

I raised an eyebrow and said, "Child abuse."

Branna let out a roar and clawed at Ryder's hands with her nails that were the most deadly things on this planet. They were like mini bloody razors. Even as big and strong as Ryder was, he snatched his hands away from her when she drew blood.

I screamed murder, stomped on Dominic's right foot so he would jump back and release me—he did with another roar—then sprinted like Usain Bolt out of the kitchen and towards the stairs so I could get up to my bedroom and put a big wooden oak door between myself and Branna.

I had made it about halfway up the stairs when she caught me by the leg and pulled hard causing me to face-plant on the stairs. I screamed as I flipped myself over and instantly put my non-injured hand up to block Branna's impending blows.

"I'm goin' to *kill* you!" she swore.

I was still screaming but managed to hold her up off me.

"I'm sorry," I pleaded. "You aren't a cow... well, not a huge one anyway—"

"Oh, that will make her less angry!" Dominic laughed.

"Fuck you, you cheatin' pig!" I hissed as I turned to look through the banisters.

Ryder and Dominic were leaned up against the hall wall observing me being viciously attacked by my so-called sibling and didn't do a single thing to stop it. They actually looked fucking amused with what they were witnessing, the pricks.

"Stop that," Branna snapped and swatted my hands away. Stop being such a little—"

"Such a little *what*?" I demanded. "Why are you defendin' Dominic? If you say it's because you are shaggin' his brother, I'm disownin' you and *never* talkin' to you again!"

Branna stopped her attack on me but didn't move off me.

"I'm not defendin' him," she said firmly. "I still think he is a little shite who needs a good clout now and then, but I do think you should let him explain himself. You really like him; you wouldn't be so upset over him otherwise. He likes you too, he wouldn't put up with you if he didn't."

I narrowed my eyes when he spoke.

"I think 'like' is puttin' things a little too strongly now after being attacked with dishes—"

"Shut up," Ryder cut Dominic off. "You see red whenever Damien talks about her and her could-be-or-could-not-be-boyfriend Gavin."

"He is *not* her boyfriend," Dominic snapped to his brother. "How many damn times do I have to keep saying that? I *told* you what went down last night!"

I felt my eyes widen as irritation set in.

"How do you know he isn't me boyfriend now?" I questioned. "I could have went to him today for all you know!"

Dominic's eye twitched when he focused his gaze on me. "Because before school today I told him that if he touched you ever again I'd kill him. I might have also mentioned something about you being mine."

Oh.

My.

God.

"What is wrong with you?" I asked. "I'm not somethin' you own. You can't tell people to not touch me—"

"I can and I will," he cut me off.

I looked back at Branna who was grinning down at me.

"What are you grinnin' about?" I growled in annoyance.

She shrugged, still lying on top of me. "He wants you to be together for good. He wants to explain what you saw in school today but is worried you won't give him the time of day."

"Why would I give him any of my time?" I frowned. "He was going to kiss her, Branna."

Dominic groaned. "I wasn't, Bronagh. I wouldn't do that no matter how much of an asshole you think I am. I'm a lot of things, but disloyal isn't one of them."

I continued to look up at my sister as he spoke, and when I saw in her eyes that she believed him, it made me rethink what I saw. I was about to let Dominic explain himself, but I watched as my sister turned her head and looked at Ryder. I looked between the pair of them and blinked. They were only gazing at one another, but it felt very intimate.

"Do you both love each other?" I asked.

Branna smiled as she looked away from Ryder and looked back down at me.

"Yeah," she nodded. "I do love him."

Shit.

"And he loves me."

Fuck.

"And we're goin' to live together."

Bollocks.

"Then get married and have babies."

Fuck. Fuck. *Fuck*!

"*What?*" I shouted, wiping the smile from my sister's face. "You're engaged to *that*?" I pointed a trembling hand to Ryder who avoided making eye contact with me.

"Him," Branna growled. "*Not* that!"

I felt tears well up in my eyes.

"I can't believe you would do this to me!" I cried. "If you marry him, that bastard over there will never be out of me life. Never!"

Tears fell from my eyes and I didn't care that Ryder or Dominic could see. Everything was changing too much, and too fast.

"Stop it, Bronagh," Branna's bottom lip quivered. "I'm not doin' this to hurt you, babe. I love you more than anythin'; you're me sister but your problems with Dominic have nothin' to do with Ryder."

"Only the fact that they're related," I stated, sniffling.

My sister frowned. "You're only cryin' because you're mad at Dominic because you thought he was kissin' Destiny in school today and it's hurtin' you."

That was part of it, but not the only reason.

"I don't want *any* part of anythin' that has to do with the Slater brothers, and if that includes you and Ryder then so be it!"

Branna stood up when I struggled against her. She let me get up, turn and run up the stairs. When I made it into my bedroom I dove onto my bed, put my face in my pillow, and sobbed. I was panting by the time I was done and lying motionless on my bed.

My world and life as I knew it was ending. Branna was engaged to Ryder. En-fucking-gaged to Ryder! She only knew him a few weeks and they were already engaged. How was that possible?

I heard my bedroom door open and my body tensed.

"Leave me alone, Branna," I muttered. "I don't wanna talk to you."

I heard shoes hitting the floor then the bottom of my bed dipped down the centre, then next to me, as she crawled up on my bed beside me.

I turned my head. "I said leave me be, Bran—get out!" I growled when Dominic's grey eyes stared back to me instead of Branna's blue ones.

"No," he frowned. "You need me right now."

I turned my head, and buried it in my pillow in a feeble attempt to get away from him and find the seclusion I desperately needed. He refused me of that, though, when his hands came around my body, and rolled me onto my back. For a moment I was looking up at my ceiling, then a better view came into focus when Dominic appeared over me, nudging his way between my legs, and resting his elbows besides my shoulders as he hovered over me.

I planned on telling him to get out of my room, and life, but he had other plans.

"Dominic," I murmured when his mouth covered mine. "Stop this."

He ignored me and simply took advantage of my open mouth to slip his tongue inside. I thought about biting him to get him to back off, but I didn't want to hurt him... not *that* much anyway.

"Shut up and kiss me, sweetheart." He bit out. "Just fucking kiss me!"

I squeezed my eyes shut and forced myself not to kiss him back even though I wanted to. I thought of all the times he gave me no reason to trust him, or to allow him to kiss or touch me, but every fabricated thought was shattered with each flick of Dominic's talented tongue.

"Stop thinking," he growled. "Just kiss me."

I opened my eyes and shook my head.

"No," I replied, licking my lips and tasting him on them. "You're up to no good. I know you well enough to know you don't like me like you think you do. You hate me just as much as I hate you and you're tryin' to—"

"I'm trying to kiss my girl, that's all," he cut me off.

"Your girl?" I asked trying to pull away from me him, but he didn't let me move.

Did he not take me seeing him almost kissing Destiny as a big fat fucking break up?

"You've been my girl since you slapped me across the face two days after I met you." Dominic grinned. "No girl has ever hit me before for touching her ass, but you did and you insulted me to no end and openly professed your hatred for me every day you encountered me after that. I like it in a weird, twisted way. You don't fall for my bullshit, Bronagh, you're yourself with me. You don't act the way you think I want you to act just so we can hook up. You avoid me at all costs and refuse to look at me most days; you're amazing."

I gaped at him. "You're so messed up, Dominic. You actually like me because I hate you?"

He chortled. "No, I like you because you stay true to yourself and aren't in the slightest bit fake. You're also gorgeous and have a great ass, but those things are just a plus. I really just like you for *you*. And I know you don't hate me, pretty girl. You might think you do, but I know you don't. Just like I don't hate you."

Dominic Slater, my archenemy, had just admitted to liking me. I knew he had liked me for a while now, and after last night I definitely knew, but hearing him saying it out loud like this for the first time still made me a little weak.

Why did my heart contract and stomach swim with butterflies over that declaration? I knew the answer to that question easily; I liked him back.

A hell of a lot.

"I'm overlookin' the pig headed comments about me looks and arse and also overlookin' your current brain fart." I began. "You don't like me, Dominic. You like Destiny or was there another reason you almost stuck your tongue down her throat in reg class today?"

I hated how much that situation actually annoyed me.

He sighed. "I didn't almost kiss her, babe. She was in my face to try and *bribe* me into kissing her, but I wasn't about to cave, not when I just got you. If it was a test though, you would have passed with flying colours."

"A test?" I quipped. "What kind of bloody test?"

"You're like a closed book sometimes, Bronagh." Dominic said as he rubbed the tip of his nose over mine. "I don't have a clue what you're feeling or thinking, but when Destiny was close to my mouth and you went red in the face, I knew it had made you mad."

I felt heat creep up my neck and spread out over my cheeks. "No it didn't. I don't care, Dominic."

"Yeah, you do." He murmured. "You don't like me kissing Destiny, and I'm betting you don't like me kissing anybody else either, do you?"

I looked away from him but he grabbed my chin and forced me to look back at him.

"Do you?" he repeated.

Did I like Dominic kissing other girls?

I really didn't.

"No," I sighed in defeat.

He smiled in triumph. "Good because I don't like kissing anyone *but* you, and I definitely don't fucking like the thought of you kissing someone else. I know I'm a prick and that you aren't my biggest fan, but I want to be with you. I think I'd kill if you belonged to someone else."

There we go with that stupid word again.

"I'm not a piece of property." I snippily replied.

Dominic's grin made me stop mid-sentence.

"What?" I quizzed. "Why're you lookin' at me like that?"

He shrugged. "Stop being so defensive with me, babe. I want you and you want me. Just admit that to yourself and we can move on from here."

I looked away from him and closed my eyes.

"I have issues, Dominic-"

"Look who you're talkin' to," he cut me off laughing. "Don't preach to me about issues."

I swallowed and opened my eyes and looking back up at him. "No, I've issues with… with… lettin' people get close to me."

He waggled his brows. "I'm pretty close to you right now, babe."

I gnawed on my inner cheek.

"No, I mean in here," I muttered and pointed to my heart, only to drop my hand and look away.

"Bronagh," he murmured.

When I wouldn't look at him, he pulled me closer to him and kissed my cheek. "Babe, there is nothing wrong with letting someone get close to you. This isn't the same as what happened with your parents."

I closed my eyes at the mention of them.

"Please, don't talk about them." I whispered. "I love and miss them, but they are gone. Talkin' about them just hurts me chest."

Dominic kissed my check again and nodded his head in understanding. "Okay, I won't mention them again, I just want you to know this isn't the same."

I grunted. "Yeah, it is. If I start to care about you—more than I already do—and somethin' happens that takes you away, then I'll be hurt. I already lost two of the loves of me life Dominic; Branna is all I have left. I don't get close to people because I can't handle knowin' they could leave me without a second's notice. It terrifies me, okay?"

"I won't ever leave you. That's something you should know about me, sweetheart," he said, nuzzling my cheek. "Once you're mine, I won't ever let you go. I'm a stubborn prick eighty percent of the time so even if you want to leave me, I still wouldn't let it happen."

I would say ninety-nine point nine percent of the time, but I kept my mouth shut.

My heart was pounding against my ribs as he spoke, my feelings for him deepening with each passing second. "You have to promise you won't leave me. Say it."

He looked me in the eye and grinned. "I'll promise never to leave you if you promise not to hurt me."

I rolled my eyes at his playfulness. "I promise."

"I promise, too."

I frowned. "What if you get bored of me?"

He looked at me like I was an idiot and said, "Babe," as if what I just said was too stupid for words.

"What if you get punched in the head and die?" I questioned.

Dominic tilted his head as he looked down at me. "I can't promise you I won't die because no one knows when that boat comes for them, but I'm not letting you out of this because you're afraid of death. Death is a part of life, babe, everyone and thing dies at some point. I just want you around me until that day comes."

I let my jaw drop.

"Deep, huh?" he snickered.

He wanted me around until he died, which could be tomorrow or seventy years from now. So yeah, it was fucking deep.

"Yeah, Dominic," I whispered. "It's deep."

He shrugged. "It's true. You have no idea what you do to me, Bronagh. You make me feel, babe, *really* feel. I want you to be mine for good this time, no bullshit. *Will* you be mine?" he asked, eyebrows raised.

My stomach was a fluttering mess at this stage.

"Can I not think about it?" I asked.

"No," he countered. "You wanted to be with me quick enough last night so answer now."

I growled. "I can't just decide right away after everythin' that happened today. I have to think."

"No, you don't," he quipped. "If you want me, answer me now and let me know."

I felt like strangling him.

"How can I be with someone who I like but really can't stand at the same time?" I asked with my eyes narrowed.

Dominic grinned. "Easily."

He was impossible.

"Will you leave me alone in school and stop bullyin' me?" I questioned.

He rolled his eyes this time. "I don't bully you, I tease you, but I won't do anything to make you mad at me."

"What does that mean exactly?" I questioned.

"I won't piss you off." He winked. "I'll just kiss you instead."

I licked my lips. "We can't kiss in school."

Dominic raised a brow. "Why not?"

"Because everyone knows we hate each other," I replied in a duh tone.

He chuckled. "No, everyone knows I have a thing for you."

I blinked, dumbly.

"Excuse me," I gulped. "How can everyone know when I didn't even know?"

"Because you get so mad at me it makes you blind to what's in front of you. You ignore me, but no one else does. Damien tells me how everyone watches me stare at you or try to annoy you just so I have your attention."

I didn't reply back to him.

I just remembered a time when my mother told me when I was little that if a boy was really mean to a girl it could mean that he liked her, but didn't know how to go about telling her so acted like a bully instead, just so he would still get her attention.

She actually told me that when Jason first started bullying me when we were kids after I refused to kiss him during yard time. I thought that was stupid, but it was a fact. Not with everyone, obviously, but with Dominic, it apparently was.

"If Ryder and Branna get married," I cringed. "You'll be me brother-in-law and I will be your sister-in-law. You can't kiss an in-law."

Dominic pecked my lips with his. "Watch me."

I breathed him in as he leaned down and pressed his forehead to mine.

"Answer me," he prompted. "Now."

I suppressed a smile as I said, "Fine."

Dominic's eyes lit up. "Fine as in you will be my girl… again?"

What was the worst that could happen? Other than him breaking what was left of my heart to a million pieces.

I shrugged and said, "Sure."

He kissed me with a hunger that sent a jolt of excitement to my core. When he propped himself up on his elbows and applied more pressure to our kiss, I groaned and gave into what he wanted and kissed him back. I lifted my arm around his neck, sliding my good hand up into his hair and knotting my fingers through his silky locks.

I didn't think it was possible, but Dominic kissed me even harder, making everything much more intense. He was starting to affect the temperature of my body so I broke the kiss off and panted.

"Slow down," I breathed.

He growled and tried to kiss me again, but I held him off by the chest.

"Seriously, slow down," I pressed. "I'm not sleepin' with you just because we're together now. I know the message I sent out to you after what we did in the hospital would make you *think* I want sex, but I don't. I'm not ready for that."

Dominic blinked a couple of times, then sighed and rolled off my body until he landed on his side next to me.

"I'm sorry; I'm not going to pressure you, I promise, but when you kiss me like that it makes it *very* hard not to give in to what my body wants."

I involuntary looked down at his lower half; I could visibly see what the effects of our kiss had on him. I felt my cheeks flush so I looked away making Dominic laugh. He reached over and pulled my body against his, nuzzling my neck.

"Don't be embarrassed," he murmured.

"I'm not," I lied still not looking at him.

He chuckled and moved quickly to roll me completely under him once again. He got between my legs and pressed himself against me, kicking my heart rate into overdrive. I wasn't ready for sex yet but that didn't mean Dominic couldn't get my body excited.

Because he could, and he knew it, the bastard.

He ground his pelvis into me and watched as my eyes slightly rolled back simply at the brief contact his hardened length had on my pulsing clit. Our clothing separated us, but that didn't stop it from feeling incredible. I arched my back as a toe curling sensation flooded my core... and I wanted more. Not a lot, but more.

"This is what you do to me and have been doing to me since I first laid eyes on you." Dominic growled. "You make my dick hurt, and my mouth dry. I want to fuck you with both. First my tongue, then I want to pound into you with my cock until you scream."

I widened my eyes at his statement and couldn't help but admit that I wanted that too. A lot.

Dominic was about to lean in and kiss me again when a bellow from our left and something hitting off his head made him quickly roll off me.

"Ow, fuck!" he snapped. "What the hell is with you two and throwing things at my head?"

I looked to my left and saw Branna storming into my bedroom and went to the side of my bed where she picked up her shoe and put it back on her foot.

I snorted; she threw her shoe at Dominic and hit him in the head with it. Nice aiming on her part.

"Get away from me little sister," she hissed. "I *told* you just to talk to her about how you feel-"

"I did and she's taking me back." Dominic argued, still rubbing his head. "We're officially together again so ease up on the throwing of things. I don't get knocked around this much in the fucking circle!"

Ryder laughed from the doorway earning a middle finger from Dominic, who was glaring at him. Branna looked to me with raised eyebrows, and a knowing look.

"What happened to all the stuff you said downstairs about him?" she questioned.

I winced.

That did make me out to be a complete eejit. I said *a lot* of stuff to contradict my current actions.

I shrugged. "Just because I'm with him doesn't mean I don't think he can be a prick, because he can."

"Thanks babe," Dominic muttered.

I ignored him and continued to stare at Branna.

"You think he is a prick and yet you're still goin' to go out with 'em?" Branna asked, astonished.

I glared at her harder. "He will work on it!" I growled then snapped my head to Dominic. "Right?"

He nodded his head. "Whatever you want, babe."

"I wish Dame was here to see this!" Ryder's voice laughed then mimicked Dominic's voice, "Whatever you want, babe."

"Fuck you, Ry!" Dominic snarled.

I shook my head at them both. "He is the oldest brother and he is currently actin' like a child. Way to go Bran, you sure know how to pick 'em!"

Branna blinked. "Like you're much better? You picked his younger brother to become your fella, if I have bad taste in lads then so do you!"

I was all ready to fire a snappy reply, but for once I didn't have one and it irked me. I liked having an answer to everything, but this time Branna had me stumped.

"I blame you!" I eventually stated.

Branna gaped at me. "You blame me for you decidin' to get together with Dominic? That's ridiculous!"

"No, it's not!" I retorted. "I'd still hate him from afar if you weren't with Ryder."

Branna rolled her eyes. "He still would have found a way to get to you."

"That's true," Dominic said from behind me.

"Can we be done with this conversation, please? It's done. I'm with Dominic and you're with Ryder. Everybody is happy. Yay for us." I deadpanned, exhausted from arguing.

For the third time, Dominic's face appeared over mine.

"You're so hot when you're angry," he smiled down at me.

I hated that my cheeks flushed with heat because Branna was snickering from across the room watching us along with Ryder.

"Some privacy, maybe?" I asked.

Branna rolled her eyes at me then flicked them to Dominic and glared. "No sex with her unless she condones it. She may be eighteen, but she is still me little sister, got it hotshot?"

Dominic nodded. "Yep."

Branna left the room with a grinning Ryder. Dominic looked back to me smiling and waggling his eyebrows before he tried to get back between my thighs.

"We just started datin'," I stated. "I'm *really* not havin' sex with you for ages yet! I wasn't talkin' shite before."

Dominic's face morphed into one of pain and nausea making me chuckle.

"*Ages*," he murmured, his voice strained. "Really?"

I giggled. "Stop actin' so heartbroken. You're eighteen, how much sex have you had in order to miss it so much—" I cut myself off when Dominic gave me a deadpanned look.

I shook my head. "I don't even want to know so keep your sexual experiences to yourself."

Dominic frowned. "I wouldn't boast about anything like that to you. You know I'm not a virgin and unless you ask, that's all you will ever know. Okay?"

I shrugged. "'Kay."

Dominic continued to look at me. "So... what are my limits?"

"Your limits?" I questioned.

"Yeah." He nodded. "What am I allowed to touch? Are your tits, ass, and pussy fair game? Be specific."

"Dominic!" I gasped. "Don't be so crude!"

He tipped his head back and laughed while I covered my face with my hands.

"Babe," he rasped through his laughter. "If I had known how much dirty words make you blush, school would have been ten times worse for you."

I growled into my hands. Dominic nuzzled my hands away from my face with his nose until I moved them away. He captured my lips with his and kissed me softly. I lifted my arms around his neck and pulled him down to me, he moved with little hesitation.

"Limits," he mumbled onto my lips. "I need you to set limits otherwise, I will do everything but actually penetrate you with my cock."

I widened my eyes and sat up straight, pushing Dominic back off me a little.

"No touchin' my private parts unless I say otherwise," I started.

Dominic groaned and then stated, "That *better* not mean your ass!"

I bit down on my lower lip. "I'm fine with you touchin' it because you seem to be an arse lad, but do *not* grope it, or I *will* be annoyed."

He smirked. "I'm all for play fights with you, pretty girl."

I snorted. "Yeah because you're bigger and stronger than me and can pin me easily!"

Dominic pumped his brows making me shake my head as I began thinking up some other limits for him. "Oh, no touchin' me boobs."

"Like, at all?"

I chuckle and repeated, "Like, at all."

Dominic groaned, and pressed his face down into the pillow under my head making me chuckle.

"You're so dramatic." I giggled. "I have small boobs, you won't be missin' out on much."

His head shot straight up. "Your tits aren't small; they aren't big but they aren't small, they will fill my hands and that is good enough for me."

I blushed again and playfully shoved him.

"Okay," he sighed. "Is that all I'm not allowed do or is there more?"

I couldn't think of anything else so I shrugged.

"That's it for now, I'll let you know when I think of more."

"Witch," he growled making me grin.

He kissed me again, and I kissed him back. This continued for a few minutes until I became so relaxed that I remembered how tired I was.

"I'm so tired," I murmured into Dominic's mouth.

He paused, pulled back a little, and just looked down at me while he panted. "I've got a raging hard on and kissing you is making it worse but I can't seem to stop. There's a huge battle going on in my head right now because I want to fuck you so bad, but I can't and you're simply… tired? Tell me I made you wet or my ego will be seriously wounded."

I shifted and tried to rub my legs together to ease the ache that *was* between them, but Dominic wouldn't let me and stopped me when I tried to turn from him.

"I made you wet?" he asked, hopeful.

He knows he did.

"Wet and achy, happy now?" I grumbled.

Dominic's full-blown smile indicated he was very happy with the knowledge of what he could do to me with a simple kiss.

"Let's get under your covers—"

"Hey!" I snapped.

Dominic laughed as he raised his hands up. "So we can sleep. Just sleep, I promise."

I glared at him. "Normal couples should be together a while before they sleep together, Dominic."

He smirked as he pulled the covers from under me and pulled them over the pair of us while he pulled me into his body and snuggled against me.

"We aren't a normal couple, pretty girl," he whispered into my ear, sending shivers down my spine.

I sighed and closed my eyes. I nestled against him, really liking how I fit against his hard body. I couldn't argue with him, for once. We just became a couple but anyone with a brain could tell we weren't normal. We had a lustful attraction towards one another. We're pretty much getting together and hoping for the best, we were so far from normal.

CHAPTER FIFTEEN

"Hello there, beautiful."

I groaned as I crossed into the entrance of school. I looked up and noticed Dominic walking towards me while Damien leaned against the wall next to the main hallway entrance that led to our registration class.

My heart hammered just seeing Dominic, but I tried to downplay my reaction to him so I didn't appear pathetic and needy.

"It's too early, don't start," I stated making Damien snort and Dominic grin as he continued to walk towards me.

I felt the eyes of students who were already in school fall upon us and it made me stop walking and focus on my boyfriend.

"I don't like attention and you're gainin' us a lot of it, so stop!" I grumbled when he was mere feet away from me.

He continued to grin at me and pulled me into his arms when he was close enough to me to do so.

"I missed you," he murmured before dipping his head to kiss me.

I actually heard gasps from girls that could see us, and I found it very dramatic and sort of staged. It was like in the films where a lad, that every girl liked, kissed a lucky girl, and the rest of the girls got all jealous and pissy about it and pretty much wanted to stab the lucky girl to death and take her place.

"Dominic," I groaned into his mouth making him smile.

He pecked my lips a couple of times before he pulled his head back. "Say 'I missed you too, Nico'."

He was going to have to give up on getting me to call him Nico, it just wasn't going to happen.

I gave him a stubborn look and said, "I missed you too, *Dominic*."

He nibbled my bottom lip lightly. "Did you really?"

My hammering heart was indication that I did, and I knew he wanted me to tell him that. I was gathering that he liked hearing those sort of things. He liked knowing I thought of him.

"Yeah," I frowned. "I woke up and you were gone."

He slide his tongue over my lower lip, teasing me before he pulled back and said, "Branna made me leave after you fell asleep."

I sighed. "I like sleepin' with you, it makes me feel safe."

Dominic rubbed his thumbs across my cheeks as he looked into my eyes. I felt myself blush, but I didn't look away because we were having a moment.

"I make you feel safe?" he murmured.

I bobbed my head up and down. "You do, I don't know what you're doin' to me but me heart is hammerin' against me chest right now just bein' with you," I whispered.

He pulled me tighter to him and brushed a few strands of hair behind my ear. "Keep that sweet talking up and I will be an emotional mess declaring my undying love for you before we even get to class."

His sense of humour didn't ruin our moment; it only added some flare to it.

"That won't do it for me," I teased. "You have to take a page out of Heath Ledger's book and serenade me in front of the whole school."

Dominic chuckled and beamed down at me. "You know I'll do that without hesitation."

I knew he would, he wasn't afraid of anything, humiliation being one of those things.

I devilishly grinned. "It has to be a Justin Bieber or One Direction song though, none of the old school stuff."

He growled and said, "Typical, you little brat," before leaning his head down and covering his mouth with mine.

"Hey, break it up lovebirds," a teacher shouted. "There is no PDA on school grounds!"

I was like a fish out of water and tried to jump away from Dominic upon hearing the warning, but he laughed and held me tight.

"Sir, don't be a cock block," he said, making the students laugh.

"I could kill you," I whispered to him and got out of his hold, moving around him and walking towards the main doors.

"See what you did, sir?" Dominic laughed. "Put me in the dog house!"

The more people laughed at him, the more I wanted to pummel him.

"Your brother is an eejit," I said as I passed Damien.

"Tell me about it," he snorted and followed me through the main doors.

"Bronagh, wait!" Dominic called out as he jogged after Damien and me.

I didn't stop until I was in our registration class and sat at my desk.

"Leave her alone," I heard Damien say. "It's too early for her to put up with you."

White-haired twin was amazing!

"Amen," I said making him laugh.

Dominic playfully hit his brother before he moved over to my desk. "Can I sit next to you?" he asked.

I felt bad because I wanted to refuse. We were together now, but this was going to take some getting used to, and him kissing and wanting to be near me all the time now wasn't taking things slow.

I shrugged at him anyway because he looked so good today, and I wanted to feel him close to me. He looked good everyday but today he was delicious. He had on his school uniform like always, but he had on a grey beanie and a grey zipped hoodie over his uniform jumper. It was hardly a fashion statement, but he looked hot... *really* hot.

"Sure," I replied as I took off my bag and put it under my desk.

Dominic pulled out the chair next to me and moved it a little closer to my chair and then put his arm around the back of my chair and looked at me.

I pulled a face at him. "Stopping lookin' at me you creep."

He snorted, leaned in, and kissed my cheek. "You look gorgeous."

My cheeks heated as he cooed

"Stop tryin' to embarrass me, please," I muttered.

He kissed the side of my head. "I'm not trying to, I promise. I'm just telling you the truth."

He was such a charmer.

"Well, thank you," I murmured. "You look good too."

"Just good?" he quizzed making me snort.

"Okay," I grinned. "You look hot."

"Better." He mused.

He turned then to talk to Damien, who was sitting in his usual seat at the back row tapping on the screen of his phone. I took out my iTouch and was about to put on a song when I looked at the camera app.

I had the sudden urge to have a photo of Dominic... or me *and* Dominic on my iTouch, and it embarrassed me because he probably would think I was a child wanting to get a picture with him. I forced myself not to care though; I mean, he was my boyfriend, and if I wanted a picture with him then I could damn well get one!

"Dominic?" I muttered as all traces of bravery left my body in one breath.

"Hmm?" he murmured, turning back to me.

"I want a picture of us so will you get in one with me?" I asked very fast and avoided all eye contact with him.

I could sense his smile though when he said, "I'm ready."

I looked up and couldn't help but smile because he looked so happy. I leaned into him, flipped the camera on my iTouch and held it out in front of us. Dominic put his arm around my waist and pressed his cheek down to mine and smiled. Both of his dimples popped up and it made me sigh; he was so gorgeous!

I smiled as well, looking at the camera, and tapped on the screen. When the picture saved and showed up on the screen I wanted to gush because we actually looked like a normal teenage couple—only Dominic had stitches and a black eye—and it made me so happy.

"I love it!" I gushed.

Dominic chuckled and kissed my cheek. "Me too, but I want one of just you."

I looked over at him and watched him take out his iPhone, unlock it, open the camera app, and aim it in my direction.

"Will I smile with or without showin' me teeth?" I asked.

He shrugged. "With your teeth showing, you have tiny dimples on your cheeks when you smile that way."

I raised a brow. "Yours are dimples, mine are just big pores."

He snorted. "Just smile, smartass."

I did, and I looked directly into the camera lens as he took the picture.

"Beautiful," he smiled when he looked at the picture then turned and showed it to me.

I grimaced. "My eyes are too big and my ears stick out."

Dominic looked at me blankly. "You're stupid."

"Rude," I frowned.

He laughed. "You look beautiful so stop picking out things that you think are flaws."

I mimicked him making him chuckle as he tapped on the screen of his phone then turned it to me. I blushed; he made me his wallpaper and lock screen photo.

I already did the same with our picture on my iTouch and smiled; I looked back to Damien then who was still messing on his phone.

"Damien?" I called.

"Hmm?" he asked and looked up at me.

I grinned. "Do you want to get in a picture with me?"

"Only if you sit on my lap," he smirked.

"Bro," Dominic growled in warning.

I chuckled.

"Okay," I said and moved towards Damien.

"Bronagh!" Dominic snapped.

"He is your brother, Dominic" I stated. "Your *twin* brother, he won't slip a hand to feel me arse."

"He *would* cop a feel; he's worse than me when it comes to that shit," he snapped, still sat at my desk.

Damien grinned at me as he patted his left leg; I snorted and sat on him, then held my iTouch out and put my arm around his shoulder.

"Smile," I beamed then laughed when Damien's hand found its way to my arse.

"Sorry, thought that was your hip," he said, chuckling.

The picture I took was of Damien smiling and me laughing with my eyes closed. We took another one, then another because Damien said he wanted loads of them just to piss Dominic off.

"Okay, that's enough picture time." Dominic's voice cut through my and Damien's chuckling. "Get off my brother now, please."

I laughed as I got up and moved back over to Dominic, who pulled me onto his lap and glared at his brother.

"Stop looking at me like that, she's practically my sis-in-law now." Damien stated. "I'm not trying anything, now or ever, even though she *is* hot."

I gasped. "We *just* started goin' out, don't use the words 'in-law' around me. Do you want me to have a heart attack?"

Dominic and Damien laughed while I moved back to my seat.

"Do you have a Facebook profile?" Dominic randomly asked when I settled into my seat.

"No, why?" I asked, curiously.

He shrugged. "I was going to add you as a friend if you did."

I glanced at him. "I'll make one later and you can add me, okay?"

He grinned. "You can put that picture of us as your profile picture."

I nodded. "Okay, sure."

"And you can mark yourself as being in a relationship with me," he added.

I looked to him with a raised eyebrow. "When did you turn into a bitch?"

Dominic cocked an eyebrow in question.

"You're actin' like a girl, wanting to add me on Facebook and change your relationship status," I teased.

"Whatever, screw you," he muttered making me laugh just as some of our classmates entered the class.

Alannah was among them and when she spotted Dominic sitting next to me, she beamed and quickly moved to take his old seat next to his brother.

"Hey, good-looking." Damien grinned when she sat down; he pocketed his phone and gave her his full attention.

"Hey," she smiled, her cheeks flushing red.

I snorted at her blushing cheeks and how she played with her hair as they talked. She did that a lot around Damien.

"What are you snorting at, Miss Piggy?" Dominic asked me poking my sides with his finger.

"The fact that girls act like complete and total fools when they talk to you or your brother." I replied.

He put his arm around me and kissed my temple. "We're the heartthrobs of this school. I'd be offended if girls *didn't* have a crush on me or Dame."

I reached down and pinched his inner thigh. "You better be kidding."

"I *am* kidding!" Dominic cut me off, laughing.

With my lip quirked I leaned against him.

"Want to go see a movie later?" he asked as more students came into the room.

I didn't look at him as I asked, "On a date?"

"Yeah." He replied.

"To see what?" I questioned, turning to look at him.

If he said *The Mortal Instruments*, I was going to cringe.

He shrugged, uncaring. "As long as it's not a romance or chick flick type of thing, I don't care."

I thought about what films were out and then gasped. "The new *Fast & Furious* film, definitely that one!"

Dominic nodded. "Good choice, baby."

I smiled proudly but stopped when I noticed students in my class were looking at me.

"She *can* smile," I heard someone say.

"Nico, did you break Bronagh? 'Cause she is laughin' and lettin' someone sit beside her, and that for her, is just... weird," Robert Moore, fellow classmate, said to Dominic.

I know no one was making fun of me, but seeing them so shocked that I could actually be social was embarrassing.

"I didn't break her, she's perfectly fine." Dominic said loudly. "She *is* allowed to sit next to her boyfriend, right?"

"*Boyfriend?*" the class chorused.

Damien's laugh stuck out like a sore thumb down the back of the class and it made me was to slap him silly.

"Oh, my God," I grumbled and looked down.

"You deserve a medal, man." Robert said in awe. "You did the impossible, you cracked Bronagh Murphy."

Now he was just being ridiculous. I wasn't like some sort of safe that no one could get into—wait, crap, for a time that's exactly what I was. Dominic was the only lad to ever get an attempt at unlocking me!

I just realised Robert was right and Dominic did the impossible of getting through to me. It made me feel apprehensive. I've never cared for anyone other than Branna and my parents but now... now I felt like Dominic was climbing his way up the ladder and onto the list.

I even liked being around Damien and Ryder when I saw them. It wouldn't be long before I got used to having them, and the other brothers, in my life.

This was unknown territory for me, and I wasn't going to lie, it was scaring the bejesus out of me.

"Thanks... I think," Dominic's voice pulled me from my thoughts so I turned my attention to him. He raised his eyebrows when he looked at me and saw my face.

"Why do you look like you've seen a ghost?" he asked me.

I moved into him, put my face into his neck and my arms around his waist. We had only started officially dating yesterday so this was the first time I ever freely did this. Even when we weren't going out, he was the one who would touch me first, so this was one for the record books.

"Hey," Dominic murmured into my hair when he lowered his head to mine. "Are you okay?"

I nodded and turned my head to look up at him. "Robert is right, you're the first person to ever get this far with me and to be honest, the reality that you managed to set up camp with me is freakin' me out a little."

His body vibrated as he chuckled. "Babe, this is only the beginning for us. Give it time and once you're used to all this, you'll just accept that you're mine and you will be happy. I guarantee it."

I licked my now dry lips making Dominic lowly growl at me, which I still found odd that he could make noises like that seem so hot.

"I'm yours?" I mumbled; still in awe that this beautiful person wanted me when he could have any girl he wanted.

Dominic smiled at me and kissed the tip of my nose as he said, "You've always been mine, pretty girl. You just didn't know it."

CHAPTER SIXTEEN

"The last time I saw you in this house was when you were stating that you were picturing Damien when you were kissing on Dominic in his room," Alec said to me, teasing playfully.

I felt my cheeks heat up as I muttered, "I was here at the party after Dominic's fight a few weeks ago."

Alec smiled at me, his eyes gleaming. "That's right, I actually forgot about that. So the last time you were here you were rejecting my little brother when he asked you to be his girlfriend?"

I flushed a deeper shade of red, which made Alec laugh.

"Leave her alone," Dominic scowled and put his arm around my shoulder giving me a squeeze before he went back to eating his dinner.

I was currently sitting at Dominic's kitchen table with all of his brothers and Branna while we ate dinner. It was a little surreal; they were all huge, and it made me feel like Branna and I were dining with giants.

I was pretty much toying with the steak and potatoes on my plate. I was hungry before I got here, but now that I was here, I just couldn't stomach the food. Dominic and I had only been dating a few days; we went on our first date to the cinema a few days ago and now, all of a sudden, we're having family dinner.

It was all happening extremely fast and to be honest, it was really freaking me out.

I licked my lips and sat back a little, looking around the table with wild eyes until my eyes landed on Branna's. She was looking directly at me.

"Bronagh," he said, "Come talk with me for a minute in the hall."

I practically jumped up from the chair, and all but ran out into the hall where I automatically moved towards the hall door. Now that I saw an exit I just wanted to bail.

"Alec," I heard Damien's voice growl. "You upset her!"

He didn't upset me; I knew he was only teasing me. I wasn't upset at all; I was just feeling a little overwhelmed with all the new things that dating Dominic introduced into my life.

"Look at me," I heard Branna's voice say from behind me.

I turned around and looked at her and blew out a breath. "I'm sorry, I'm tryin'. I swear that I am, but it just feels weird. All of us havin' dinner and actin' like a big happy family; it's hard to break from the habit of just being with you all the time. I... I don't know if I like sharin' you and being social, and that makes me a horrible sister and a loser."

I didn't realise I was crying until I felt Branna's arm come around me and her voice softly shushing me.

"To be honest with you, Bee," she whispered. "This is takin' some gettin' used to for me, as well. There are times when I just want to be with you after I get home from work or school, and that's normal. For a long time it was just you, and me, but I *do* think we're tryin' to break from that habit too fast. So what do you say we go out tomorrow, just the two of us, for a girls' day? We can go see a film, get some new clothes and go out to dinner, then go home and just chill."

I felt the weight of the world drop off my shoulders when she finished speaking. She was feeling this too. The new people in our lives were changing things, and I wasn't a freak for thinking it was weird that I felt like I was living someone else's life all of a sudden.

"That sounds perfect." I nodded.

Branna gave me another hug and when we separated Dominic was next to us.

"Let's go up to my room, we can relax," he said as he took my hand.

Branna smiled as I went up the stairs with him before heading back into the kitchen to the rest of the brothers.

"I hate stairs," I grumbled breathlessly when we reached the top floor, making Dominic grunt.

When we entered his bedroom I suddenly became extremely shy and self-conscious as I folded my arms across my chest. The last time I was here was at the party and we were kissing on his bed.

"Why are you blushing?" He smiled when he rounded on me after closing his bedroom door.

I looked down and murmured, "I'm not."

He laughed. "You're adorable, pretty girl."

I suppressed a smile.

He unfolded my arms and led me across the room to his bed. "What movie do you want to watch? I have Netflix, so we have a lot of options."

I watched Dominic switch on his television and his Xbox before he closed the curtains, covering the room in darkness. The only light was that of the television so when I stepped forward, I stumbled over something and crashed into Dominic, which sent us both falling onto the bed.

"Someone is eager to get me into bed," he teased as I sat upwards.

I was half on his body and was pressed against his face. I couldn't push up and support myself 'cause my bad hand was under me so when I looked at Dominic's smiling face, I couldn't help but laugh. "This is your fault, I tripped—"

"—and fell for me? Awe, babe!"

I playfully snapped my teeth at him and tried to bite him, which made him screech like a girl. Which, of course, sent me into a fit of laughter. Dominic smiled at me for a few moments, watching me laugh before grabbing my shoulders and flipping me over.

I gasped when he straddled my hips and pinned my good arm above my head.

"I like you like this," he commented.

I raised an eyebrow. "Like what?"

"At my mercy," he grinned devilishly.

I gave him a warning look. "Don't even think of tryin' to seduce me, you aren't gettin' into me knickers."

He groaned as he leaned forward, pressing his body weight down on me.

"Dominic," I rasped, "can't... breathe."

He sat up off me and glared down on me. "I weigh two hundred and ten pounds not four hundred, you little shit."

I laughed as I tried to get my breath back. "I'm one fifty-eight, so you just added fifty extra pounds than I'm not used too; that's all."

His gaze travelled down my body and stopped at my belly where he was straddling me. "You don't look like you weigh in the one fifties."

I shrugged. "I'm pear shaped, that means I carry the majority of me weight below my belly. I'm sure you've heard Jason call me lard arse or thunder thighs since you started school."

Dominic's lips straightened in a tight, grim line. "That dick wouldn't know a woman's body from a girl's, so his opinion is irrelevant."

I chuckled. "I do have a big arse though—"

"A sexy phat ass is what you have," he cut me off.

My lip twitched. "I'm not gettin' into this argument with you again. I still have a headache from that day in Dunnes Stores where we engaged in a battle of words, verbal assault if you wish to say—"

"And physical. You hit me, remember?"

I playfully growled. "You put your arms around me and tried to take my cookies! A judge would understand that, and thank me for not doin' further damage."

Dominic started laughing and it lightened my mood almost instantly.

"I really like you, pretty girl," he beamed as he rolled off me making me instantly miss the feel of his body on mine.

I sat up, kicked off my shoes, crossed my legs, and stared at him as he leaned back on his pillow with his hands laced together across the back of his head, making his biceps stand at attention.

I swallowed and avoided looking directly at them.

"I would hope you like me, being a couple wouldn't work otherwise," I teased.

Dominic grinned. "No, I mean I *really* like you. I need you to be a part of my daily routine for me to feel good now. Everything I do centres around you."

I felt my heart constrict. "Dominic, we've only been goin' out a few days—"

"So?" he cut me off. "I don't believe in all the bullshit about it taking a lot of time to build a connection. I *already* connect with you on a deep level, pretty girl."

I let his words sink in and I smiled. "You know I might be the last girl you ever kiss or have sex with, when we get to the sex part I mean."

Dominic winked. "You *will* be the last girl I kiss and have sex with."

I winked. "Because you know I will murder you if you stray away?"

He playfully rolled his eyes and shoved me a little with his leg and muttered, "Smartass."

I pulled a face. "It's *smartarse*, not smartass."

Dominic smirked. "Babe, do you *really* want to get into what words should be pronounced what way? Because you don't even pronounce half of your words correctly, the 'th' sound doesn't exist over here!"

I gasped. "It does too!"

It didn't, but I wasn't about to bow down and say Dominic was right.

Dominic smiled at me. "Say 'the'."

I glared at him and said the word in question.

Dominic burst out laughing. "See? You put a 'd' where the 'th' should be."

I glared at him. "Yeah, well, you sound like a... ghetto person sometimes."

Dominic snickered, "I'm from New York; it's not really a surprise if I sound like that."

I moved closer to him until I was sitting directly next to him; he removed one hand from behind his head and brought it around to my back where he lazily stroked up and down, making me shiver.

"What's New York like?" I quizzed. "I wanna go there someday, do the whole tourist thing."

Dominic beamed at me. "It's a beautiful city but pretty chaotic. I've lived in the city my entire life and that's why I like it here so much. We live on the side of the mountain; I mean, how awesome is the view we get to see every day?"

I shrugged. "I've seen that view every day for me entire life, and while it *is* beautiful, I'd still like to visit New York. Not to live or anythin', just to tour it. I'll live here forever; I'm a small town girl at heart and always will be."

Dominic's lip quirked. "Well, what do you know? I went and got my fortune told when I was sixteen and the lady said I would find me a nice small town Irish girl."

I looked away. "Stop makin' things up to embarrass me, you eejit."

Dominic guffawed.

I was quiet for a moment until I looked around his room and noticed how gorgeous it was; his entire house was beautiful. I remembered thinking his family had to be rich in order to live here in Upton back when I first came here, and I now wondered how they could afford it.

"Dominic?" I murmured.

"Hmmm?"

"What do your brothers do for work?" I questioned.

He was silent for a moment. "We have a family business but I don't really want to talk about it. It's boring and not important."

I frowned, not liking his answer but said, "Okay."

Dominic then used the hand on my back to reach around and grip my waist so he could pull me down next to him. I settled beside him even though I was stiff as a board.

"Relax," he told me. "I may want to tear your clothes off but I won't... unless you ask me to."

I lightly slapped his chest making him yelp and me laugh.

"Oh, shut up!" I teased. "You get kicked around the fightin' circle at Darkness; my slaps don't hurt."

Dominic kissed the crown of my head while rubbing where I hit him with my hand. "Firstly, I don't get kicked around the circle, I do the kicking around, and—"

"You do get hurt a lot though," I cut him off with a grin.

Dominic raised an eyebrow at me. "I get bruises here and there, but they can't be avoided. I don't care how good of a fighter you are; you *never* leave a circle without some sort of swelling and bruising. Anyone who tells you different is lying to make themselves look better than they are."

I shivered when he poked my side. "Anyway, I could be weak as hell and still pin your tiny self."

I barked with laughter and sat upright, looking down at him. "I'm not small—"

"You weigh fifty pounds less than me and you're a foot shorter. You're a tiny thing, pretty girl."

I glared at him. "I'm not a *whole* foot shorter—"

"Branna said you're five foot three. I'm six foot three, so that *is* a whole foot," Dominic cut me off with a grin.

I stared at him. "You're really six foot three?"

Dominic nodded, and I let out a puffy breath of air. "Lads grow until they're twenty-one, you're eighteen... what if you get even taller?"

He laughed. "The tallest I'll get to be is six foot four. Alec is six foot four and so are Ryder and Kane. Dame is an inch shorter than me at six foot two."

I shook my head. "You're all so tall while Branna and I are short. That's not fair!"

Dominic was amused. "I like that you're shorter than me, makes you more adorable."

I growled at him. "Six foot three or not, you call me adorable again, and I'm gonna pound the head off you."

His eyes lit up. "Which head?"

"Dominic!" I spluttered.

He burst out laughing and pulled me back down next to him. I put my arms over his stomach and gave him a little squeeze.

"You're actually really nice to cuddle," I commented. "I thought the muscles would make it uncomfortable."

Dominic grunted and started to stroke my back again. "It would be uncomfortable if I tensed. You would feel them more then, but not so much now. I'm too relaxed to try and flex."

I chuckled as I ran my finger over his abs, I could feel the outline of each one through his t-shirt.

"You like my stomach?" he asked me.

Was I being that obvious? I thought.

"Why?" I asked, lowly.

"'Cause you're rubbing it with your fingers," he said with an amused tone of voice.

I shrugged but didn't answer him.

I sat back a little when Dominic moved under my head and hand. He sat up, shrugged out of his shirt and lay back down.

"There you go, trace away," he said and lay back down, his hands went back behind his head.

I stopped breathing and just stared.

His biceps, triceps, and the rest of his 'ceps were flexed now, and it was making me want to lick him all over. I moved my eyes to his tattoo and had to shift because the sight of it made my insides quiver.

"I thought you said you were too relaxed to flex." I whispered.

"Your fuck-me-now look changed my mind." He replied, his voice low and husky.

I flicked my eyes away from his tattoo and up to meet his gaze; he dropped his grin when he saw my face. I could only imagine what I looked like because I felt all hot and bothered.

"Can I try somethin'?" I asked him shyly.

Dominic nodded quickly while licking his lips.

I moved closer to him and then before I lost my nerve, I cocked my leg over his stomach and straddled him. I looked down and decided that the view from on top of Dominic was one I wanted to see often, *very* often. I leaned down until my mouth was a breath away from his.

"You're gorgeous," I whispered.

Dominic groaned a little, then moved his hands from behind his head and brought them down to my arse.

"You're fucking sexy," he growled back.

I smiled, my inner-self delighted that I could be sexy.

"I love your body," I whispered again and brushed my lips over his.

He growled, the low rumble deep in his throat. "I love yours too baby, all curves and ass. My *perfect* body in a woman."

Talk about feeling empowered.

I kissed him and smiled when he squeezed my arse with his hands. He rubbed up and down the back of my thighs, back up over my arse, and all the way up to my hips.

I melted against him when his hands left my lower body and suddenly touched my face as he kissed me deeply. He flipped us over then; I squeaked into his mouth while he settled me under him.

He pressed some of his weight against me, and because he was between my legs I felt *everything*. I began to panic then.

"Dominic," I breathed. "Wait—"

"I just want to do what I did the day at the hospital, I promise," he purred as he hooked his fingers around the waist band of my leggings and pulled them down, my knickers going south with them.

I nearly came up off the bed.

"Dominic!" I whisper shouted at him and tried to close my legs but couldn't because he was between them.

He kept eye contact with me. "Trust me, pretty girl."

I was shaking with nerves.

"Just… just like in the hospital?" I questioned.

He nodded slowly, and then leaned his head down to mine. "I'm going to make you come again."

I felt my body flush with heat and need.

He kissed me then, thoroughly. I began to feel achy and needed to be touched, and Dominic seemed to know this.

"Is that pretty clit of yours ready for me?" he asked against my mouth.

If I wasn't so worked up and hot, I would have been mortified at his crude words.

"Uh huh," I nodded against him.

"Are you wet for me?" he asked, his voice a rumble.

I jolted when I felt his finger slide over my folds and took one long swipe upwards until it rested on my clit.

I began panting. "Dominic, please!"

"You are. You're so wet, baby," he groaned and began to circle his finger around the sensitive bundle of nerves.

It felt good but like he was teasing me at the same time, because he never made direct contact.

"Does that feel good?" he asked, his voice huskier than before.

"More," I groaned.

He smiled, and then dropped it as he slid his finger over my clit causing my eyes to roll back a little.

"Damn, Bronagh," he grunted. "I could come from just watching your face, sweetheart."

I felt his hand pull away from me, and his weight came up off me. I was a second away from sitting up and asking what he was doing when I felt a soft, hot, wet tongue lick me. Down *there!*

I went cross-eyed and flat-out screamed. Dominic reached up with his hand and covered my mouth, muting the sound of my cries. His tongue swirled around and sucked on my clit until my body vibrated with pleasure and dots spotted my vision.

Dominic removed his hand and moved back up my body until his mouth was on mine again, and I was acutely aware of what I tasted on his tongue.

Me!

"Oh, God," I breathed as he moved his lips down to my neck.

"No, baby," he growled. "Dominic."

I was still twitching in the aftermath of my orgasm; my mind was cloudy as hell, too.

"Have sex with me," I breathed.

Dominic lifted up off me a little and smiled down at my panting self. "Sex drunk suits you."

I furrowed my eyebrows in confusion making him chuckle.

"I would love nothin' more than to sink into you, baby, but you're only asking me because I made you come and you feel really good, not because you're ready."

I frowned at him. "But I really, really want you inside me. Please."

He groaned and rested his head against mine. "You're killing me, baby. Killing. Me."

"I'm yours for the takin'," I pressed. "Fuck me, please."

"Bronagh," Dominic growled. "Stop it. I only have so much self-control. If you want me to fuck you after you wake up, I will, but until then sleep."

I yawned making him smile.

"You're so beautiful, my pretty girl," he murmured and kissed the tip of my nose.

I inwardly snorted at his wording; he saw me as something I wasn't.

"Sleep," he urged again. "You will need your energy for Darkness tonight."

I closed my eyes and sighed, my body feeling as light as a feather. "Are you fightin' tonight?"

Dominic chuckled at what I assumed was my sleepy voice. "Yeah, I am, and my girl has to be there and fully rested for when I take my good luck kiss."

CHAPTER SEVENTEEN

I was in Dominic's room stomping around because he was rushing me to get dressed for Darkness. We had overslept and since I had zero clothes here—why would I? It wasn't my house—it meant I would have to go home to get changed, but if I did that then we would be late. So Branna hooked me up with a dress and a pair of heels that she had in Ryder's room.

Dominic was grateful, and so was I until I saw the dress.

You see, Branna was two sizes smaller than me in the hip area. My arse took up a decent amount of space so when I put the dress on and found it to be a second skin that barely covered my arse, I cried wolf and said I wasn't going.

Dominic argued with me until he saw me in the dress. Alec and Kane had to argue with him then because he kept touching me and trying to kiss me.

He settled on being okay with me wearing it once I had a blazer covering it. A blazer wouldn't do any good for hiding my arse, but he said that he would just stand behind me all night if he had to… and get himself a front row seat to the view.

He was disgusting.

That and the fact that I wasn't ready yet had me rushing around Dominic's room trying to put my heels on. I got the left one on then tried to put the right one on and that was when it happened, I lost my balance and fell on something that made a huge cracking sound that honestly made my heart stop beating.

"Oh, no," I breathed. "Please, Jesus, no!"

I quickly stood up, dropped my high heel to the floor and spun around and looked down at my crime scene. I stared at Dominic's Xbox and wanted to cry, it looked like a cannonball was dropped on top of it, that's how big the dent was.

My arse *actually* caused a dent on it!

"Fuck," I whispered and covered my mouth with my hand.

He was going to break up with me; we've just about been dating a week and already I had done something to give him a reason to dump my fat arse.

"*Fuck!*" I said again, this time a little louder. "Fuckin' fuck!"

"Bronagh?" Dominic's voice called out from the other side of his bedroom door. "Babe, are you ready yet?"

Oh, Christ!

I kicked off my left heel and sprinted towards the door. Dominic stepped inside the room and widened his eyes a little before he opened his arms and caught me when I launched myself at him.

I usually would never jump on someone because I'd be afraid my weight would hurt them but I knew that Dominic was heavier than me—thank God—and would be able to hold me up with all his muscle. It might not be comfortable, he might even not be able to hold me up for long, but I just needed to distract him for a few minutes and keep him away from the right side of his room.

"You're so sexy," I breathed and covered my mouth with his.

He was either stunned or confused… or probably both because it took him a good five seconds to kiss me back and hoist me up a little further on him so he could hold me in an easier position.

"Babe—" he said trying to pull away from my kiss, but I wouldn't let him. I pushed my mouth harder against his and forced my tongue back into his mouth while I fisted my hands into his hair and tugged.

He groaned and tried to pull back twice more and when I

wouldn't let up he growled and gave me such a wallop on my arse that I yelped into his mouth and pulled back.

"I have a fight in forty fucking minutes. I can't fuck you because I would get my fucking ass kicked inside the circle. You're making turning you down very fucking hard and making my dick turn to diamond in the process! Fuck's sakes woman, why are you fucking doing this to me?"

The word 'fuck' was starting to sound weird to me because he had said it so much. He cursed a hell of a lot but I could understand why, so what did I answer him with?

Truth or lie?

Lie.

No, truth.

Yes, truth was always better.

"IthinkIbrokeyourXboxbutIdidn'tmeantoIswear," I blurted out in one breath.

Dominic just stared at me for a moment, and then slowly set me down onto my feet.

"Move so I can check on her," he growled.

I widened my eyes for two reasons. Firstly, he actually understood my rapid-fire admission, and secondly he called his Xbox her.

"It's a machine, not a female," I grumbled, but instantly looked down and shut my mouth when Dominic shot me a look that promised painful slaps for my arse if I kept it up.

"Move, Bronagh."

The way he said my name gave me shivers.

"I don't wanna 'cause you will be mad. I didn't mean to do it, I was trying to put my heel on and I fell on it. It's your fault when you think about it, you're the one who left it on the floor and not up on the unit."

I flicked my eyes up for a second then lowered them back down; his face was red indicating he was pissed.

"I'm overlooking your blame game, because I'm in a rush and don't want our first fight as a couple to be over a machine. Let me check my hard drive, the rest can be replaced but if my hard drive is fucked then I'll probably be charged with murder after my fight to-night."

I snapped my head up and blinked but did as he asked—or told—and stepped aside. I watched as Dominic walked over to his Xbox. He covered his face with his hands and let out a puff of air into them that sounded dangerously close to a whimper.

"Um… Dominic—"

"What the hell did you do to her?" he cut me off.

I played with my fingers. "I told you, I fell on it."

"Ass first?" he asked.

I grunted. "Yeah."

He shook his head. "You're fucking lucky I love that phat ass otherwise I'd chop the thing clean off. It broke my Xbox. It actually *broke* it. Jesus Christ!"

I felt beyond offended for my arse.

"I'm sorry, I didn't mean it." I frowned. "I tripped and fell!"

Dominic cut me a look. "Were you hurt? Is your hand injured further?"

I paused. "Well, no."

He grunted and laughed at the same time. "Right, I forgot you landed ass first and I doubt you would feel any impact on that ass."

Well, excuse the fuck out of me!

"I said sorry, what more do you want me to do?" I shouted.

He shook his head. "There's nothing you can do, you cracked my hard drive and dented the body cover. It's ruined."

I felt bad and was very sorry, but I was still mad that he wasn't being the least bit understanding.

"Well, I'll take me fat arse out of here where it won't cause any more damage," I snapped and stormed over to collect my shoes.

Dominic rolled his eyes at me so I threw a heel at him, and then screamed in anger when he caught it, which he found funny.

"Fine. Keep it, I don't even care, they are Branna's anyway," I snapped and stormed out of the room with my left shoe in my hand

and Dominic on my heels.

"I don't know why you're even mad. I'm the one whose baby was just murdered by a phat ass crushing her!"

I turned around when I reached the bottom floor and attacked Dominic with my remaining high heel. He jumped backwards and watched my movements. When I reach for him again he grabbed my arms and then spun me around so my back was to him and held my arms across my chest like an X. He was careful not to press on my injured hand though, which earned him a point or two.

"Yeah, and you said you wouldn't be able to hold your own against Micah. If you came at her like you do me, that bitch wouldn't have got a hit in!"

I hated him for bringing that fight up. Regardless of what he thought, I wouldn't win a fight with Micah. She was a kickboxer and I was just someone who gunned her boyfriend when he got too lippy.

"I'm cheerin' for whoever you're fightin' tonight, you big bastard!" I grunted as I struggled to break free of Dominic's hold.

"If I hear anything other than Rampage or Dominic come out of your mouth tonight then your ass is mine when we get home!" he growled in my ear.

My arse would be his… *what the fuck did that mean?*

"Hey, don't threaten my baby sister with spankin's you little shite," I heard Branna's voice snap, then Dominic's yelp in my ear, making me wince.

"Hey, put me down right now. Ryder!" I watched as Ryder hauled Branna out of the house, tugging on her dress when it began to ride up.

Kane, Alec and Damien followed suit all laughing in our direction.

"Twenty bucks says she kicks his ass before they leave the house," Kane grinned over his shoulder at Dominic and me.

I growled, "It's twenty Euros not bucks. Eejit!"

Damien howled with laughter as he closed the door behind himself and the lads. I huffed and puffed to break out of the arms caged around me, but when they wouldn't budge I gave in and sagged back into Dominic, who didn't move an inch.

"You finished with your temper tantrum, sweetie?" he asked, his tone annoyed.

I shrugged. "Give me a minute, I'll get an energy boost from somewhere and scratch your eyes out."

"As amusing as you being batshit crazy is, can you cut me some slack until *after* my fight? We can go fifty rounds of arguing then. Okay?"

"No!" I protested. "Let me go. I'm not goin' to your fight. I wanna go home, somewhere you and your stupid fightin' pit, or circle, or whatever that stupid thing is, *won't* be."

He let go of me and I stumbled forward. "Fine, fuck off home then. I don't need this bullshit before a fight."

Him and his stupid bloody fight.

"Bloody gobshite!" I growled as I spun around to face him.

His eyes raked over my body in my tight fitting dress and he licked his lips. I glared at him so hard, holes should have appeared in his head. I turned and stormed out of the house—barefoot—and down the driveway and climbed into the back of the Jeep.

"Drop me home first, I'm not goin' to that stupid fight," I stated and kept my eyes straight ahead after I settled between Alec and Kane, who wouldn't even look at me after I spoke.

Dominic got into the Jeep and since he didn't have a seat, he half-shared with Damien. They were muttering the entire ride to my house, and it pissed me off because I heard Damien say things like 'tell her' and 'she has a right to know what you do' and it was freaking me out.

"Do you want me to—"

"No, it's fine. It's Friday, *Supernatural* is on tonight. I'll watch that before I go to bed," I muttered to Branna after I cut her off then leaned forward and kissed her cheek.

"Touch her," Dominic suddenly growled. "I fucking dare you, bro!"

Alec's voice laughed. "I'm not doing anything."

"You're looking at her ass!"

I shuffled out of the car, angrily climbing over Damien and Dominic making them grunt, and hiss when my knees pressed into sensitive areas.

"It was in my face, what am I supposed to do, be rude and look away?" Alec asked, making Kane and Ryder chuckle.

I ignored him and his teasing and took the key Branna held out from her side of the car.

I said goodbye to my sister, gave Dominic the finger, everyone else got a smile then I walked up the garden.

"Jesus, Bronagh! It's freezin', girly! Get your arse inside and into warm clothes!" Mrs. Brown, my elderly neighbour, shouted from my right as she exited her house.

I heard chuckles from behind me but I ignored them.

"Will do, Mrs. Brown." I smiled to her.

I didn't look back as I entered my house and closed the door. I shook myself out, noticing my legs were tingling from the cold. I headed straight upstairs and jumped into a warm shower then got out and changed into my pyjamas. I took my time drying and straightening my hair before I went downstairs, stocked up on ice-cream and cookies, and headed back up to my room.

I turned the station on for *Supernatural* and dug into my food while I waited for it to come on. When it finally did come up, I lasted only twenty minutes before I turned it off and snuggled under my covers. Good thing I always recorded the episodes.

I was in bed tossing and turning even though I was knackered tired, I still couldn't sleep. It took me a few minutes to realise that I was worried about Dominic and the thought alone made me bolt upright and break out in a sweat.

If I was worried about him getting hurt during his fight that obviously meant I really cared for him. I groaned then because I knew I more than cared for him. Just thinking about him made my heart race. I knew everyone risked their hearts going into a relationship, but when I really thought about the impact that hurt could have on me, I shuddered. I would just die altogether if it felt as bad as when I lost my parents. I couldn't survive that again, no way.

I shook my head at my train of thought and inwardly kicked myself for thinking so negative. I had to have a positive outlook, things would just be miserable otherwise.

I sighed as I got out of bed and grabbed my phone off my locker.

Is he okay? Did he win his fight?

I went into the bathroom after I hit send and went to the toilet, then came back into my dark room. My phone lit up, and I found myself rushing towards it.

His fight got delayed, he just left the circle now, but yeah he is fine. He won by knockout, which isn't surprising since he was mad from your fight from earlier. The lad he was fighting didn't have a chance.

The knowledge that he was okay lifted a weight off my shoulder and gave me some of my stubbornness back.

Whatever. He started it by saying me arse had its own postcode!

Okay, he didn't say that, but he was clearly thinking it after the way he described the damage my arse did to his stupid Xbox.

I tucked my phone under my pillow and climbed back into bed; sleep came very easily then, and not even the sensation from the phone vibrating made me move.

I wasn't fully asleep, but I wasn't awake either, so when I heard the door open and people talking downstairs I knew Dominic had somehow talked Branna into letting him come back here.

"No, shower first." I heard Branna hiss from outside my door.

"She will drop kick you if you go in there and get in her bed all sweaty."

I ignored her voice and fell into a deeper sleep that again was disturbed, but this time by arms, legs, and a body entangling itself around me.

"Dominic," I groaned. "I'm sleepin' here... move over."

He kissed the back of my neck freely because my hair was tied up and it made me squirm and shudder. I blinked my eyes open and squinted through the darkness. I sighed and rested back against him when I realised he wasn't going to let me go.

"I didn't say your ass had its own postcode," his voice suddenly murmured.

I groaned. "That bitch can't keep anythin' to herself!"

Dominic snorted from behind me.

I sighed. "I was jokin'."

"Hmmm."

I felt his hand slide over my stomach, and I grabbed it, stopping its movements.

"I'm lyin' on my side, any fat that I have just hangs down when I'm on my side, and you aren't touchin' it," I stated through my tired voice.

Dominic groaned from behind me. "Havin' some meat doesn't make you fat, it makes you human."

I gnawed on my inner cheek. "You have like zero fat, so you don't get a say."

"I'm twelve percent body fat and weigh two ten. The reason I'm so heavy is because muscle is heavier than fat. I train for muscle, so I'm fit and powerful."

I didn't care about any of this.

"Why are you even here?" I asked. "How did you talk Branna into lettin' you come in here?"

He kissed the back of my head and forced his hand around mine and rested it on my stomach. "I told her the truth—that I missed you and just wanted to sleep next to you."

The layer of ice that had formed around my heart because of our fight melted after he finished speaking. I turned around to face him.

"You missed me?" I murmured.

He nodded his head in the dark; I couldn't really see him, but the moonlight gave off some of his profile.

"Yeah, babe, I missed you, and I hated that you weren't at my fight. I wanted my good luck kiss," he said and pulled me closer to him.

My lip twitched. "You won, so you didn't need a good luck kiss from me."

He kissed the tip of my nose. "I'll always need your good luck kisses, pretty girl."

He was undoing me!

"I missed you too," I admitted and leaned my head against his. "I'm sorry for breaking your Xbox and for fightin' with you. I didn't mean any of what I said."

He stroked my back with his hand. "Me too, I overreacted."

Not really, I broke an expensive machine. He was calmer than I would have been if it were something of mine. Way calmer.

"Let me make it up to you?" I whispered.

I heard him swallow. "How?"

I moved up, pushed him onto his back and straddled him. He winced, and I frowned and looked down but I couldn't see a thing so I reached over and flipped on my lamp. I looked back to Dominic and gasped.

His left ribcage was bruised, and his poor face was busted up again.

"I'm gettin' fed up with them hittin' your face! Why do they always go for the face?" I asked and leaned down to him, placing kisses over his bruised jaw and eyes.

Dominic smiled, and it sent a wave of need through me. No one had the right to look so stunning with a bruised up face. No one!

I looked down to where I was sitting then slid down until I was straddling Dominic's shins instead of his hips.

"Bronagh?" Dominic sat as he leaned up on his elbows and looked at me.

I smiled at him shyly.

"Just tell me what to do?" I asked. "I want to do this."

He looked a little torn, so I frowned. "Please?"

He let out a choked laugh. "Don't beg to suck my cock, babe. You can do it whenever you want; I just want you to be sure that it's what you want to do. I'm always up—pun intended—for your mouth and hands on me, I just want you to be sure that you're doing it because you want to and not because I want you to."

I gave him another smile and reached up for his boxer briefs—it was all he had on—and gripped the waistband. They were already tented before I even touched them so that relaxed me knowing he was turned on and ready for me to attempt this... *task*?

No, not a task, this was something I wanted to do.

Lots of girls liked making their boyfriends feel good and apparently I was no different. The knowledge that I was doing stuff a normal girlfriend would do made me happy.

"Dominic," I breathed when I pulled his boxers to his knees.

It might have been rude, but I couldn't help it. I stared for a solid minute before flicking my eyes upwards.

"That will really hurt me, won't it?" I asked, my voice cracking with nerves.

"The first time is usually uncomfortable for girls, but when we do come together for the first time I'll be *really* gentle." He assured me. "I promise."

I was amazed that he could sound so sweet and sincere while his fully erect penis was resting up against his stomach; that was how big it was. It was thick and long; I really was afraid it would hurt me when we eventually did have sex, but I pushed the thought away.

"A blowjob." I cleared my throat. "How do I give you one? Educate me."

Dominic spluttered with laughter, lay back on the pillow, and carefully scrubbed his face with his hands.

"Don't say it like that!" he pleaded. "I'm trying to think of how to ask you to lick and suck on me without sounding—Jesus!"

I smiled when I looked upwards and drew my tongue away from the salty tip of Dominic's cock and looked at his face and how it changed when I put my mouth on him.

I repeated the lick and started from the base this time and dragged my tongue and then sucked around the tip. It was shockingly surprising how similar it was to sucking on a lollipop.

I just had to remember not to bite.

"Use your hand as well, put it on my cock and work it up and down in time with your mouth and—oh yeah, that's it. Just like that, fuck that's good," he groaned. "Suck a little harder... flick your tongue around the head, yes! Keep doing that, fuck, *just* like that."

Being praised for giving a blowjob was actually empowering, it made me feel very womanly.

"Bronagh, ease up on the sucking now, I can't—Fuck! Baby, please, I want this to last."

He was panting, literally panting, and I felt bloody amazing that I was reducing him to that.

I removed my mouth from his cock with a pop and kissed down his length until I lifted it up and came to his balls. I knew they were the sensitive part; Jason dropped enough times when I kneed him there, and even Dominic before we got together, so I wondered if they would be sensitive to a kiss.

I tested it out and earned a little groan; I licked one, then the other, and his hips bucked into my face a little. I went for the grand prize and carefully sucked one into my mouth and swirled my tongue around it.

Dominic was making low noises and kept bucking his hips into my face, so I took it as a good sign and repeated my actions with the other ball.

I was sucking on his ball!

I wanted to laugh at my thoughts, but I didn't because that would just be a mood killer. I felt his hands on my hair as I licked my way back up to the tip of his cock and looked at his face as I took the head into my mouth.

"Fuck me," he breathed as he watched me. "I could come just with the sight of you sucking my cock alone, baby."

I was practically purring with glee as I moved my hand back under my mouth and worked it up and down, sucking hard every so often earning a loud groan that shocked me a little. I didn't think males could make that type of groaning noises, but apparently they could.

"Damien in drag clothes, Kane in high heels. Alec in a tutu—"

I looked up at Dominic as I continued my work and found his eyes closed as he talked to himself about his brothers in all types of get-ups.

I wanted to ask what the fuck he was doing but didn't want to stop, because I wanted him to orgasm soon. My jaw was starting to kill me and my arm felt like it was about to fall off.

I picked up my pace; sucking harder until I was sure my jaw would lock. Dominic's sentences got quicker as well and fell perfectly in time with my strokes.

"Ryder naked, Alec naked, Damien naked, Kane naked. All of them fucking—Oh fuck, Bronagh, I'm coming!" I felt the hot spurts of his salty liquid coat my tongue as he finished talking.

I resisted the urge to gag as I swallowed it down; it was very salty and not good at all. It was actually disgusting.

I sat back on my heels and looked at Dominic with his arms spread across the bed; his cock slowly softening against his stomach, and his face looked like he was already asleep.

"Dominic?" I poked his belly.

He popped an eye open, so I smiled at him.

"I did good?" I asked.

He lazily lifted his hand, gave me a thumbs up, and winked at me. "A fucking plus, baby girl. A fucking plus."

I inwardly did a happy dance; it wasn't as hard—no pun intended—as I thought it would be. My mouth and hand hurt more than I thought it would, but it wasn't hard!

"Why were you talkin' about your brothers in weird clothes?" I asked with a smile.

He shrugged. "Trying to think of anything but what you were doing so I wouldn't come."

I frowned. "Wait, so lads think about sex all the time but durin' sex and sex acts they think of anythin' but it?"

"Yep."

I laughed. "That's so stupid, why not just embrace it—"

"'Cause it would be over before it started if I did that. I wasn't joking when I said the sight of your mouth on my cock was enough to make me come."

I understood what he meant but still found it silly. I settled in next to him then and relaxed.

"You swallowed my come," he murmured to me when I snuggled up beside him.

I gaped as he covered us with a blanket. I shouldn't have been so shocked, I mean I just gave him a blowjob, and he was my boyfriend after all, but he was still naked in my bed.

Another bunch of firsts!

"I'm sorry, was I not supposed to?" I asked, feeling worried that I ruined the whole thing.

"Are you fucking with me? That is beyond sexy, baby," he assured me.

I blew out a breath. "I'm glad you think so because it is the saltiest thing I've ever tasted."

Dominic laughed and cuddled me to him. "I live you, pretty girl."

I pulled back and stared at him. "You live me?" I questioned.

He had his eyes closed and was drifting off, so I shook him.

"You live me? You said the word *live*, Dominic," I repeated when he blinked his eyes open.

He nodded and lazily smiled again.

God, he was so gorgeous.

"I more than like you but don't feel quite near love yet, so I put the word love and like together and got live so I live you. I'm in live with you, pretty girl."

I knew that was possibly the sweetest thing he has ever said to me, but be that as it may, I looked down at him with a raised eyebrow, I never heard an expression like that before so I said, "Did you just make that expression up?"

He shook his head. "Nah, a girl I was fucking last year said it to me, she said it was a reference from a book she read. I can't remember the name of it. I just thought it was cute and figured this was a fitting time to say it."

He did not just say that.

I thumped him in the stomach. "You're a prick!"

He grunted out and then laughed and he gripped his stomach. "You're amazing."

I went to thump him again but he quickly grabbed me and pulled him down to his side, he lowered his head and ran his nose from the tip of mine to between my eyes then kissed that spot. "I do live you, I swear it."

"Dominic," I breathed, my stomach twisting in knots and my chest constricting. It was almost painful, but a good type of pain; that was how I knew I felt the same as him. "I live you, too."

He closed his eyes and smiled again, tugging me towards him. I closed my eyes as well and fell asleep in his arms, perfectly and happily content.

"Stop smiling like that Dominic, it's starting to freak me out!" Ryder snapped to Dominic as we finished having breakfast the next morning.

Dominic snorted at Ryder then looked at me. "I'm just happy."

I felt my cheeks flush.

"Please tell me you used a condom?" Branna swore across the table. "I'll kill you if you get pregnant, Bronagh!"

I gaped at her. "We didn't have sex!"

My sister raised an eyebrow at me. "I heard groanin' comin' from your room last night, don't lie to me!"

My face must have gone beetroot purple!

"We didn't have sex!" I repeated and looked away from her and everyone else.

"She's right, we didn't have sex," Dominic stated. "What you heard was me getting a fucking *amazing* blow—"

"Dominic!" I shrieked.

He burst out laughing and so did Ryder.

Branna blushed a little herself. "Oh Lord, me little sister was givin' head to her fella—"

"Branna!" I screamed.

Why were they doing this to me? I angrily thought. *That stuff was supposed to be private!*

I tried to make a break up to my room, but Dominic caught me at the end of the stairs and lifted me back against him.

"Don't be embarrassed, those two were fucking last night so they can't say shit about what we did."

I really didn't need to know that bit of information.

"I don't care, you shouldn't have opened your mouth; that's supposed to be private!" I scowled. I won't ever be givin' you oral again if—"

"I'll never mention anything like it for as long as I live, I promise. Don't cut me off when I've only started getting some, *please.*"

I smiled to myself; I had all the power here, and it felt good, *really* good.

"Okay," I said firmly. "But no more talkin' about it, I don't like it."

Dominic kissed my cheek. "Deal."

He just hugged me from behind then and it made me smile.

"You have to leave now," I said.

He squeezed me. "Yeah, yeah, I know. It's girl's day. Blah, blah, blah."

I laughed. "I'll see you tomorrow. We can hang out all day, okay?"

"I'm holding you to that, pretty girl."

He put me down and turned me to face him. He then leaned in, pecked my lips before shouting, "Bro, move it!"

Ryder walked out to the hallway, stretching his arms above his head.

"Let's go bro," he said to Dominic. "We've got business to attend to."

I looked from Dominic to Ryder and said, "What business?"

He scratched his neck. "Just some family business."

I raised an eyebrow and turned to Dominic. "What *is* the family business? You never talk about it, you told me it's not important but I still want to know about it."

The silence that followed gave me a sick feeling in my stomach.

"I'll fill her in." Branna said from behind Ryder. "Go on, get goin'."

Both Ryder and Dominic looked at her and after some sort of silent communication; they nodded and left the house. I stood staring after them for a moment before turning to Branna.

"Please tell me they aren't drug dealers," I joked.

Branna grumbled. "They aren't drug dealers, unfortunately things they are into are a little worse than that."

What?

"What is worse than being a drug dealer?" I asked, my voice barely audible.

Branna sighed and looked me dead in the eye as she said, "Workin' for one."

CHAPTER EIGHTEEN

I stared at Branna in horror then flat-out gaped at her back when she turned and walked into the kitchen.

"You can't just say somethin' like that and then walk away!" I bellowed as I stormed into the kitchen after her.

She glanced at me over her shoulder and shrugged. "I'm puttin' the kettle on. This is a conversation that requires a cuppa."

I knew she was right when I felt my hands shake and my knees start to knock together, so I made my way over to our kitchen table and slumped down onto a chair.

"Run this by me again," I asked. "Our boyfriends work for a drug dealer?"

Branna scrubbed her face with her hands before she folded them across her chest, rested her hip against the kitchen counter, and looked me in the eye. Her left eye twitched a little.

"You're jokin'!" I snapped. "I don't find this funny at all!"

She didn't say a word, not a peep, and that made me feel sicker than I already felt.

"Dominic would have told me if he was into shite like that!" I pressed. "He wouldn't have pestered me into goin' out with him if he was tangled up in things as bad as *drugs*! He doesn't even smoke Branna, and he rarely drinks because of his trainin' for his fights."

"I never said he took drugs." Branna said. "None of the lads do drugs, but they are all involved with them. Except Damien."

I stared at her for a long, long moment as it all began to make sense in my head. All the hushed conversations between Damien and Dominic, then Ryder saying Dominic fighting in school brought them unwanted attention, and *then* Dominic telling me he didn't fight for fun but for 'family business', a family business he wouldn't tell me about.

I suddenly burst into tears. "I can't b-believe... why would he... oh my God, I'm goin' out with a drug dealer!"

I covered my face with both my good and injured hand and sobbed like a baby. My chest was hurting me, and my stomach was lurching something terrible. I knew I was going to be sick. And I was, all over the floor next to me.

"Don't move, okay? I'll clean it up." Branna said to me in a soft tone. "Just stay put and focus on breathin' so you can calm yourself."

I numbly nodded at her while staring out to our back garden through the back door glass. I ignored the vile taste in my mouth and forced myself not to think of the pain in my stomach. But nothing I did stopped my chest from constricting in pain.

"I'm breakin' up with him," I said as I continued to look out at the back garden.

Branna sighed next to me as she finished cleaning up my vomit. I glanced at her as she moved over to the fridge to get some juice then filled a glass full of it. She came back over to my side and handed me the juice. I drank it as she stroked my back with her hand.

"If it makes you look at this differently," she murmured, "they don't want to be involved with this man, they just don't have a choice."

I snapped my head to her; I felt my face go red when she didn't explain that any further.

"Branna," I growled. "*Stop* cuttin' yourself off when you're tellin' me somethin' as important as this!"

She smiled a little at me. "I'm sorry, Bee, but I'm not sayin' any more. This is a conversation you need to have with Dominic alone. Just know that I fully stand by him, Ryder, and the rest of the lads. I would *never* go out with someone who would involve us in somethin' as dangerous as this, and I wouldn't allow you to go out with someone like that unless there was a good reason. The lads have got a handle on this so we don't need to worry."

I stared at her blankly, unblinking.

How in God's name was she so calm about this?

I shook my head at her, got up and left the kitchen and went up to my room where I flung myself onto my bed. I was still coming to grips with just dating Dominic and allowing myself to let him in. And now I had to deal with this fucking bombshell?

I shook my head into my pillow.

Was this why he fought at Darkness? Was it why he fought at all? Was this the reason why he was always battered and bruised when he came to school? Was this why he and his brothers were here in Ireland?

I had so many questions and zero answers.

I sat up, got my phone from my dresser and unlocked it.

I need to speak to you!!

I sent a text to his phone and sat back on my bed and closed my eyes and started thinking.

How the hell did my life get so complicated?

Only a few months ago I was invisible, boyfriend-less, bullied, and a complete and total loner until Dominic happened. I couldn't even remember how it felt not to feel for someone. I cared about no one, bar Branna, until he stormed into my life and turned my world upside down. I did care about Dominic, I cared about him so much; I lived him, but this was something I didn't know if I could deal with. The things he was involved in were so much bigger than me.

I opened my eyes when my phone beeped and tapped on Dominic's face when his text came through.

I know I have a lot of explaining to do baby, but don't make any decisions until you hear me out. Please?

I frowned; he knew my automatic reaction would be to break up with him and that upset me. The whole point of being with Dominic was to let go of my old insecurities and I wasn't going back to running away from things that scared me or threatened my bubbled world. No, I was going to pull up my big girl trousers and listen to what he had to say. Any decisions I made about us would come after I'd heard everything and thought things over. I nodded my head as I tapped on my phone, replying to Dominic.

Okay, but know I'm beyond upset with you. This—you—have really hurt me.

I wasn't lying; I was hurting because of this. I didn't know if it was because Dominic kept the secret from me for so long or because of what the secret actually was. *Both*, I thought.

I looked at my phone when it beeped.

I'm sry, pretty girl. I'll be over 2nite. I've some stuff to sort with Ryder 1st but once I'm done, I'm coming str8 to you. Have your girl's day with Bran and try not to overthink on this. Don't give yourself a headache. I know you will understand once I lay everything out for you. I live you, babe.

I started crying again because I prayed he was right; I really did.

"What have you done with Dominic?" Branna randomly asked me as we sat on the sofa in our sitting room. "Like how far have you gotten with him?"

It was past nine at night and after a long day of shopping on

Grafton Street, we were watching *In Her Shoes*. But the film was forgotten once that question was asked, even though we continued to eat the pizza in our hands.

I looked at Branna and tried to glare, but I was pretty sure I looked stupid because I could feel my cheeks getting warm.

Branna cackled. "Don't be embarrassed, sisters talk about things like this all the time."

I sighed and just shrugged. "Not as far as you've gotten with Ryder, which I'm sure is all the way and back again multiple times, but probably way too far for only a week of goin' out."

My sister pumped her eyebrows at me, and it made me laugh and cough around the pizza that was in my mouth, making her crack up and slap her knee. I shook my head at her, still smiling as she wiped her eyes.

"Details Bee," she pressed. "I need details."

I groaned. "I gave him a… you know."

She only raised her eyebrows at me, and I hated her, because I knew she was going to make me say the word.

"A blow job," I blurted out then squeaked and covered my face.

It was weird knowing I've done something so intimate with Dominic, and I just told my sister about it!

"You dirty minx!" Branna teased playfully making me kick her leg, which she snorted at.

"He also… you know… went down on me too and he… put his fingers up there as well."

Branna widened her eyes. "Holy shite, the lad doesn't waste any time does he?"

I frowned. "What do you mean?"

"He has been tryin' to get with you since he moved here." She grinned. "He must have envisioned doing dirty stuff with you for ages and can't hold back now that you're together."

I rolled my eyes. "Well, tough shite for him because I've set limits. I won't go any further than the stuff we have done already until I know in meself that I am ready. He won't pressure me either;

he values his life and dick too much to do otherwise."

Branna burst out laughing, and her laughter made me laugh. We stopped when we heard a knock on the door. I instantly knew it wasn't the lads because Ryder had a key, and so did Dominic—he stole Ryder's and made a copy for himself. I looked to Branna and shrugged. "I'll get it."

She continued to eat her pizza, but she watched me until I disappeared out of her view as I walked out to the hall. I opened the hall door and froze a little because of who was on the other side.

"Hey, Bronagh. Can I talk to you for a second?"

I cleared my throat and said, "Sure, Gavin. Come on in."

CHAPTER NINETEEN

"Who is it?" Branna's voice called out from the sitting room.

I closed the door when Gavin stepped inside. "It's Gavin Collins, he wants to have a chat."

I smiled at Gavin then gestured towards the stairs and whispered, "We can go up to my room to talk. She will only listen in if we stay down here."

Gavin chuckled under his breath making me chuckle as well. We headed upstairs then, with Branna's quizzical gaze on our backs until we were out of sight and safely inside my room.

"So... what's up?" I asked as I awkwardly walked towards my bed and sat on it, facing Gavin.

He sighed and ran his hands through his thick, wavy dirty blond locks and for a moment I found myself just staring at him. I was Dominic's girlfriend, but I was only human and Gavin was hot. Anyone with eyes could see that.

"I wanted to tell you I'm sorry," he sighed. "I was a complete fuckin' dickhead for bailin' on our date. I know things won't work out for us like a couple and that you're with Nico now, but I do want to be your mate. I've been feelin' like crap since that night and even worse when I saw your hand bandaged up at school."

I raised my eyebrows; I didn't know what I was expecting him to talk to me about, but an apology from him definitely wasn't it.

"Is it bad?" he asked, gesturing to my hand.

I looked down at my hand, looked back up and shook my head. "No, it's fine now, only a little stiff. The bruisin' on it has faded to yellow. After I get a check-up at the hospital next week, I can take the bandage off," I explained.

Gavin nodded at me then sighed as he stared. "You look good."

I felt myself blush.

He smiled. "I'm not chattin' you up, I mean you just look... good," he said with a shrug.

I still continued to blush while he continued to smile.

I cleared my throat. "I'm not gonna lie, I did call you a few choice names in my head when you just left me last week in McDonald's but I *do* understand why. Dominic... he can be very persistent and overwhelmin' to deal with."

Gavin grunted as he came to sit next to me on my bed. "Understatement, Bee."

I smiled at him. "I forgive you, if that's what you need to hear. I don't hold grudges... unless you're Jason Bane. But since you aren't, no worries."

Gavin laughed and relaxed completely next to me. "I'll be thankin' God for small favours tonight before I go to bed."

I snorted, and it made Gavin cackle, which sent me over the edge with laughter. I could not handle it when people cackle, it got me every time, and I had to laugh.

"I'll get goin', I just stopped by to get that off me chest. I hope we can be mates though? Like hangin' out and shite like that," Gavin said as he turned his head to me.

I looked back at him and ignored the voice in my head that shouted 'no, we don't want any more change!' and gave Gavin a smile and said, "Yeah, I think a friend is just what I need."

Gavin beamed at me and it made me feel shy; I actually had a beautiful lad as my friend and a complete stunner as my boyfriend... little me wasn't doing too badly for herself.

Gavin leaned in to hug me and I returned it. "I'll see you on Monday and—"

"No, Ryder, stop him!" Branna's voice suddenly screamed from downstairs.

Gavin and I pulled apart from our hug and turned to my door as footsteps pounded up the stairs.

"Oh, shite," Gavin breathed when the door was flung open.

I winced when it smacked against the wall, but full-on recoiled when I saw Dominic filling up the doorway, his face twisted in rage. I jumped out in front of Gavin and raised my hands up in surrender.

"Dominic," I shouted. "He just came over to apologise to me. He isn't tryin' to ask me out again or anythin', he just wants to be friends—"

Dominic shot forward and I had to fling myself at him so he wouldn't dodge around me and get Gavin, whom I could sense was standing behind me waiting for a blow to hit him.

Dominic's arms were tight around me as I squeezed myself to him. He growled into my temple and tried to shake me off him, but I wasn't letting go for anything, and he realised this after a moment and relaxed a tiny bit to settle me against him.

"First and only warning you're getting, Collins," he snarled. "She's mine, if you try and take her away from me, I will kill you."

Holy. Fuck!

"Dominic," I whispered. "It's okay."

"Fuck you, Nico," Gavin spat. "She can be me friend if she wants to be!"

Dominic tried to push me away from him, but my arms were locked around his waist and weren't coming apart any time soon.

"GET OUT!" Dominic roared, which caused me to duck my head because the noise of it stung my ears.

"I'm goin', man. Don't worry," Gavin snarled and moved towards the door. "See you in school, Bee."

Dominic swung his arm and missed Gavin because he ducked away and left the room, passing Branna and Ryder who were both standing outside my room looking in and watching.

I locked eyes with Branna and nodded for her and Ryder to leave. She nodded back at me and reached inside my room and closed the door leaving Dominic and myself alone. I removed my arms from around him and made a move to step backwards to give him some space but he kept me in place and it made me sigh.

"I'm just tryin' to give you some space to cool off—"

"Why was he here?" he growled down at me, cutting me off mid-sentence. "In your room?"

I shrugged. "He wanted to apologise and—"

"I got that," he angrily cut me off. "But. Why. Was. He. In. Your. Room?"

I blinked at him for a moment then shook my head. "Because he wanted to talk."

Dominic's gaze on me was hard as he looked down at me. "Why in here? Why not downstairs?"

I sighed. "I don't know, I figured it would be easier to talk up here and—"

"*You* suggested you both come up to your room?" he roared.

I flinched away from him. I knew he wouldn't hit me or hurt me physically, but that still didn't change the fact that he was scaring me.

"Dominic, you're frightenin' me," I said, my voice shaking.

He grunted and moved his arms from around me and began pacing my room. I got a headache looking at him, so I moved to my bed, climbed onto it, and snuggled under my covers. I was already in my pyjamas and I was content enough to stay for the night now that I was there.

I heard Dominic sigh after another few minutes of pacing. "Bronagh?"

I didn't answer, which caused another deep sigh to escape his mouth. I heard him moving about and then came the noise of things hitting the floor, and I instantly knew it was his clothes and shoes.

He was stripping.

I mentally kicked myself; we're having serious problems, and I was melting over him getting semi-naked. My mind was apparently stuck in the gutter where Dominic was involved.

I tensed when he climbed into my bed behind me. I didn't fight him off when he tangled his limbs up with mine. First his arms came around my waist and he pulled me against him until I was moulded into the front of his body, then he tangled his legs up with mine and put his head resting above mine.

"I live you, pretty girl," he murmured and kissed the crown of my head.

I squeezed my eyes shut for a second then opened them. "I live you, too."

He turned me to him then, lowered his head and brushed his lips over mine. I knew I should have lightly kissed him back or even attempted to tease him with a whisper kiss, but I just couldn't. I pressed my mouth hard on his and forced my tongue into his mouth.

Dominic groaned, tensed, and then quickly pulled back away from me.

"Bronagh," he growled, "I want to fuck you when you kiss me like that!"

I smiled at him; I loved getting him so worked up. It made me feel empowered.

I leaned forward and lightly kissed him then, but he groaned again. "Still makes me want to fuck you."

I laughed. "So will I just stop kissin' you then?"

"Never stop kissing me. *Never*!" he growled, making me shudder and lazily smile at him.

He kissed my forehead and sighed. "I'm sorry for upsetting you. You know I would never put my hands on you to hurt you. Right?"

I nodded. "I know, but you're still very intimidatin' when you get like that. It's fine if I'm just as mad because sometimes I think I scare you when I'm like that."

"You do but I think it's sexy as well," Dominic mumbled.

I shook my head. "We need to talk."

He nodded and locked eyes with me. "Tell me what Branna told you."

I did as he asked and when I finished speaking he was nodding.

"Have you ever heard of a man called Marco Miles?" Dominic asked me.

I thought on it, and then shook my head—answering no.

"Damn, baby, you really are sheltered," he murmured.

I frowned. "I don't know any bad people, Dominic. I made it my business for years not to talk to anyone or listen to gossip."

Dominic nodded again. "I know that but everyone knows of Marco, his name is known all over the world. He is... a very bad person."

I closed my eyes and asked, "And he is your boss?"

"Yes."

My heart broke in two.

"Oh, my God," I whispered.

Dominic pulled me even closer to him. "I don't sell drugs, I don't take them, and I don't kill people or go on any jobs that would land me in prison for life."

I opened my eyes feeling a little more than confused. "What do you do then?"

His jaw tensed. "I'm paying off a loan, you could say, by fighting."

I frowned. "Money?"

He sighed and closed his eyes. "No, not money. It's more complicated than that."

I sat up and pulled him upright with me. I turned to him, crossed my legs, and gestured him with my hand to carry on talking. "I've got nothin' but time so start talkin'."

Dominic's lip twitched. "Bossy."

I shrugged.

He scrubbed his face with his hands before locking eyes with me again.

"My dad was Marco's best friend since they were kids. They

were both bad people and started up their empire from scratch. They had links to a number of Dons from different Mafias, nearly every drug cartel known to man, and they pretty much had the law in their back pocket." He grunted and shook his head.

"My brothers and I grew up around violence and that lifestyle not knowing any better. We were treated like princes, and got everything we wanted because of who our dad was. High-end escorts were servicing me from the time I was thirteen because I didn't want to jerk myself off. Our lives were a blur up until my mom and dad got killed just after my and Damien's fifteenth birthday." He set his jaw as he spoke.

"Dad crossed Marco looking to get some extra money on a drug cartel deal so Marco had my dad and mom killed before they could take him out. They were best friends, but their greed for money and power changed them, made them hollow... evil. My mom was no better; the only thing she loved were money and materialistic things. She encouraged my dad to keep our lifestyle up... it got them both killed in the end."

Dominic watched me while he was speaking and stopped when he saw I was now crying.

"Baby, please don't cry." He frowned and reached for me.

I moved forward and engulfed him in a hug, holding him to me tighter than I ever had before.

"I'm so sorry." I whispered.

Dominic swayed us from side to side. "What are you sorry for?"

"For your upbringin'," I sniffled. "I wish you and your brothers had the love Branna and I had from our parents."

He rubbed his thumb across my cheek and murmured, "No one has ever cried for me before."

"Well, I live you so of course I'm goin' to cry when I hear about your childhood," I sobbed.

Dominic lightly smiled at me. "Bar my brothers, you're the most important thing in the world to me, you mean everything to me. I just want you to know that before I finish what I need to tell you, okay?"

There was more?

Oh, God!

"Okay," I whispered.

He blew out a breath and licked his lips before he said, "It's disgusting to say, but I genuinely don't care that Marco had my parents killed. I hate him, but not for that. We never saw my parents and when we did they were cold people so them being dead wasn't hurting anyone… except Damien. He really is a lover and not a fighter in all aspects. He was the only one who held out hope that our mom would someday love us instead of her clothes and bags, and that our dad would be proud of us instead of Marco's nephews, Trent and Carter. After they were killed he wouldn't let us speak a bad word about them; he got very violent if we did."

I blinked my eyes in shock while Dominic nodded his head and said, "I know it's hard to think of him as being violent but after our parents were gone he just changed."

I felt sick as I listened to him, my heart hurt for Dominic and all his brothers. I just wanted to squeeze them all.

"Marco's nephew Carter doesn't look like the family at all, but he *is* evil like them and Trent was even *worse*. He really was a younger version of Marco in all aspects from looks to personality."

I furrowed my eyebrows.

"Was?" I questioned.

Dominic nodded, closed his eyes for a moment before opening them and locking his gaze on mine. "He is dead. His death is the reason my family is in debt to Marco."

"Do you owe him a lot of money or somethin'?" I asked, confused.

Dominic shook his head. "Not money but we do have to work off our debt to him. My brothers, bar Damien, have certain jobs they do for Marco. My job is fighting."

I frowned. "I don't understand. Why are you and your brothers in debt with Marco over his nephew's death?"

243

Dominic sighed. "We have to work for Marco in order to keep Damien safe."

I felt my heart stop. "Why just Damien? Why is he always singled out?"

"Because Damien is the reason why Trent is dead." Dominic watched me as he said, "He killed him."

CHAPTER TWENTY

"What did you just say?" I whispered, hoping I had heard him wrong.

Dominic lifted his hands to my face. "Please don't think less of him, Bronagh," he begged me. "You have to understand what our parents' death did to him, what it *still* does to him. You think you have problems with letting people get close to you? Damien barely loves me, and I'm his twin."

I widened my eyes. "Don't say that, he does love you. You just have to see you two together to see that."

Dominic sighed and rubbed my cheek with his thumb. "He has opened up a lot lately since we've been here. I know he hasn't forgotten our past, but he seems different here, he isn't as cold anymore."

I gave him a stern look and said, "Say that to the trail of heartbroken girls at our school and around town."

Dominic smiled a little. "He makes them no promises, Bronagh. Having sex is the only intimate thing he does with girls. He doesn't feel for them, he doesn't feel for anybody and not by choice; he's just hollow inside. He's a nice guy, but if you're looking for someone who is sensitive or someone to have a talk with about feelings and shit, you might as well pass him by because he doesn't do anything like that with anyone."

I held up my finger. "That is where you're wrong, dear boy-friend. He randomly told me the other day that I was growing on him and not just because I'm hot." I grimaced at the last part of my sentence, making Dominic snort.

"That's unheard of for him, babe. He never talks to girls much, unless he is hitting on them or fucking them."

I swallowed. "I'll consider myself very lucky then."

Dominic grinned at me. "You should. You're important to me, and he knows that. You don't know how happy it makes me feel knowing that my brother is coming out of his funk and it's because of my girl."

I shook my head. "I don't think it's because of me, I think it's because he sees that you're in a relationship and are happy—"

"I'm with you, and I'm happy because of you, so it's still down to you that he is coming around," Dominic cut me off.

I suppressed a beaming smile. "Yeah, well, I'm just happy he is thawin' out."

Dominic sighed. "I don't think he will ever thaw out completely, that shit with our parents and Trent really fucked him up."

I swallowed, then chewed on my lip a little before asking, "Can I ask why he…"

"Killed Trent?" Dominic finished my question for me.

I nodded and settled into his side when he motioned for me to do so.

"We turned fifteen two weeks before our parents were killed, over three and a half years ago, and Trent stood by us through it all. Carter did too for a time, but he was more of a loner unlike Trent. The three of us were practically best friends; we were raised together in the same environment, so he thought like we did and accepted the shit we had seen and done as normal. The only difference with him and us was that he enjoyed all the evil things, and we didn't.

"We never voiced it, because we didn't want to appear weak, but Dame and I talked some nights, and we both agreed the life our dad and Marco led wasn't for us. We were going to tell our dad that we wanted to leave New York and go anywhere else the day they died." Dominic frowned as he played with my hair.

"Damien didn't want to leave the compound we lived in after that day. All the things we talked about were forgotten because he wanted no part in them if it involved him leaving New York. He started to pull away from all of us, except Trent and Nala."

The female name peaked my interest. "Who is Nala?"

"Nala was Damien's girlfriend, but before that she was just the cute Asian chick who followed us everywhere," Dominic said, and he smiled like he was reliving a memory with Nala in it.

I smiled also then asked, "Is she a nice person?"

Dominic shrugged. "Her dad was into the same shit as my dad and Marco but she hated what he did for 'business' like Damien and I did. She was quiet but nice, and she had a thing for Damien. She said it was his blond hair that attracted her to him and that his— our—beautiful face had nothing to do it."

I snorted. "You vain fucker, you're makin' that up!"

Dominic grinned. "Okay, she never said we had a beautiful face, but she *was* obsessed with Dame's hair colour. She came to the compound when we were all around ten. Damien had a crush on her as well so when he asked her to be his girlfriend when we were thirteen and she said yeah it wasn't a surprise." He chuckled for a moment before sighing.

"The only thing that was a surprise was that Trent hated them together. I think he had a thing for Nala as well and was just jealous of her and Dame, but I'm not really sure if that is the exact reason." Dominic shrugged then stretched and settled back next to me.

"Dame and Nala were still together after our parents were killed but he eventually grew distant from her as well. No matter how hard she tried to help him feel better, she just couldn't. Trent was sort of her shoulder to lean on through that time; he made the mistake of trying to kiss her one night though. Damien saw the whole thing and went crazy. He attacked Trent and beat the shit out of him for touching his girl."

Dominic looked up to the ceiling then and tightened his hold on me. "I think he loved Nala. I know we were only kids, but they were dating for a solid two years and knew everything about each other and did everything together. They were literally the others half and were happy until all hell broke loose. After Trent tried to kiss her and Damien kicked his ass, he spewed a lot of bullshit towards Damien, and that only made him angrier. He said Damien wasn't good enough to be Nala's boyfriend and that he belonged in the ground with our traitorous father."

Dominic shook his head. "It was a bad thing to say to a friend over a girl. Don't get me wrong, Nala was great, but she was still a girl, and I found it stupid that they were fighting over her. Loyalty wise, though, I was pissed at Trent for trying something with my bro's girl. I didn't care what he called our dad but when he wished Damien were dead, I got my turn at kicking his ass. It was the first time I was ever in a fight and I beat the shit out of him. Damien got me off him, though, because he wanted to do it himself. I was fine with that 'cause I had gotten a few hits in. Trent got to his feet after Damien got me off him, and the crazy fucker pulled out a gun, a real fucking gun." I rubbed his arms when he started to get a little bit twitchy as he spoke which seemed to calm him down some.

"I wasn't afraid of being shot by him. I was afraid for Damien though, because Trent looked at him with such hatred before he pointed the gun at him. It was then that I knew how much he truly was like Marco. If Nala hadn't jumped on Trent's back and caused him to drop the gun, there is no doubt in my mind that he would have shot and killed Dame; I feel sick just thinking about it."

My eyes were wide.

"Where did he get a gun from?" I asked.

Dominic shrugged. "The compound we lived in never kept weapons or product onsite because we got raided a lot, but my guess is he swiped the licensed gun Marco kept in his office. After it was knocked out of Trent's hand it somehow ended up in Damien's hand, and that was when I started to panic. I still remember crying like a bitch for him to throw the gun away and that we weren't like our dad or Marco. He was listening to me until Trent laughed at me and called me a bitch like our dad, who deserved to be six feet under with lead in his head. Trent had already knocked Nala off him so when Damien fired the gun and hit Trent, she was safe from a follow through bullet." He shook he said, like he still couldn't believe what he was saying had actually happened.

"Trent was hit either in his heart or his shoulder. I couldn't tell because the blood that came from his wound soaked his shirt, so I couldn't pinpoint where he was hit. He wasn't moving so I guess Damien got him with one shot." Dominic shook his head then and cleared his throat. "Shit hit the fan after that. Everything went by fast, Marco had his boys clear the courtyard and wash away Trent's blood while he called the doctor but it was too late. We were told he was already dead by the time the doc got there. Ryder being the oldest out of us met with Marco to 'discuss' things. Ryder, Kane and Alec were already involved in the business but after Dame killed Trent, they were in even deeper.

"We weren't stupid; we knew that the meeting with Ryder and Marco was to keep us all alive. When Ryder came out of Marco's office he told us Damien was safe, but we had to work for that safety. I knew Marco wouldn't give anything unless he received something out of the deal, so I was game for working once I knew it would keep Dame safe."

I was surprised when he snorted but didn't interrupt him.

"I was expecting to run product and sell it or some shit like that, but Marco had certain 'jobs' for us all set out. I was apparently his main man; he is really into gambling and making his money in an exciting way, and it was around that time that underground fighting got big. He wanted a fighter in the underground to represent him, and after he watched the CCTV of me kicking Trent's ass that's what I became. We have been to more countries than I can remember in the last three and half years. It seems every couple of months Marco calls me and tells me about a new underground circuit that he wants me to represent him in.”

I gripped onto him as I felt my heart hammer into my chest. “He can call you whenever and tell you to leave here at any time to go to a different country to fight then, right? If he has done it in the past then he can do it again—”

“Bronagh,” Dominic cut me off and shook me. “Listen to me very carefully, I am *not* leaving you. Ireland is the last country I am fighting in. I already told Marco this, and he has agreed because he was getting bored with my fights since I always win. Apparently it’s not exciting unless I have an even match, and I’m fighting like an animal to please him. We’re all getting released from him after my current circuit is over. Another few weeks, and it’s all done with.”

I sat up and just looked at him. “So that’s it? Marco is going to let your family off the hook that easily? Damien *killed* his nephew.”

Dominic shrugged. “Men like Marco don’t care about family or honour. He knew that Ryder was planning to get us out of New York whether Damien wanted to leave or not, and after Trent was killed it was the perfect pitch for him to play and keep us with him.”

I pulled a face. “I hate him already, and I haven’t even met him.”

Dominic pulled my head down to his. “You won’t ever meet him either.”

I nodded. “Good.”

He brushed a light kiss over my mouth before pulling back. “Do you understand why I do what I do now?” he asked.

I nodded, again. “You’re protectin’ your brother.”

Dominic kissed my forehead. “I knew you would understand once I told you everything.”

I gave him a hard look. “That *is* everythin’, right? There is nothin’ else you’re keepin’ from me?”

He shook his head. “You know everything about my past, most of it isn’t even mine, it’s Damien’s, but you still know about it.”

I released a huge breath. “I do understand it, but I’m still pro-cessin’ it. It’s a big pill to swallow.”

Dominic rubbed my crossed legs. "I know, baby."

I remained quiet for a moment then asked, "Are you and Damien goin' to school as a cover for the 'family business' to make your family look normal?"

That question made him snicker.

"No, we *want* to go to school. It's the only normal thing in our lives that we can control."

I nodded then thought of his brothers.

"What do the other lads do for Marco if you fight for him?"

Dominic chewed on his lip before he said, "Kane is his debt collector and what Marco calls his bruiser. If someone is late on payments or just in need of a 'talking' to, then Kane is the man Marco sends in to get the job done."

I gasped. "But Kane is lovely!"

Dominic frowned. "You've seen his scars, he didn't get them from being *lovely*."

Holy shite!

Kane with his big beautiful smile had hurt people for this Marco creep. It was his bit to help keep Damien safe, I got that, but still, it was beyond shocking!

"Alec, what does he do?" I asked. "If you tell me that the flirt hurts people then I will go to the corner and just cry."

Dominic laughed. "Alec, fight people? Get real, he fucks Marco's problems away. Literally."

I stared at my boyfriend with wide eyes. "You better fuckin' explain that."

Dominic rubbed his eyes. "Marco deals in things from drugs to weapons to all types of entertainment, including, but not limited to, fighting and sex."

I stared at him still waiting for him to get to Alec's role in all this.

He scrubbed his face. "Alec is an escort for Marco's clients, Bronagh. Usually the wives or husband of his clients, his job is to keep them happy."

"What?" I screeched.

Dominic jumped with fright. "Out of everything I just told you, *that* is what freaks you out?"

No, but still!

"Alec is *gay*?" I asked, shocked beyond belief.

Dominic shook his head. "He is bisexual."

Oh, my God.

"I did not pick up on that at all, I thought he was straight," I stated.

Dominic snickered. "He loves pussy *and* cock, the greedy fucker simply can't choose between them."

I blinked at him then opened my mouth to speak only to close it again. Dominic laughed at this while I just sat next to him in shock.

"So you're an underground fighter; Kane is a bruiser and Alec is an… escort. Am I right so far?" I asked then shook my head.

There was a sentence I never thought I would hear myself say.

"Yeah, and Ryder runs drugs and weapons for Marco, so he is technically a drug and weapons dealer."

Oh, my fucking God!

"And Damien?" I squeaked.

"And Damien's nothin'," he said firmly. "He isn't involved with Marco. It's part of our deal to keep him safe. He keeps out of everything while we deal with it."

I blew out a breath. "Thank God *one* of you is normal."

Dominic moved and had me on my back with himself nestled between my legs in only a few seconds. "What's not normal about me, pretty girl?" he teased.

"You're supposed to be an eighteen-year-old foreign exchange student, *not* a secret underground fighter who is tied up with one of the most dangerous men in the entire world!" I wasn't shocked that my eyes filled with tears, and neither was Dominic because he had a bit of a grin on his face when my tears fell, which made me think of him as a huge bastard.

He pressed his forehead to mine. "I was wondering when the

tears were going to come. I'm surprised you got through me telling you everything without crying."

I sniffled, "Thanks for the vote of confidence."

He kissed my nose. "I know this shit is crazy and hard to believe and hard to accept, but I need you to trust me, okay? I know what I'm doing; I can handle this."

"I do trust you." I murmured. "I can't believe all this shite, but I trust you on it."

He kissed me then and kissed me hard, but stopped when I reached down and not so gently gripped his dick in my hand and squeezed.

"Fuck!" He growled. "Why are you doing that?"

I released him and grinned when he whimpered a little on top of me.

"You just told me some of the most shocking things I have ever heard in my entire life and you're trying to kiss me like *that* while I'm trying to process it? Get fucked."

Dominic was laughing and wincing at the same time when he rolled off me and cupped himself. "I live you, pretty girl," he said through his pain.

My lip twitched. "Live you too, Fuckface."

CHAPTER TWENTY-ONE

"This is the first time you have come to school on a Monday with no fresh bruises on your face in weeks," Miss McKesson said to me as I entered her classroom on Monday morning.

I was a little surprised that she was in class already; I was usually the first person in the room.

I forced a smile to the miss, but didn't say anything to her.

She nodded towards the door. "Will you pop down to the main hall and give Alannah and some of the others a hand with some things down there?"

I furrowed my eyebrows. "A hand with what? What is she doin' down there when school doesn't even start for another ten minutes?"

The miss smiled. "She and some other students are gettin' a head start on gettin' the hall ready for the Christmas concert. It's only a week away after all."

I widened my eyes. "Holy shite, the dates really got away from me. I had no idea Christmas was so close."

The miss frowned at me. "You have been a little detached in school lately so I'm not surprised some things slipped your mind."

I swallowed. "Some things at home had my attention, but everythin' is fine now." I shook my head and chuckled a little. "I feel like my head has been buried in the sand to not know it is almost Christmas time."

The miss snorted. "It happens to the best of us."

I nodded my head then looked to the door. "I'll go help Alannah and the others then."

The miss waved me on. "Brilliant, the rest of the class will be down to help when the bell rings in ten minutes."

I nodded and left the classroom. I headed down the empty hallways until I came to the main hall entrance. I thought it was funny that in ten minutes these hallways would be flooded with students, but now it was like a silent ghost town. When I entered the main hall it was anything but silent though.

I silently groaned when I spotted Micah bossing some of her friends and classmates around while Alannah was off to the side painting some of the Christmas posters. I would rather help out by doing something by myself but if I had to choose between helping Alannah or Micah, I would pick Alannah every time.

"Hey," I said when I got to her side.

She glanced at me and widened her eyes a little when she saw it was me standing next to her saying hello.

"Hey me?" she asked and glanced around us to see if I could be talking to someone else.

I nodded and she smiled wide. "Hey back, Bronagh. Are you here to help?"

I nodded again, and she clapped her hands together. "Brilliant, you can help me get this poster done if you want to? You don't have to, of course, you can do somethin' else if you want to be alone and—"

"Alannah," I cut her off, chuckling at her. "Helpin' with the poster is fine."

She stared at me. "Really? It is? You know I'll be here right next to you helpin' too, right?"

I smiled at her again. She was being very nice and considerate, offering me an out to work on my own so I wouldn't feel uncomfortable being so close to her, but it wasn't necessary. I didn't think

255

Alannah was the type to ask me a million questions or randomly strike up a conversation to fill the silence and that was a cool person by my standards.

"Yep, I'm aware that you will be next to me," I chuckled again.

Alannah only continued to stare at me, but when she blinked and shook her head a little she seemed to snap out of it. She turned and picked up a clean paintbrush then turned backwards in my direction and handed it to me.

"Thank you," I said.

Alannah just nodded and smiled before pointing to the blank section of the poster and pushed some red paint my way. "I was thinkin' you could fill in the title words with red paint then use a smaller brush to outline them in black paint? We can swap though if you want to?"

I looked at what she was doing and felt my jaw drop open. "Did you *draw* that reindeer?" I asked, my voice a little higher than it was a few seconds ago.

Alannah nodded. "I drew up all the posters with the art teacher, Mr. Wall, last week. No one else in art class wanted to help so it was just the two of us. I drew the animals and other little characters, and Mr. Wall did the all the wording in a stylish font and filled in the background with mistletoe and stuff. It turned out nice, didn't it?"

Understatement.

I nodded my head. "It really did. Seriously Alannah, it looks brilliant!"

She blushed and gave a modest shrug. "Thanks, I'm afraid I might ruin them with the paint so that's why it's takin' me awhile to paint them. I'm bein' *extra* careful," she chuckled.

I blew out a breath. "I'm goin' to get chairs for us to sit on while we paint 'cause there is less chance of us makin' a mistake that way."

Alannah gave me a thumbs up. "Good thinkin', Sherlock."

I grinned. "Anytime, Watson."

Alannah shook her head and laughed while I moved over to the folded up chairs hanging on their hooks on the hall wall and lifted two off. They were light chairs so carrying them wasn't a problem. When I got back to Alannah and our worktable, I opened them up and looked over to Micah and her crew as I did so. She was sitting cross-legged on the floor while she instructed her friends on what to do. They were decorating the big Christmas tree that goes to the back of the hall; it's huge so it has to go there. I shook my head at how bossy Micah was. She was literally directing where her friends placed decorations on the tree instead of helping herself and just placing them anywhere.

I turned back to Alannah, and we got to work on our poster. Five minutes passed by when the bell for first period rang aloud. I jumped a little, and almost went outside the lines with the red paint, making Alannah laugh.

"Fuck," I gasped.

"Shite," she cackled. "That was too close."

I lost it when she started laughing like that and burst into a fit of giggles which only made her point at me and laugh harder. We were still chuckling when shadows appeared over our worktop and, like a sixth sense; I knew he was there before I even looked to check.

"What do you want, stalker?" I asked without turning around while Alannah looked over her shoulder to see who was behind us.

She blushed a little before going back to her section of the poster after she had seen who was there. Her blush and small smile gave away that Damien was standing behind us as well. I've noticed her doing that a lot when he looked at her over the last few weeks in class.

"Stalker? If you're going to title me with something, I think you should go with magic fingers. Or tongue. I'm not fussy."

Damien laughed while Dominic grunted thanks to the elbow I threw back into his stomach. He put his arms around me and leaned his head down to kiss my cheek and nuzzle his nose into my neck, inhaling. I closed my eyes and embraced the butterflies that consumed my stomach.

I shivered when he nipped my neck with his teeth, which made me moan a little. I nudged his head with mine. "Go make yourself useful. You and Damien can help with the heavy liftin'."

Damien laughed and said, "You just want to see me work, pervert."

I shook my head slightly and glanced to his grinning face. We hadn't talked about any of the stuff that I was told last week, even though he knew I knew about what he did, and we didn't have to. It didn't change my opinion of Damien; he was still a sweetheart and was rapidly becoming one of my favourite people.

"Oh yeah, because you're so hot I just need to see that body of yours do some *hard* labour."

Damien shot me a smirk while Dominic bit my neck again. "Cut out the flirting."

I grunted. "If you make me mess up on this picture I am goin' to kick your arse."

Dominic stood up straight and leaned over to check out what I was doing and kissed me on the crown of my head. "It looks good, babe."

I pointed to Alannah. "She drew up all the posters, I'm just fillin' in the lines with paint."

Damien moved behind Alannah and looked at her section of the poster and whistled. "Damn, Lana, you drew these?"

Lana?

Alannah's face went purple. "No, not all by meself. Mr. Wall did the letters, mistletoe, and holly."

Damien grinned. "So you drew the awesome animals and characters?"

Alannah shrugged her shoulders so I reached over and shoved her a little. "Stop bein' so modest."

She pulled a face at me and then flicked her eyes up towards Damien who was still behind her looking down at her work. I thought it was some type of girl code gesture, but I honestly had no clue what it meant so I cleared my throat.

"Lads, go help the girls with the tree. We have this under control," I said and gestured them to move on.

Dominic crunched down to my side and nudged me with his forehead. "I missed you last night, again. I'm thinking of just sneaking into your room at night so I can be with you."

Was he trying to reduce me to an emotional mess?

I smiled and leaned into him. "It's probably best you don't stay over, I'm startin' to lose an ongoin' battle within myself, and you bein' next to me will make me cave instantly."

Dominic's eyes locked onto mine.

"What battle?" he whispered.

I smiled as I leaned in and licked his bottom lip. "A personal battle to *not* fuck you until we are together longer."

Dominic audibly groaned and latched onto my bottom lip with his teeth making me hiss in pain and him grin. "That will teach you to control that filthy mouth while we're in school."

I snapped my teeth at him making him grin as I said, "Go on, get."

"If I didn't know any better I would think you're trying to get rid of Dame and me."

I smiled. "Would I do such a thing?"

"Yes," Dominic and Damien said in unison.

"Go on, get," I repeated, shooing them away.

They both did as I asked and left chuckling.

I looked to Alannah who was also flicking her eyes over her shoulders watching the twins leave.

"What was that about?" I asked her.

"I was about to stop breathin'! Did you see how close he was to me?" she whispered.

I chuckled at her. "Yeah, he also called you Lana. Is that your preferred nickname or somethin'?" I asked.

She shrugged. "No one has ever called me that but Damien. He randomly started callin' me that last week in class. I like it though, I've never had a nickname."

I smiled and stored that bit of information away. "So if I said you liked him—"

"You would be absolutely correct, but *please* don't tell him or Nico, I try me best not to be obvious about it," she said and flicked her eyes around us making sure we were still out of hearing range.

I raised my eyebrow at her. "Why not just be honest with him?"

She sighed. "You know he doesn't do relationships. He has been with more girls than I care to count since he moved here, and even though I really like him, I'm not about to be added to his 'hit' list."

I laughed at her meaning but nodded my head. "I understand what you mean. Dominic was a slut, too, before we got together. If he can change, then so can Damien. Don't give up hope is all I'm sayin'."

Alannah sighed and went back to painting. I joined her but kept flicking my eyes towards her every so often.

"What?" she eventually asked me with a sigh.

I smiled to her. "I didn't say anythin'."

"Why are you lookin' at me and smilin' then?" she asked.

I shrugged and gestured to what we were doing. "I kind of like this."

"Paintin'?" Alannah questioned.

"The paintin' is fun but I meant the talkin' part with you. It's nicer than I thought it would be," I admitted.

Alannah laughed. "I'm not like everyone else in school, Bronagh. I don't judge you because you prefer to be on your own. If it makes you happy, then leave you be I say."

"I always liked you for that; you always respected me and never bugged me into talkin', makin' friends, or doin' anythin' to make me uncomfortable," I said, smiling wide only to frown and blow out a big breath.

"I wasn't happy on my own though; being with Dominic is makin' me realise I wasn't really livin' at all, I was just existin' and not even in a fun way. I am literally way out of my comfort zone by bein' with him, and every day I'm venturin' further away from it. I mean, an example is just sittin' here and talkin' with you. Oh and a bigger example is that Gavin Collins is me friend now, how crazy is that?"

Alannah smiled. "Not crazy, just extremely lucky because Gavin is a hottie!"

I laughed. "I agree. I can try and set somethin' up for you—"

"Oh, Jesus, no!" Alannah cut me off, making me laugh.

She smiled at me then. "I appreciate the offer to help, I really do, but since I can't have the one person I want in the way I want him, I'm just gonna steer clear of lads and focus on preparin' for the Leavin' Cert. It's only six months away, after all."

I groaned.

"*Why* did you have to tell me that?" I whined.

Alannah rolled her eyes. "Oh, shut up! You're probably the most prepared student for those exams out of the entire group of sixth years!"

My lip twitched. "Okay, I'm probably a *bit* more prepared, because before Dominic happened I literally just did school work and revision all the time, but now that he is in me life I've noticed that I haven't picked up a book in weeks! Havin' a boyfriend durin' this year in school is probably goin' to kill me."

Alannah flicked her eyes over my shoulder and a bit to the right then chewed on her lip. "Because he distracts you?" she asked, still looking in that direction.

I nodded. "Yeah, he distracts me big time."

Alannah snorted then. "You aren't the only one he distracts."

I furrowed my eyebrows in confusion then turned to see what she was looking at. I blew a large amount of air out through my nose and folded my arms angrily across my chest as I watched my boyfriend and his brother being stared at by twenty or more female students... and one or two male ones!

Dominic, Damien, and a bunch of other lads from the sixth year class were helping hang up finished posters around the hall. They were up on ladders or each other's shoulders to get them to where they needed to be on the wall. Dominic and Damien didn't use a ladder though; Damien was standing on Dominic's shoulders while he reached up and pinned the posters to the wall.

When Damien reached up you could see the flex of the muscles in his back contract with each movement. On Dominic you could see his biceps practically ripping through his already too tight school shirt, because he had them completely tense and flexed as he braced his body against the wall so he could hold Damien up. I didn't understand why they had their school jumpers off in the first place, but I didn't really care about that. I cared about the tilted heads bluntly staring at my man's body!

"I could slap them all," I grunted.

Alannah laughed. "I'm jealous of those bitches checkin' Damien out and he isn't even mine, so I can only imagine how you feel about them checkin' out your actual fella. I guess this is a downfall in goin' out with someone who is so good-lookin'."

I sighed. "You don't know the half of it."

Alannah chuckled. "I'm goin' to get some more brown paint. I'll mix up some others for us in the art room and be back in a second."

I nodded and didn't pay any attention to Alannah as she grabbed some stuff and moved towards the entrance of the hall. I was too busy watching the girls in the hall watch Dominic but the crashing noise from the hallway outside got my attention... and so did the shouting.

No one else in the hall seemed to hear it over all the voices and music but I could. The fact that Alannah had just went out there made me a little worried so before I even thought about it I got up and headed out into the hallway.

When I got outside I was more than shocked to see Micah standing over Alannah and squirting what was left in her almost empty paint bottles onto her hair, face, and uniform.

"There bitch, I'll pay for my uniform to be cleaned and you can pay for yours. Watch where you're fuckin' goin' next time, look up when you're walkin' instead of down at the ground!" Micah snapped.

I was so disgusted with what I was seeing, but when Alannah sniffled and rubbed her face to try and stop her tears from falling, I became furious.

"Who the fuck do you think you are?" I snapped and rushed forward, shoving Micah in the back and knocking her and Alannah onto the ground.

I quickly reached down and helped Alannah to her feet. She was crying and had paint everywhere. Her hair was messed up like it had been pulled on, and I instantly knew who caused that. I turned to Micah who was getting to her feet and brushing herself off.

"Mind your own business, this has *nothin'* to do with you!" Micah snapped at me.

I glared at her and didn't move an inch. "It *is* me business when you hurt me friend."

"*Your friend?* Since when do *you* have a friend?" Micah scoffed.

I was about to reply when I felt a hand on my shoulder.

"Since now," Alannah's voice answered.

I looked over my shoulder and smiled at her tear and paint streaked face.

"Isn't that touchin', a loner and a book lover are friends. Excuse me while I puke."

I shook my head when Micah brushed by us.

"Leave us alone, Micah. We won't bother you, and you won't bother us from now on. Deal?" I said to her when she paused by the main hall entrance.

She looked at me for a long moment before nodding her head and saying, "Just stay out of me way and we won't have problems."

I didn't know why but in that moment I knew she wouldn't bother me anymore and not because Dominic warned her not to, but because I stood up for myself. She didn't know how to react.

It was a great feeling, not only would she be staying away from me but Destiny hadn't so much as looked in my direction since our spat in the hall a few weeks ago. Both girls had been problems over the last few weeks, and I could breathe easy now knowing that those problems wouldn't come about ever again.

Even dickhead Jason hadn't muttered an insult my way in ages. Sure he still glared at me and probably thought all sorts of horrible things, but he didn't voice them anymore, and he didn't bug me which was just Heaven. I knew him staying away from me was *completely* due to Dominic but whatever; once he kept to himself I was happy.

When Micah went inside the hall the noise of the door shutting got my attention. I fully turned to Alannah and sighed. "She is such a bitch, she got paint everywhere."

Alannah surprised me then by wrapping her arms around my body and pressing her cheek to mine. "Thank you."

I felt a huge wave of emotion suddenly hit me so I hugged her back. I felt like the last layer of the brick wall I had built up so long ago around my heart just came crashing down, and it felt good, really good. "No problem, that's what friends are for, right? We look out for each other."

Alannah pulled back from me and smiled. "Right."

When she got a good look at me, she burst out laughing. "I got a bit of paint on you."

I looked down to my uniform and laughed as well; she got more than a bit on me. I reached up to my face, touching my cheek then looked to my now blue fingers. I laughed as I looked to myself and to Alannah. "We look gorgeous."

"Stunners is what we are," she sarcastically replied then bent down to pick up her things.

I helped her then went with her to the art room so she could re-fill the paint bottle and mix the new colours we needed for the rest of the posters we had to do. I was looking around the art room while Alannah was busy and read the label on some of the new paint bottles.

"It says that all the paint is clothes friendly and can be washed out of fabrics," I said aloud then looked to Alannah.

She nodded. "I know, I tried to tell Micah that but she didn't listen. She just pushed me down and pulled my hair."

"What a cunt," I grunted making Alannah laugh.

I chuckled along with her then helped her carry the paint and some clean brushes and palettes back to the main hall.

"Girls, what happened?" Miss McKesson's voice shouted when we entered the hall.

This got everyone's attention to fall on us.

Alannah looked at me with a panicked face, so I put on a playful one and said, "Things got a bit wild in the art room while we were mixin' some paint but don't worry, nothin' was damaged. Well, not beyond repair anyway."

Miss McKesson shook her head and waved us on as she chuckled.

Alannah and I blew out a breath and headed back over to our section where our posters still awaited us. We were sorting out our things when I felt a presence beyond me followed by a shadow falling over my worktop.

"Is there a reason why Micah is covered in paint and has a mad look about her?" Dominic's voice asked.

I turned around and smiled widely at him. "I have no idea what you're talkin' about, boyfriend."

He smirked at me and flicked his eyes over my face then down to the front of my uniform. He looked to Alannah as well; who made a big show of looking around like Damien wasn't standing directly in front of her asking why her eye was swelling.

I grabbed Alannah's hand and tugged her to me then murmured, "You said she just pulled your hair! Did she punch you in the face too?"

"Just once but it's fine," she murmured back.

"You know we can hear everything you're saying," Damien's voice interrupted our murmuring chat.

I looked to him then to Dominic, who stood like he was waiting for an explanation.

I glared at him. "Don't give me that look. Micah was hittin' her over a stupid accident, like I'm goin' to stand by and not help me friend out when she needs me!"

Dominic simply beamed at me as he said, *"Friend?"*

I felt myself flush. "Yeah, we're friends, it's not *that* shockin'!"

He laughed, reached forward and pulled me into him.

"I'm gettin' paint on you," I gasped.

"It's school paint, it will wash out," he replied.

"If only Micah had that logic," Alannah mumbled making me laugh.

I glanced at her and watched as she blatantly ignored Damien's attempts at flirting to get her attention. I grinned when he frowned at the back of her paint stained head; he looked so confused as to why he didn't have her attention. The poor sod didn't realise he wasn't going to get her for the dirty romp he wanted.

"I'm going to finish helping with hanging up the posters," Damien said to the back of Alannah's head.

"Bye," Alannah chirped and began lowly singing along to the song that was playing through the speakers in the hall.

Damien grunted then turned and walked off. No, more like stormed off.

"What's eating him?" Dominic murmured as he watched his brother walk away.

I tugged on Dominic's shirt for his attention, and when I got it, I flicked my eyes Alannah's way. "He wants someone he can't have," I whispered.

Dominic looked to Alannah and then to Damien, who was already straight into flirting with girls across the hall, probably to make himself feel better about Alannah ignoring him.

Dominic fully smiled when he looked back to me. "You made a friend and stood up to Micah. Damien got shut down by a girl and I haven't gotten into a fight this week. What the hell is happening around here?"

I chuckled and hugged him tight. "Things are changin' for the better," I said as I flicked my eyes to my new friend then to Damien, who was watching her from across the hall with a look of determination about him. "*Definitely* for the better."

CHAPTER TWENTY-TWO

"Bronagh?" Dominic's voice called from downstairs.

I peeked my head from under the covers of my bed. "What?" I shouted back.

"Come here!" he shouted even louder.

I groaned as I pushed my blankets from my body and got out of my bed. I slipped my feet into my fuzzy slippers and walked zombie-like out of my room, down the hall, and down the stairs. No one was in the sitting room so I went into the kitchen and froze when I caught sight of all the Slater brothers seated at my kitchen table. They made the room look tiny.

"Is someone dead?" I asked, wariness in my voice.

Ryder gave me a weird look. "No, why?"

I shrugged. "The last time this many people were sat around me kitchen table was when a bunch of people were tellin' me that me ma and da were gone to Heaven and wouldn't be comin' home. I was young, but I still knew that meant they were dead."

Ryder blinked at me while the others just looked at me with different expressions on their faces.

"Then of course the Garda tried to take me away and put me into care, and that resulted in Branna almost gettin' arrested for assaultin' a Garda," I smirked making the five brothers snort and laugh as well.

"How come she wasn't charged?" Damien asked me as I turned and began looking through the fridge for something to eat.

"They said she was shocked over our parents death and that someone tryin' to take me from her was askin' to be punched in the face, which is exactly what Branna did." I stood up when I had the makings for a sandwich and turned to Ryder with a grin on my face. "She used to kickbox before our parents died, so remember that when you make her mad."

Ryder laughed and rubbed his jaw. "I could have done with knowing that information a few months ago."

I smiled. "She has a mean right hook, huh?"

Ryder pouted and nodded, making his brothers laugh. I chuckled as well then turned and began making my sandwich.

"What has you all here tonight? Do you all have a night off from criminal activities or somethin'?" I asked and was met with complete and utter silence.

I looked over my shoulder and smiled to the wide-eyed stares looking back at me. "I know a creepy man, Mr. Doyle, down the road in an apartment complex who stares for too long if you all need to scratch a need-for-crime itch. I'll turn a blind eye while you deliver it as well, won't rat or anythin'."

Alec was the first to smile at me. "You're a regular fucking comedian aren't you?"

I snorted. "Yep, because I insinuated you, Mr. Escort, would be *kickin'* someone's arse instead of *fuckin'* it."

I couldn't hear Alec's reply because the rest of the brothers burst out laughing and banged on the table with their hands.

When my sandwich was made I picked it up and bit into it before turning around and leaning against the counter while I looked at the still chuckling group of brothers. Dominic was smiling wide at me, which made me straighten up.

"What?" I asked him nervously.

"Oh, look at her face, she is nervous that little brother will redden that ass," Kane teased.

I looked at Kane and gave him an are-you-serious look. "The day he spanks me arse is the day pigs fly."

All the lads oh'd and teased Dominic saying I was challenging him, which only caused Dominic to stand up and shake his arms and legs out which instantly made me place my sandwich on the counter so I could have free hands.

"You want some of this, stretch? Let's go," I said, and put my hands up into fists, which only made the lot of them crack up laughing again.

Dominic all but fell back into his chair while Damien was falling against him from laughing so hard. I turned back to my sandwich, but just as I was about to pick it up, I heard the noise of a chair scrap against the floor and then felt pain as it filled my behind.

"Ow, that sounded like a sore spanking," Ryder laughed.

"Oh, is that a pig I see flying across the night sky?" Alec snickered.

I ignored them both as I turned and dove on Dominic who was behind me and ready to grab me. The fucker was so fast; he blocked every single one of my attempts at hitting him. Even trying to kick him failed miserably. The laughing from the lads and Dominic's smug face reduced me to tears. Fake tears, of course.

I covered my face with my hands and cried into them and turned myself outwards from Dominic's body. It took only three or four seconds for silence to fill the room and for Dominic to tense around me.

"Shit, babe, I'm sorry I didn't mean to—oft!" Dominic grunted as I delivered him a gut full of elbow.

He was gasping for air as he bent forward trying to ease the pain, but I only heightened his pain by hitting him down below. I didn't hit him hard in any sense, but he still dropped to his knees and groaned like he was dying. All his brothers groaned and grabbed between their legs as if they could feel his pain. I rolled my eyes and stepped away from Dominic. I picked up my sandwich and continued to eat it until I was finished.

"You're an evil woman," Alec said and winced as he looked at his little brother on the floor.

I smiled at Alec who shivered as if I was creeping him out.

"I think I am in love with you," Damien said to me, his tone one of awe.

I snorted. "Love you too, Dame."

I widened my eyes a little because even though I said it playfully, I did actually love him. I loved him and his brothers like they were *my* brothers.

This knowledge made my heart beat faster and caused a feeling of happiness settle over me, and I really liked it. I loved that by caring for other people it was making me feel so complete. I didn't know why I had hidden from these feelings for so many years.

Damien winked at me while Dominic carefully got himself to his feet and stepped towards me, wincing as he wrapped himself around me. "I'm in pain," he groaned into my hair.

I rolled my eyes and put my arms around his waist and rubbed his back. "It'll teach you not to spank me ever again, won't it?"

"Yeah," Dominic answered in unison with his brothers.

I looked around Dominic and raised my eyebrows at them. "Why are you all sayin' yeah?"

Ryder shrugged at me and said, "We all just learned never to smack your ass even if we're playing, because the repercussions will be deadly."

I snorted and turned back behind Dominic who still had his head bent down pressed against my hair. I nudged him until he turned his head a little and gave me access to his cheek, which I kissed before I leaned up to his ear and whispered, "I'll kiss it better for you later."

Dominic increased the tightness of his hold on me as he growled, which made me laugh. He was trying to kiss me then but I ducked and weaved so he couldn't.

"Why are you all here? Where is me sister?" I asked aloud when Dominic gave up trying to get a kiss and put his face back down in my hair.

"She is gone to pick up Alannah," Ryder answered me.

Alannah?

"*My* Alannah?" I asked.

Dominic chuckled into my hair as he slid his hands down to my behind and began to rub the sting from his slap away only to receive a nip on the shoulder from me, which he found funny.

"Yeah, *your* Alannah," Damien answered me.

"Why?" I asked. "It's half eleven at night!"

"We're going to Darkness," Dominic murmured into my hair.

I pulled back away from him until he was looking at my face. "It's Wednesday, not Friday."

Dominic grinned. "So?"

I grunted. "Do you not only fight on a Friday?"

He shrugged. "I fight whenever Marco calls me and tells me I'm fighting."

I frowned. "I'm so sorry. I wouldn't have hurt you if I knew you were fightin'."

"Calm it, I'm fine." Dominic said. "Barely felt a thing."

"You were just lying on the floor groaning in pain for show then?" Damien asked.

Dominic cut his eyes to his twin and nodded. "Yup."

Damien and his brothers shook their heads at Dominic's obvious lie while I looked down to my pyjamas and yelped as I moved Dominic out of my way. "I have to get dressed!" I shouted and ran all the way up to my bedroom with Dominic's laughter following me.

I pulled out a royal blue dress from my wardrobe that Branna got me while she was shopping last week and grabbed my usual black heels and little clutch thing to go with it. The clutch was pointless; it was always empty since I held my phone in my hand, but Branna made me carry it anyway.

The top of the dress was fitted and tight while the bottom was loose and swayed nicely and came up to my mid-thigh. The thing I loved about it besides the colour was that it was backless; it really was absolutely gorgeous.

I stripped out of my pyjamas, changed my underwear, and froze when I heard my door creak open.

"Oh, *hell yes*," Dominic's voice growled as my door clicked shut.

I turned to him and just stared at him while I was naked except for my knickers being on. Dominic was looking at my breasts then my hips, legs and back up again. I forced myself not to cover my chest or my stomach, because the look on his face in that moment made me feel absolutely beautiful.

I smiled at him. "Don't be gettin' ideas, I have to get dressed."

He took a step towards me so I took one back. He grinned as he took another step forward, and I again took a step back.

"Dominic, don't!" I screamed with laughter as he lunged forward and lifted me into his arms. I screamed again when he all but jumped with me in his arms until we landed on the bed. I grunted and tried to shove him off me, but he grabbed my hands and pinned them above my head with his right hand while his left was roaming freely over my body. I felt my nipples pebble and was uncomfortable with the pain so I tried to rub myself against Dominic's chest, hoping his t-shirt would lessen the ache.

He chuckled at me and moved back a little so his chest was out of my reach. I groaned and gave him a pleading look, which caused him to smile before he dipped his head and encased my left nipple in his mouth.

"Fuck!" I hissed as his warm, wet tongue swirled around causing an eye rolling sensation to wash over me. I bucked up against him when he switched breasts and showed the same care and attention to my right nipple.

I was panting and trying to squeeze my thighs together but groaned out loud, because Dominic's body was between my legs preventing that from happening. I tried pulling my hands free so I could touch my fingers against my clit to see if it would stop the throbbing. Dominic let my left hand go and without a single thought I reached down into my knickers and started to rub my clit better.

"Fuck me," Dominic breathed as he sat back on his heels and just watched me masturbate. I felt too good to be embarrassed or stop what I was doing. If anything, I was more turned on as Dominic's gaze stayed locked onto my hand between my legs.

"You look beautiful," Dominic growled as he sucked his bottom lip into his mouth.

I moaned, wanting to feel his mouth on mine.

"Kiss me," I panted.

Dominic crawled up next to me, propped himself up on his elbow and leaned his head to kiss me. His lips were the only part of his body touching me, and it was driving me crazy.

"Oh, please," I moaned into his mouth.

He pulled back a little and glanced down at my rotating wrist and grinned. "You don't want to make yourself come?" he asked me.

I shook my head. "You. Please."

He smiled. "You want me to—"

"Make me come," I cried out.

With a growl Dominic pulled my hand out of my knickers and replaced it with his own. He dipped his fingers into me, swirling them to get them wet before he quickly moved to my clit and rubbed at an even faster pace than I was previously doing. I felt myself go cross-eyed, and my legs opened wider than they already were.

"Yes, YES!" I cried out, only to be silenced by Dominic's mouth as it covered mine.

I bucked up into Dominic's hand when it happened. A hot, burning sensation spread throughout my core; my eyes rolled back, and I stopped breathing. My body jerked and twisted under Dominic's hold until the wave of pleasure that hit had washed away.

"Oh, my God," I whispered when I came to.

Dominic nuzzled his nose with mine and lightly kissed my lips. "I love making you come and watching you come, it's the most beautiful thing I have ever seen. You're fucking perfect." He pressed his forehead against mine then and smiled. "You're everything to me, pretty girl."

I lifted my hands up, encircled his neck and held tight as I made eye contact with him. I let out a relaxed sigh and smiled as I said, "I love you."

I was momentarily worried when those words left my mouth because we hadn't been together what was considered long enough to have feelings like love. I couldn't help it though. It was a fact that I wholeheartedly knew I loved him. It had hit me full force, and I decided that I never ever wanted to be without him. He was it for me and the look of awe on his face touched my heart so much that I just needed to be with him completely, in every single way. I should feel terrified that this had actually happened to me but I didn't. It felt amazing to feel this way for someone.

"Bronagh, I—"

"Make love to me," I breathed.

He widened his eyes and *really* looked at me before he said, "Are you sure you want this?"

I nodded and smiled. "I want this more than you can ever imagine, I *need* this to happen."

He looked at me for a second longer before he moved his mouth down and kissed me. He kissed me for a few minutes before he stood up off the bed and began pulling his shirt off. I quickly got up and stopped him though, I wanted to undress him and touch him.

"Let me," I whispered.

Dominic didn't smile, he only removed his hands from the hem of his tee and watched me with such intensity that I began to shake. I gripped the hem of his tee and slowly lifted it up and over his head. When his torso was bare, I ran my hand up his arms admiring the ink on his skin, and then moved them down his chest and across his abs.

"I love these," I whispered.

I felt hands slide up my thighs and around to my behind and after a tight squeeze of each cheek Dominic growled, "I love these."

I smiled and lowered my hands to his belt buckle. My breath picked up when I undid the button and zip to his jeans. He lowered his jeans, and then stepped out of them. I didn't make a move to lower his boxer briefs so Dominic lifted my hands and guided me to lower them with him.

"You're hard," I said, my voice a little breathless as we lowered his underwear.

Dominic lowered his head and nuzzled his face into my neck then said, "I'm always hard when I'm with you, when I see you... when I think of you."

My heart began to beat faster. "Babe," I whispered.

He reached down to his jeans and pulled out his wallet and took a condom packet out from the back of it, which made my breath quicken.

"Lay back for me, pretty girl."

I did as he asked and lay back on my bed. Dominic kept eye contact with me when he reached for the hem of my underwear and lowered them until they slid over my ankles and then off onto the floor. He dropped his eyes then and spread my legs. He groaned as he bent forward and pressed a kiss to each of my inner thighs, then centred his mouth over me and flicked his tongue over my clit. I groaned then reached down and gripped his hair with my right hand, I went to the hospital the other day and got the all clear on it. It was healed fine.

"Dominic," I groaned, "I need you inside me. *Now*!"

He shushed me. "I need you fully ready before you take my cock, pretty girl. It's might hurt and I want to lessen that if I can."

He sucked my clit into his mouth then and it caused me to almost come up off the bed. He entered a finger into me then and slowly pumped in and out. I jerked when he curved his fingers inside me like a hook and rubbed it against a part of me that made me scream into my hands after I quickly covered my mouth. I began to panic then, because whatever Dominic was doing made me feel amazing but also like I wanted to pee so when I thought that was about to happen I told him to stop, but he instead nipped my clit with his teeth and the pain of that mixed with the pleasure sent me into a whirlwind of fucking brilliance. I barely registered that Dominic was moving over me, but I did register when he slowly pushed inside me, because I felt the pain and pressure through my orgasm.

"Ow," I cried but bucked my hips up to meet him because I was still riding out my orgasm as he pushed inside me.

"Shhh," Dominic whispered and kissed me all over my face.

After he fully pushed inside me and was buried up to the hilt, he stayed put and didn't move. The only part of him that moved was his mouth as he kissed all over my face. I melted when he kissed the tiny tears that gathered in the corners of my eyes and I wrapped my arms around his back and pressed my nails into his shoulders making him growl.

I nudged his face with mine until he pulled back and looked at me, "You can move," I said quietly.

He very carefully pulled out then thrust back in. I groaned and threw my head back trying to decipher what my body was feeling. I felt mellow and relaxed but also slightly uncomfortable. I wasn't going to lie and say having sex for the first time with Dominic was amazing sensation wise, because it wasn't. I could feel him stretching me as he moved in and out. That didn't feel like anything other than pressure and slight pinching pain. What I would say, despite being uncomfortable, was that it was the best thing that I had ever experienced.

My heart was so full with the knowledge that I was giving away something precious to me to someone I wanted to be with as long as I lived. This was the moment I read about in books and had seen in films. I knew I *really* was in love with him and knowing that couldn't have made me happier.

I lifted my head to kiss Dominic, but he had me completely pressed back into the mattress as he thrust in and out of me. I could see the sweat bead around his forehead and felt it gather on his back. He was grunting and shivering as he moved inside me.

"Are you okay?" he whispered to me when our eyes locked.

I nodded. "I'm perfect, *this* is perfect."

I jerked a little then when he changed the angle of his hips as his cock thrust inside me, touching the spot that his finger had found a few minutes ago. The sensation suddenly changed from pinching pain and pressure to pure toe curling ecstasy.

"Oh, what is that?" I moaned.

"That," Dominic said when he thrust forward and watched me shiver in pleasure, "is your g-spot, baby."

Damn.

"It feels *so* good!" I panted, and then groaned when he hit the spot again as he thrust into me.

"You feel so fucking good, baby, your pussy is wrapped around my cock like a vice," Dominic grunted as he dipped his head down and encased my left nipple in his mouth.

I gasped. "Yes, YES!"

He released my nipple with a pop and moved his head directly over mine. "You like that? You like me fucking this pretty little pussy?"

I frantically nodded my head, his dirty words turning me on.

He thrust into me hard and growled, *"Tell me."*

"Yes," I cried out. "I love it, don't stop."

He lowered his head and sucked my bottom lip into his mouth. "Not a fucking chance, pretty girl."

I began to pant and even though I was tired I forced my body to move in time with Dominic's thrusts so I met him for each one.

"Can I fuck you harder?" Dominic suddenly asked though his voice sounded strained.

This wasn't hard?

"Yes," I breathed.

The next thrust he delivered caused a loud slapping noise to fill the room. As his body connected to mine, the vibrations it sent up my body had me twisting under him.

"Oh, God. Yes!" I growled and clawed at Dominic's back, which only made him kiss and thrust into me harder.

"I love you, Bronagh," he growled then pumped harder, his fast-paced thrusts now matching my hammering heart.

"Fucking." Thrust. "Love." Thrust. "You." Thrust.

I wrapped my legs around his hips and screamed, "I love you, too."

Six thrusts later Dominic came. His head was thrown back, his eyes were closed, and his body slightly jerked and spasmed. After a minute or so he carefully withdrew from me and just as I was about to sit up and embrace him with a hug, he pushed me back down and zeroed his mouth between my legs.

I gasped. "*What* are you doin'?"

"You didn't come," Dominic replied as he worshiped my clit with his mouth, but stayed away from my entrance after he inserted a finger and I hissed a little from its tenderness.

"I came… *twice*." I panted out my words because the pressure of his tongue started to put me on edge again.

"You come first and you come last, *always*!" Dominic said, then reached his hands up and encased my breasts with them.

He rolled my nipples between his fingers and sucked a little harder on my clit. My heart was hammering against my chest and my body felt like it was about to explode. Dominic chose this moment to pinch my nipples and nip my clit with his teeth, which not only sent me over the edge, but fucking threw me over. I thought I screamed and said 'oh, my God' a hundred or so times but when I opened my eyes and found Dominic's face looking back at mine, I smiled and forgot about everything but him.

"Love you," he said, and then kissed me.

I kissed him back, but half-arsed at best because I was completely spent.

Dominic chuckled into my mouth and reached down to my now overly sensitive clit and gave it a pinch, which made me shoot up off the bed and sway on my feet until Dominic jumped up laughing and steadied me.

I sagged into him and yawned. "I'm so tired, can we sleep?"

Dominic kissed the crown of my head. "I wish I could keep you naked in here for days, babe, but I have a fight in an hour."

I groaned making him chuckle then yawn himself. I looked up to him, lifted my hand then pressed my fingers into his mouth making him jump back and me laugh. "Yawn rape," I chuckled.

Dominic growled. "That was evil!"

I smiled, sweetly. "But you still love me, right?"

He moved back to me, brushed my hair out of my eyes, and kissed my nose. "Yeah, I still love you."

I beamed. "Good, 'cause I sort of love you too."

Dominic closed his eyes and leaned his forehead down until it was against mine. He opened his eyes and grinned when I pinched his arse and told him to get dressed. I watched him as he removed the used condom, tied a knot in it, and threw it in my bin. I had to tell him to get dressed again and this time he did as asked while watching me get dressed. He helped me put my dress on and then tried to talk me out of it.

"I want to fuck you again," he snarled.

"You won't be gettin' near me until me vagina stops throbbin', so back off!" I laughed then went into the bathroom.

I came back into the room when I was all cleaned up and looked to him. "I'm bleeding a little."

Dominic frowned. "I hurt you."

I rolled my eyes. "You took me virginity is all."

Saying that out loud was so surreal.

He glanced to me. "One of the many precious gifts you have given me."

I raised my eyebrows. "One of *many*?"

Dominic nodded. "Yup, your virginity is one. Your love is another. Your future vows to me will be a big one but the best one of all will be a baby."

What?

I stared at him. "You want marriage *and* babies with me?"

"I want *everything* with you. You *are* my everything," Dominic replied and reached for me when my bottom lip started to wobble.

"Don't cry," he chuckled.

I squeezed him to me. "I really do love you."

I did, I really did.

"I love you too, pretty girl," he said, then stood up and took me with him. "Now finish getting dressed. I want to get to the club early so I can get a quick session in to warm me up."

I frowned. "You said before that sex before a fight is bad. Maybe you should call up Marco and tell him you can't fight tonight."

Dominic snorted. "And say what? I can't fight, because I had mind-blowing sex with my girlfriend? Yeah, he will *love* that."

Mind-blowing was a perfect word to describe that experience.

"All I'm sayin' is—"

"Can you drop this, please?" Dominic cut me off with a grunt. "Don't annoy me with talk of Marco after making me so happy."

I gave him a look and said, "Shut up with the backtalk, if I wanted lip from you, I'd sit on your face."

He choked on air as he looked at me with wide eyes, making me laugh. He shook off his shock and was about to say what I was sure was a dirty reply, but I held my hand up, which stopped him from speaking, and said, "I just don't want you to get hurt, that's all."

Dominic smiled at me as he moved towards me and engulfed me in his arms. "Don't worry, I'll be fine. I haven't lost a fight yet, and I'm not going to start on the best night of my life. I've got this, baby."

I hoped he was right.

CHAPTER TWENTY-THREE

"**A**ll I'm saying is little brother has skills that he *obviously* picked up from me. His girl called out to God more times than I could count. He was in control of that puss—"

"Finish that sentence, you slapper, and I will end you!" I snarled to Alec, who had not stopped teasing me since I emerged from my bedroom with Dominic to leave for Darkness.

Apparently everyone heard mine and Dominic's first time together, and it mortified me. Of course, Dominic received high-fucking-fives from his brothers. After Branna and Alannah arrived, they saw to me to make sure I was feeling okay after I told them what the lads were teasing me about. It was just so wrong, I felt so uncomfortable that everyone knew I had sex and was no longer a virgin. I planned on buying a fucking gag to shut me up in the future because enduring this humiliation was just horrible.

I was red-faced talking to Alannah, which she found hilarious. We were friends now but hadn't built up a solid bond or anything like that yet. It was technically our fifth real conversation since we became friends last week, and I had to deal with the fact that she knew in graphic detail what Dominic and I did in my bedroom thanks to his stupid brothers. Damien was the only one telling them to shut up, and I wanted to squeeze him because of it. It was baffling to me that he killed a person; he was a flat-out sweetheart!

We had been at Darkness for about twenty minutes. The music was pounding, people were dancing and Dominic was shadow boxing in the corner near the circle to 'get warm', or something like that. I was shattered and a bit tender and sore. I was sitting in a large booth with Alannah, Branna, and the lads and I forced myself not to lean my head on Kane's shoulder because he was sitting next to me and was slouched down so his shoulder was at my head height. It was as if he was tempting me to use him as a pillow.

"I should have stayed at home," I yawned and stretched.

Alannah, who was on her second vodka and Coke, snapped her head to me and rolled her eyes. "Have a drink and loosen up. This is fun!"

I gave her a look. "We have school in the mornin' so I'm passin' on havin' a drink. You should just stop altogether; you're goin' to be dyin' with a hangover when you wake up otherwise."

Alannah blew me a kiss. "Thanks Ma, I'll keep that in mind."

The cheeky sod!

"Bitch," I grunted, making her laugh and me grin.

I liked this; she was so easy to talk with and didn't get offended when I called her names which was brilliant because, at one stage or another, I called everyone a bitch.

"Let's dance," Alannah announced to me because Branna was now on Ryder's lap, whispering what I was sure were nasty things in his ear.

I looked at my friend and sighed.

Did she not see or hear me yawning and stretching a few moments ago?

"Don't even think about sayin' no, Bronagh. We have to bond and dancin' helps with that so come on," she whined.

I couldn't help but groan as she frowned and targeted me with her puppy dog brown eyes. It wasn't fair; the things tripled in size when she pinned me with them and it made me feel bloody terrible.

"Okay," I groaned and reached for her outstretched hand.

God help the lad she ended up with, the poor sod wouldn't have any resistance against those eyes when she asked him for something.

"Yay," Alannah beamed.

"We will be back later," Alannah said to the table without looking at any of the lads.

I looked at each of them and said, "By later, she hopefully means after the next song."

The lads chuckled when Alannah cackled and, of course, her cackles made me snicker.

"Fat chance of that. Now come on, I love this song!"

Ten seconds later we were on the edge of the dance floor dancing to *Best Love Song* by T-Pain and Chris Brown. Both Alannah and I shouted the lyrics to the song instead of singing them, which we found hilarious. I rolled my hips a little with my hands swaying up in the air while Alannah went to town on shaking her arse and rolling her hips like a belly dancer. I was okay on the dancing front, but Alannah was killing it. Not in a choreographed styled way; just in a plain seductive way. I found myself dancing but staring at her as well.

When hands came around me from behind it made me jump because I wasn't expecting it. I quickly looked over my shoulder and upwards ready to tell whoever it was to back off but I stopped myself when my eyes landed on his. I smiled then and sagged my back into his chest.

He leaned his head down to my ear as he moved his body with mine and said, "You're fucking killing me. What the fuck is with moving your hips and ass so much? Are you *trying* to cause a riot?"

I rolled my eyes. "I'm just dancin'."

"Dancing like a fucking seductress," Dominic growled as his hands landed on my hips and pulled my arse into his groin so I was sort of slowly grinding on him.

"A seductress? *Me*? That title belongs to Alannah. Did you not see how she was dancin'?" I asked then looked forward to where Alannah was, only to find she wasn't there anymore or anywhere in my line of sight.

"I wasn't watching Alannah, or anybody else for that matter. My eyes were locked on you... and that ass."

I ignored him and got on my tiptoes looking for Alannah.

My stomach started to churn. "Where did she go? She was *right there* a minute ago. I have to find her—"

"There she is," Dominic said and pointed to the lowly lit section of the club that had hallways leading to private rooms.

I squinted my eyes and then widened them. "That's Damien she is with!" I all but screamed over the loud music.

Dominic laughed as we watched Damien and Alannah necking across the room. They weren't just kissing; they were all but fucking each other through their clothes, and it actually made me blush.

"I have to stop her, she is not thinkin' clearly and will regret this in the mornin'. She told me she wasn't addin' herself onto Damien's hit list even though she fancies him."

Dominic burst out laughing. "Damien's *what*?"

I turned to him. "His hit list, you know the number of girls he has shagged since you all moved here."

Dominic was vibrating with laughter as he led me from the dance floor and back towards the booth that was now full of girls and a good-looking lad that was seated directly next to Alec. He had a girl on his lap but also had his hand on the thigh of the lad and it made me stare, and I don't know why. Other thoughts filled my head the more I looked at him.

"Do you mind Alec being bisexual?" Dominic asked me when he noticed me staring.

I shook my head. "Nope, I'm just curious to find out if he is a giver or a receiver."

Dominic looked horrified. "We're *never* discussing my brother's sexual orientation ever again."

I laughed but stopped when a screeching voice made me wince.

"RAMPAGE!" two girls screamed, making me jump with fright.

I moved to the left away from Dominic a bit when they flanked him on both sides. I hated that my stomach lurched at the sight of them gushing over him.

I knew he was gorgeous and I knew he was a hot fighter, but he was mine, and these girls, and everyone else, better realise that.

"I can't wait to see you fight, you're always *so* good," a girl with fiery red hair purred to Dominic.

He smiled to her and winked before he said, "Thanks, beautiful. With ladies like you cheering for me it's no surprise."

They giggled and I glared hard at Dominic before I stepped forward and literally shoved them away from him. "Fan girl time is over ladies, so get."

They were easily seven or eight years older than me but I didn't care. If I had to stake my claim on Dominic for people to realise that I was his girlfriend then I bloody well would.

"Bee, relax," Branna's voice came from my left.

I glanced at her; she was still on Ryder's lap. I shook my head and said, "Tell him to stop it then and I will."

"Stop *what*?"

I turned and glared at Dominic before clearing my throat and repeated his words in his accent. "Thanks, beautiful. With ladies like you cheering for me it's no surprise."

Alec, Kane, Ryder, and Branna cracked up when I finished talking, but I wasn't in the slightest bit trying to be funny. I was actually pretty annoyed. "Pull that flirtin' bullshit again whether I'm around or not and I'll castrate you," I snapped to Dominic, who was just staring at me as I turned and began to walk away.

"Where are you goin'?" Branna asked me.

"To find Alannah," I said loudly so she could hear over the music as I walked away.

I knew he was following me without even looking over my shoulder and it made the hair on the back of my neck rise up. I forced myself to ignore him as I walked over to the dimly lit area of the club where the hallway that led to the private rooms was located.

Alannah and Damien weren't in sight, so I walked up to the

bouncers standing guard at the hallway entrance. I didn't want to know what happened in those rooms; it couldn't have been anything good if they needed huge bouncers to keep guard outside of it.

"VIPs only, sweetheart," Skull said to me when I reached him.

He wasn't looking at me, but when he glanced up a huge smile spread across his face. "Bronagh! Nice to see you, kid, you're lookin' well."

I felt myself blush at the compliment and was about to thank Skull when I wasn't so gently pulled behind a body.

A hard body.

"I don't want any trouble, Nico, I was just sayin' hello to your misses. That's it," Skull's voice said loudly to be heard over the music that seemed to be getting louder by the minute.

Dominic had his hand twisted around to his back so he could hold my hand in his. He didn't hold on gently either, so I yanked and pulled until he released me. When he let go, I kicked the back of his leg, which caused him to snap his entire body around to me and put his back to Skull and the other bouncer.

"I'm speaking to the nice bouncer, sweetheart. Can you hold off on your childish antics for a moment while the grown-ups converse? You can? *Great*," Dominic chirped and snarled at the same time, which just made me stare at him for a moment until a huge pissed off feeling settled over me.

I gripped onto his arm and forced my way around to be in front of him. He kept hold of me and had my back and arse pressed against the front of his body, but I ignored that and focused on Skull. "Ignore caveman behind me and tell me if you've seen me friend, you know the girl you let in with us tonight? Black hair, around five foot six, big boobs, pretty face. Does any of that ring a bell?"

Skull glanced to the other bouncer when he signalled for a private conversation. Skull leaned into the man, grinned when said man spoke in his ear then straightened up and looked back to me. He nodded in the direction of the hallway behind him. "She is back there with the white-haired Slater brother. Your lad's twin."

I felt my eyes widen. "She is in one of those rooms with him? She has been drinkin'! Let me in now—"

"Bronagh!" Dominic snapped, making me jump as he turned me in his arms. "You're making it out that it's dangerous for her to be alone with Damien. He wouldn't hurt her so back the fuck off!"

I glared at Dominic. "I bet Trent thought that as well once upon a time."

I regretted those words as soon as they left my mouth, because I didn't think badly of Damien. I only said it because Dominic made me mad, but I hated myself when I saw the look of hurt on his face.

"I can't believe you said that," he said, and then did something that made my stomach twist in knots.

He pushed me away from him. Not hard enough that he knocked me over but with enough force that he got me out of his space; I wanted to cry when he did it. A lump formed in my throat, and my chest felt heavy. I wanted to apologise, but I couldn't form the words. Dominic didn't stick around to listen anyway. He looked me up and down, shook his head then turned and walked back across the room to the booth. I watched him sit down in the booth and lock his eyes on the floor. He didn't move, not even when his brothers nudged him or shouted over the music.

I felt sick; this was the best night of my life. Dominic and I were together and said I love you for the first time so we shouldn't be fighting right now. I wanted to fix it, but I also wanted to find Alannah because I knew she would regret sleeping with Damien in the morning. She would be crushed when he didn't want anything more than sex, and it was my duty as her friend to protect her from that hurt if I could.

Everything would just have to wait until later, so with a sigh I turned to Skull and said, "I need to get me friend. Which room is she and Damien in?"

Skull chewed on his lip before stepping aside. "Back room on your left. It might be locked so just knock in case."

I nodded and took off walking down the hallway. I passed nine rooms by the time I reached the one Skull said Damien and Alannah were inside. I cleared my throat, raised my hand and knocked hard on the door. I had to wait outside knocking for a good fifteen minutes, and I couldn't hear a thing from inside the room so when the door suddenly opened, I almost jumped out of my skin as I flung my hand over my heart.

"You scared me, you bastard," I snapped to a shirtless Damien, who only grinned at me.

"Where is she?" I growled.

He raised his eyebrows and stopped grinning. "In the bath-room—"

"Did you have sex with her?" I cut him off.

He narrowed his eyes at me then. "I don't think that is any of your business, Bee."

I glared right back at him and said, "It's me fuckin' business when it's me friend you're fuckin' over."

I pushed by him into the room. I had made it a few steps before he grabbed my arm and pulled me close to him.

"I didn't fucking rape her!" he snarled.

I almost wet myself, because I had never seen him this mad; I actually had never seen him mad at all.

"Let go of me arm or I'm tellin' Dominic," I said in a tone that left no room for jokes.

Damien shook his head but let me go. "Is that how you deal with problems? You have my brother fix them?"

I was shocked at that and also enraged. "Fuck you, Damien. You know fuckin' well that I deal with me problems meself. I don't need Dominic to defend me from anybody!"

Damien laughed. "Jason Bane and Gavin Collins would disa-gree."

I shook my head. "You can seriously go and fuck yourself."

He laughed as I turned and stormed over to the side of the room where another door was; I knocked on it and called out, "Alannah?"

"I'm in here," she replied.

"Are you okay?" I asked through the door.

"Yes and no," she replied.

My stomach lurched as I said, "Explain."

"Well, I know I sa-said I wasn't goin' to do it but I ha-had sex with Damien and it was gr-great. A little sore but still great… however, he said that nothin' will come of it, and we can just be friends because he doesn't d-do relationships… I'm sa-sad over it."

She was tipsy earlier, but she didn't exactly sound drunk right now; she just sounded really upset. I turned to face Damien, who was looking at the bathroom door with a frown on his face. He looked like it bothered him that he upset Alannah.

I walked forward and pushed him by the chest and he made no move to fight me off this time. He locked eyes with me and silently willed me to hit him, to hurt him. I didn't touch him again though. I instead looked him up and down, utterly disgusted with him.

"I was very wrong about you. I thought you were a good person; I didn't let what Dominic told me about your past change me opinion of you, because what you did wasn't planned or even thought on. You did it to protect yourself, your brother, and Nala, but this? You *knew* how much Alannah liked you, you *knew* she was a virgin and you *knew* she didn't want to be a one hit wonder, but yet you *still* pursued her and persuaded your way into her knickers all because she rejected you and you liked the challenge of pullin' her." I shook my head in disgust.

"You're no fuckin' better than any other scumbag out there who uses girls, and I hope you realise what a cold and cruel person you are for doin' this, Damien Slater!" I made a move to turn away from his stone cold face but paused and shook my head before I glanced up at him again.

I gave him a hard glare as I said, "After hearin' a description of your ma and da from Dominic, it looks like the apple didn't fall too far from the tree after all because you only think about one person just like they did. Yourself. I bet they are so fuckin' proud."

His face completely dropped and he looked a little unsteady on his feet like he could fall over at any second. I didn't care though; I turned and went back over to the bathroom to where Alannah was still holed up inside. I gently knocked on the door and gripped the handle when I heard sniffling.

"Lana?" I said softly, using her nickname for the first time. "It's me, can I come in?"

I ignored the banging behind me. I knew Damien had to get dressed and he was clearly pissed as he banged around the room but whatever. Fuck him.

I entered the bathroom when the door clicked open and locked it behind me. I kicked off my heels, bent down to my knees and then reached forward and engulfed Alannah, who was sitting on the closed lid of the toilet with her head in her hands. When I put my arms around her she cried and wrapped her arms around my back and just held me tight.

"It's goin' to be okay, Lana. You're strong and won't let an annoyin' American prick get you down, right?" I asked.

Alannah sniffled and snorted a little as she pulled back from me to get some tissue to wipe up the snot that was running from her nose.

"You know somethin'? I know Nico is your fella, but I thought he was the prick and Damien was the nice one. I was so wrong. Nico is honest and has always been himself whether you like him or hate him. Damien though... he is like a snake in human form. I hate him."

I hugged her again when fresh tears began to stream down her face; I wanted to kill Damien for doing this to her.

Who could do this to another person and not feel guilty?

Dominic wasn't joking when he said Damien was hollow; he was stone fucking cold!

"If it makes you feel better, Dominic really *is* a prick."

Alannah started laughing through her tears then pulled back to clean herself up again. I switched from kneeling on my knees to sitting on my arse. I winced making Alannah frown.

"I just realised we both lost our virginity tonight to the twins."

I raised my eyebrows. "Well... at least we can be sore and hate them together."

Alannah started chuckling again and, even though she was still really upset, I could already see the wall she was starting to build up around her heart whenever she spat something about Damien. She was never going to forgive him for this, and if she did he would really have to prove himself to her. It wouldn't happen anytime soon though. Alannah seems to be a lot like me so I knew she would hold onto it for years and keep her guard up until her walls got smashed down, just like mine did.

"Bee?" Alannah said getting my attention.

I looked to her. "Yeah?"

"Ready to go back outside?" she asked. "I can hear 'RAM-PAGE' being cheered now that they stopped the music for the fight."

I was on my feet in seconds and shoving my feet back into my heels. I had completely forgotten about Dominic's fight! Fuck! I grabbed Alannah's hand and we all but ran out of the private room, down the hallway, and around Skull and his buddy. I widened my eyes when I looked to the platform that Dominic was on with a guy twice his size.

They were even in height but this man must have been thirty years old and was at least forty pounds heavier than Dominic. The man had muscular arms but his gut looked more flab than ab. It made me grimace when Dominic punched him there because I doubt he even felt it.

"Fuckin' kill 'em, RAMPAGE, you beaut!"

I couldn't tell which girl shouted it and I didn't care to pinpoint her either because she wasn't the only female shouting things like that at my boyfriend. Women a lot older than us were shouting extremely crude things that honestly made my blood boil. Dominic was a man, not a fucking piece of meat... and if he was a piece of meat then he was *my* piece of meat and I didn't share my food!

"You looked pissed, bumble bee."

I was still holding onto Alannah's hand as I looked to my left and up at Kane's marred, yet stunning, face. "I am pissed," I said over the noise of the on-going crude remarks directed at my boyfriend. I looked to the crowd of pulsing vaginas and growled, "They are disgustin'!"

Kane put his arm around my shoulder and chuckled. "He only has eyes for you, no if, and, or but about it. Only you."

I looked at Kane and smiled, and I put my free arm around him and squeezed. "You know, I kind of love you."

Kane's eyes widened for a moment as he looked at me. He gave me a squeeze before he said, "Yeah? Well, I think I kind of love you too, bumble bee."

I playfully rolled my eyes at the nickname he came up with last week after deciding Bee was too short and not interesting. He added the bumble onto my nickname and has thought himself Albert Einstein since that day. He told everyone to call me that, but anyone who called me Bee still called me that while Kane was the only one who added on the bumble. It's beyond adorable, and I'd never tell him, but I secretly loved it.

I looked away from Kane and back to the platform Dominic was up on and chewed on my lip then screamed when the man he was fighting suddenly speared Dominic to the ground. I could hear his back slap off the ground from where I stood. I pushed away from Kane and Alannah and made a beeline for the platform. I pushed through the crowd of people while screaming for the fight to be stopped; it wasn't stopped though. If anything, Dominic losing the upper hand was getting people more pumped and hyper.

I started to panic when I looked up and saw the man on top of Dominic, viciously punching him. I screamed bloody murder but no one heard me and if they did, they thought I was cheering the fight on. I even tried to jump for the platform but I couldn't reach it. I was choking on my sobs and blinded by my tears when arms came around me from behind. I felt myself being lifted up and out of the crowd.

"He is okay," Ryder's voice said in my ear.

I was set down in front of my sister and Alannah who both hugged me and asked if I was okay. I shook my head and looked back at the platform and felt my heart leap when Dominic wrapped his legs around the man he was fighting and somehow pinned him to the ground. It was then Dominic's turn to deliver blows, and he did, but the man didn't—or couldn't—guard his head to lessen the impact of the blows. He smacked his hand off the ground and a second later Dominic stopped hitting him and was on his feet. He was bleeding from his eyebrow and nose and sweat covered his body, but other than that, he actually looked okay. The other man, however, was on the ground writhing in pain.

"Give it up for the undefeated champion of Darkness... RAMPAGE!"

I jumped at the sound of the voice coming through the club's speakers but I ignored it when Dominic jumped down from the platform and was swarmed by people. I moved towards his direction and pushed through the crowd until I managed to get in front of him. I didn't think he knew it was me when I jumped at him, because he didn't put his arms around me until he tried to look down to see who I was.

When he realised I wasn't a crazy fan girl, he put his arms around me and lifted me up. My mouth was right next to his ear so I kissed it and cried as I said, "I'm so sorry."

Dominic squeezed me and kept walking. I had my head buried in the crook of his neck so I didn't know where he was heading until I heard Skull's voice, a door opening and closing, then nothing but complete silence. Well, except for my sobs.

I felt myself being set down on a bed and then Dominic kneeled down in front of me, which made him the same height as me since I was sitting down too.

He wiped at my tear-stained face and sighed. "Why do you do this to yourself?" he asked me, frowning.

"I can't help it; he was *killin'* you! I can't stomach the sight of it; it kills me when they hurt you. I hate it!" I cried and shoved him at his shoulder.

"I'm okay, pretty girl," he gave me a small smile. "I've got a hard head."

"What about the rest of your body?" I snapped and wiped at my running nose.

Dominic grinned at me. "The rest of me is always hard, especially when you're around—"

"Cut the messin' out, I'm being serious with you!" I growled.

Dominic sighed. "We had a blow out before my fight so there was no way I was going to lose. I was too pissed not to take it out on that guy and win."

I frowned… that guy was beaten pretty badly.

"I made you that mad then?" I asked and looked down.

"Look at me," Dominic murmured.

I did and almost started to cry again.

"Why is it always the face?" I whispered and wiped away some of his blood from his eyebrow with the back of my hand.

Dominic smiled and closed his eyes. "Yes, to your question about making me mad. You did sink your claws in with that remark about Damien."

Well, I was glad he wasn't in the room when I said even worse things to Damien. I didn't regret them though; he needed to hear what a prick he was for doing Alannah wrong.

"He did her wrong, Dominic. He took her virginity then said he would only be her friend 'cause he didn't do relationships. I fuckin' hate him for hurtin' her so bad. He *knew* she liked him and yet he still did this to her and treated her like nothin' more than a hole to stick his dick into. I thought he was nothin' but a nice lad, but I was very wrong. What he did was cruel, and I told him exactly what I thought of him and if you can't deal with that, then I am sorry you feel that way," I said, and then looked away from his burning eyes.

"What did you say to him?" Dominic asked, struggling to keep his temper in check.

I shrugged. "I'm not gettin' into it. If he wants to tell you what I said then he will, but I doubt it."

"Why do you doubt it?" Dominic questioned.

"'Cause I said some things that almost knocked him off his feet. I wasn't kind, but he needed to hear what I said. He can't continue treatin' girls the way he has. He has no respect for women, and it was time someone put him in his place, so I did."

Dominic lifted my chin so I was looking at him. "Bronagh, what did you say to my brother?"

My heart was pounding, but I didn't answer.

"I saw him practically run out of the club. I haven't seen him that upset in a long time. He doesn't lose it unless my parents are somehow brought into... the mix."

I wanted to die when his eyes flashed with realisation.

"*Tell* me you didn't mention my parents to him," Dominic snarled.

CHAPTER TWENTY-FOUR

I almost swallowed my tongue as I looked away from Dominic's burning eyes. That didn't last for long though. He gripped my chin and forced my head up until I was looking him in the eye again.

"Answer me, Bronagh," he growled. "*Now.*"

I felt my eyes well up with tears—he was so mad that it scared me. I wasn't scared of him doing anything to lash out and hurt me. I was just scared of all the other damage he could do without actually laying a finger on me.

"I told him that based on the description you gave of your parents he wasn't very different from them. They only looked out for themselves and nobody else and so does he," I whispered, and then held my breath for Dominic's reaction.

The silence that followed felt longer than only a few seconds.

"I *told* you he is the way he is because of my parents and then you throw them in his face by saying he is exactly fucking like them?" Dominic said in a tone that wasn't aggressive but merely calm, and it frightened the life out of me.

I knew it wasn't right to answer him back when he was this angry but I couldn't let him defend someone that hurt my friend so badly. "He *is* like them! How can you say he isn't? He isn't into the bullshit they were into, but he does carry the trait of not carin' about other people. He would use and abuse girls—"

"He *doesn't* abuse them," Dominic cut me off with a scream, making me jump back on the bed.

Dominic followed me though and when I realised he was following me, my heart jumped up into my throat.

"He fucks bitches that *want* to be fucked by him," Dominic snapped as he grabbed my hands, got between my legs and applied his weight onto my body pinning me in place. "He doesn't spew false promises to get pussy because pussy falls directly onto his lap... or onto his cock, it would seem."

I tried to lash out at him. I hated when he referred to women as 'pussy'. I hated when he referred to me as that word back when he first kissed me in his bedroom, so I wasn't about to lay quietly while he referred to other women as that word, especially when one of those women was my friend.

"*Don't* call Alannah that word." I snarled. She is more than just a hole for Damien to stick his dick into and so is every other female he and any other lad come into contact with. I know the majority of the girls he has shagged just wanted sex with him, but a lot didn't and it is disgustin' that he will be nice and romantic before he touches them but afterwards he doesn't even speak to them! *How* can you condone that?" I bellowed.

"Because he is my brother and I love him!" Dominic shouted into my face.

I shook my head and glared. "You can still love him but not agree with what he does. If you talked to him about—"

"About what, Bronagh? You want me to sit my brother down and ask him to take a break from the only thing that makes him feel something?" Dominic growled.

I set my jaw. "His purpose on this Earth isn't to fuck everythin' with a vagina and pulse, Dominic! If he needs sex all the time then maybe you should consider that fact that he is a sex addict—"

"You need to shut the fuck up because you have no idea what you're fucking talking about," he spat. "He isn't an addict, he just fucks girls because he likes to. Loads of people like sex without attachment, and Dame is one of those people!"

I used my forehead to push his head away from mine when he tried to press it against me. "Well, he needs to revaluate his life because he hurts people by usin' them, and that is *exactly* what he did to Alannah. He knew she wouldn't be one of those girls who didn't care. It was written across her face how much he hurt her!"

Dominic glared at me. "She had sex with him too, Bronagh. She didn't have to if she didn't want to!"

I screamed and struggled under him. "You don't get it; he used her attraction to him against her!"

Dominic shook his head. "I'll talk to him about that then but you just stay away from him. Throwing someone's dead parents in their face is disgusting. I thought you would be more sensitive than that since you know what it's like to lose both your parents."

I was dumbstruck as he got up off me but quickly sat up and said, "*My* parents were *nothin'* like yours!"

Dominic shrugged. "You loved them and Damien loved ours regardless of their choices in life, and yet you still used them as a verbal weapon to hurt him. I never thought I would be disappointed in you. I know you speak your mind but that was low, Bronagh. Real low."

A lump formed in my throat when he turned and walked towards the door of the room.

"*Where* are you goin'?" I demanded.

Dominic didn't turn around as he said, "To find my brother and make sure he is okay. I'm going to do what you want and speak to him about hurting Alannah since it means so much to you."

The cloud of anger that hovered over me started to fade away as I said, "Thank you—"

"But I'm doing it alone, I need to be away from you right now."

My heart broke as he started to walk away from me.

"Are you breakin' up with me?" I asked, my voice shaking.

Dominic paused and hesitated before he said, "No, I'm not. I love you, Bronagh, but I would be lying if I said I didn't hate you a little bit right now. I need to leave just until we cool off."

I felt tears fall from my eyes as I said, "You said you would never leave me… you promised you wouldn't."

Dominic sighed as he reached the door of the room. "And you promised you would never hurt me. I guess we both broke our promises."

When he opened the door and closed it after him, I burst into tears and fell back onto the bed. There was a pain in my chest that hurt so much, it felt like there was a weight pressing on it. I forced myself to breathe in order to control my sobbing.

I knew I was sticking up for my friend when I lashed out at Damien, but there was no escaping the fact that I had formed the divide that was just placed between Dominic and me. I could have chosen my words differently when speaking to Damien, but no, I had to go for his heart by bringing up his parents. Dominic was right; I should have never thrown them in his face, all the things I spewed before I said that would have been hurtful enough.

"Stupid!" I cried and punched the pillow next to my head.

I continued to cry for what felt like an age and eventually cried myself to sleep.

I woke up with a jolt some time later and groggily crawled from the bed I was on until I was standing on the floor. I was a bit unsteady on my feet because of the heels I was wearing, but after a moment or two I got a handle on my legs and walked steadily towards the door of the private room.

When I opened the door, I was met by laughter and some low music that was nothing like the volume that had been blaring earlier before Dominic's fight. I closed my eyes at the thought of him and tried to overlook the pain in my chest. I repeated in my head that we didn't break up, and we were only apart because we were cooling off. We would speak soon; he was probably at my house right now pissed off that I wasn't there waiting for him.

I reached for the handle of the door and closed it behind me after I stepped out into the hall. I walked down the hallway in the direction that led back into the nightclub. The laughter and wolf whistles I heard made the hairs on the back of my neck stand up and I got goose bumps when I stepped out from the hallway and looked around the club.

The dance floor was empty except for two girls dirty dancing with each other in time with the sensual music that was playing low. I glanced towards the circle but found that section of the club to be black because the lights were switched off. I jumped when I heard a deep, rumbling chuckle come from my far left. I looked in the direction and spotted three men sitting around the very booth Dominic and his brothers always sat at. Two of the men were in their forties or fifties while the other was a younger lad, probably nineteen or so.

The man who was chuckling looked in my direction and stared at me for a moment before he gestured with his finger for me to go to him. I didn't know why but instead of walking straight towards the exit, I kept my eyes on the man's as I walked towards him. He smiled at me when I reached the booth and held out his hand for me. I took hold of it and moved when he gently pulled me down to the spot next to him.

"What is your name, beauty?" he asked me, his accent not Irish but American.

"Bronagh," I replied as I still just stared at him.

His hair was jet black, his eyes were a light hazel colour, and his skin was lightly tanned. There wasn't anything exceptionally remarkable about him; he was just a good-looking man, average even, but he had something about him that made me want to be close to him. It was the weirdest feeling I had ever gotten in my entire life; I knew he was somebody important just by looking at him. He had a dominant status about him and, to be honest, I was curious to know who he was.

"Such a pretty name for such a pretty girl," the man smiled before reaching out and wiping under my eyes with his thumbs. He smiled at my eyes lingering on his, and then asked, "Why are you here?"

I swallowed before I said, "I came here to watch the fight that was on earlier, but I fell asleep in one of the private rooms."

He grinned and asked, "You like watching the brawls?"

I shook my head. "No way, I actually hate them but me boyfriend fights in them, so I have to come along for support or he gets mad."

He raised his eyebrows then, but lowered them as he reached out again and smoothed my hair back from my face. He was very gentle when he asked, "Who is your boyfriend? I bet on the fights; he might have won me some money in the past."

The other men in the booth snickered at this, but I didn't look at them, I kept my eyes on the man next to me and answered, "Dominic Slater, he's the undefeated champion of Darkness. He always wins his fights."

I didn't know what I was expecting when I answered the man's question, but growling from the young lad across from me wasn't it. "That pussy gets lucky in his fights."

I was instantly mad.

"He just happens to get lucky in *every single fight* then?" I asked the young lad as I looked away from the man next to me. I was instantly aware that he was somehow related to the man next to me because he looked so much like him, just a younger version.

"He is a pussy, *bitch*," the young lad snarled.

"Well, you know what they say?" I glared right back at him. "You are what you eat."

The young lad grinned at me while the two other men burst into laughter. I jumped a little when the man next to me put his arm over my shoulder as he laughed. "Get my picture with this Irish beauty. It's not often someone shuts my nephew up."

I looked to the man as the other older man across the table snapped a picture on his phone. I looked to him then when he began tapping on it and reached over handing it back to the man next to me.

Referring to them as just 'men' was hurting my head so I asked,

"What is your name?"

The man next to me opened his mouth to speak when the phone in his hand rang, causing a smile to light up his face. "I don't think he has ever called me back so quick before." He chuckled then answered the phone and said, "Nico, my boy, how are you?"

My full attention was on the man next to me when he said the name Nico.

The man held his phone away from his ear a little when screaming spewed from the receiver. The man nodded to the other man across the table. After the nod, the man got up and walked in the direction of the hallway where all the private rooms were. I furrowed my eyes as I watched him disappear down the hallway; I kept looking in that direction waiting for him to reappear and when he did, he was dragging a person's body by their legs in our direction.

"Omigod," I screamed in horror at what I was seeing.

The man next to me suddenly fisted my hair in his hand and snarled, "Bronagh, I don't like screaming so cut it out or I'll cut your tongue out, your choice."

I was breathing heavily as I snapped my mouth shut.

"Good girl," the man said then chuckled. "You trained your bitch well, Nico, I'm proud of you, son. Your woman knows her place."

I began to cry as the man dragging the male body by the legs neared the booth. I could tell it was a male but the closer he got, the more things I noticed. I furrowed my eyebrow and blinked through my tears when I recognised who the person was. When the person's face came into view I screamed out and tried to go to him.

"Damien!" I cried.

He was out cold on the ground and his face was all busted up. If you didn't know who he was you wouldn't have been able to recognise him; that's how swollen his face was.

"Shut it, bitch, you look better when your mouth is closed," the man that fisted my hair growled.

He pulled me by the hair until I was standing up from the booth.

He turned me and shoved me forward until I landed on the younger lad whose hands latched onto me and pulled me down onto him so my arse was directly on his groin.

"Fuck me, you have some ass," he commented making my stomach lurch. "Marco, *please* let me test this one out."

I widened my eyes as I stared at the man who was grinning at me as he still held his phone to his ear. "Be here in one hour or I'll kill the girl and paralyse your brother." He hung up and dropped his phone on the table in front me.

"Marco Miles?" I whispered.

He grinned and asked, "Nico told you about me then?"

I set my jaw.

"He told me *everythin'* about you," I growled.

Marco chuckled. "I hope it was all good?"

I curled my lip in disgust making him laugh as he dropped back down into the booth. "I thought the trip to this country wouldn't be worth it. I figured Nico and his brothers would be hard to keep employed, but you and Damien have made it very easy. Damien left Darkness just as we arrived so grabbing him was easy. Then when we went to put him in one of the back rooms, Trent found you passed out. One of the bouncers identified who you were and just so happened to mention whose girlfriend you were." Marco snickered. "You confirmed it when you admitted Nico was your guy."

I processed what he just said and my mind lingered on one thing, the name 'Trent'. I looked over my shoulder to the scumbag who was rubbing my thighs and asked, "Trent Miles?"

He evil smiled at me. "In the flesh, bitch."

CHAPTER TWENTY-FIVE

"You're supposed to be dead!" I shouted and struggled in Trent's arms. "Damien *killed* you!"

Marco laughed from across the table. "No, Damien shot him in the shoulder, and I told Ryder it went in his heart and that he was dead. I was about to lose those boys and after their father and I had been grooming them all their lives for our line of work, I couldn't let it happen. So when I got the opportunity to put them where I wanted them, I took it with both hands."

I glared at him in disgust. "You pretended your nephew was dead just so you could hold it over the brothers and make them work for you?"

"Genius wasn't it?" Marco chortled. "The Slater brothers are nothin' if not loyal to each other. They would give up everything to keep each other safe, and holding Damien's life in my hands got me their lives in return. I *own* that family."

I shook my head. "They want out. Dominic told me they were cuttin' ties with you!"

Marco snorted. "Yeah, he told me that as well, but I'm not very happy with my best boys jumping ship. They each provide substantial income for me, and I really like my money so we're just going to have to talk about extending their work contracts instead of terminating them."

I felt like getting sick. "You can't make them work for you anymore. Trent isn't dead; you held somethin' over them that didn't exist in order to keep them in line!"

Marco laughed at me again. "That was an illusion; what I *really* held was the threat of killing their brother over them, and I *still* hold it over them... the threat of killing you is new, but I'm sure it will prove just as effective."

He was fucking crazy!

"You *won't* get away with this!" I snapped.

Trent laughed, and he gripped my hair. "He already has," he said as he whacked the back of my head causing darkness to consume me instantly.

I woke up when someone called my name. I groaned but didn't answer. I had a killer headache and just wanted to sleep until it went away

I groaned in response.

"Bee?" a familiar voice murmured. "Wake up, please."

I groaned as I blinked my eyes open. I flicked my eyes around until I realised I wasn't in my bedroom. I shot up and gripped the back of my head when pain filled it. I pulled my hand away and found some blood, fresh and hard, on it.

What the fuck?

"What happened?" I asked as I looked around.

I felt an arm come around my waist, making me jump. I looked to the person who was holding me and gasped. I knew it was Damien but his face was so swollen and cut up that it was hard to recognise him.

"Damien," I whimpered and threw my arms around him. He winced but squeezed me with the arm that was already around my waist.

"Are you okay?" I cried as I pulled back from him.

He nodded his head as I brushed his hair from his face and

kissed his forehead. "It's goin' to be okay, I promise."

He squeezed me again. "I know."

I looked at him as tears streamed down my face. "I'm sorry for everything I said to you. You're still a dick, but what I said was wrong."

Damien laughed but his face wouldn't allow him to smile. "Shut up, Bee, you were right about everything you said and I only reacted the way I did because I knew it was true and I hated it. I never want to be like my parents, and the shit I've being doing just proves that I am."

I frowned as I looked at him.

"I don't set out to break hearts. I actually don't set out to have anything to do with hearts at all but some girls get attached to me. I swear I never meant to hurt Alannah. I know this will make me sound like a prick. I am a prick, but I just wanted to be with her in the only way I know how to be. She's different."

I gave him a look. "Is that your cryptic way of sayin' you like Alannah?"

Damien shrugged but didn't answer.

I glanced around the room then and groaned. "I can't believe I was knocked out."

"Tell me about it," he growled. "They did this to me *after* I was knocked out, the fucking pussies!"

I shook my head then winced. "The back of me head is throbbin', it's bleedin' as well."

Damien turned me so my back was to him and he placed his hands gently on my neck and tipped my head forward. He moved his fingers through my hair and stopped when I hissed in pain. "It's not a deep cut and it's starting to clot. I can see all the dried blood."

I breathed sigh of relief. "Thank God for that."

"Who hit you? Marco?" he asked, his voice a snarl. "I saw his face before I was hit."

I swallowed and turned to face Damien. "It wasn't Marco, Damien... it was Trent."

Damien's eyebrows shot up, and his mouth dropped open.

"Trent... *Trent Miles*?" Damien spluttered.

I nodded my head. "He isn't dead. Marco said he just pretended he was so that he could hold the threat of killin' you over your brothers' heads. He lied to you all, Damien."

Damien looked at me for a moment then turned his head and stared off into space. I was about to ask if he was okay when he said, "For the last three and a half years I've seen his face every night when I've gone to sleep. I was convinced he was haunting me for what I did to him but now I realise it's all just been in my head."

I swallowed the lump that formed in my throat and said, "You can let go of all that now."

Damien nodded then looked to me just as the door of the room we were in opened and asked, "Is he really alive?"

Laughter from the doorway caused us to look in that direction. I set my jaw when I saw him while Damien just stared, his mouth hanging open. Trent smirked at Damien and gestured to himself with open arms and said, "I'm really alive. Did you miss me, buddy?"

CHAPTER TWENTY-SIX

"It looks like I've got to work on my aim," Damien snarled, making Trent laugh.

He tapped his shoulder and winked. "I'm glad you have shit aim. Things wouldn't have worked out for me the way they have otherwise."

Damien got to his feet but froze when Trent pulled out a gun and pointed it at him, "Oh, déjà vu." He laughed. "Does this scene remind you of something, *bro*?"

I scoffed in disgust as I got up from the bed and grabbed Damien's arm. "Leave us alone," I said to Trent.

Trent grinned at me and nodded behind him. "Can't do that, baby. Uncle Marco wants a chat."

He gestured for us to exit the room with the gun. Damien held my hand tight as we did so without argument. I was shaking like a leaf knowing Trent was behind us with a real gun in his hand; I was expecting a bang to go off at any second.

When Damien and I re-entered the club from the hallway, we walked up to the booth we were at earlier and just stood there while Marco received a lap dance from one of the girls I had seen dancing earlier. I moved a little behind Damien when Marco flicked his eyes to me and winked. He laughed when he saw me trying to hide. He then slapped the arse of the girl dancing on him and told her to leave, which she did without a word.

I looked around the room and noticed two big men, one of which was the man who dragged Damien out from the private rooms earlier, walking towards the private rooms only to stand outside the hallway like Skull and his bouncer friend did earlier in the night. I tore my eyes away from them and looked at Damien when he started to tense up next to me.

"You let me believe I killed him!" he growled to Marco.

Marco nodded his head and said, "I did."

I wanted to punch him. He answered that question as casually as if accepting a cup of tea from someone.

"Just to keep my family in the business?" Damien asked, his voice laced with venom.

Marco shrugged as he lit up a cigarette, inhaled then exhaled and blew the smoke in our direction causing me to cough a little.

"Your brothers were born for this line of work, *literally*." He said, his lip quirked. "I've heard lately that you have a way of getting pussy by just blinking. I could tie you into what Alec does if you're interested? Brothers on Demand, it will be my, or your, next big *hit*."

Marco, Trent, and the two men across the room chuckled at this, so I glowered at them.

"You're nothin' but a scumbag!" I snapped.

Damien fully stood in front of me then, which only made Marco laugh.

"Calm down, blondie." He said. "I'm not going to touch your brother's bit on the side."

Damien glared at Marco. "He will kill you for this, I hope you know that. Dragging me here was strike one, knocking Bronagh out was strike two, and using her life as a bargaining chip to keep him in the business is strike fucking three."

Marco had a bored look about him. "I can be *very* persuasive, Damien."

Damien shook his head. "You won't be able to talk your way

out of this one, or make up some bullshit story like you did with Trent. We aren't the same people you took advantage of back in New York."

Marco raised his eyebrows and glared at Damien. "You're the men you are today because I fucking made you that way!"

"Which is *exactly* why this is going to blow up in your face," Damien countered. "We know all the tricks of your trades. Each one of my brothers knows the ins and outs of how you do business; they do all your work while you sit back and reap the rewards. You would be nothing without them!"

"Nothing?" Marco roared. "Who the fuck built up this empire? *Me!*"

Damien snorted. "You *and* my dad until it went to your heads. His head is full of lead now and, trust me when I say, soon so will yours."

Marco looked like he was about to clock Damien until he chuckled and shook his head then glanced to Trent and shrugged his shoulders. "I guess this side of him was what that little chinky bitch loved so much."

I furrowed my eyebrows because I had no clue what or whom he was talking about and neither did Damien. Trent snorted at our expressions and said, "She only liked him for his hair colour, which is exactly why I put a blond wig in my hole with her. No one can ever say I gave the bitch nothing."

Once again, what?

"Who did you bury in Trent's grave if he is here?" Damien asked, his voice shaking.

Trent only smiled at him, which caused my heart to beat faster than it already was.

"Who did you bury if he is alive?" Damien screamed.

Marco shrugged. "That little Asian chick you were dating or fucking. What was her name? Gala? She came to the house looking for you the day after the 'incident' and walked in on Trent being treated by a doc. Of course I couldn't let her walk out of there alive.

She would have told you Trent was alive, and then I wouldn't have been able to cash in on Dominic's talent. Your brothers running shit for me was a plus but getting Dominic where I wanted him was my true prize.

"After I saw the CCTV footage of him attacking Trent before you shot him I knew your brother was a born fighter. Another plus was that kid's body was the weight I needed for the coffin that was for Trent. She probably weighed as much as him back then."

Marco and his goons chuckled while Trent growled, "Fuck you, I was a late bloomer!"

Marco continued to chuckle before turning back to Damien whose face was so red, I thought his head might pop.

"You killed Nala and buried her in Trent's grave?" he asked lowly, because his voice was shaking.

Marco snapped his fingers. "*Nala*, that's her name! Cute little chick, put up quite a fight."

I almost missed Damien when he moved; he was almost as fast as Dominic when he charged at someone. He wasn't fast enough though because just as he neared Marco, the man that was across the room by the hallway shot forward and hit Damien in the face repeatedly with the butt of his gun. The other man appeared next to me and fisted his hand into my hair to keep me put.

"Damien!" I screamed and tried to move forward to help him but the grip on my hair tightened, causing strands to be pulled from my head. I howled in pain and tried kicking back at the arsehole that held onto me, but it only resulted in me being dragged to the ground by my hair, which hurt even more than just being tugged on.

"Let her go!" Damien's voice bellowed just as a knee was pressed to the back of my neck pinning me to the ground while cutting off my oxygen supply.

"Matt, I need her *alive*. Nico won't be reasoned with if she is dead!" Marco snapped as I began to kick out with my arms and legs, trying to break free so I could breathe again.

The burning that was building in my chest was suddenly eased when the thug pinning me down let up on the pressure of Matt's knee. I gasped and choked for air when he moved his body off me completely, then lifted my hands to the back of my neck and down the left side because those parts were throbbing and hurting badly.

I lay down on the ground for a moment and flinched when I felt a hand wrap around my arm.

"It's me, Bee," Damien's voice said.

I looked up at him and whimpered. He was bleeding from both of his nostrils, he had a large cut above his eyebrow, and his left jaw and eye were swollen shut; he looked a wreck. I reached up and ran my fingers over the swelling before whimpering and leaning into him. He hoisted me up onto his lap and held me tightly to him, swaying me from left to right.

"It's going to be okay, Bee." Damien whispered and kissed the crown of my sore head. "He will come for us."

I knew he was talking about Dominic, and I prayed he was right. If he didn't get here soon I didn't think things were going to end very well. I didn't think Marco was holding us captive just for a good ol' chat about the lads' past.

"Are you fucking your brother's girl, D?" Trent asked, chortling. "That would be boss if you were."

Damien's hold on me tightened. "Don't."

I looked at Trent as he laughed again and said, "Always the protector of females. That particular trait had you swimming in pussy when we were kids. I'm glad to see nothing has changed."

I was disgusted that Trent nodded in my direction as if the only reason Damien was trying to keep me safe was because he wanted to have sex with me.

"He is a good person you fuckin' prick. He doesn't need a reason to keep people safe!" I snapped, and then went into a coughing fit because my voice was raspy and my throat was bloody killing me.

Trent snapped his teeth at me. "Say fucking one more time, baby. Your accent has me tied up in knots over here."

I curled my lip in disgusted. "You're a vile creature."

Trent smiled at me. "You haven't seen anything yet, baby. Let's see what names you call me after I fuck that smart mouth right out of you."

My stomach lurched while Damien pushed us up to our feet. "You touch her, and I will kill you for real this time!"

Trent switched his gaze from me to Damien and his face hardened. "Oh, I'll be touching her; I seem to have a need to fuck Slater bitches. Nala was a fighter, but I'm betting little Irish here will give me one hell of a time."

I widened my eyes, not because he said he was going to rape me, but because he just admitted to raping Nala. Damien went deathly still, so I moved directly to his side and gripped onto him as he looked to Marco who was watching the three of us with mild amusement.

"You said you killed her," Damien said to Marco.

Marco shook his head. "I never said that. I said I couldn't let her leave my house alive. She did die that day but not by my hand; she died by *his*."

I let out a whimper when Marco nodded to a grinning Trent, who was looking at Damien with a smugness that made me feel physically sick.

"I knew you loved her and after she rejected me, what better revenge could I get on you for almost killing me? Killing your heart, of course. She screamed as well, so loud I almost wanted to cap her before I was even finished fucking her, but I didn't. I got a shot at all her holes before I blew her mind. Literally."

I didn't even try to hold Damien back when he tore away from me and charged at Trent. No one was quick enough to stop him from getting to his target this time. He crashed into Trent and knocked them both to the ground. If I pretended Damien's hair was brown, I would have sworn that I was watching Dominic beat someone up because Damien was throwing punches exactly like him.

Damien got about five or six hits in before Marco's men intervened and pulled him off Trent.

"She was ten weeks pregnant!" Damien screamed as he tried to break free of the men's hold on him and charge for Trent again.

I flung my hand over my mouth and let the tears that filled my eyes fall down my cheeks. Damien let out a male cry that broke my heart and made me cry out for him and Nala.

She was pregnant when she was raped and murdered?

"I'll kill you for this!" Damien swore to Trent, who was getting up from the ground and swiping away the blood from under his nose and from his lip.

Trent looked at Damien and smiled a smile so evil it made me shiver. "So I killed your bitch *and* your kid? Fuck me, talk about killing two birds with one stone, or one bullet as it was."

Damien roared again and tried to break out of the hold the arms had on him but he couldn't. Nobody held me or was paying me any attention though, so with anger and grief for Nala I charged at Trent and dug my nails into his face and scratched with every bit of power in me. Trent screamed so loud and knocked me off him to the ground, but it was too late. I had already raked his face with deep scratches and cuts that would scar no matter how many stitches he got.

I laughed but then screamed when he let out a roar and gave me a kick in the stomach with such force it caused me to heave and throw up all over the floor.

"I'm going to make you scream, bitch. You will see how much of a vile creature I can fucking be," Trent growled down as he stood over me with blood running down his neck and under his shirt from the cuts I had caused.

He made a move to hit me again but stopped when Marco appeared over me and grabbed his raised arm, halting his movements.

"Enough! I need her *alive*. How many times do I have to fucking say that?" Marco snapped to Trent.

Trent lowered his hand when Marco let go of it and swallowed. "But uncle—"

"No buts, you can have the other one. This one belongs to Nico, and I need him, and he needs her, so she is off limits. Do you understand that, boy?" Marco asked Trent, his gaze now a glare.

Trent nodded his head and swallowed again. "Yes, sir."

Marco sighed a little then waved his hand to two men who were standing guard over a whimpering Damien. They let him fall to the floor and walked off towards the hallway and down to the private rooms.

"If you keep it together for the rest of this meeting then you can have this one to play with."

I carefully pushed myself up into a sitting position wincing at the pain in my side so I could look past Marco and see who he was talking about. I felt like throwing up again when the unconscious body of a female was dragged into the room and dropped a few feet away from me.

"Alannah!" I whimpered when I saw her face. I crawled over to her body and my fingers instantly went to her throat looking for a pulse and when I found one I cried out in relief.

"Is she alive?" Damien shouted, his voice filled with emotion.

"Yes," I called back to him and gathered Alannah in my arms before I looked up to Marco, daring him with my eyes to try and let Trent take her from me.

Marco seemed to know what I was thinking because he laughed and shook his head at me. "I like you, kiddo. You have heart, but I'm not sure if that makes you brave or stupid."

I glared at him and said, "Probably both."

He pointed his finger at me. "Definitely like you."

"Yeah, well I fuckin' *hate* you!" I growled.

Marco snorted. "You wouldn't be the first or the last to hate me, kiddo."

I held tight to Alannah and looked at Damien as he crawled over to us. He could barely pull himself, but he managed to put himself in front of Alannah and me, which made me cry even more than I already was. I was shaking with Alannah in my arms, I had vomit and blood on me and felt like I was about to fall over at any second, but I forced myself to stay upright. I couldn't allow Trent to get her and drag her to one of the private rooms. I would die before I let that happen.

Trent was laughing at our little huddle but stopped when he heard the noise of gunshots come from the stairway entrance to Darkness; the doors were slightly open allowing us to hear them. I gripped onto Alannah and reached for Damien's arm and gave him a squeeze.

I looked at Marco and found him grinning as he said, "The Slater brothers are here."

Trent moved into the shadows to my left while Marco's men drew guns from inside their coats. Marco, too, took out a handgun. Twenty seconds passed before the doors to the entrance to the stairway were fully kicked open. I felt my heart leap when Dominic, Ryder, Alec, and Kane all walked in with guns in their hands. They didn't raise and point them at anyone though, and I was pretty sure it was because Marco's men were standing over Damien, Alannah, and I with *their* guns pointed at *us*.

I looked to the brothers and made eye contact with Dominic who looked like he was having an internal battle with himself; I gave him a small smile and mouthed, "I love you," just in case it was my last chance to tell him.

His eyes swam with emotion before he switched them from me to Marco and his face morphed to one of anger. "Let my brother, my girl, and her friend go and I *won't* make you suffer when I kill you."

Marco laughed as he sat down in the booth that I decided I wholeheartedly hated. "You haven't seen me in months and that is the greeting you give your uncle?"

"You're *nothing* to us!" Kane growled.

I widened my eyes, shocked at how different his voice sounded. He looked absolutely terrifying now that he wasn't smiling. He looked as, if he had the chance, Marco and all his men would be dead. I looked at Marco when he chuckled and shook my head at him; he was only pissing them off more by laughing.

I got a bit lightheaded then and felt myself droop a bit but the leg behind me held me up. The man who was behind me whistled for Marco's attention and when he got it he said, "She is going to go any minute."

"Put her up here then," Marco snapped.

Damien grabbed a hold of Alannah when the man who was behind me lifted me to my feet and held onto me as he moved me over to the booth where Marco was sitting. I instantly slumped forward onto the table, and Dominic's roar barely registered with me.

"Give it a rest, *bro*." Trent's voice sang merrily. "She took a knock to the head, but she is okay."

"Trent?" all the brothers said in unison.

I couldn't see them, but I could hear the shock in their voices.

"Happy to see me?" Trent snickered.

"What the fuck is going on?" Alec shouted, confusion laced in his tone.

"I'll tell you," Damien growled from the floor. "Marco lied when he said I killed Trent. He just wanted an easy way to pull you four deep into the business, and saying that working for him would be protection for me was the perfect opportunity."

"We *buried* the little prick though," Ryder's voice snapped.

"No," Damien said, his voice hollow. "We buried Nala. Trent killed her when she found out he wasn't really dead."

The room filled with silence until Trent said, "And the slut was pregnant with his kid as well. Talk about shit luck for her."

"*Pregnant*?" the brothers spluttered.

"She told me the day mom and dad were killed," Damien said sadly.

"That was why you'd been distant?" Dominic asked. "Not because of mom and dad but because of Nala?"

"I thought she fucking left on purpose with my kid so yeah, I've been messed up about that, but now I know she is dead and so is my kid. Having this prick haunting me every night because I thought I had killed him wasn't fun either."

"Does that make me the man of your dreams, D?" Trent voice asked.

I forced my eyes open when Marco chuckled under his breath. He wasn't looking at me; he was looking down at Damien and Alannah. He had his gun on the table but it wasn't in his hand, it was next to him. Either he was cocky or just plain stupid because all the brothers had guns in their hands and he was sitting on the booth with his gun just casually lying on the table in front of him like they weren't a threat.

Either he thought I was out cold, or he didn't think I would make a play for his gun. He was wrong on both counts because as soon as he lifted his hand to reach for another cigarette inside his coat pocket, I shot my hand forward and grabbed the gun.

I fumbled with it for a second but once I got a grip on the handle, I placed my finger on the trigger and pointed it directly at Marco's head. Marco's eyebrows almost touched his hairline as he looked down the barrel of his own gun. When he flicked his eyes to me, he smiled and said, "Damn, Irish, you sure know how to play a man."

I forced my eyes to stay open and my arm to hold the gun up. "Tell your men to back off or I swear to God, I will pull this trigger and kill you." I warned him. "I'm not afraid to do it."

"Stay where you are!" I heard one of Marco's men growl.

"Unless you want your boss's brains all over the place, I'd advise you to let me go to my girl or she will kill him." Dominic said, lowly. "Trust me on that."

Trent growled from behind Damien and Alannah. He stepped fully into my view and spat in my direction before he said, "She's bluffing, she doesn't have it in her to pull that trigger."

"I wouldn't put money on that," Kane's voice said as I heard footsteps come from behind me.

"Hey, pretty girl," Dominic's voice said from my right as he slid into the booth next to me.

My hand was shaking and tears were in my eyes.

"I could kill him and make all this go away, I could do it," I said to Dominic without looking away from Marco, who actually started to look nervous.

"I know you can baby, but this piece of shit isn't worth it," Dominic said and carefully reached for me.

I leaned a little away from him.

"He wants to take you away from me, and I won't let him." I swore. "You're mine, *not* his!"

I could feel Dominic get closer to me, he kissed my shoulder and whispered, "I'm already yours, pretty girl. Always."

I started to cry then.

"Give me the gun," he whispered. "That's it, good girl,"

I lowered my arm down a little but still had the gun in my hand when a bang sounded around the room. I screamed and my hand instinctively pulled the trigger on the gun causing an even louder bang to ring in my ears. I dropped the gun as a shockwave of pain flew up my arm. I thought I was somehow shot, but after a second, I realised it was the force of the gun going off that hurt me.

When more shots went off around the room Dominic dove on me and covered me with his body. I felt like he was crushing me. When he moved off me I gasped for air and greedily sucked it into my lungs.

I opened my eyes and widened them when I looked to Marco who was still sitting across from me in the booth but he was holding his shoulder and groaning in pain. I gasped and looked around Dominic and found both of Marco's men on the ground unmoving with blood splotches on their chest. Trent was on the ground too but he was alive; I could tell from his crying, and how he was writhing in pain.

I looked back to Marco and widened my eyes as blood started to soak around the material of his shirt even though his hand was pressed against the gunshot wound in his shoulder.

I shot him. I actually shot somebody.

Oh, my God.

"'I didn't mean to, I got a fright and—"

"Bronagh!" Dominic snapped, cutting me off. "It's okay baby, it's going to be okay."

I shook my head. "We're going to go to prison, those men—"

"Will be disposed of, as will Marco and Trent when we're finished with them."

I snapped my head in the direction of Kane's voice and felt myself tremble under his stare. "We won't get in trouble then?" I asked.

He smiled at me and for some reason, with just a small smile from him; things didn't seem to be that messed up.

"I did a lot more for this scumbag than just hurt people Bronagh." He assured me. "He is about to get the experience of me *fully* displaying my 'services'."

Forget what I just said, things were *beyond* messed up.

"Nico, Kane... we can talk about this," Marco said then cried out in pain when Alec rounded on the booth and pressed a finger into Marco's wound, making me almost vomit.

"Out of all the things on the to-do list, Marco," he growled. "Talking to you won't be one of them."

Oh, my God.

I felt myself droop again when arms came around me. "Bring Alannah to the room I'm putting Bronagh in. They're soundproof so they won't hear a thing if they wake up."

Oh, my *fucking* God!

I was then being lifted into the air and, after a minute or two; I was placed down on a soft surface that made me groan out loud. I felt a kiss on my forehead then a voice whispered, "I'm going to make all this go away, pretty girl."

"We can't leave them for long. Bronagh has a concussion and Lana hasn't woken up since one of those pricks knocked her out."

I heard knuckles crack before Dominic replied, "Trust me bro, this *won't* take long."

"Promise me something," Damien said to Dominic.

"What?" Dominic asked.

"Leave Trent to me."

My mind picked that exact moment to go black and send me into a sea of darkness.

CHAPTER TWENTY-SEVEN

"**Y**ou want me to *lie* to me best friend, Dominic?" I snapped to my irritating boyfriend as Branna stood behind me carefully brushing my hair out.

I couldn't do it myself because every time I tried to, the bristles of the hairbrush scraped on my head wound, which hurt like hell itself. Branna was careful though, so I didn't mind her doing it, and that was the only thing I didn't mind her doing. Since shite hit the fan a week ago in Darkness, everyone has treated me like a glass doll.

Sure, I was hit in the head and got cut from it. Sure I received a minor concussion. And sure I was beaten and subjected to the hands of one of the most dangerous men in the world and have had nightmares about it ever since, but I wasn't that fucking fragile. I could happily deal with this on my own; I just wish everyone else would realise that.

"She doesn't know who hit her, and she didn't wake up until the morning after, so it is best to keep her in the dark about what happened," Dominic pleaded. "I understand she's your friend, but the fewer people who know about what happened, the better. Ryder already cut all ties with Marco's business associates. Everyone believes he is missing, and since Trent was thought dead all these years, no one knows about him. We took care of Marco's men upstairs and downstairs, and we cleaned every part of Darkness. No one knew he was at Darkness anyway since he flew in on his own plane unannounced to catch us off-guard. That shit blew up in his face."

I nodded; I understood this but hated talking about it. I didn't ask for details about that night and I didn't want them. The brother told me that Marco and Trent were dead, and that was all I needed to know to feel safe. Any more information on how they died would make my current nightmares worse than they already were.

"There you go," Branna announced. "Hair is all done so we can finally go collect our shoppin'!"

I groaned. Branna was the only person who would tackle Dublin's city centre on Christmas Eve. "I think the lads will understand if we have no presents for them to open tomorrow mornin' after everythin' that's happened this week."

Branna rounded on me and pinned me with a look that told me to shut my mouth, so I did.

"I don't care if Jesus himself shows up at the door for dinner, we're collectin' those presents," she stated. "Besides, everythin' is paid for, we just need to collect them, and that is final, understood?"

I saluted her. "Yes, Mother."

She chuckled as she kissed my shoulder. She bumped Dominic with her hip as she passed him at my bedroom door, which made him smile. He looked over his shoulder and watched her go, which led to me taking off my shoe and throwing it at him. It clocked him right in the chest and caused him to yelp.

"Fuck, what was that for?" Dominic snapped when he turned to face me.

"Lookin' at me sister's arse, you pervy bastard!" I growled.

I heard Branna's laughter come from down the hallway, and it made Dominic grin as he rubbed his chest and walked towards my bed.

He climbed up beside me and pulled me close to him. He was quiet for a moment then said, "Damien booked his flight."

I frowned; Damien was going back to America one last time to say goodbye to Nala. He knew he couldn't have her taken out of Trent's marked grave because it would raise too many questions, so the best he could do was ignore the gravestone that was engraved for Trent and laid fresh flowers for her.

He said he was coming back to Ireland; he promised me he would. He just never promised when and that made me sad because I knew deep down it wouldn't be anytime soon.

"You know he is goin' to be gone away for a while, right?" I murmured to Dominic.

He nodded his head. "I know, he won't come back here for a few years at least, but if it helps him sort out his head then good for him."

"What if he never comes back?" I whispered and clamped my mouth shut when my voice shook.

Dominic squeezed. "He will come back; this is our home, Bronagh. We're his family... plus, Lana is here and even though she kicked him in the nuts yesterday when he tried to say sorry for what he had done; he will still come back for her. Kicking him in the nuts just put the final stamp on things. No girl will measure up to her now."

"I *still* can't believe she did that." I blinked. "I understand it but still can't believe it."

"I don't know what it is about my family but once a girl knocks us about, we set our sights on them. You're a prime example of that, you mouthed off at me from day one and slapped me when I tried to get a spider off your ass-"

I elbowed him in the stomach cutting him off. "You're a lyin' piece of crap. You were trying to feel me arse, not wipe anythin' off it!"

Dominic shrugged and chuckled. "I love that phat ass."

I playfully rolled my eyes and said, "I invited Gavin over for Christmas Eve drinks tonight after our family dinner so you have to be on your best behaviour or you won't get any fat *arse* again."

He grunted. "You mean I'm not allowed to pound on any guy that gets close to you? Not even your friend?"

I looked up to him and smiled. "When Christmas holidays are over, and we're back in school, you can target and pound on Jason Bane all you like."

Dominic burst out laughing. "I love you, babe, even though you're a bit of an evil wench."

I traced my fingers over his abs. "I love you too, babe, even though you turned my world upside down."

"But in a good way, right?" he murmured.

I smiled and looked up at him. "In the best way."

He suddenly flipped me over then and smirked down at me, his dimples waving at me. I screamed with laughter when he tried to undo the tie on my trousers.

"Don't even think about it, Dominic." Branna shouted from downstairs. "We're leavin' in exactly thirty seconds. Leave her alone!"

Dominic groaned as he fell next me and grunted. "Your sister is a huge fucking cock block."

I laughed and leaned over kissing his cheek. "I'll be back soon."

"You better," Dominic grunted as I jumped up from the bed and headed downstairs to my impatient big sister.

"We're fucking starving," Dominic groaned for the tenth time since Branna and I got home from town an hour ago.

While we prepared dinner, we gave the lads the jobs of wrapping the presents from them to other people that we had picked up for them. I checked on them a few times and found each grown man either complaining about the wrapping present process or popping the bubbles on the bubble wrap we gave them.

"If you complain one more time you won't be gettin' any dinner," I snapped to Dominic as I poured the gravy into our gravy boat.

I felt hands on my hips and a kiss on the back of my neck. "Sorry," he mumbled.

"I've never heard you apologise so fast before." Branna laughed from my right.

"He'll apologise at the speed of light if his pussy and food are threatened," Damien said.

I growled as I looked over my shoulder to the white-haired Slater brother. "You're disgustin'."

Damien smiled as much as his still swollen face would allow. "You still love me."

My lip twitched. "Only a little bit."

Dominic chuckled, as did Damien as they both moved to the large kitchen table. Branna was already putting out plates with food on them and the smell was attracting the brothers like a bunch of wild animals.

"Touch those roast potatoes, Dominic, and I will end you," I said without turning around.

"How did you know I was going to take one?" he asked, sounding surprised.

"Because you're impatient and greedy," I answered, making him chuckle.

I turned and smiled at everyone taking their seats at the table while I walked over and put the gravy boat on a coaster. I took my seat next to Dominic and smiled when he gave my hand a squeeze.

I looked to all the food and grinned. "Not to toot my own horn, but this looks amazin'."

Ryder chuckled. "It does look amazing, you and Branna did an awesome job."

Branna and I perked up with the praise and beamed when the other brothers agreed. Damien reached for a roast potato and because he was seated to my right, I smacked his hand away making him yelp which his brothers found funny.

"Rude!" Damien snapped.

I raised my eyebrow. "Says the greedy fecker who is takin' food before we pray!"

Damien sighed. "Sorry."

I nodded and looked to everyone. "Hold hands."

No one moved except Branna and it made me snort. "We don't pray before every meal but Christmas time is different. Besides, after all the shite you lot did over the past few years, you *need* to be prayin' to God."

Branna chuckled when all the brothers practically grabbed each other hands and held them; they all bowed their heads and so did Branna so I guess it left me to say a prayer.

"Thank you for blessin' us with this meal we're about to receive and thank you for keepin' us all safe and sound throughout our struggles over the past few weeks." I smiled. "Thank you for makin' my and Branna's family whole again by bringin' the brothers into our lives. Please keep Damien safe when he travels to America and when he is ready, guide him safely back home to us. I ask this in Jesus' name. Amen."

"Amen," everyone said in unison.

I looked up and reached for the bowl of mashed potatoes but froze when I realised everyone was looking at me. I felt my entire face flush as I cleared my throat and said, "Branna always says the prayers. I never do, did I mess it up?"

Dominic leaned over, pressed his hand to the back of my neck and pulled my face to his. He covered my mouth with his and gave me a long, gentle kiss. "No, pretty girl, it was perfect."

I smiled when we broke apart and looked to everyone else and found them smiling at me, I felt like I was about to combust when Damien reached over and kissed my cheek. "Love you, Bee," he said.

I forced myself not to cry but it was hard because this was a damn touching moment.

"I love you, too, Dame."

Alec's overplayed clearing of his throat made me snort. "Love you as well, Alec."

I flicked my eyes to Kane and found him already looking at me, his eyebrows raised. "I love you Kane, and I love you Ryder, and you Branna. I love you all."

Everyone chuckled as more declarations of love got thrown around, making everyone beam with happiness. We all dug into our food then, and drank our beers as the lads started up random conversations about the future. Dominic wanted to finish school and go on to college and become a personal trainer; Damien was going back to America for a while; Alec wanted to remain a bachelor; Kane wanted to see if he could do something with the abandoned community centre in town for the kids in the area, and Ryder just wanted to marry Branna.

A few times I just stopped to look around at the faces of the people who had all done what I thought was impossible; they had set up camp in my heart and wouldn't leave no matter what. It was the best feeling in the world.

I had a family again; a *whole* family, and I felt truly blessed because of it.

"Are you okay, phat ass?" Dominic asked in a teasing tone from my left.

I looked at him; I looked past his bruises and saw him. He was perfect; he saved me from myself, and he was all mine.

I gave him a wink that made him smile as I said, "I've never been better, Fuckface."

ACKNOWLEDGEMENTS

To write and self-publish *DOMINIC* took a crew of people, people I wouldn't have been able to do without during this journey. I couldn't have done any of this without you all.

My daughter – you're everything to me, mini me. I love you with all my heart.

My sister – the genius behind our late night brainstorming sessions, I wouldn't have been able to do any of this without you. You're crazy, annoying and sometimes brilliant. I love you!

My family – your support has been second to none. I love you all.

My beta readers – Neeny and Yessi, who broke *DOMINIC* down piece by piece and gave me incredible feedback and helped me mould it into the story it is today. Even though my stomach was twisted in knots as I awaited your input, you made my first beta experience a brilliant one, thank you both from the bottom of my heart!

Yessi – I can't tell you how much you have helped me throughout this entire process. From the random conversations to answering endless newbie book related questions from me, you have been absolutely brilliant. I would have been lost without you.

Jenny over at Editing4Indies for proofreading! Thank you for everything!

Jennifer Van Wyk over at JaVa Editing for editing. Thank you so much for making the editing process a fun one.

Julie over at JT Formatting, thank you for the beautiful interior.

L.J. Anderson over at Mayhem Cover Creations for creating a cover that I am in love with.

Last, but never least, my readers. I hope you enjoyed Dominic and Bronagh's story as much as I did writing it. Watch out for the rest of the books in the *Slater Brothers* series. I'm not nearly finished with them ;)

ABOUT THE AUTHOR

L.A. Casey is a *New York Times* and *USA Today* best-selling author who juggles her time between her mini-me and writing. She was born, raised and currently resides in Dublin, Ireland. She enjoys chatting with her readers, who love her humour and Irish accent as much as her books.

Casey's first book, *DOMINIC*, was independently published in 2014 and became an instant success on Amazon. She is both traditionally and independently published and is represented by Mark Gottlieb from Trident Media Group.

To read more about this author, visit her website
at www.lacaseyauthor.com.

21467124R00189

Printed in Great Britain
by Amazon